The Miracle at St. Bruno's

Philippa Carr

THE MIRACLE AT ST. BRUNO'S

G. P. Putnam's Sons, New York

Contents

The Miracle at St. Bruno's

Prologue

Early on Christmas Day of the year 1522 the Abbot of St. Bruno's Abbey drew aside the curtains which shut off the Lady Chapel from the rest of the Abbey Church and there, in the Christmas crib, which Brother Thomas had so skillfully carved, lay, not the wooden figure of the Christ which had been put there the night before, but a living child.

The Abbot, an old man, immediately thought that the candles flickering on the altar had played some trick on his failing eyesight. He looked from the crib to the inanimate figures of Joseph, Mary and the three wise men; and from them to the statue of the Virgin set high above the altar. His eyes went back to the child expecting it to have been replaced by the wooden image. But it was still there.

He hurried from the chapel. He must have witnesses.

In the cloister he came face to face with Brother Valerian.

"My son," said the Abbot, his voice trembling with emotion. "I have seen a vision."

He led Brother Valerian to the chapel and together they gazed down on the child in the crib.

"It is a miracle," said Brother Valerian.

About the crib stood a circle of black-robed figures—Brother Thomas from the woodhouse, Brother Clement from the bakehouse, Brothers Arnold and Eugene from the brewhouse, Brother Valerian whose delight was the scriptorium where he worked on his manuscripts, and Brother Ambrose, whose task was to till the soil.

The Abbot watched them closely. All were silent with awe and wonder, except Brother Ambrose, who exclaimed, his voice tense with excitement, "Unto us a child is given." His eyes were gleaming with an emotion he could not suppress. He was a young monk—twenty-two years of age—and of all his sons Ambrose gave the Abbot most concern. Often he had wondered whether Ambrose should remain in the community; yet at times this monk seemed to embrace monasticism more fervently than his fellows. The Abbot had recently come to the conclusion that Brother Ambrose could either be a saint or a sinner and whosoever it was who claimed him—God or the Devil—Brother Ambrose would be a most devoted disciple.

"We must care for this child," said Brother Ambrose earnestly.

"Is he sent to stay with us then?" asked Brother Clement, the gentle, simple one.

"How did he come here?" asked Brother Eugene, the worldly one.

"It is a miracle," retorted Brother Ambrose. "Does one question a miracle?"

So this was the miracle of St. Bruno's Abbey. Soon the news spread through the countryside and people traveled far to visit the blessed spot. They brought gifts for the Child like the wise men of old and in the years that followed rich men and women remembered St. Bruno's in their wills; so that in due time the Abbey, which had been in dire decline—a fact which caused its Abbot grave concern—became one of the most prosperous in the south of England.

Part I

The Jeweled Madonna

I was born in the September of 1523, nine months after the monks had discovered the Child in the crib on that Christmas morning. My birth was, my father used to say, another miracle. He was not young at the time, being forty years of age; he had recently married my mother who was more than twenty years his junior. His first wife had died giving birth to a stillborn son after having made several attempts to bear children all of which had failed; and because my father at last had a child, he called that a miracle.

It is not difficult to imagine the rejoicing in the household. Keziah, who was my nurse and mentor in those early days, was constantly telling me about it.

"Mercy me!" she said. "The feasting. It was like a wedding. You could smell the venison and sucking pig all over the house. And there was tansy cake and saffron cake with mead to wash it down for all who cared to call for it. The beggars came from miles around. What a time of plenty! Poor souls! Up to St. Bruno's for a night's shelter, a bite to eat and a blessing and then to the Big House for tansy and saffron. And all on account of you."

"And the Child," I reminded her, for I had very quickly become aware of the miracle of St. Bruno's.

"And the Child," she agreed; and whenever she spoke of the Child, a certain smile illumined her face and made her beautiful.

My mother, whose great pleasure was tending her gardens, called me Damask, after the rose which Dr. Linacre, the King's physician, had brought into England that year. I began to grow up with a sense of my own importance, for my mother's attempts to bear more children were frustrated. There were three miscarriages in the five years that followed. I was cosseted, watched over, cherished.

My father was a good and gentle man, who went into the city to do his business. Each day one of the boats at our privy steps would be untied and a servant in dark-blue livery would row him upriver. Sometimes my mother would carry me down to the steps to watch him go; she would tell me to wave so that my father would gaze lovingly at me until he was carried too far away to see me.

The big house with its timber frame and gables had been built by my father's father; it was commodious with its great hall, its numerous bedchambers and reception rooms, its winter parlor and its three staircases. At the east wing a stone spiral one led to the attic bedrooms occupied by our servants; and in addition there was the buttery, the scalding house, the washhouse, the bakehouse and the stables. My father owned many acres which were farmed by men who lived on his estate; and there were animals too—horses, cows and pigs. Our land adjoined that of St. Bruno's Abbey and my father was a friend of several of the lay brothers for he had once been on the point of becoming a monk.

Between the house and the river were the gardens by which my mother set such store. There she grew flowers most of the year round—irises and tiger lilies; lavender, rosemary, gillyflowers and of course roses. The damask rose was always her favorite though.

Her lawns were smooth and beautiful; the river kept them green and both she and my father loved animals. We had our dogs and our peacocks too; how often we laughed at the strutting birds flaunting their beautiful tails while the far less glorious peahens followed in the wake of their vainglorious lords and masters. One of my first memories was feeding them with the peas they so loved.

To sit on the stone wall and look at the river always delighted me. When I see it now it suggests serenity and perfect peace more than anything else I know. And in those days in my happy home I believed I was not altogether unconscious of the deep satisfying sense of security, although I didn't appreciate it then; I was not wise enough to do so, but took it for granted. But I was quickly to be jerked out of my complacent youth.

I remember a day when I was four years old. I loved to watch the craft moving along the river and because my parents could not deny themselves the pleasure of indulging me, my father would often take me to the river's edge—I was forbidden to go there alone because they were terrified that some accident would befall their beloved only child. There he would sit on the low stone wall while I stood on it. He would keep his arm tightly about me, he would point out the boats as they passed, and sometimes he would say: "That is my lord of Norfolk." Or, "That is the Duke of Suffolk's barge." He knew these people slightly because sometimes in the course of his business he met them.

On this summer's day as the strains of music came from a grand barge which was sailing down the river my father's arm tightened about me. Someone was playing a lute and there was singing.

"Damask," he said speaking quietly as though we could be overheard, "it's the royal barge."

It was a fine one—grander than any I had ever seen. A line of silken flags adorned it; it was gaily colored and I saw people in it; the sun caught the jewels on their doublets so that they glittered.

I thought my father was about to pick me up and go back to the house.

"Oh, no," I protested.

He did not seem to hear me, but I was aware of his hesitation and he seemed different from his usual strong and clever self. Young as I was, I sensed a certain fear.

He stood up, holding me even more firmly. The barge was very near now; the music was quite loud; I heard the sound of laughter and then I was aware of a giant of a man—a man with red-gold beard and a face that seemed enormous and on his head was a cap that glittered with jewels; on his doublet gems shone too. Beside him was a man in scarlet robes, and the giant and the man in red stood very close.

My father took off his hat and stood bareheaded. He whispered to me: "Curtsy, Damask."

I hardly needed to be told. I knew I was in the presence of a godlike creature.

My curtsy appeared to be a success for the giant laughed pleasantly and waved a glittering hand. The barge passed on; my father breathed more easily but he still stood with his arms tightly about me staring after it.

"Father," I cried, "who was that?"

He answered: "My child, you have just been recognized by the King and the Cardinal."

I had caught his excitement. I wanted to know more of this great man. So he was the King. I had heard of the King; people said his name in hushed tones. They revered him; they worshiped him as they were supposed to worship God alone. And more than anything they were afraid of him.

My parents, I had already noticed, were wary when they spoke of him, but this encounter had caught my father off his guard. I was quick to realize this.

"Where are they going?" I wanted to know.

"They are on their way to Hampton Court. You have seen Hampton Court, my love."

Beautiful Hampton! Yes, I had seen it. It was grand and imposing, even more so than my father's house.

"Whose house is it, Father?" I asked.

"It is the King's house."

"But his house is at Greenwich. You showed me."

"The King has many houses and now he has yet another. Hampton Court. The Cardinal has given it to him."

"Why, Father? Why did he give the King Hampton Court?"

"Because he was forced to."

"The King . . . stole it?"

"Hush, hush, my child. You speak treason."

I wondered what treason was. I remembered the word but I did not ask then because I was more interested in knowing why the King had taken that beautiful house from the Cardinal. But my father would tell me no more.

"The Cardinal did not want to lose it," I said.

"You have too old a head on those shoulders," said my father fondly.

It was a fact of which he was proud. He wanted me to be clever. That was why even at such an age I already had a tutor and knew my letters and could read simple words. Already I had felt the burning desire to know—and this was applauded and encouraged by my father so I suppose I was precocious.

"But he was sad to lose it," I insisted. "And, Father, you are sad too. You do not like the Cardinal to lose his house."

"You must not say that, my dearest," he said. "The happier our King is the happier I as a true subject must be and you must be. . . ."

"And the Cardinal must be," I said, "because he is the King's subject too."

"You're a clever girl," he said fondly.

"Laugh, Father," I said. "Really laugh with your mouth and your eyes and your voice. It is only the Cardinal who has lost his house. . . . It is not us."

He stared at me as though I had said something very strange and then he spoke to me as though I were as old and wise as Brother John who came to visit him sometimes from St. Bruno's.

"My love," he said, "no one stands alone. The tragedy of one could well be the tragedy of us all."

I did not understand the words. I did know what tragedy was and silently puzzled over what he had said. But I did remember it later and I thought how prophetic were his words that day by the river.

Then he diverted my attention. "Look how pretty the loose-strife is! Shall we gather some for your mother?"

"Oh, yes," I cried. For I loved gathering flowers and my mother was always so pleased with what I found for her; so as I made a nosegay of purple loosestrife with the flowers we called cream-and-codlings I forgot the sadness the sight of the King and the Cardinal in the royal barge together had wrought in my father.

That had been a terrible summer. News came to us that the plague was raging through Europe and that thousands had died in France and Germany.

The heat was terrible and the fragrance of the flowers of the garden was overlaid by the stench that came off the river.

I heard what was happening from Keziah. I had discovered that I could learn far more from her than from my parents, who were always cautious in my hearing and a little afraid, while they were immensely proud, of my precocity.

She had been along to the Chepe and found that several of the shops were boarded up because their owners had fallen victim to the sweating sickness.

"The dreaded sweat," she called it and rolled her eyes upward when she spoke of it. It carried off people in the thousands.

Keziah went to the woods to see Mother Salter whom everyone was afraid of offending; at the same time she was said to have cures for every kind of ailment. Keziah was on very good terms with her. She would proudly toss her thick fair curly hair, her eyes would crinkle with merriment and she would smile knowingly when she talked of Mother Salter. "She's my old Granny," she told me once in sudden confidence.

"Then are you a witch, Kezzie?" I asked.

"There's some that have called me so, little 'un." Then she made claws of her hands and prowled toward me. "So you'd better be a good girl or I'll be after you." I squealed with the delight Keziah could arouse in me and pretended to be afraid. With her laughter, sometimes sly, sometimes warm and loving, Keziah was for me the most exciting person in the household. She it was who first told me of the miracle and one day when we were out walking she said that if I were a good girl she might be able to show me the Child.

We had come to that wall where our lands joined those of the Abbey. Keziah hoisted me up. "Sit still," she commanded. "Don't dare move." Then she climbed up beside me.

"This is his favorite place," she said. "You may well see him today."

She was right. I did. He came across the grass and looked straight up at us perched on the wall.

I was struck by his beauty although I did not realize it then; all I knew was that I wanted to go on looking at him. His face was pale; his eyes the most startling dark blue I had ever seen; and his fair hair curled about his head. He was taller than I and even at that age there was an air of superiority about him which immediately overawed me.

"He don't look holy," whispered Keziah, "but he's too young for it to show."

"Who are you?" he asked, giving me a cold direct stare.

"Damask Farland," I said. "I live at the big house."

"You should not be here," answered the Child.

"Now, darling, we've a right to be here," replied Keziah.

"This is Abbey land," retorted the boy.

Keziah chuckled. "Not where we are. We're on the wall."

The boy picked up a stone and looked about him as though to see if he would be observed throwing it at us.

"Oh, that's wicked," cried Keziah. "You wouldn't think he was holy, would you? He is though. Only holiness don't show till they get older. Some of the saints have been very naughty boys. Do you know that, Dammy? It's in some of the stories. They get their halos later on."

"But this one was *born* holy, Keziah," I whispered.

"*You* are wicked," cried the boy; and at that moment one of the monks came walking across the grass.

"Bruno," called the monk; and then he saw us on the wall.

Keziah smiled at him rather strangely, I thought, because after all he was a monk, and I knew by his robes that he was not one of the lay brothers who left the Abbey and mingled with the world.

"What are you doing here?" he cried; and I thought Keziah would jump down, lift me down and run, for he was clearly very shocked to see us.

"I'm looking at the Child," said Keziah. "He's a bonny sight."

The monk appeared to be distressed by our wickedness.

"It's only me and my little 'un," said Keziah in that comfortable easy way which made everything less serious than others were trying to make it out to be. "He was going to throw a stone at us."

"That was wrong, Bruno," said the monk.

The boy lifted his head and said: "They shouldn't be here, Brother Ambrose."

"But you must not throw stones. You know that Brother Valerian teaches you to love everybody."

"Not sinners," said the Child.

I felt very wicked then. I was a sinner. *He* had said so and he was the Holy Child.

I thought of Jesus who had been in His crib on Christmas Day and how different He must have been. He was humble, my mother told me, and tried to help sinners. I could not believe that He would ever have wanted to throw stones at them.

"You're looking well, Brother Ambrose," said Keziah. She might have been talking to Tom Skillen, one of our gardeners to whom she did talk very often. There was a little trill at the end of her sentence which was not quite a laugh but served the same purpose since it betrayed her refusal to admit anything was very serious in any situation.

The Child was watching us intently, but strangely enough I found my attention becoming fixed on Keziah and the monk. The Child might become a prophet, I had heard, but at this time he was simply a *child*, though an unusual one, and I accepted the fact that he had been found in the Christmas crib as I accepted the stories of witches and fairies which Keziah told me; but grown-up people interested me because they often seemed to be hiding something from me and to discover what was a kind of challenge which I could not resist meeting.

We saw the lay brothers now and then in the lanes, but not the monks who lived the enclosed life; and I had heard that in the last years when the fame of St. Bruno's had spread the number of lay brothers had increased. Sometimes they went into the city because there were the products of the Abbey to be disposed of and business to discuss; but they always went into the world outside the Abbey in twos. Wealthy parents sent their sons to the Abbey to be educated by the monks; men seeking work often found it in the Abbey farm, mill or bake and brew houses. There was a great deal of activity, for not only was there the monastic community but mendicants, and poor travelers would always be given a meal and a night's shelter for it was a rule that none who lacked these should be turned away.

But although I had seen the brothers in pairs walking along the lanes, usually silent, their eyes averted from worldly sights, I had never before seen a monk and a woman together. I did not know then what kind of woman Keziah was, but in spite of my youth I was very curious on this occasion and surprised by the challenging and the jocular disrespect which Keziah seemed to show toward Brother Ambrose. I could not understand why he did not reprove her.

All he did say was: "You should not look on what you are not meant to see."

Then he took the Child firmly by the hand and led him away. I hoped the boy would look around but he did not.

When they had gone Keziah jumped down and lifted me off the wall.

I chattered excitedly about our adventure.

"His name's Bruno."

"Yes, after the Abbey."

"How did they know that was his name?"

"They gave it to him, and right and proper it is."

"Is he Saint Bruno?"

"Not yet—that's to come."

"I don't think he liked us."

Keziah did not answer. She seemed to be thinking of something else.

As we were about to enter the house she said: "That was our adventure, wasn't it? Our secret, eh, Dammy? We won't tell anyone, will we?"

"Why not?"

"Oh, better not. Promise."

I promised.

Sometimes John and James, two of the lay brothers, came to see my father, who told me that once, long ago, he had lived at St. Bruno's Abbey.

"I thought I would be a monk and I lived there for two years. After that I came out into the world."

"You would have made a better monk than Brothers John and James."

"You should not say that, my love."

"But you have said I must say what is true. Brother John is old and he wheezes, which Keziah says means his chest is bad. He needs some herbs from Mother Salter. And Brother James always looks so cross. Why did you not stay a monk?"

"Because the world called me. I wanted a home and a wife and a little girl."

"Like me!" I cried triumphantly. It seemed a good enough reason for leaving the Abbey. "Monks can't have little girls," I went on. "But they have the Child."

"Ah, but his coming was a miracle."

Later I thought how sad it was for my father for I came to believe he craved for the monastic life of solitude, study and contemplation. He had wanted a large family—stalwart sons and beautiful daughters. And all those years he had longed for a child and had been denied his wish—until I came.

I always liked to be near when Brothers John and James called at our house. In their fusty robes they repelled while they fascinated me. Sometimes the sight of James's sad face and John's pale one made a lump come into my throat, and when I heard them call my father Brother, I was strangely moved.

One day I had been playing with the dogs in the garden and was tired suddenly so I climbed onto my father's knee and in the quick way that children do I fell asleep.

When I awoke Brothers John and James were in the garden sitting on the bench beside my father talking to him, so I just lay still with my eyes closed, listening. They were talking about the Abbey.

"Sometimes I wonder, William," said Brother John to my father. "The Abbey has changed very much since the miracle. It is comforting to talk and we can talk to you, can we not, James, as to no other outside the Abbey walls?"

"That is true," said James.

"It was a sad day," went on Brother John, "when you made up your mind to leave us. But mayhap you were wise. You have this life. . . . Has it brought you the peace you wanted? You have a good wife. You have your child."

"I am content if everything can remain as it is at this time."

"Nothing remains static, William."

"And times are changing," said my father sadly. "I like not the manner of their change."

"The King is fierce in his desires. He will have his pleasure no matter at what price. And the Queen must suffer for the sake of her who comes from Hever to disrupt our peace."

"And what of her, John? How long will she keep her hold on his heart and his senses?"

They were all silent for a while.

Then Brother John said, "One would have thought we should have become spiritual with the coming of the Child. It is quite different. I remember a day . . . a June day some six months before he came. The heat was great and I came out into the gardens hoping to catch a cool breeze from the river. I was uneasy, William. We were very poor. The year before our harvest had been ruined. We were forced to buy our corn. There had been sickness among us; we were not paying our way. It seemed that St. Bruno's for the first time in two hundred years would fall into decline. We would stay here and starve. And in the gardens that day I said to myself, 'Only a miracle can save us.' I am not sure whether I prayed for a miracle. I believe I *willed* a miracle to happen. I did not ask in humility as one does in prayer. I did not say, 'Holy Mother, if it is thy will that St. Bruno's be saved, save us.' I was angry within me, in no mood for prayer. It seems to me now that my spirit was bold and arrogant. I *demanded* a miracle. And afterward when it came I remembered that day."

"But whatever it was your words were heeded. In a few years the Abbey has become rich. You have no fear now that Bruno will fall into decay. Never in the Abbey's history can it have been so prosperous."

"It's true and yet I wonder. We have changed, William. We have become worldly, have we not, Brother James?"

James grunted agreement.

"You do great good to the community," my father reminded them. "You are leading useful lives. Perhaps it is more commendable to help one's fellow men than to shut oneself away in meditation and prayer."

"I had thought so. But the change is marked. The Child obsesses everyone."

"I can understand that," said my father, putting his lips on my hair. I nestled closer and then remembered that I did not want them to know that I was listening. I did not understand a great deal of what they said, but I enjoyed the rise and fall of their voices and now and then I got a glimmer of light.

"They vie with each other to please the boy. Brother Arnold is jealous of Brother Clement because the boy is more often in the bakehouse than in the brewhouse; he accuses him of bribing the Child with cake. The rule of silence is scarcely ever observed. I hear them whispering together and believe it is about the boy.

They play games with him. It seems strange behavior for men dedicated to the monastic life."

"It is a strange situation—monks with a child to bring up!"

"Perhaps we should have put him out with some woman to care for him. Mayhap your good wife could have taken him and brought him up here."

I stopped myself protesting in time. I did not want the boy here. This was my home—I was the center of attraction. If he came people would take more notice of him than of me.

"But of a surety he was meant to remain at the Abbey," said my father. "That was where he was sent."

"You speak truth. But we can talk to you of our misgivings. There is in the Abbey a restiveness which was not there before. We have gained in worldly goods but we have lost our peace. Clement and Arnold, as I have said, share this rivalry. Brother Ambrose is restive. He speaks of this to James. It seems as though he cannot resist this indulgence. He says that the Devil is constantly at his elbow and his flesh overpowers his spirit. . . . He mortifies the flesh but it is of no avail. He breaks the rule of silence constantly. Sometimes I think he should go out into the world. He finds solace in the Child, who loves Brother Ambrose as he loves no other."

"He has come to be a blessing to you all. That much is clear. The Abbey was founded three hundred years ago by a Bruno who became a saint; now there is another Bruno at the Abbey and it prospers as it did in the beginning. This young Bruno has removed your anxieties and you say he comforts Brother Ambrose."

"Yet he is a child with a child's ways. Yesterday Brother Valerian found him eating hot cakes which he had stolen from the kitchen. Brother Valerian was shocked. The Holy Child to steal! Then Clement pretended that he had given the Child the cakes and was caught by Valerian winking in some sort of collusion. You see. . . ."

"Innocent mischief," said my father.

"Innocent to steal . . . to lie?"

"Yet the lie showed a kindness in Clement."

"He would never have lied before. He is becoming fat. He eats too much. I believe he and the boy eat together in the bakehouse.

And in the cellars Arnold and Eugene are constantly testing their brew. I have seen them emerge flushed and merry. I have seen them slap each other on the back—forgetting that one of our rules is never to come into physical contact with another human being. We are changing, changing, William. We have become rich and self-indulgent. It is not what we were intended for."

"It is well to be rich in these days. Is it true that certain monasteries have been suppressed in order to found the King's colleges at Eton and Cambridge?"

"It is indeed true and it is true that there is talk of linking the smaller monasteries with larger ones," said Brother James.

"Then it is well for you that St. Bruno's has become one of the more powerful abbeys."

"Perhaps so. But we live in changing times and the King has some unscrupulous ministers about him."

"Hush," said my father. "It is unwise to talk so."

"There spoke the lawyer," said Brother John. "But I am uneasy —more so than I was on that day when I asked for a miracle. The King is deeply worried by a conscience which appears to have come into being now that he wishes to put away an aging wife and take to his bed one who is called a witch and a siren."

"A divorce will not be granted him," said my father. "He will keep the Queen and the lady will remain what she is now for evermore—the Concubine."

"I pray it may be so," said Brother James.

"And have you heard," went on my father, "that the lady is at this time sick of the sweat and that her life is in danger and the King is well nigh mad with anxiety lest she be taken from him?"

"If she were it would save a good many people a great deal of trouble."

"You will not pray for *that* miracle, Brothers?"

"I shall never ask for miracles again," said Brother John.

They went on to talk of matters which I did not understand and I dozed.

I was awakened next time by my mother's voice.

She had come into the garden and was clearly agitated.

"There is bad news, William," she said. "My Cousin Mary and her husband are both dead of the sweat. Oh, it is so tragic."

"My dear Dulce," said my father, "this is indeed terrible news. When did it happen?"

"Three weeks ago or thereabouts. My cousin died first; her husband followed in a few days."

"And the children?"

"Fortunately my sister sent them away to an old servant who had married and was some miles off. It is this servant who sends the messenger to me now. She wants to know what is to become of little Rupert and Katherine."

"By my soul," said my father, "there is no question. Their home must be with us now."

And so Kate and Rupert came to live with us.

Everything was different. We seemed to be a household of children, and I was the youngest for Kate was two years my senior, Rupert two years hers. At first I was resentful; then I began to realize that life was more exciting if not so comfortable now that my cousins had come.

Kate was beautiful even in those days when she was inclined to be overplump. Her hair was reddish, her eyes green, and her skin creamy with a sprinkle of freckles across the bridge of her nose. She was vain of her looks even at seven, and used to worry a great deal about the freckles. Her mother had used a freckle lotion because she had had the same kind of fair skin and Kate used to steal it. She could not do that now. She was more knowledgeable than I—sharp and shrewd, but in spite of her two years' advantage, I was ahead of her in the Greek, Latin and English which I had been studying since the age of three, a fact which I knew gave great satisfaction to my father.

Rupert was quieter than Kate; one would have thought she was the elder, but he was much taller and slender; he had the same color hair but lacked the green eyes—his were almost colorless— gray sometimes, faintly blue at others. Water color, I called them, for they reflected colors as water did. He was very anxious to please my parents; he was self-effacing and the sort of person people didn't notice was there. My father thought he might learn to become a lawyer in which case he would go to one of the Inns of Chancery after leaving Oxford as Father had done, but Rupert was enamored of the land. He loved being in the hayfield cutting and carrying and at such times he seemed more alive than we had ever seen him.

My parents were very kind to them. They guessed how sad they must be to lose father and mother and they were constantly indicating how welcome they were in our house. I was told secretly that I must treat them as though they were my brother and sister and must always remember if I was inclined to be unkind to them that I was more fortunate than they because I had two beloved parents and they had lost both theirs.

Kate was naturally more often with me than Rupert was. When we had finished our lessons, he liked to wander off into the fields and he would talk with the cowherds or shepherds or those of our servants who worked on the land while Kate turned her attention to me; and she always managed to score as soon as we left the schoolroom to make up for my ascendancy there.

She told me that we were not very fashionable people. Her parents had been different. Her father had gone often to Court. She told me, erroneously as it turned out, that Rupert would have a fine estate when he came of age and that it was being looked after for him by my father, who was a lawyer and so qualified to do so. "You see we are favoring him by allowing him to look after our affairs." That was typical of Kate. She made a favor of accepting anything.

"Then he will be able to grow his own corn," I commented.

As for herself, she would marry, she told me. No one less than a Duke would do for her. She would have a mansion in London and she supposed there would have to be an estate in the country but she would live mainly in London and go to Court.

London was amusing. Why did we not go there more often? We were very near. It was just up the river. All we had to do was get into a boat and go there. But we rarely went. She herself had been taken to see the great Cardinal go to Westminster in state.

What a sight it had been! Kate could act; she took my red cloak and wrapped it around her and seized an orange and held it to her nose as she strutted before me.

" 'I am the great Cardinal,' " she cried. " 'Friend of the King.' This is how he walked, Damask. You should have seen him. And all about him were his servants. They say he keeps greater state than the King. There were the crossbearers and the ushers—and my lord himself in crimson . . . a much brighter red than this cloak of yours. And his tippet was of sable and the orange was to preserve him from the smell of the people. But you don't understand. You've never seen anything . . . you're too *young*."

She might have seen the Cardinal with his orange, I retorted, but I had seen him with the King.

Her green eyes sparkled at the mention of the King and she had a little more respect for me after that. But we were rivals from the beginning. She was always trying to prove to me not how much more learned she was than I—she cared not a berry for the learning such as our tutors had to impart—but how much more clever, how much more worldly.

Keziah admired her from the start. "Mercy me!" she would cry. "The men will be round her like bees round the honeysuckle." And that, according to Keziah, was the most desirable state for any woman to be in.

Kate was nearly eight years old when she came to us but she seemed more like eleven—so said Keziah; and there were some at eleven who knew a thing or two—Keziah herself, for instance. I was a little jealous of the effect she had on Keziah, although I was always her Little 'Un, her baby, and she always defended me, when defense was needed, against the dazzling Kate.

But after Kate came all the little pleasures seemed to be slightly less exciting. Romping with dogs, feeding the peacocks, gathering wild flowers for my mother and seeing how many different kinds I could find and name—all that was childish. Kate liked dressing up, pretending she was someone else, climbing the trees in the nuttery, hiding there and throwing nuts down on people as they passed; she liked wrapping a sheet around her and frightening the maids. Once in the cellar she startled one of them so badly that the poor girl fell down the steps and sprained her ankle. She made me swear that I wouldn't tell she was the ghost and from then on the servants were convinced the cellar was haunted.

There was always drama around Kate; she would listen at keyholes to what people said and then she would tell her own highly colored version of it; she plagued our tutor and used to put her tongue out at him when his back was turned. "You're as wicked as I am, Damask," she would tell me, "because you laughed. If I go to hell, you will go too."

It was a terrifying thought. But my father had taught me to be logical and I insisted that it wasn't so bad to laugh at something wicked as to do it. It was every bit as bad, Kate assured me. I would ask Father, I said; at which she told me that if I did she would invent such wickedness and swear that I was guilty of it that he would turn me out of the house.

"He never would," I said. "He gave up being a monk so that he could have me."

She was scornful. "You wait till he hears."

"But I have done nothing," I protested tearfully.

"I will tell it so that it will be just as though you had."

"You'll go to hell for it."

"I'm going there already—you said so. So what does a bit more wickedness matter?"

Usually she insisted that I obey her. The worst punishment she could inflict on me was to remove her exciting presence and this she quickly discovered. It delighted her that she was so important to me.

"Of course," she was fond of saying, "you are really only a baby."

I wished that Rupert would have been with us more often, but we seemed so very young to him. He was kind to me always and very polite but he didn't want to be with me, of course. One of the occasions I remember most vividly of him was in the winter at the lambing time and how he went out into the snow and brought in a lamb and sat nursing it all the evening. He was very tender and I thought how kind he was and how I could love him if he would only let me.

Once my father took me down to the river's edge as he used to before my cousins came and he sat on the wall while I stood there with his arm supporting me as we watched the barges going by.

"It's a different house now, eh, Damask?" he said.

I knew what he meant and I nodded.

"And you're as happy as you used to be?"

I was unsure and he gave me a little squeeze.

"It's better for you," he said. "Children should not be brought up alone."

I reminded him of the time we had seen the King and the Cardinal go by in the royal barge. "We never saw him again," I said.

"Nor ever shall," said my father.

"Kate saw him in his scarlet robes and fur tippet holding his orange in his hand."

"The pomp and glory has passed away, poor man," said my father quietly.

"What are they?" I asked.

And my father replied, "What the Cardinal had to excess and has no longer. Poor sad man, his fall is imminent."

I could not believe that the mighty Cardinal was a poor sad man. I was about to ask for explanations. But I didn't. Instead I would ask Kate. That was the difference in our household. Kate had become my instructress; I no longer asked my father to explain what I did not know.

My cousins had been with us two years when the Cardinal died and by that time it seemed to me that they had always been there. I was seven years old at that time and two years of Kate's tuition had matured me considerably. Kate at nine—grown a little plumper—seemed at least three years older, and at twelve girls began to be considered for marriage in their not very distant future.

I had worked hard in the schoolroom. My tutors told my father that I should be quite a scholar in a few years' time; he compared me with the daughters of my father's friend Sir Thomas More and they were notoriously clever. I needed the reassurance of being able to rise above Kate's ascendancy in some ways. She pooh-poohed Latin and Greek. "Are they going to make you a Duchess? All your little quips and tags! What are they? Just repeating what someone has said before!"

She was wonderful in the saddle and to see her there in her green riding habit and the hat with the green feather lifted the spirits like the sudden sight of bluebells misty under trees or the first call of the cuckoo. I suppose others felt the same; they always turned to look at her; and she would ignore the stares but I knew by the way she held her head and smiled secretly that she was aware of the effect she had and enjoyed it.

She loved to dance and she did so with a natural grace which delighted our dancing teacher; and she could play the lute in a strange untutored way which was somehow more effective than my pieces which were in tune and time. She dominated the scene whether it was at Christmas when we gathered holly and ivy and decorated the great hall or at May Day when we watched the villagers dancing around the Maypole. When the Morris Dancers came to the house she danced with them and my parents, I think, were about to reprove her but she enchanted them as she did all others and soon they were applauding with the rest. She loved to dress up as Robin Hood and I would have to be Maid Marian. I must always take the lesser part.

The servants were always laughing and shaking their heads over Mistress Kate, and Keziah used to say with her throaty chuckle, "You wait . . . you just wait till Mistress Kate's a woman."

I had more freedom than I had before she came. My parents seemed to realize that they could not coddle me forever; and sometimes when Kate was charming everyone, I would catch my father's eye on me and he would smile and that smile told me that I was still and always would be the darling of his heart and no one however beautiful and exciting could ever oust me from my place there.

Kate knew that the Cardinal was dead and she gave me her version of the affair.

"It is all due to the King's passion for Anne Boleyn. He is determined to have her and she says, 'No, your mistress I will not be; your wife I cannot be.' Which shows how clever she is." Kate threw up her hands as though warding off a persistent lover. She was Anne Boleyn. I could see in that moment that she was wondering whether a Duke was good enough to be her future husband. Why not a King?

"What of the Queen?" I asked.

Kate's lips curled. "She is old and no longer beautiful. And she can't give the King a son."

"Why not?"

"Why not what, idiot? Why is she not beautiful? Because she is old and it's horrid to be old. And why can't she give him a son? I can't explain that to you. You are too young to understand." Kate's favorite explanation when she did not know herself was that I was too young. I had pointed this out to her and it had the effect of making her use it more than ever.

She went on: "The Cardinal tried to stop the King. Silly man! So . . . he died."

"The King killed him?"

"In a manner of speaking. Old Brother John told your father he died of a broken heart."

"How terrible!"

I thought of that day when I had seen them in the barge together, standing close, laughing.

"He should not have annoyed the King. He was silly so his heart broke. The King is going to divorce the Queen and then he can marry Anne Boleyn and they will have a son who will be King in his turn. It's all very simple."

I said it didn't seem simple to me.

"That's because you're too young to understand."

What I did understand and what she failed to was the difference in our household since the death of the Cardinal. A gloom seemed to have fallen over it. My father often looked sad and when I talked to him he would smile and draw me to him as in the old days, but I fancied that his gaiety was forced. He seemed to be over-watchful; and when we were at meals I would catch him listening as though he expected some messenger who would not be very welcome.

Friends often called at the house and they would join us at table. Father had many friends both in Law and at Court. During their visits the conversation would be lively at the table and when they had drunk freely of the wine my father served them they would often talk about the affairs of the country. One thing that occupied most of the conversation was "The King's Secret Matter." I noticed how Kate's eyes glistened when it was referred to; and my father said on one occasion: "Remember, my friends, it is The King's Secret Matter, and therefore it is not for us to discuss or pass judgment."

That sobered them; and I noticed how they almost glanced

furtively over their shoulders and were very insistent that it was indeed The King's Secret Matter and none of his subjects should attempt to question royal decisions.

Yes, it was uneasy.

But Brother John and Brother James were perhaps more uneasy than anyone. They used to come often and sit and talk with my father. I was too old now to curl up on his lap and listen. Kate was not very interested in them. She wrinkled her little nose with disgust and said: "Monks. Silly old men who go and live in monasteries and kneel for hours in prayer. Their knees must be quite sore. Mine get sore in church. And they live on bread and water and are always telling God how sinful they are—as if He doesn't know without their telling Him! They wear hair shirts. Ugh. I like silk and satin and cloth of gold. When I grow up I shall always wear cloth of gold—or do you think silver tissue would suit me better?"

So I did not know of what Brother John and Brother James talked to my father, but I believed that their conversation was full of forebodings and I caught their lack of ease. But only temporarily for Kate soon dispelled it. Life for her was gay and it must be for me if I was to share it. She discovered so much. She told me that Jim, the chief stableman, who had a wife and six children and lived in a cottage on our estate, crept out into the woods to meet Bess, one of the housemaids, and she had seen them lying in the bracken.

"What would she do about it?" I asked. "Would she tell my father, or Jim's wife?"

She narrowed her eyes. "I'll tell no one but you . . . and you don't count. I'll remember it. It will be useful when I want to use it." Then she burst out laughing. She liked power. She wanted to have control over us like the puppeteer had over the dolls which he had shown us at Christmastime when he had come with the mummers.

And then she became interested in the boy.

One day she came to me when I was in the orchard sitting under a tree whither I had taken my Latin exercise. It was a beautiful day and I decided that I could work more easily out of doors.

"Put down that silly old book," commanded Kate.

"It's far from silly, Kate. In fact it is very difficult to read. I need all my powers of concentration."

"Powers of rubbish!" cried Kate. "I want to show you something."

"What?"

"First," said Kate, "you have to swear to tell no one. Swear."

"I swear."

"Hold your hand up and swear by the saints and the Holy Mother of God."

"Oh, Kate, that sounds like blasphemy."

"Swear or you will be told nothing."

So I swore.

"Now come on," she said.

I followed her out of the orchard, across our land to that stone wall which separated us from the Abbey. Tangled ivy grew thick over certain parts of this wall. At one spot she drew it aside and to my surprise disclosed the outline of a door.

"I noticed that the ivy looked as though it had been disturbed and I investigated," she said with a laugh. "And so I found this door. It's hard to open. You have to push it. Come on. Heave with me."

I obeyed. The door gave a protesting creak and then swung open. She stepped through onto Abbey land.

I stood on the other side of the door. "We are not supposed to. It's trespassing."

She laughed at me. "Of course I knew you'd be a coward. I wonder I bother with you, Damask Farland."

I was already stepping through the door and when I had done so the ivy swept back into place covering it. I looked about me, expecting the Abbey land to be different from any other. The grass was the same luscious green; the trees about to break into leaf. No one would guess that we were in what had always seemed to be sacred ground.

"Come on," said Kate and seizing my hand drew me across the grass. I followed her reluctantly. We went through the trees and suddenly she stopped because we had come in sight of the gray walls of the Abbey. "Better not go too near. They might see us and find out how we got in. They might stop up the door. That would never do, for I intend to come here whenever I wish."

We drew back into the shelter of the bushes and sat down on the grass. Kate watched me intently, knowing exactly how I was feeling and that I was really longing to go back through the door because I hated being where I knew I should not be.

"I wonder what musty old John and James would say if they found us here?" said Kate.

A voice behind us startled us. "They would take you down to the dungeons and hang you up by your wrists and there you would stay until your hands dropped off and you fell to the ground . . . dead."

We turned around and standing behind us was the boy.

"What are you doing here?" demanded Kate. She did not scramble to her feet as I did. She merely sat there calmly looking up at him.

"You ask such a question of *me?*" said the boy haughtily. "That I find amusing."

"You should never creep up on people," said Kate. "It could be alarming."

"Particularly when they are where they should not be."

"Who says not? The Abbey door should always be open."

"To those who are in need," said the boy. "Are you in need?"

"I'm always in need . . . of something different . . . something exciting. Life is very dull."

I was hot with indignation for I thought her very ungrateful and I resented the reference to life in our household.

"My parents are very good to you," I said. "If they hadn't taken you in. . . ."

Kate's mocking laughter rang out. "My brother and I are not beggars. Your father is paid well to manage our estate. Besides he is a sort of cousin."

The boy had turned his gaze from Kate to me and I felt a strange exultation possess me. I thought of his being placed in the Christmas crib by angels and a great destiny awaiting him. There was a quality about him of which, young as I was, I was aware. He was aloof, seeming to be conscious of the difference between himself and ordinary mortals. It was a sort of sublime arrogance. Kate had it too but hers was the result of her beauty and vitality. Although I was apprehensive I rejoiced that Kate had found the door in the wall and thus given me a chance to see him so closely. He seemed a good deal older than I although there was not a year between us. He was taller than Kate and capable of subduing even her.

Kate was bubbling over with questions. What was it like to be a holy child? she wanted to know. Did he remember anything about Heaven because he must have come from there, mustn't he? What was God like? What about the angels? Were they really as good as people said they were? That must be very *dull*.

He studied her with a sort of amused tolerance. "I cannot speak of these things to you," he said coldly.

"Why not? Holy people ought to be able to do anything. Being holy seems to be no different from anything else."

She was deeply impressed by him however much she might pretend not to be, and it must have been clear to her that she could not tease or torment him as she did me. He was too grave and yet there was a strange gleam in his eyes which I couldn't understand. I thought of what I had overheard about his stealing cakes from the kitchen.

"Do you have lessons like everyone else?" I asked.

He replied that he studied Latin and Greek.

I told him enthusiastically that I studied with Mr. Brunton and at what stage I had reached.

"We didn't come through the door in the wall to talk of lessons," complained Kate.

She rose and turned a somersault on the lawn—she was adept at this and practiced it frequently. Keziah called it wanton behavior. Her object in doing it now, I knew, was to divert attention from me to herself.

We both looked on at Kate turning somersaults and suddenly she stopped and challenged the boy to join her.

"It would not be seemly," he said.

"Ah." Kate laughed triumphantly. "You mean you can't do it?"

"I could. I could do anything."

"Prove it."

He appeared to be at a loss for a moment and then I had the strange experience of seeing wayward Kate and the Holy Child turning somersaults on the Abbey grass.

"Come on, Damask," she commanded.

I joined them.

It was an afternoon to remember. When Kate had proved that she could turn somersaults at a greater speed than either of us, she called a halt and we sat on the grass and talked. We learned a little about the boy, who was called Bruno after the founder of the Abbey. He had never spoken to any other children. He took lessons with Brother Valerian and he learned about plants and herbs from Brother Ambrose. He was often with the Abbot whose house was the Abbot's Lodging and the Abbot had a servant who was a deaf-mute and as tall as a giant and as strong as a horse.

"It must be very lonely in an Abbey," I said.

"I have the monks. They are like brothers. It is not lonely all the time."

"Listen," said Kate in her commanding way. "We'll come again. Don't tell anyone about the door under the ivy. We three shall meet again here. It'll be our secret."

And we did. Any afternoon that we could get away we went through the secret door and very often we were joined by Bruno. It was a strange experience because at times we forgot how he had appeared in the Christmas crib and he seemed just like an ordinary boy, and sometimes we played games together—boisterous games at which Kate scored, but he liked guessing games too and that was when I had a chance. He and I were rivals in that just as he and Kate were at those which involved physical effort. He was always determined though to beat us both—his wits were sharper than mine and he had a physical strength which Kate could not match.

Of course, I said, it was what was to be expected of a Holy Child.

Rupert, though not quite fifteen years old, was working more and more in the fields. He could talk knowledgeably with my fa-

ther of the crops and the animals. He found such joy in the new-
born creatures and he liked to share that excitement with others,
particularly me. I remember his taking me out to see a recently
born foal and pointing out the grace of the creature. Animals
knew him and were his friends as soon as they saw him; he had
that special gift. He could shear a sheep with greater skill than
the shearers; and he always knew the precise moment to start to
cut the corn. He could predict the weather and smell rain a day
or so off. My father said he was a true man of the soil.

Haymaking was a happy time; then we would all go into the
fields, even Kate rather grudgingly, and then she would begin to
enjoy it when the home-brewed ale was brought around and when
we rode in on the hay cart. The harvest was the best time though;
and when it had been bound and cocked and the poor had finished
their gleaning there would be a merry harvest supper. From the
kitchens all that day would have come the smell of roasting
goose and baking pies. My mother would fill the house with
flowers and there would be general excitement everywhere. Kate
and I would hang up the miniature corn sheaves which would
be kept all through the year to bring good luck to the next harvest.
Then we would dance and Kate would come into her own; but
my father always liked Rupert to take me out to the floor and
open the harvest ball.

At this time conversation seemed to center about the King's
marriage with Anne Boleyn. He had put away Queen Katharine
who had gone to Ampthill. Bruno used to tell us a great deal more
than we learned elsewhere because visiting friars brought news to
the Abbey.

One day as we sat on the grass keeping within the shelter of
the bushes lest we should be seen, we talked about the poor sad
Queen and he and Kate were once more in conflict.

"Queen Katharine was a saint," said Bruno; and he went on
to describe her sufferings. I loved to watch him as he talked. His
face seemed to me so beautiful; his profile was clear-cut, proud
and yet innocent in a way; and the manner in which his hair
curled about his head reminded me of the pictures I had seen of
Greek heroes. He was tall and slender; and I believe now that
what I found so attractive was that blending of saintliness and

paganism and the manner in which he changed from being a boy, fallible and quarrelsome, into a superior being who looked down on Kate and me from heights which we could never hope to reach. I believe Kate felt this too although she would not admit it and fought against it. To be with Bruno was so different from being with Rupert. My cousin was so gentle, so careful of me that sometimes I thought he regarded me as one of his newborn foals or lambs. I enjoyed being cherished, I always had; but when I was in the presence of Bruno an exultation took possession of me; and I was excited as I could never be in the company of any other person. I knew that Kate shared this feeling with me, because she never lost an opportunity of trying to score over him, as though she must convince herself, as well as us, of her superiority.

Now because Bruno talked so sympathetically of Queen Katharine she retorted that the Queen was old and plain. It was said that she had no right to be Queen and that Anne Boleyn with her Frenchified ways and her beautiful clothes was as fascinating as a siren.

"She is a siren who has lured the King to dishonor with her singing," said Bruno.

Kate had no use for metaphor and she was bored with old legends. Whenever she talked of Anne Boleyn her eyes danced and I knew she imagined herself in her place. How she would have enjoyed it! To have had the eyes of everyone upon her; she would have reveled in the admiration and the envy. The jewels and the flattery would have delighted her and she would have snapped her fingers at those who showed their hatred of her.

"And the true Queen," insisted Bruno, "reproves her women when they curse Anne Boleyn. 'Pray for her,' she says. 'Lament her case for the time is coming when she will need your prayers.'"

"*She'll* not need their prayers," cried Kate. "She is Queen in truth though there are many to say she is not."

"How can she be Queen when we have a Queen already?"

"You speak treason, Holy Child," said Kate with a sneer. "Take care I do not inform on you."

"Would you do that?" he asked intently.

She smiled at him slyly. "You don't believe I would? Well, I shan't tell you. I shall keep you guessing."

"Then since we are unsure we should not speak of these things to you," I ventured.

"Hold your tongue, Silly Child." She had made that my title when she was angry with me, just as he was Holy Child. The terms expressed her exasperation or her desire to mock. "You will hide nothing from me."

"We do not want to be informed against," I said.

"He is safe," she said pointing a finger at Bruno. "If anyone tried to harm him the whole countryside would be in arms. Besides he only has to work a miracle."

"The Holy Innocents were murdered," I said.

"This is child's talk," said Bruno loftily. "And if Kate wants to inform, let her. She will not go free because she talked with us and informers rarely go free."

Kate was silent and he went on: "The Queen spends her life in prayer and she does needlework. She is making a magnificent altar cloth for the glory of God."

"You may like saints," said Kate, "but I don't. They are all old and plain and that's why they're saints."

"It's not true," I said.

"Don't try to be clever, Silly Child." But she was piqued, and said we must get back or they might come to look for us, and what if they found us? Then they would find the door too, it would no longer be a secret and our meetings would be discontinued.

This was a thought which horrified us all.

It was May and proclamations were sent out that a coronation was to take place. Queen Anne Boleyn would set out from Greenwich to the Tower and after a sojourn there go to Westminster Abbey. It would be a spectacle such as had rarely been seen before.

Kate was impatient with what she called our unfashionable household. This was a coronation—even better than a wedding, she said. Crowds would be gathered in the streets and on the banks of the river to see the Queen pass by. And yet according to some it might be a funeral!

I pointed out that there had been some funerals because of this coronation.

"Never mind that now," said Kate. "I am going to see the coronation."

"My father would not wish us to," I said.

She narrowed her eyes. "It's treason not to go to the coronation of the King's chosen Queen."

Treason! It was a word of which people were becoming increasingly fearful.

On that lovely May day when Anne Boleyn was to start on the first stage of her coronation Kate came to the nuttery where I was seated in my favorite spot under a tree, reading. Her eyes were alight with excitement.

"Get up at once," she said, "and come with me."

"Why?" I demanded.

"Never mind why. Just come."

I followed her, as I always did, and she led me by a devious route through the orchards down to the privy steps and there was a barge in which sat Tom Skillen, looking somewhat sheepish.

"Tom is going to row us down to Greenwich," said Kate.

"Has my father given his permission?"

Tom was about to speak when Kate silenced him and said: "There's no need to worry. Everything is all right. No one can manage a boat better than Tom."

She pushed me into the boat and Tom grinned at me, still sheepish. I supposed it was all right because Tom would not take us anywhere without my father's permission.

He began to row us rapidly up the river and very soon I knew the reason for Kate's excitement. We were going toward Greenwich and the river was becoming more and more crowded with craft. I was as excited as she was to see so much activity. There was the great city state barge in which sat the Lord Mayor in scarlet with a heavy gold chain about his neck; and all the companies and guilds were there in all their different barges. The sound of music filled the air and there was laughter and chatter from the smaller craft. Salutes from guns could be heard in the distance.

"We shall soon see the Queen," Kate whispered. "This is the start of the coronation festivities."

"Shall we see her?"

"That is why we are here," answered Kate with exaggerated patience.

And we did see her. Tom's skillful oar work brought us close to the palace itself so we saw the new Queen with her retinue of pretty girls board her barge. She was dressed in cloth of gold and she looked strangely attractive . . . not beautiful perhaps but more elegant than anyone I had ever seen; and her enormous dark eyes were as bright as her flashing jewels.

Kate could not take her eyes from her.

"They say she is a witch," she whispered.

"Perhaps she is," I answered.

"She's the most fascinating woman I ever saw! If I were in her place. . . ."

Kate held her head high; I knew that she was imagining herself in that barge sailing down the river to the Tower where the King would be waiting for her.

The Queen's barge had passed by; a passing boat rammed us and the water shot up soaking me to the skin. Kate burst into peals of laughter.

"We'd better go straight back," said Tom nervously.

"Certainly not!" cried Kate.

"The Queen's barge has gone."

"*I* shall say when *we* shall go," retorted Kate.

I was surprised that Tom was so meek. I had not noticed that he was before.

But Kate seemed suddenly to realize that everything she could see now after the passing of the Queen would be dull in comparison so she said: "Very well, we'll go now."

I was shivering in spite of the warm weather. I said: "We could have seen them pass from our privy stairs."

"We could not have seen the Queen so close," said Kate, "and I wished to see her close."

"I'm surprised they gave us permission," I said.

"*I* gave the permission," retorted Kate.

"Do you mean my parents did not know that we were on the river?"

Tom looked uneasy.

"But who said Tom might row us out on such a day?"

"I did," said Kate, and she was looking at Tom as she spoke. I wondered that she should have such power over him.

We were seen disembarking and my mother came hurrying out; when she saw my drenched clothes there was a great fuss. I was shivering! Where had I been? On the river! On a day like this! What had Tom been thinking of!

Tom scratched his head. "Well, Mistress," he said, "I didn't see the harm. . . ."

My mother said nothing but I was hustled off to my bedchamber with instructions to take off my damp clothes and drink a posset.

Kate came up to tell me that Tom had been questioned and he had said that the young ladies wanted to go and he had thought there was no harm in taking them.

"Didn't you tell them that you made Tom?"

"So you know I made him?"

"I couldn't understand why he took us. He didn't really want to."

"You are right, Damask. He didn't. But he dared do aught else when I commanded."

"You talk as though you own him."

"That's what I'd like to do . . . to own people. I'd like to be the King or the Queen, with everyone afraid of offending me."

"That shows an unpleasant nature."

"Who wants a pleasant nature? Does that command people? Does that make them afraid of you?"

"Why do you want them afraid of you?"

"So that they do what I say."

"Like poor Tom."

"Like Tom." She hesitated but she was so anxious that I should be aware of her cleverness that she blurted out: "I heard him coming out of Keziah's bedroom early one morning. He wouldn't want anyone to know, would he? Nor would Keziah. So if they want me not to tell they have to do as I say."

I stared at her in amazement.

"I don't believe it," I said.

"That they sleep together or that I have discovered them?"

"Neither."

"You get on with your Greek and Latin. It's all you can do. You know nothing . . . nothing at all. And I'll tell you something else. We are going to see the coronation. We are going to have a window in your father's house of business."

"Father would not wish us to see it."

"Oh, yes, he does, and I'll tell you why. *I* have made him."

"You are not going to tell me *he* dares not obey you?"

"In this he dare not. You see, I said: 'Uncle, why do you not wish us to see the coronation procession? Is it because you don't believe the Queen to be the true Queen?' Very innocent I was . . . none could look more so. And he grew pale for there were servants there. You see, he dare not keep us away now and I knew it because if it were said that he would not allow his family to see the coronation, people would say he was a traitor and so. . . ."

"You are wicked, Kate."

"The way to get what you want," said Kate, "is to make people afraid of not giving it."

She was right. We did see the procession pass through the city. Father and Mother took us and we sat there at the upper window of his business premises looking down on the street which had been graveled like all those from the Tower to Temple Bar. Rails had been set up so that the people should not be hurt by the horses. My father's house was in Gracechurch Street and it was a goodly sight to see the decorations of crimson and velvet and cloth of gold.

What a sight that was! All the nobility were present. There was the French ambassador with his retinue of servants in blue velvet; the archbishops were there and for the first time I saw Cranmer, the Archbishop of Canterbury, who looked very stern and serious. There were the Dukes and the Earls, the highest in state and church; and at last the one on whom all attention was centered—the new Queen herself. She lay in a litter made of cloth of gold shot with silver and two palfreys supported the litter and these were led by the Queen's footmen. But it was the Queen on whom one must gaze, for she was magnificent with long dark hair flowing from the ruby-studded coif to fall around her shoulders like a silken cape. Her dress and surcoat were of silver tissue, ermine trimmed. She looked indeed a Queen, lying there in her litter with four handsome men to hold a canopy of cloth of gold over her.

I could not forget her; nor, I guessed, could Kate. She stared at her as though in a daze and I was sure that her imagination had transported her and *she* was that young woman in the litter, going to the Abbey to be crowned; she was the woman whom the King had delighted to honor even though he had to send many to their deaths in order to reach her. There were wonderful pageants in the street set about the fountain from which on this day wine flowed instead of water; but when the Queen had passed I knew that Kate lost interest in what followed.

My father's men of business joined us for refreshments afterward and for the first time I met Simon Caseman—a man then in his early twenties.

My father said: "Ah, Damask, this is Simon Caseman, who will be joining our household shortly. He is learning to be a lawyer and will live with us for a while."

We had had a young man living with us before, but he had made so little impression on me that I had scarcely been aware of him. He had stayed for about three years, I supposed. That was when I was much younger; but it was not unusual for men in my father's position to take those whom they were tutoring into their households.

Simon Caseman bowed. Then Kate came forward. Kate was always interested to make an impression and I could see that she had. I was not quite sure what I thought of Simon Caseman. One thing I did know was that he was different from that other young man whose name I could not recall and who although a part of our household had somehow made so little impression on me.

Simon Caseman asked Kate what she thought of the procession and she expressed her delight in it. I noticed my father looked rather sad so I didn't join in quite so ecstatically, although I had been as delighted as Kate with the glittering pageantry.

It was necessary to wait until the press of people had diminished before we could make our way to the stairs and our barge. Father continued silent and rather sad.

When we entered the house, I said to Kate: "I wonder what she was thinking lying there in her litter."

"What should she think of," demanded Kate, "but her crown and the power it will bring her?"

During the September of that year there was great excitement everywhere because the new Queen was about to give birth to a child. Everyone confidently expected a boy. It was, the King had tried to make the people believe, the very reason for his change of wives. After all Queen Katharine had already borne him the Lady Mary.

"There will be great rejoicing," my father said to me as we took one of our walks to the river's edge, "but if the Queen should fail. . . ."

"Father, she will not fail. She will give the King his son and then we shall be dancing in the big hall. The mummers will come, the bells will ring out, and the guns will boom."

"My dearest child," he said, "let us pray that this will be so."

I was touched that he, whose sympathies were with poor Queen Katharine, could now be sorry for Queen Anne Boleyn.

"Poor soul," he said.

"Many have suffered because of her, Father," I answered.

"Yes, indeed," he replied sadly. "Many have lost their heads for her. Who knows when she will be in like case?"

"But she is beloved of the King."

"So were others, my child, and what of them when they cease to inspire that love? Many now rest in their quiet graves. When my time comes I should like to lie in the Abbey burial grounds. I spoke to Brother John about it. He thinks it can be arranged."

"Father, I forbid you to talk of death! And it all began by talking of birth!"

He smiled rather sadly. "There is a link, dear child. We are all born and we all must die."

A few days later the royal child was born. We heard that the King was bitterly disappointed, for the child, though healthy, was a girl.

There was rejoicing at her christening and she was named Elizabeth.

"The next one," everyone said, "*must* be a boy."

Christmas came with its festivities: mummers, carols, feasting and the decorations with the holly and the ivy. We were growing up and the following spring I heard Elizabeth Barton's name for the first time because everyone was talking of her; she was known as the Holy Maid of Kent and she had prophesied that if the King put away Queen Katharine and set up Anne Boleyn as his Queen he would soon die; and now that he had done so, many people were certain that he had not long to live.

Brother John and Brother James came to see my father and the three of them walked about the garden in earnest conversation because they thought the Holy Maid could make the King realize his error. It might well be a sign from heaven, said Brother John. I don't know what my father felt because he never talked to me about these matters. I realize now that he was afraid that I might, in my innocence, say something that would incriminate not only him but me, for young people could be deemed traitors. I understand now that the King was swept on by his desire for the woman who had fascinated him and his wariness with the Queen who no longer did. His senses were in command but he greatly feared the wrath of God toward sinners. Therefore he must convince himself that he was in the right. He must believe—what he said so constantly—that it was not his senses which dictated his actions but his conscience. He insisted that Queen Katharine's previous marriage to his brother Arthur meant that she was not legally his wife because the marriage had been consummated, although the Queen swore it had not been. The reason his marriage had failed to be blessed with children—except one girl, the Lady Mary—was due to God's displeasure, said the King. It was not his desire for Anne Boleyn which had made him demand a divorce from Katharine. It was his duty to provide England with a male heir. The new

Queen had now one daughter and had proved herself fertile; the next child would be a son.

So the King reasoned and there was no logic which could defeat his conscience. This I learned later, but at the time I forgot the brooding sense of insecurity for hours at a stretch.

My mother did too. She was a gentle, pliable woman, who perhaps because she was so much younger than my father relied on him for everything and had few opinions of her own; but she kept our house in order and our servants were devoted to her; moreover she was becoming known as one of the best gardeners in the south of England. She was always excited when new plants were introduced into England; the musk rose had now arrived; and she grew that side by side with the damask. Corinthian grapes too had been brought from the Isle of Zante and she planned a vinery which gave her a great deal of pleasure.

She was, I gradually learned, the sort of woman who believes that if she shuts her eyes to unpleasantness it ceases to exist. I was fond of her and she doted on me; but I was never close to her as I was to my father. My greatest pleasure was to be with him, to walk with him down to the river or through the orchards and as I was growing older he could talk seriously to me, which I think gave him great pleasure.

It was at the time when Elizabeth Barton became prominent that my father did talk to me.

I remember the day she was executed he put his arm through mine and we walked down to the river. He liked this way better because it was open lawn and we could talk without being overheard as we might be in the orchard or the nuttery.

He told me the Holy Maid had been a servant to a member of Archbishop Warham's retinue and how she became ill and subject to fits. This state had turned into trances and she had declared herself to be under deep spiritual influence.

"It may well be that she was used," he said, "poor soul. It may be that she spoke half-truths, but as you know, Damask, she has uttered against the King; she had prophesied his death if he should put Queen Katharine from him."

"Which he has done, Father."

"And taken to him Anne Boleyn."

"Why shouldn't *we* forget it?" I said. "If the King has sinned it is he who will be called upon to answer for it."

My father smiled. "Do you remember, my child, when you and I saw the once-great Cardinal sail by with the King?"

"I shall never forget it. I think it was the time I first began to notice things."

"And I said to you . . . what did I say to you? Do you remember?"

"You said: We are not alone. The misfortune of one is that of us all."

"What a clever child you are! Oh, Damask, I shall enjoy seeing you a woman . . . if I live as long."

"Please don't say that. Of course you are going to live to see me a woman. I am almost that now and we shall always be together."

"And one day you will marry."

"Do you think that will part me from my father? Any husband who wished to separate me from you would not find much favor with me."

He laughed. "This house and all I possess will be for you and your children."

"But it will remain yours for many many years to come," I insisted.

"Damask, don't lose sight of this: We live in troublous times. The King has tired of one wife and wanted another. That may concern us, Damask. I want you to be prepared." He pressed my hand. "You are such a little wiseacre that I forget your youth. I talk to you as I might talk to Brother John or Brother James. I forget you are just a child."

"Kate constantly reminds me of it."

"Ah, Kate. She lacks your wisdom. But one could not expect two such clever people in one household."

"You are a fond parent," I said.

"I admit it," he told me. And he went on: "This day they are taking the Maid of Kent to Tyburn. She will be executed there."

"Just for a prophecy?"

"For prophesying what the King does not wish to be prophesied." He shivered and went on: "Enough of talk of death. Let us go and see how your mother's musk roses are faring."

* * *

The Maid of Kent was dead. On the scaffold she had admitted her guilt.

"I am a poor wench without learning," she had said. "I have been puffed up by the praises of learned men. They made me pretend to revelations which would be useful to them."

The learned men who had supported her were such as Sir Thomas More and Bishop Fisher.

Because I was so young I was only vaguely and intermittently aware of the tension all about me. I could not at that time accept the fact that the world outside our household was of any great importance to us. My father aged considerably in the months that followed the new Queen's coronation. He used to row up the river to Chelsea and visited Sir Thomas More who was a very well-known gentleman. He had been Lord Chancellor before his resignation, having taken the post vacated by the great Cardinal. My father had a great deal in common with Sir Thomas, for their lives had not been dissimilar; they were both lawyers; they had both toyed with the idea of becoming monks and had chosen the family life instead. Sir Thomas had a house not unlike ours but his family was grown up and they were a large household because his children were married and their families formed part of that household. It used to be such a merry household; Sir Thomas, although so learned and a man of great integrity, loved a joke; but everything was changed now. It seemed as though they were all waiting for something terrible to happen, and because of this a certain foreboding had crept into our house.

Kate and I could escape from it, although I doubt whether Kate was even aware of it. She could go into such a storm with Keziah over the manner in which a dress had been washed, or if a favorite ribbon had been lost, and these matters seemed so much more important to her than anything else. She was so forceful and I was so used to following her that I began to feel as she did. I had discovered too that there was an inclination in my nature to ignore that which was unpleasant (no doubt inherited from my mother), so I tried not to be aware of the growing tension and to assure myself that it did not exist.

Simon Caseman had now joined us. Father said he was an extremely clever young man and he thought he would be very successful. He had shown a shrewd ability in my father's business and seemed determined to ingratiate himself with our household. He was always very deferential toward Father and at meals he would say very humbly: "Do you think, sir—" and then go on to discuss some law matter which was incomprehensible to the rest of us. He would put forward a view and if Father didn't agree would immediately apologize and say he was only a kind of apprentice after all. Father used to chide him a little and say that he was not necessarily wrong because they did not agree; every man should have his own opinion and so on; I could see that Father was very pleased with Simon. "He's the cleverest of any young man I've trained," he used to say.

Then Simon made himself useful to Mother. He very quickly learned the names of flowers and how best they should be tended. Mother was delighted with him and he was often to be seen carrying her basket for her while she went about the garden, snipping blooms here and there.

Often I would find him watching me speculatively and he even tried to interest himself in what I liked. He would attempt to discuss the Greek philosophers with me—for I had a reputation for being something of a scholar, largely because I was so much better at my lessons than Kate or Rupert, which did not mean I had reached such a really high standard; he would also discuss horses with me because I loved to ride.

With Rupert he could talk fairly knowledgeably on farming and the raising of animals; and he always treated Kate with that mixture of deference and boldness which she provoked and expected from most men.

In fact he took considerable pains to cause no inconvenience in the household—indeed to make himself an agreeable part of it. During the long summer evenings of that year the time passed pleasantly. We went Maying, riding, and on Midsummer Eve we stayed up to see the sun rise; we picnicked; we made the hay, always something of a ritual, and we cut the corn and when the harvest was in we hung our sheaves on the walls of the kitchen to be left there until next year; then we gathered in the fruits of the orchards and the nuttery and stored them away. When the evenings drew in we played games at the fireside. We had treasure hunts around the house, and sometimes guessing games at which I usually excelled, much to Kate's chagrin.

It was that summer that I saw the jeweled Madonna. We had no right to see it and I am sure Bruno would never have taken us into the chapel had Kate not lured him into it.

We had gone through the secret door to find Bruno waiting for us. I believe he looked forward to these meetings as much as we did. I suppose it was because had it been known that we were trespassing on the Abbey grounds and that Bruno was meeting us, there would have been such an outcry, that we all found the meetings so exciting. Bruno fascinated us both because we could never forget the mystery of his birth. For this reason I was in awe of him; so was Kate. I believed she would have refused to admit this and to deceive herself constantly attempted to lead him into some kind of mischief. She told me once that she could well understand how the Devil felt when he tempted Christ to cast himself down and prove his divinity because she was always wanting to make Bruno do something like that. "There must be quite a bit of the Devil in me," she said; and I assured her that she was no doubt right about that.

We were lying on the grass and Kate was talking as she often did about the Queen's coronation and how she had lain in her litter of cloth of gold.

"She sparkled with jewels such as *you've* never seen," she told Bruno.

"Oh, yes, I have," he replied. "I've seen better jewels than hers."

"There aren't any better. These were royal jewels."

"I've seen *holy* jewels," said Bruno.

"Holy jewels! There aren't such things. Jewels are a symbol of worldly pomp. So how could they be holy, pray?"

"If they're the Madonna's jewels they're holy," said Bruno.

"Madonnas don't have jewels."

"They do. Our Madonna has. She has finer jewels than the King has."

"I don't believe you."

Bruno plucked a blade of grass and began to chew it in a very unholy manner. He remained silent and there was nothing like that kind of silence to infuriate Kate.

"Well?" she demanded. "You're lying, aren't you? You're making up stories about your silly old Madonna."

Kate looked over her shoulder as she spoke for she was very superstitious and she wondered whether she had gone too far in referring to the Madonna as silly and old.

Bruno said: "I'm not. I wish I could show you. You never believe anything that you're not shown."

"Then show us," cried Kate.

"How could I? It's in the sacred chapel."

"All things are possible," said Kate virtuously.

"The jeweled Madonna is in the sacred chapel and only those monks who are enclosed visit it."

"Then how have you seen it?"

"I was taken there. I blessed her and she blessed me."

"Oh," said Kate, "the Holy Child of course."

"Brother Valerian has the key and it hangs on a chain he wears round his waist."

"You could steal it when he sleeps. He often sleeps when you are doing your lessons. You told us so."

"I could not do that."

"You mean you dare not. You call yourself a Holy Child and you are afraid of an old monk! Where are all your miracles? If you're really a Holy Child you should be able to get the key . . . just like that."

"I never said I could work miracles all the time."

"But it's what we all expect of you. How dare you appear in a Christmas crib if you're not a holy child? It's sacrilege. You ought to be turned out of the Abbey. You're not a holy child, you're a fraud."

I had discovered that there was one thing Bruno could not endure and that was to have his holiness doubted. I was beginning to realize how much it meant to him to see himself apart from others. His face was suffused with fury. I had never seen him so put out before.

"I am," he cried. "And don't dare say otherwise."

Kate, who could not learn a few lines of poetry, who could not without great difficulty add a few figures or memorize a Latin verb, was knowledgeable in the ways of people. She was immediately aware of their weaknesses and knew how to exploit them. She was determined to see the jeweled Madonna and set to work to achieve that end.

It took her a few days; but during that time she so played on Bruno's fear that perhaps after all he was not so different from other boys that she prevailed upon him to steal the key from Brother Valerian's girdle.

I had become caught up in the adventure so that I was as eager to see the Madonna as Kate was. I shall never forget the moment when we entered that cold gray building. I felt that at any moment we should be struck dead for daring to set foot on sacred ground but I was driven on not so much by my great desire to see the Madonna as to share in the triumph of these two—Kate for getting her own way and Bruno for proving that he was capable of acts beyond the power of mortal beings. For who but he would dare to bring outsiders into the sacred precincts of the Abbey.

He went on ahead of us and when he was sure that the way was clear beckoned for Kate and me to follow. We crept through those dank gray cloisters, into the narrow flagged corridors and up a spiral staircase. It was very eerie and so still that Kate said afterward that it was like being with the dead.

Bruno was very pale, his lips were firmly set though and I knew that nothing would deter him. Kate too, her eyes dilated it seemed, silent for once, overawed. Before we had entered the Abbey I had visualized our being discovered and the pain and surprise this would cause my father; but now I forgot that. I was as eager as Kate and as careless of flouting authority. It was a strange feeling; a certain knowledge that I was doing something very wrong and yet an inability to resist doing it.

It seemed a long time before we came to the chapel and Bruno fitted the stolen key into the lock; the door creaked as it moved inward so loudly I thought that the monks in their cells would hear.

Then we were in the chapel.

We crept across the stone flags, past the pews each guarded by a stone angel with what I presumed to be a flaming sword. There was a hush over the place. The stained-glass windows gave a bluish light to the place; the great stone buttresses were very cold.

We crept behind Bruno to the altar on which was a magnificent cloth wrought in gold and silver thread. The ornaments on the cloth were of silver and gold encrusted with jewels. We stared at them in wonder.

Then Bruno drew aside the heavy curtain decorated with gold embroidery. We were in a small holy of holies and facing us was the Madonna.

Kate caught her breath in wonder for she was beautiful. She was carved out of marble but her cape was of real lace and she was wearing a flowing gown of some thick embroidered material. This gown was aflame with the most glittering jewels imaginable. It was dazzling. Rubies, emeralds, diamonds and pearls had been fixed onto it. I remember thinking how heavy it must be. The Madonna's hands had been beautifully carved and rings glittered on her fingers. There were diamonds, sapphires and pearls in the bracelets which adorned her arms. But it was her crown which was almost blinding in its brilliance. In the center of this glittered an enormous diamond; and about this was clustered gems of all colors.

I thought to myself Kate will have to admit that the Madonna is richer and more sparkling than the new Queen on the way to her coronation.

Kate clasped her hands in ecstasy. She had never seen such jewels. She wanted to touch the jeweled robe but Bruno restrained her.

"You daren't. You would be struck dead," he said.

And even Kate drew back.

Having proved his point Bruno was now eager to get us out of the chapel; and I think that we were anxious to go although it was difficult to take one's eyes from that glittering figure.

Cautiously we tiptoed out, and how relieved Bruno was when he turned the key in the lock. The journey through the stone corridors seemed almost an anticlimax after being in the sacred chapel. If we were caught we would be reprimanded but he would not mention that we had seen the Madonna. We instinctively knew that in looking on that we had committed a greater sin than by merely trespassing into the Abbey.

We came out into the open and hurried to our secret meeting place. Bruno threw himself onto the ground, face downward. He was shaken by what he had done. Kate was silent; I guessed she was thinking of herself wearing that jeweled crown. But even she was subdued as we went home.

Murder at the Abbey

Outside events had thrust themselves upon us now, intruding into our home, destroying its peace. Even my mother could not escape from this. My father said the very foundations of the Church were shaken. Brother John and Brother James sat in the garden with him; they talked in whispers, their voices grave. My father talked to me as he always did. He wanted me to know what was going on and as he said to me often: "You are not a frivolous girl, Damask. You are not like Kate, concerned with ribbons and frills. We live in dangerous times."

I knew of the tragedy surrounding our neighbors, the Mores. Sir Thomas had made clear his refusal to sign the Oath of Supremacy which was an admission that the King was Head of the Church as well as State and that his marriage to Queen Katharine of Aragon had been no marriage; it was an admission that the heirs the King might have by Queen Anne Boleyn were the true heirs. And Lady Mary, Katharine's daughter, illegitimate.

"I am afraid for Sir Thomas, Damask," said my father. "He is a brave man and will adhere to his principles whatever evil may befall him. He has, as you know, been taken to the Tower by way of the Traitors' Gate and I greatly fear we may never see him again."

There was infinite sadness in my father's face and fear too.

"Such a sad household it is now, Damask," he went on, "and you know full well what a merry one it once was. Poor Dame Alice, she is bewildered and angry. She doesn't understand. 'Why does he have to be obstinate?' she keeps asking. 'I say to him, Master More, you are a fool.' Poor Alice, she never did understand her brilliant saint of a husband. And there is Meg. Oh, Damask, it breaks my heart to see poor Meg. She is his favorite daughter and none closer to him than Meg. Meg is like a poor lost soul, and I thank God she has a good husband in Will Roper to comfort her."

"Father, if he would sign the Oath this need not be."

"If he signed the Oath it would be to him as though he had betrayed his God. He has been a good servant to the King but as he has said to me, 'William, I am the King's servant, but God's first.'"

"And yet because of this they are so unhappy."

"You will understand when you are older, Damask. Oh, how I wish you were a little older. I wish you were of Meg's age."

I wondered why Father wished I was older then; and I understood later.

I remember the day Bishop Fisher was executed. Then there were the monks of the Charterhouse who were most cruelly killed. They were drawn to the place of their execution, hanged and cut down when alive and fearful agonies inflicted on them. That day Brother John and Brother James came to see my father. I heard Brother John say: "What is to become of us, William? What is to become of us all?"

Bruno told us that there was continuous prayer in the Abbey for Bishop Fisher, for the monks of the Charterhouse and for Sir Thomas More; and that Brother Valerian had said what happened to them could happen to others and much hung on the fate of Sir Thomas More. He was a man who was greatly loved; if the King allowed him to die the people would be angry. Some said it was more than the King dared do; but the King dared all. He would brook no interference and he had declared that any who denied his supremacy were traitors, be they onetime Chancellors and friends of his. No man was his friend who stood against him and none who did so should escape his wrath.

There came the terrible day when Sir Thomas came from the Court in procession with the ax turned toward him. We heard of it from those who witnessed it; and how poor Meg ran to him and threw her arms about his neck before she fell fainting to the ground.

"They'll never do it," said my father. "The King cannot kill a man he once professed to love; he cannot murder a saint."

But the King would allow no one to defy him. I often thought of him as I had seen him on his barge laughing with the Cardinal . . . another who had died, they said, through his displeasure. No man could afford to displease the King.

And then on that day of mourning the bell tolled for Sir Thomas, and his head was severed from his body and stuck on a pole on London Bridge, from which spot Meg later retrieved it.

My father shut himself into his room; I knew that he spent the hours of that day on his knees and I did not believe he was praying for himself.

He talked to me again, his arm through mine down there by the loosestrife and the long grass that grew on the riverbank, there where we could talk with no fear of being overheard.

"You are nearly twelve years old, Damask," he said; and he repeated: "I would you were older."

"Why so, Father?" I asked. "Is it because you wish I could understand more easily?"

"You are wise beyond your years, my child. If you were fifteen or sixteen perhaps you might marry and then I would know that you had someone to care for you."

"Why should I want a husband when I have the best of fathers? And I have Mother too."

"And we shall care for you as long as we shall live," he said fervently. "I think that if by some mischance. . . ."

"Father!"

He went on: "If we should not be here . . . if *I* should not be here. . . ."

"But you are not going away."

"In these times, Damask, how can we know when our time shall come? Who would have believed a few years ago that Sir Thomas would be taken from us?"

"Father, you will not be asked to sign the Oath?"

"Who can say?"

I clung to his arm suddenly.

Then he said soothingly: "The times are dangerous. It may be that we may be called upon to do what our consciences will not permit. And then. . . ."

"Oh, but that is cruel."

"We live in cruel times, child."

"Father," I whispered, "do you believe that the new Queen is no true Queen?"

" 'Tis better not to say such words."

"Then do not answer that question. When I think of her . . . lying in the litter smiling, so proud, so glad because all that pomp and ceremony was for her. . . . Oh, Father, do you think that she spared a thought for all the blood that would be shed for her. . . . Men like Sir Thomas, the monks. . . ."

"Hush, child. Sir Thomas expressed his pity for her. Heads have been cut off because of her. Who can say how long she will keep her own?"

"Kate heard it said that the King was growing tired of her, that she has given him no son . . . only the Princess Elizabeth . . . and that he is already looking at others."

"Tell Kate to keep a curb on her tongue, Damask. She's a reckless girl. I fear for Kate—yet somehow I fancy she has a talent for self-preservation. I fear more for you, my beloved daughter. I would you were old enough to take a husband. What think you of Rupert?"

"Rupert? As a husband, you mean? I had not thought of that."

"Yet, my child, he is a good boy. Reserved in temperament, good-natured, hardworking; it is true he has very little of his own but he is our own flesh and blood and I would like to see him continue to care for the estate. But most of all I would feel I was putting you into safe hands."

"Oh, Father, I hadn't thought of . . . marriage."

"At twelve it is time you gave that important matter a little consideration. Perhaps in four years' time. Four years! It is long."

"You sound as though I am a burden you would be relieved to be rid of."

"My darling child, you know you are my life."

"I know it and I spoke carelessly. Father, are you so much afraid for yourself that you wish I had another protector?"

He was silent for a while and he gazed along the river and I knew he was thinking of that bereaved house in Chelsea.

And never before had I been so aware of the uncertainty of our lives.

* * *

That summer seemed long and the days filled with perpetual sunshine. Whenever we had visitors to the house, which we did frequently for no travelers were ever turned away—rich or poor —there was usually a place for them at the table. If they came from Court, Kate would waylay them and try to lure them out of earshot of my father, perhaps into the gardens to see the peacocks or the dogs that she might talk of the Court.

Thus we learned that the King was indeed tiring of the Queen; that they quarreled and that the Queen was reckless and showed little respect for the King's Majesty; we heard that the King had cast his eyes on a rather sly and not very handsome young woman who was one of the Queen's maids of honor. Jane Seymour was meek and pliable, but with a very ambitious family who did not see why since the King had cast off Katharine of Aragon, a Spanish Princess and aunt of the great Emperor Charles, he should not mete out the same treatment to the daughter of comparatively humble Thomas Boleyn.

If there had been a son, we heard, all would have been different. But Anne could not get a son any more than Katharine had and there were rumors that Jane was already pregnant by the King.

Kate used to stretch out on the long grass and talk endlessly about Court affairs. She had ceased to fancy herself as Queen Anne. She was now Jane Seymour, but the role of meek Jane subservient to ambitious brothers did not suit her as well as that of proud Anne Boleyn. She was inclined to be scornful of Jane.

"How long does she think she will last?" she demanded almost angrily.

Sometimes we went through the secret door into the Abbey, and there she would talk about the jeweled Madonna. The thought of all those jewels looked at only by monks was maddening, she said. How she would like to wear them!

Her attitude toward Bruno was changing, as mine was too. I looked forward to our secret visits. I liked to watch his face as he talked and I always tried to take the conversation out of Kate's range. It made me feel closer to him. He liked to talk to me but he liked to look at Kate; in fact he rarely glanced at me when she was there. She bullied him; she was inclined to order him about, a fact which exasperated and angered him but only seemed to increase his interest in her. Once or twice she made veiled allusions to the fact that he had taken us into the Abbey and shown us the Madonna.

"But it was you who wanted to go," I said, for I always contrived to be on the side of Bruno against her.

"Ah," she replied, "but *he* was the one who took us." She pointed at him gleefully. "His was the greater sin."

Then she taunted him with being the Holy Child so unbearably that he ran after her and I heard her laughing as he chased and when he caught her they rolled on the grass together and he pretended that he was going to hurt her. She goaded him as though she wanted him to do so, so that she would have something else with which to taunt him; I was always a little apart from these frolics; I could only look on; but I was aware of the excitement that seemed to grip them both when they played these rough games.

I grew up fast that summer; I passed out of my childhood. I knew that Kate had special privileges with Keziah because Keziah used to let Tom Skillen into her room at night, and not only Tom Skillen. Keziah was like Kate in as much as she had great interest in men; she changed in their presence even as Kate did; but whereas Keziah was soft and yielding, Kate was arrogant and demanding. But I did notice the men were immediately aware of them both, as they were of men.

Kate took me into her confidence a little. "It's time you grew up, young Damask."

One night she came into my room and said, "Get up. I want to show you something. She made me go with her up the spiral staircase to the servants' rooms and listening at Keziah's door I heard whisperings. Kate looked through the keyhole and made me look too. I could just see Keziah in bed with one of the grooms. Kate took out a key and locked the door and then we tiptoed down the stairs to the landing and went across to our own staircase and so to her room. Kate was stifling laughter. "Wait till he tries to get out and finds himself locked in!" she cried.

I said, "You had better unlock the door."

"Why?" she demanded. "Then they wouldn't know I'd seen them."

She thought it was a great joke but I was worried about Keziah for I was fond of her and somehow I knew that these adventures with men were necessary to her, and that she would not have been Keziah without them.

Her companion of that night turned out to be Walt Freeman; he broke his leg when he scrambled out of her window soon after the dawn. As for Keziah, she couldn't climb out of the window, and how could she get out while the door was locked? Walt told some story about his thinking he heard robbers and coming out early had tripped over a root. Kate made me come with her when she unlocked the door on a distraught Keziah.

"So it was you, you minx!" cried Keziah.

"We crept up and saw you and Walt in bed," Kate told her.

Keziah looked at me and a slow flush spread across her face. I felt sorry because Kate had exposed her to me.

"You really are a wanton, Keziah," said Kate, shaking with laughter.

"There's more ways than one of being that," said Keziah meaningfully, which made Kate laugh all the more.

Keziah explained to me when we were alone.

"I've always had too much love to give away, you see, Dammy," she told me. "It would have been different if I'd had a husband. That's what I'd have liked—a husband and lots of little 'uns like you. Not like that Mistress Kate."

"Do you love many men, Keziah?" I asked her.

"Well, my ducky, the trouble with me is that I love them all and not being the sort that likes to say no . . . there it is. So it'll be our little secret, eh, and you'll not tell anyone?"

"Kezzie," I said, "I think they all know."

It was a lovely May day when we heard the news of the Queen's arrest. It shook us all although we had been expecting something like it to happen; there had been so many rumors of the King's dissatisfaction with his Queen and it was hinted that she was a witch and a sorceress who had tricked him into marriage. He was tired of her witchery; he wanted a good quiet wife who would give him sons. Already he had laid eyes and hands on Jane Seymour and her brothers were coaching her for the role of Queen. This we had heard; but there were many rumors and it was not until that May that we knew there was truth in them.

The King and Queen had gone to the joust together; then suddenly the King had left and the next thing was that the Queen was arrested and sent to the Tower—and some of those who were alleged to be her lovers were sent there too. One of these included her musician, a poor boy named Mark Smeaton, on whom it was impossible to believe the haughty Queen could have bestowed her favors; and more scandalous still her own brother was accused of being her lover.

My father had never believed that Anne Boleyn was the true Queen but now he was filled with pity for her, as I believed many others were too. Kate had seen herself so clearly as the fascinating Queen that to her this seemed almost a personal tragedy. That three short years ago she had ridden through the city in her triumph and was now in a dismal dungeon in the Tower had a sobering effect on us all.

As for Keziah she was full of compassion.

"Mercy me!" she mourned. "The poor soul! And what will become of her? That proud head will roll off her shoulders like as not and all because she fancied a man."

"So you believe her guilty, Keziah?" I asked.

"Guilty," cried Keziah, her eyes flashing. "Is it guilty to bring a little comfort to those who need it?" She had been frank with me since that night when Kate had locked her bedroom door, shutting her in with her lover. I was no longer a child. I had to learn about life, she had said, and the sooner the better. Life to Keziah was the relationship between men and women. "Men." Her eyes flashed with anger and it was rarely that she was angry with men. She adored them, joked with them, placated them, soothed them, satisfied them, and if they were rough or gentle, pleading or demanding, she loved them all; but she did resent that what they might do with impunity was considered a crime in a woman; they might go their way and follow their will as far as she was concerned as long as the women who pleased them were not blamed for doing the same. But when a woman was shamed for sharing in what for a man was considered natural, she could be angry; and she was angry now.

"The King," she said, "is not above a bit of fun and frolic. And if the Queen, poor soul, wishes for the same . . . well, then, why not?"

"But she will bear the King and the future King must be the son of the reigning one."

"My patience, we are clever! We're growing up and I'm glad. We can have some cozy chats now, Mistress Damask. But don't you go thinking hard of the Queen."

"What does it matter what I think of her? It's what the King thinks that counts and he is determined to think ill because he is off after Mistress Seymour."

Keziah put her finger to her lips. "Ah, that's the root of it all, Mistress. This pale beauty has caught his fancy and he wants change. Men are rare ones for change, though there's some that'll be faithful. I'll tell you this, Mistress Damask, there's little about men that I don't know. But you find out a little more every time. I knew about men before I was your age. I'd had my first by then. A handsome gentleman who came riding in the woods when I was with my Granny and he said to me, 'Meet me in the woods close by the cottage' . . . that was my Granny's cottage . . . 'and I'll have a fairing for you.' And I met him and our bed was the bracken which, when all's said and done, can prove as good a virgin's couch as feathers. It was dusk, I remember, and the air full of the scent of spring and when I got back my Granny was sitting there by the fire she always kept and the pot was brewing and her black cat that she used to say had more wisdom in his tail than most folk had in their whole bodies mewed and rubbed himself round my legs when I came in. She said, 'What's that you've got, Keziah?' I said, 'A fairing.' It had blue ribbons on it and was made of marchpane. 'Oh,' she said, 'so you've gained a fairing and lost your virginity.' And I was afraid being less than your age. But Granny said, 'Well, you can't learn the ways of the world too soon and you'll always be one who'll never say no to the men nor they to you, so whether you take your first now or in two years' time it's of no matter.' He came back . . . that fine gentleman, and we tried it under the hedge and even in a good feather bed and it was better every time. And then he disappeared and I was sad but soon another came riding by . . . and so it's been."

I said, "Keziah, are you not what is called a wanton?"

"Well, my love, I've always kept it quiet. I'm not one to brazen it round, I've always tried to make it so that it was just a little matter between the two of us. My word, my tongue runs away with me and all because of the King and his Queen."

I thought a great deal about the Queen lying in her dismal prison. I shuddered when the barge carried us up the river past that grim gray fortress. I averted my eyes when we passed the Mores' house. It was now deserted and I thought how it used to be when the peacocks strutted on the lawns and there was usually a glimpse of some members of that family walking in earnest conversation, or laughing together as they played some game.

Then came the day when the Queen walked out of her prison to Tower Hill where her head was cut off by the executioner's sword which had been brought from France for this purpose; and the guns boomed out and the King rode off to Wolf Hall to be married to Jane Seymour.

I kept thinking of her lying in her litter, proud and triumphant. That she had come to this was tragic and I remember my father's comment that the tragedy of one could be the tragedy of us all.

Meals were more silent than they used to be; guests who called on us and shared our meals no longer talked as freely as they once had.

We heard the new Queen was expecting a child and then one day the guns boomed; there was great rejoicing for Jane Seymour had given the King what he desired more than anything—a son. In conferring this great blessing she lost her life but the important matter seemed to be that at last the King had his heir. We were all commanded to drink to the new Prince; and we loyally did so.

Poor motherless Edward, the King's heir! Doubtless he would join his sisters in their nursery—Mary, the daughter of Queen Katharine, who was now a young woman of twenty-one, and Elizabeth, the daughter of Anne Boleyn, who was but four years old.

We all guessed it would not be long before the King was seeking a new wife. Poor Queens—Katharine, Anne and Jane! Who would be the next?

It was not of the King's next Queen that we heard but of something quite different. Keziah was laughing about it with Tom Skillen.

"Mercy me. Well, it seems nuns and monks are human after all."

"Ain't what you'd expect 'em to be," said Tom; and they giggled together.

Others took the matter more seriously. My father was very grave. It seemed that there had been several complaints concerning the conduct of nuns and monks in various nunneries and monasteries all over the country and this was giving rise to great scandals.

Kate told me about it. "A monk was found in bed with a woman," she said. "And he was blackmailed and has been paying for months. One Abbot has two sons and he has been making sure that they both have good positions in churches."

"But monks don't go out into the world. How could they do these things?"

Kate laughed. "Oh, there are stories. They say that there's a tunnel connecting a nunnery and a monastery and that the nuns and monks meet for orgies. They say that there is a burial ground where they bury the babies the nuns have, and that sometimes they smuggle them out."

"It's all nonsense," I said.

"There may be some truth in it," insisted Kate.

"But why should monks and nuns suddenly become depraved?"

"They've been so for a long time and only just been found out."

She couldn't wait to see Bruno. She wanted to taunt him with what she had learned.

"So it seems you're not so holy in your abbeys," she said as she lay in the grass kicking her heels in the air.

Bruno watched her with a strange expression in his eyes which I had seen before and never been able to understand.

"This is a plot," he cried hotly. "It's a plot to discredit the Faith."

"But the Faith should not be in a position to be discredited."

"Any lies can be told."

"Are they all lies? How could they all be?"

"Perhaps there are faults."

"So you admit it!"

"I admit that perhaps a few of these stories may be true but why should monasteries be discredited because of one or two evil ones?"

"People who pretend to be holy rarely are. They all do wicked things. Look at you, Holy One, who took us to see the Madonna."

"That's not fair, Kate," I said.

"Little children should speak only when spoken to."

"I am not a little child," I said hotly.

"You don't know anything, so be silent."

I knew that Bruno was very uneasy and I guessed this was due to the state of tension within the Abbey. My father told me of it. He was very unhappy.

"Life is full of trials," he said sadly. "One does not know when to expect the next thunderclap nor from what direction."

"It all seems to have changed when the King changed wives," I said. "Before that it seemed so peaceful."

"That may have been so," admitted my father, "or it may have been that you were too young to be aware of troubles. Some people never are. I verily believe that your mother is unaware of these storm clouds."

"She is too concerned whether or not there is blight on her roses."

"I would have her so," said my father with a tender smile. And I thought what a good man he was and how content he could have been if he could have lived happily with his family, sailing up the river to his business, dealing with his cases and then coming home to hear of our domestic affairs. We could have been a serene family surely. I had my differences with Kate; I saw all too little of Rupert; and Simon Caseman although he was so adaptable and did his utmost to please everyone did not somehow make me fond of him; my mother sometimes exasperated me by her absorption in the gardens, as though nothing were of much importance outside them; and there was my father, the center of my world, of whose moods I was always aware, so that when he was uneasy so was I. I was therefore very disturbed at this time. I was fond of the servants and some of our neighbors. My mother was the lady bountiful of the place and she always saw that her needy neighbors were supplied with bread and meat. No beggars were ever sent away empty-handed. Our house was noted for its liberality. All could have been so happy but for the murmurs which surrounded us and the fact that Sir Thomas More had lost his head and his household was disbanded. These were signs that even my mother found it difficult to ignore. She did mention to me once that she thought Sir Thomas should have considered his family rather than his principles. Then he would have signed the Oath and all would have been well.

And then St. Bruno's was threatened.

My father talked to me about it. I was fast becoming his confidante in these matters. He talked with Rupert and Simon now and then and they discussed affairs but I believe he spoke more freely of his innermost thoughts to me.

As we walked to the river he said to me: "I fear for the Abbey. Since the miracle it has become very rich. I believe it is one of those on which Thomas Cromwell in the name of the King has cast covetous eyes."

"What would happen to it then?"

"What has happened to others? You know that some of the smaller monasteries and abbeys have already been seized."

"It is said that the monks in them have been guilty of unmonkly behavior."

"It is said . . . it is said. . . ." My father passed his hand wearily across his eyes. "How easy it is to say, Damask. It is so easy to find those who will testify against others—particularly when it is made worth their while to do so."

"Simon Caseman was saying that only those monasteries whose inmates had been guilty of abominations have been suppressed."

"Oh, Damask, these are sad times. Think of all the years the monasteries have flourished. They have done so much good for the country. They have provided a sobering influence. They have tended the sick. They have employed people, brought them up in the ways of God. But now that the King has become Supreme

Head of the Church and a man can lose his head for denying this is so, Cromwell seeks to enrich the King by suppressing the monasteries and transferring their wealth from church to state. And since the miracle St. Bruno's has become one of the richest in the land. I tremble. Brother John tells me the Abbot has had to take to his bed. He is a very sick man and a fearful one, and Brother John fears he could not survive the loss of St. Bruno's and I verily believe he could not."

"Oh, Father, let us hope the King's men do not come to our Abbey."

"We will pray for it, but it will be a miracle if they do not."

"There was a miracle once before," I said.

My father bowed his head.

I tried to comfort him and I believe I did to some extent. But what uneasy days they were!

My mother had sent me out to take a basket of fish and bread to old Mother Garnet who was bedridden. She lived in a tiny cottage with but one room and relied on our house for sustenance. She had lost her husband and six children through plague and sweat but nothing, it seemed, could remove Mother Garnet. Everyone had forgotten how old she was and so had she, but it was a ripe age. My mother used to send one of the maids down with clean rushes for her floor every now and again and herbs and unguents would be taken too. One of my tasks was to make sure that there was always something in her larder and on this occasion Keziah came with me to carry a basket.

Keziah was full of the tales she had heard about the goings-on of monks and nuns. In fact it was the main topic with everyone. Each day there seemed to be a new and more shocking tale.

We had been to the cottage, heard Mother Garnet tell us the story she told us every time of how she had buried all her children, and were on our way back when in the lane we heard the sound of horses' hooves approaching and there came into sight a party of about four men led by a man on a big black horse.

He hailed us.

"Hey!" he cried. "Pray direct us to St. Bruno's Abbey."

His manner was arrogant, insolent almost, but Keziah did not seem to notice.

"Why, Master," she cried, bobbing a curtsy, "you're but a stone's throw from it."

I noticed his eyes on Keziah; his tight mouth slackened a little and his little black eyes seemed to disappear into his head as his lids came down over them.

He walked his horse forward. Briefly his eyes swept over me; then he was looking at Keziah again.

"Who are you?" he asked.

"I'm from the big house and this is my little mistress."

The man nodded again; he leaned forward in his saddle and taking Keziah's ear in his finger pulled her toward him by it. She shrieked in pain and the men in the party laughed.

"What's your name?" he said.

"I'm Keziah, sir, and the young lady is. . . ."

"I'll make a bet that you're a fine wench, Keziah," he said. "Sometime we'll put it to the test." Then he released her and went on: "A stone's throw, eh? And this is the road."

As they rode off I looked at Keziah, whose ear was scarlet where he had nipped it.

"He was all of a man, did you think, Mistress?" said Keziah with a giggle.

"All of a beast," I replied vehemently.

I was shivering from the encounter for there *was* something bestial about the man which had horrified me. It had appeared to have the opposite effect on Keziah. He had excited her; I could hear that familiar trill in her voice.

"He hurt you," I cried indignantly.

"Oh, it was a friendly kind of hurt," said Keziah happily.

Later I discovered that the man was a Rolf Weaver, the leader of a band of men who had come to assess the treasures of the Abbey.

My father was deeply distressed. "Cromwell's men are at the Abbey," he said. "This will kill the Abbot."

What it did mean was that this was the beginning of the end of St. Bruno's as we had known it. Its sanctity was immediately destroyed. Weaver's men made the cloisters noisy; they raided the Abbey cellars and were often drunk; they took girls in and forced them to lie with them on the monks' pallets and took a profane delight in defiling the cells. The girls' stories were that they went because they daren't disobey Cromwell's men; and I knew it would not be long before Keziah was there; and when I pictured her with Rolf Weaver I felt sick.

Brother John came alone to see my father; he told him that the Abbot had been so grievously stricken that he had had a seizure and was unable to move from his bed.

"I fear his end is near," said my father. "This will kill him."

When the following day neither Brother John nor Brother James came to the house my father went to the Abbey in an attempt to see them. His way was barred and one of Rolf Weaver's men demanded to know his business and when my father told him that he had come to see two lay brothers he was told that no one was allowed into the Abbey and no one out.

"How is the Abbot?" asked my father. "I heard he was very ill."

"Ill with fright" was the answer. "He's frightened because he's been found out. That's all it is. Fear."

"The Abbot has lived a saintly life," said my father indignantly.

"That's what you think" was the answer. "Wait till we tell you all we've found out."

"I know that any accusation which is brought against him will be false."

"Then you'd better be careful. The King's men don't like those that are too friendly with monks."

My father could only walk away; and I had not seen him so depressed since the execution of Sir Thomas More.

That very night Kate and I saw Keziah come in staggering a little. She had been to the Abbey, I gathered.

Kate sniffed her breath.

"You've been drinking, Keziah," she accused.

"Oh, Kezzie," I said reproachfully, "you've been with that man."

Keziah kept nodding. I had never seen her drunk before although she liked her ale, and drank it freely. She must have had something strong to make her as she was.

Kate's eyes gleamed with excitement. She shook Keziah and said: "Tell us what happened. You've been at your tricks again."

Keziah started to giggle. "What a one," she murmured. "What a one! Never in all my life. . . ."

"It was Rolf Weaver, was it?"

Keziah kept nodding. "He sent for me. 'Bring Keziah,' he said. So I had to go."

"And most willingly you went," said Kate. "Go on."

"And there he was and he. . . ." She started to giggle again.

"It was no new experience to you," said Kate, "so why are you in this state?"

But apparently it had been a new experience. She could only keep nodding and giggling. So Kate and I put her to bed. We noticed there were bruises on her big soft white body. I shivered but Kate was very excited.

A gibbet had been erected outside the gates of the Abbey. On it swung the body of a monk. He looked grotesque, like a great black crow, with his robes flapping about him. His crime was that he had tried to take some of the Abbey's treasures to a goldsmith in London. No doubt he planned to make his escape on the proceeds, but Weaver's men had caught him. This was a lesson to any who tried to flout their authority and divert Abbey treasure from the King who now laid claim to it.

It was horrible. None of us would pass the Abbey gates. We stayed indoors, afraid to go out.

Of everything that had happened this was the most terrible. It seemed as though our entire world was collapsing about us. No matter what else had happened the Abbey had always stood there, powerful and solid; now it was shaken to its foundations.

I often thought of Bruno and wondered what was happening to him. He would see those crude men sprawling at the refectory table where once the monks had sat observing their rules of silence. He would see them invading the cells, taking shrieking girls in there and just for the joy of abominating sacred places. I remembered that day when on Kate's insistence he had taken us into the sacred chapel and shown us the jeweled Madonna. I caught my breath. Those men would find her; they would tear off those glittering gems. The silent chapel would be desecrated.

I prayed for Bruno while my father prayed that no ill should come to the Abbot and the Abbey be saved—although that was a forlorn hope since Cromwell's men had come to make their inventories. Bruno was in my thoughts constantly. Perhaps he always had been, ever since we had found him that day when we went through the door for the first time. He was proud—apart from us all. The Holy Child. Sometimes I wondered what I should have been like if instead of being born in a normal way I had been found in a crib in a holy place.

Kate and I talked about Bruno while other people talked about the Abbey.

"We ought to try and see him," she said. "We could go through the door."

I thought of all those rough men wandering about the Abbey. "We dare not now," I said.

Kate saw my point for once. Perhaps she had visions of being seized by one of them and forced into one of the cells for many of the girls had talked of having been forced. That offended Kate's fastidious nature. Kate wanted to receive admiration rather than give physical satisfaction. She was the sort of woman, I was to discover later, who wishes to be perpetually wooed and rarely won.

She did not consider the idea that we should go through the door now. But she talked of Bruno and there was something in her manner when she spoke of him that made me sure that he was almost as important to her as he was to me.

"There'll be a miracle," she said to me. "You'll see. This is what it was for. This is why he was sent. He was put in the crib so that he could be here at this time. You'll see."

She voiced the thoughts of us all. We were all waiting for a miracle; and it would come from the Holy Child.

The atmosphere was tense with expectancy.

And then the climax came. But it was not the miracle we were expecting.

Kate came to my room. It was past midnight. She looked beautiful in a blue robe with her long tawny hair about her shoulders.

"Wake up," she said. But I had not been asleep. I don't know whether it was some premonition which kept me awake on that night. It was almost as though I was aware that this was going to be the end of an era.

She said: "Keziah's not in her room."

I sat up in bed. "She's with one of the men."

"Yes, she's with a man. She's at the Abbey, I dareswear."

"That man. He's sent for her again!"

"She went willingly enough. It's . . . horrible."

"Keziah was always like that."

"Yes, I know. A man only had to beckon and she was after him. I wonder your father allows her in the house."

"I don't think he knows."

"His head is in the clouds. One day he will lose it if he is not careful."

"Kate, don't dare say such things!"

"I must say what I feel. Everything has changed so much. Do you remember when we went to see Queen Anne? How different it seemed then. Now everything has changed."

"No, it was changing then. It has always been changing, but it seems now that tragedy is coming near . . . nearer to us."

Kate sitting on the edge of my bed clasping her knees looked thoughtful. She did not want this kind of excitement. She wanted balls and gaiety, the pleasure of wearing fine clothes and jewels and men desiring her.

"It's time your father thought of a match for me," she said. "And all he thinks of is what is happening at the Abbey."

"We all think of it."

"It's so long since we've seen Bruno," said Kate. "I wonder. . . ."

I had never seen her so concerned for anyone before. She said: "Let's talk of pleasant things. Let's forget Weaver and his men and the Abbey."

"We could not forget it for long," I said, "because it is so much a part of our lives and what is happening there is happening to us."

But Kate wanted to talk of pleasant things. Her marriage, for instance. The Duke or Earl who would take her to Court. He would be rich and doting; but she was halfhearted and as she talked of the splendors to come I knew she was thinking of Bruno.

Was it premonition?

It was five of the clock when Keziah came in. Kate had seen her staggering across the courtyard and brought her to my room. She was without shoes or stockings and her feet were bleeding; her gown was torn and I saw a great bruise across her shoulder. She seemed as though she were intoxicated but I could smell no drink on her breath.

I cried out: "What has happened?"

"She seems to be demented," said Kate. "Something's certainly happened to her."

Keziah looked at me and held out a hand. I took it. She was trembling.

I said: "Keziah, what is it? What happened? You've been hurt."

She said: "Mistress Damask. I'm a sinner. The gates of hell are yawning for me."

I said, "Pull yourself together, Keziah. What happened? How did you get into this state?"

"She's come from the Abbey," said Kate. "You've come from the Abbey, Keziah. Don't try to deny it."

Keziah shook her head. "No. Not the Abbey," she said. "I've sinned. . . . I've sinned something awful. I've told what should be locked away in here." She beat her breast with such violence that I thought she would injure herself.

I said: "For God's sake, Keziah, what have you done?"

"I've told them. I've told *him* and now 'tis for the whole world to know what was a sacred secret. What'll they do now, Mistress Damask? What'll they do now they know?"

"You'd better tell us what they know," said Kate. "And you'd better be quick about it."

Keziah rolled her eyes up to the ceiling and then burst into bitter sobbing.

I felt I had strayed into a nightmare. I knew that something portentous had happened. I had never seen careless, sensuous Keziah in such a state before. Had she been an innocent young girl I should have thought that she had been raped by the monsters who had invaded the Abbey, but Keziah was no innocent girl, she was one who would find rape an enjoyable experience.

But this was real sorrow—abandoned sorrow. Keziah was in torment.

I said gently: "Tell us, Kezzie. It'll help. Start at the beginning and tell us all."

She turned to me and I put my arms about her. She winced with pain. Her big rather flaccid body trembled.

"I've told," she babbled. "I've told what ought never to be told. I've done something terrible. I wonder Satan himself don't come down for me."

"Begin at the beginning," commanded Kate. "Tell us everything. You're just babbling nonsense."

"Yes, it'll help you to talk, Kezzie," I said. "I doubt it's as bad as you think."

"It's terrible, Mistress Damask, I'm doomed. The gates of hell be yawning. . . ."

"Don't start that again," Kate said impatiently. "Now what happened? That man sent for you and you went willingly. In fact you could scarcely wait to get there. We know that."

"Oh, it were before that, Mistress Kate. It were long before that. It was when I found the gate in the wall. That's when it all began."

The gate in the wall! Kate and I exchanged glances.

"It were covered by the ivy and none would guess there was a gate there, but I found it . . . and I went through. I walked into sacred ground. I should have known I was damned from then."

"Don't talk nonsense," said Kate sharply. "There shouldn't have been a gate and then you wouldn't have found it. You couldn't be blamed for opening and walking through. That was natural."

"But it didn't stop there, Mistress. I saw him there . . . and he'd thrown off his monk's robe and he didn't seem the same without it—a man, nothing more. He was tending the herbs and plucking some and he was a fine man, that much was clear. I watched him and then I called to him and when he saw me he was that startled. He bade me begone quickly. He said after he thought I was some vision sent by the devil to tempt him, which in a way I was. The devil tempted us both."

"Go on," said Kate excitedly, and a glimmer of understanding came to me, for I had a hazy notion as to where all this was leading.

I could picture it so clearly. Brother Ambrose working there and Keziah tempting him with that blatant sensuality which was inherent and would prove her ruin.

"I watched him working and I told him it was a pity all that fine manhood going to waste and all he could say was 'Get thee behind me, Satan.' But I was wicked and I knew it was only a matter of waiting. I went away but I came back and I could see that he was expecting me and I couldn't think of any other man but him and I knew how it was with him. So we lay in the long grass and we did what was only natural for most men but him being a monk made it all the more exciting like for me. For him too, I reckon. And I went back and he wouldn't come that time because he was busy in his cell itching in his hair shirt or kneeling before the cross asking for purification or something like that. So he used to tell me, but I didn't listen. I always knew he'd come back and that he wanted to be there as much as I did. And so it was. But then I was with child. I know it had happened to others before me but this was different. This was with child by a monk."

"It's not the first time that's happened to you, I'll swear," said Kate, her eyes gleaming with excitement.

"That was the first time—though it's happened since, and I've rid myself of my burdens with my old Granny's help. If it hadn't been the first time I might have acted different. But there I was with child . . . by a monk. I was frightened. So I said nothing . . . nothing to him, nothing to nobody, and then it was six months and beginning to show so I went to my old Granny in the woods. She was a wise woman. She'd know what to do. 'You've left it too late, Kez!' she said. 'You should have come three months since. It would be dangerous now. You'll have to have the child.' So I told her all and that it was a monk's seed that had made my baby and she laughed then, she laughed so long and loud that she made me feel better. 'Go back to the house,' she said, 'and wear your biggest petticoats. Tell them that your aunt in Black Heath is ill and calling for you. You're going to her for a spell.' So I did as she said and I set out with a few things in my saddlebags and I was to travel with a party that my Granny was arranging. But I stayed with Granny and she kept me in her cottage so that no one knew because she had this idea of what we should do when the child was born. She sent for Ambrose and he came to her cottage— though he were living enclosed and that were breaking his vows— and the child was to be born about Christmastime. He didn't want to do it but my Granny had wonderful powers. He thought she was the Devil in petticoats for he believed by now that he sold his soul to the Devil. She tempted him. 'It's your own child,' she said. 'The seed of your loins. You'll want to see it sometimes, watch over it.' When the boy child was born—it being Christmas, this plan came to my Granny. She sat by the fire rocking herself

and talking to the cat. The child was to go into the crib, so they'd
think it was a Holy Child. My Granny said they'd bring him up in
the Abbey and perhaps he'd be Abbot one day. They made an
educated gentleman of him which would be different from his being a serving wench's bastard. So we planned it and on that Christmas Eve I carried my baby through the secret door and Ambrose
took him and laid him in the crib. . . ."

Kate and I were astounded. We could not believe this. Bruno
—the Holy Child, whose coming had been a miracle which had
changed St. Bruno's from a struggling to a prosperous Abbey, the
son of a monk and a serving girl! Yet although we cried out
against this fantastic story we believed that it was true.

"You wicked creature," cried Kate. "All this time you have been
deceiving us . . . and the world."

I thought she was going to strike Keziah. She was so angry; and
I knew that she could not bear to think of the change in Bruno's
status. She had jeered at the Holy Child but she had wanted him
to be set apart from the rest of us.

Keziah began to sob. "But I'm not deceiving now," she said.
"And this is the most wicked thing of all. Now the whole world
knows."

"Keziah," I cried, "you have told that . . . *man!*"

She rocked herself to and fro in her misery. "Mistress, I could
not help it. He sent for me to go to the inn—the Abbey Inn. I was
taken to a room there and he ordered me to strip and lie down on
the bed. So I did and waited for him because I thought. . . ."

"We know what you thought, you harlot," cried Kate.

"But it wasn't," said Keziah. "He came and he bent over me
and he fondled me rough like and said, 'You're not a *young* harlot
anymore, Keziah, but there's a lot of the harlot still left in you,
eh?' And I laughed and I thought it was a sort of love play and
then he took a rope and tied me by the ankles to the bedposts. I
struggled a bit but not so much."

"You thought it was going to be some new kind of what do you
call it . . . love play?" said Kate.

"I thought that, Mistress . . . right till I saw the whip. Then I
screamed and he hit me across the face and said, 'None of that
noise, you slut.'

"I asked him what he wanted of me more than he'd had and

more than he could take as he wished for I had nothing more to give. 'Oh, but you have, Keziah,' he said. 'You've got something I want and you're going to give it too if I have to kill you to get it.' I was frightened, Mistress, too frightened to cry for he looked like a fiend there bending over me, gloating as a man might when he looks on a naked woman but a gloating I hadn't seen before. Then he said, 'You've had something to do with the monks. You're not going to tell me a woman like you hasn't done a little frolicking behind the gray walls. You'd have had your fill of grooms and stablemen and gardeners and any travelers that came this way. You'd want a little change, wouldn't you?' Then with my sin heavy on me I began to tremble and he saw it and that made him laugh the more. 'You're going to tell me, Keziah?' he said. 'You're going to tell me all about this tumbling on the altar and in the holy chapels.' I cried out, 'It weren't there. It weren't there. We weren't as sinful as that.' And he said, 'Where were you sinful then, Keziah?' I shut my mouth tight and I wouldn't speak. Then he brought the whip down across me, Mistress. I screamed and he said, 'Scream all you like, Keziah. They're used to screams in this place and they daren't complain. That was a taste, a starter.' I could feel the blood warm on my thighs. He bent over me then and caressed me, in his rough way. He took my ear between his teeth and bit it. He said: 'Keziah, if you don't talk I'll make your body so that no man will ever want to lie with you again. I'll make your face so scarred men will shudder when they look at you. You'll want them just the same but they'll not want you. You won't find it so easy to give that I'm-willing-and-ready-sir look you gave me in the lane when we first met.' And I was trembling and I said to myself: I must not tell. I must not tell. And I said nothing and he bent over me and he said, 'Just once more to remind you how you enjoy it, eh?' And then he was on me in that fierce sort of way that was almost more pain than pleasure. Oh, Mistress, what have I done?"

"You never told that beast!" cried Kate.

She nodded. "He had the whip. He was saying all the things he would do to me and so I cried out, 'I'll tell you. . . . I'll tell you everything. . . .' And I told him about Ambrose and how I tempted him and how my Granny persuaded him to put the child in the crib and make him holy. . . . And he just stared at me and

I've never seen such a change in a man. He laughed so much I thought he was going mad. Then he untied the ropes. He said, 'You'll soon heal, Keziah. You'll be better than ever. You're a good girl, and this has been a good night's work.'

"So I put on my clothes and couldn't find my shoes. . . . I stumbled out of the inn and home and now it's out. The secret's out."

How right she was.

The secret was out.

How quickly, how suddenly I was becoming aware of the violent passions of men. Those few days will always stand out in my mind as the most horrifying I have ever known. I have perhaps since known greater horror, certainly greater suffering, but in those days I was shocked forever out of my childhood. It seemed to me that since the day I had stood with my father at the river's edge and seen the King pass by with the great Cardinal I had moved slowly but certainly toward this climax. Death and destruction were growing up all around me, like weeds in an ill-kept garden; but during those days I saw a man murdered and that is something that must make an impression on the mind for evermore. I had heard the bells toll for Queen Anne and for Sir Thomas More and the memory made me serious; but this was different.

All next morning we waited for the news to break. We knew it could not be long. But both Kate and I had been too shaken by it to speak of it to anyone. We hardly mentioned it to each other and when we did spoke in hushed tones.

Did Bruno know? I wondered. I couldn't bear to think of his knowing. I knew that it meant so much to him to be the Holy Child.

I had to see Bruno. I was amazed by the strength of my feelings. I didn't care what danger I faced. I wanted to tell him that it made no difference to me that he was the son of Keziah and a monk. In fact I felt a certain relief—although I realized what disaster this would bring to the Abbey. But I must see him; so I went out alone and I ran to the secret door, I pulled aside the ivy and entered the Abbey grounds. My heart was beating so rapidly that I felt as though I were choking. I dared not pause to think what would happen to me if I were caught there. I went to the spot where we used to meet Bruno and I hid under the clump of bushes where Kate and I used to hide, hoping, rather absurdly, that he would come. It was thus that I witnessed this terrifying scene.

I must have waited there almost half an hour, and at the end of that time he did come, but he was not alone. The monk Ambrose was with him.

I remembered him because I had seen him when Keziah had set me on the wall and I had been so bewildered by Keziah's badinage with the monk.

It was obvious as soon as I saw Bruno that he knew. There was a strange lost look in his face. Ambrose was talking to him. They must have come here because it was an uncultivated spot in the grounds and rarely used by anyone from the Abbey.

"You cannot understand," Ambrose was saying; and his voice came to me clearly. "I wanted to watch over you. I wanted to play my part in bringing you up. It was wrong. It was wicked. It was a form of blasphemy . . . but I did it because I could not bear to be parted from you."

There was anguish in his voice which wrung my heart. I could well understand the terrible remorse and tribulation he had suffered, this man who should never have become a monk. I could picture his torturing himself in the solitude of his cell. The sinner whose actions had shut him out of paradise. Thus must Adam have felt when he had eaten of the forbidden fruit.

I was deeply moved by Brother Ambrose. I think because I remembered that my father had wanted a family; he had left the Abbey because of that, which was clearly what Ambrose should have done. Instead he had tried to have the best of both worlds— his monk's cell and his son. I understood very well and I wanted Bruno to tell him that he did.

But Bruno was silent.

"I have suffered for my sin a million times," went on Brother Ambrose. "But I have had great joy in watching you. Did you not sense that extra care that I gave you? Did you not feel as I did that you were my very own boy? I was jealous of your fondness for Clement, for the hours you spent with Valerian. I wanted to be the one who taught you your Greek and Latin; I wanted to cook you tidbits in my oven. And all I could do was teach you about the herbs and their healing properties and their cruel ones too. But I grudged everyone else the time they spent with you. They loved you in their way . . . but I was your father. I would like to hear you call me by that name . . . once."

Still Bruno did not speak.

I could picture it all so clearly—the child's growing up, the anxious father, his love for the child, his delight in him in contrast to his terrible remorse. I could understand his exultation and his suffering, and I wanted to cry out: "Bruno, speak to him tenderly. Let him know that you are glad to call him Father."

But Bruno remained silent as though stunned.

And then the scene changed because I heard a loud coarse voice calling out: "So you are there. Father and son, eh?" And to my horror Rolf Weaver had appeared.

I shrank into the bushes. I began to think of Keziah lying on the bed naked with ropes about her ankles and prayed that the bushes would hide me. I could not imagine what my fate would be if I were detected. This man, so bestial, so crude, who was capable of acts which I did not fully understand, was a terrifying spectacle. His doublet was open almost to his waist and I could see the black hair on his chest; his face was ruddy and his black hair grew low on his forehead. He was a beast personified. He was capable of committing any cruelty, I was well aware. I marveled that Keziah could ever have found him attractive even before he had treated her so vilely. But Kate had said that women like Keziah found pleasure in a certain sort of cruelty. I remembered what she had said about his rough love play. I had seen Kate's lips curl with disgust as she had said that. Kate knew so much that I did not. I wished that she were with me now. I could have done with the comfort she would have given me; and I wondered that I had been so bold as to come here alone. But at this moment they would not have been interested in me. Rolf Weaver had two people to torture and they occupied his attention to the exclusion of aught else.

"Now," he cried, "what does it feel like to know you're the son of this whoresome monk and the village harlot?"

I watched Bruno's face. It was as white as the marble face of the jeweled Madonna.

He did not speak. Ambrose had taken a step toward Rolf Weaver.

"Have a care, Monk," cried Weaver. "By God. I'll have you flayed alive if you raise a hand to me. Is it not enough that you have lied to your Abbot, that you have desecrated his Abbey, that you have committed the mortal sin—must you threaten the King's man?" He laughed. "She's a fruity wench, I grant you. So ready and willing. By God, you have only to take one look at her and you know it's here-and-now-and-no-waiting-please-sir. That's your mother, my boy. Wouldn't I have liked to see them frolicking in the grass! And that's how you were made. I don't doubt it was a shock for the holy monk and his little piece of any-man's-for-the-taking when they found you were on the way."

He let out a string of words which I did not understand. I only knew that I wanted to stop my ears and get away. But I could not move for if I did I would show myself, and I was oddly enough more afraid of Bruno's knowing that I had witnessed his shame than of what Rolf Weaver could do to me.

Then it happened. Brother Ambrose had sprung at Rolf Weaver; he had him by the throat, and the two men were rolling on the ground. Bruno stood as though unable to move, just staring at them. I saw that Brother Ambrose was on top of Rolf Weaver and, his hands still about his throat, lifted him and banged his head several times on the earth.

I stared in horror. I could see the purple color of Rolf Weaver's face; I heard him gasping for his breath and then suddenly there was silence.

Brother Ambrose stood up; he took Bruno by the hand and slowly they walked toward the Abbey.

I cowered in the bushes for a second or so and then I ran, taking care not to pass too close to the man who lay inert on the grass.

At sundown the following day the body of Brother Ambrose hung on a gibbet at the Abbey's Gate. My father forbade my mother, Kate and me to go near it.

He was deeply distressed, for in addition to this awful tragedy the Abbot was dead.

He said to me: "We live in terrible times, my child."

Our house was silent for when we spoke it was in whispers. We all seemed to be waiting for what calamity could befall our community next. My father did say that he was glad of one thing. His friend Sir Thomas More at least was spared the apparently endless tragedies which resulted from the King's desire to have his pleasure at no matter what cost. I was glad he said that only to me, and I cried out in horror that he should ever repeat to any other what he had said to me. He comforted me; he would take care, he promised—as much care as it was possible to take in this dangerous world.

The commissioners had broken the Seal and the Abbey was now the King's. Because of the abominations which were said to have occurred within its precincts there were to be no pensions for any of the members. The Abbot, who might have been honored with a bishopric if no scandals had been discovered, fortunately for himself had died while the King's men were in his Abbey. It was said he died of a broken heart; and I could believe it, and I guessed it must have been almost the cruelest blow that could have been dealt him to learn that he had been deluded by one of his monks who had dared defile the holy crib with his bastard child; but the greatest blow was the loss of his Abbey.

All through those miserable days there was the sound of men's voices as the packhorses were loaded with treasures and led away. Thieves were responsible for the loss of some of the treasures. They came by night and tore the beautiful vestments for the sake of the gold and silver thread in them. If they were caught they were hanged at once; but they did not care about this. There was too much to be gained.

Many of the manuscripts, the work of Brother Valerian, were piled up before the Abbey and burned. The lead on the roofs was of great value and the man who had taken over Rolf Weaver's duties gave instructions for it to be removed.

The monks were turned adrift to find some means of making a livelihood in a world for which they were ill-fitted. Brother John and Brother James came to see my father and were immediately offered a home which they declined. "Were we to accept your offer," they explained, "we could place you in jeopardy and as lay brothers we are not so ill-equipped as some. We have been out in the world and have done business for the Abbey and know a wool merchant in London who might give us work."

Seeing that they were adamant my father insisted that they take a well-filled purse and they went on their way.

Later that day I was in my father's study and we were talking of the terrible thing which had befallen St. Bruno's, when Simon Caseman joined us. My father was saying that he greatly wished that the Brothers had stayed when we saw two monks coming across the lawn. My father hurried down to meet them, followed by Simon Caseman and myself.

The monks told my father that they were Brother Clement and Brother Eugene and they had worked respectively in the Abbey's bake and brew houses. Now they were bewildered and did not know where to go. There was an unworldliness about the pair which moved me deeply; to turn them into the world would be like sending two lambs among wolves.

My father immediately offered them work in our kitchens and brewhouse. When they wore fustian doublets and trunk hose they would look exactly like other servants, he said, and it would be wise not to mention whence they had come.

Simon Caseman was alarmed. He assured my father that taking in dispossessed monks might be construed as an act of treachery to the King. My father was aware of this but he demanded to know how he could turn such men away. I believe that he would have taken in all the monks as he had tried to take in John and James, if they had not all scattered before he was able to do so.

It was later the same day that Bruno appeared. I was walking with my father in the garden and we were talking of the terrible debacle and what it would mean to those men who had passed the greater part of their lives in the Abbey suddenly to be thrust out into the world.

"There may well be more of them to join Clement and Eugene," he was saying when we saw Bruno.

"Bruno!" I cried. "Oh, I am so relieved to see you. I have been thinking of you all the time."

My father looked surprised and with a little shock I realized that he did not know Bruno.

I said: "Father, this is he who was found in the Christmas crib."

"My poor boy," cried my father. "And where will you go now?"

Bruno replied: "I must find a roof to shelter me until a time when I no longer need it."

I thought it a strange reply but nothing Bruno did had ever been ordinary.

My father said: "You have your roof. You will stay here."

"Thank you," replied Bruno. "I shall make sure that you do not regret this day."

I was happier than I had been for a long time as we took Bruno into the house. He was given a room. We could not expect him to sleep in the servants' quarters, I told my father, and when we were alone I explained my acquaintance with Bruno and told him about the ivy-covered door.

"You did wrong," said my father, "but perhaps there was a purpose in it. Damask, that boy still believes that there is a divinity within him."

He was right. No one could treat Bruno as a servant. My father told the household that he came to us from people who were his friends. He was to share lessons with us.

He accepted this; he had lost none of that arrogance which overawed both Kate and me and exasperated her so much.

He insisted that Keziah had lied under torture and so had Ambrose. Everything that had happened, he said he had foreseen. It was all part of a divine plan and we should see it unfold in time; and although when I was alone I believed that he reasoned thus because he could not endure to do otherwise, when I was with him I half-believed him.

The King's men left and because they had taken the lead from the church roof owls and bats began to nest there. The rotting corpses were removed from the gibbets by my father's orders and given decent burial. We trembled for several weeks after that for fear it should be construed as an act of treason while we waited for someone to come and claim the Abbey and its lands. But no one came.

The Abbey remained, like the skeleton of some great monster, to remind us of a way of life that had now passed and gone forever.

Lord Remus

There was change everywhere. It was unsafe to go out after dark because the lanes and woods abounded with robbers who would not hesitate to maim or even kill for the sake of a little money. Beggars and vagabonds had in the past been sure of a meal and often shelter under the monastic roofs; these benefits no longer existed. Added to the beggars were those monks who had been deprived of the only life they understood. They must either beg or starve. It was true that some could work but few wished to take monks into their household as my father had done, for Simon Caseman was right when he said this could be construed as an act of treason.

Brother Clement settled in easily and one would not have guessed that he had lived the greater part of his life in the Abbey. Sometimes he would burst into song in a rich baritone voice as he worked; and we had never tasted such cob loaves or manchets as came from his oven. Brother Eugene was equally content in the brewhouse; he made slow gin and dandelion and elder flower wine; and was constantly experimenting with berries to improve his brew. When they discovered that Bruno was in the house they could not hide their delight; and I knew his identity could not be kept a secret.

When Clement and Eugene were together they would whisper about the old days; and whenever Ambrose's name was mentioned they would hastily cross themselves. I don't know what shocked them more—the knowledge of his sin in first begetting a child and the placing it in the crib to make a miracle, or the violent manner of his death.

As for the inhabitants of the house, we all seemed to be cowering under a blow that had momentarily stunned us. My father wore an air of resignation, almost of waiting. I knew he spent long hours on his knees in prayer. He would go into our little chapel in the west wing of the house and stay there for hours. It was as though he were preparing himself for an ordeal. My mother worked feverishly on her gardens and there was often a puzzled look on her usually placid face. She seemed to be relying more and more on Simon who, whenever he had the leisure, would carry her baskets for her and help her plant out her seedlings. Even Kate was subdued. She had craved excitement but not of the kind we had lately suffered. Rupert seemed least affected. Calmly and quietly he went about his work of tending the land as though nothing had happened.

Bruno concerned me most. His eyes would blaze with anger if Kate or I suggested that it was Brother Ambrose who had placed him in the crib. He told us fiercely that many lies had been told and one day he would prove it.

Kate recovered more quickly from the shock of events than I did, and as Bruno had come to the house she constantly sought him out. Sometimes the three of us were together as we had been in the Abbey grounds in the old days and then it was almost as it had been long ago when there had been an Abbey and we had trespassed there.

Kate teased him. "If he was divine why did he not call down the fury of the heavens on Cromwell's men?" she wanted to know.

His eyes would blaze with fury but because she was Kate she could inspire some feeling in him which I was sure he had for no one else.

The servingwoman and the monk lied, he insisted.

And as I said, I believed him when I was with him. Rupert was twenty years old now. He should have been managing his own lands but it turned out that he had none to manage. When his parents had died their possessions had been sold to pay their debts and there was very little left. This my father had set aside for Rupert when he was of age, but he had never told Kate or Rupert the true state of affairs as he had not wished them to think they were living on charity.

Rupert told me this himself when he came on me one day in the nuttery. I was seated in my favorite spot under a filbert tree reading and he came and sprawled beside me. He picked up a nut and idly threw it from him and then he started to talk to me and I realized that I was receiving a proposal of marriage.

"My uncle is the best man alive," he began; and he had certainly chosen the best opening to please me. I agreed fervently.

"Sometimes," I said, "I fear that he is too good."

Could anyone be too good? Rupert wondered; and I answered, yes, because then they endangered themselves for the sake of others. My father had taken in the monks and that might be considered an unwise thing to do. There was Sir Thomas. Had he forgotten him? He was a man who was *too* good and what had happened to him? He had lost his head and his once happy household was no more.

"Life is cruel sometimes, Damask," said Rupert. "And then it is good to have someone to stand beside you."

I agreed.

"I had thought," he went on, "that one day I should leave here to manage my own estate and I have learned that I have no estate. Your father did not wish us to know that we were paupers so he let us believe that our lands had not been seized by our parents' creditors when they died. So, I have nothing, Damask."

"But you have us. This is your home."

"As I hope it will always be."

"My father says that the land has never been tended as you tend it. The men work for you as they work for no one else."

"I have a feeling for the land, Damask, this land. I know your father hopes I will stay here forever."

"And will you?"

"It depends."

"On what?" I asked.

"On you perhaps. This will be yours one day . . . yours and your husband's. When that day comes you would not want me here."

"Nonsense, Rupert. I'd always want you here . . . you and Kate. You are as my brother and sister."

"Kate will marry, doubtless."

"You too, Rupert. And you will bring your wife here. Why, the house is big enough and we can always make it bigger. We have so much land. You are looking sad."

"This has become as my home," he said. "I love the land. I love the animals. Your father is as my own."

"And I am as much a sister to you as Kate is. Oh, I couldn't bear for all this to be broken up . . . as the Abbey has been."

He picked up another nut and threw it. He said: "I believe your father hopes that you and I will marry."

I said sharply: "That is not something that can be done because it would be comfortable and convenient to do it."

"Oh, no, no," said Rupert quickly.

I felt a little hurt. It was in a way a proposal, my first, and it had been offered to me as a convenient arrangement for the disposal of my father's lands.

I murmured that I had a Latin exercise to complete and Rupert, flushing a little, rose to his feet and went away.

I thought of marriage with Rupert and children growing up in this house. I would like a large family; I flushed uneasily, because the father I visualized for them was not Rupert.

I went up to my room. I sat on the window seat looking out through the latticed window. I saw Kate and Bruno walking together. They were talking earnestly. I felt sad because Bruno never talked to me in that earnest manner. In fact he talked to no one like that—but Kate.

When Keziah had heard that Ambrose was hanged at the Abbey's Gate she had gone to the gibbet and stood there gazing at him. It was difficult to get her away. One of her fellow servants had brought her home but she was back again and the first night that he hung there she kept her vigil at the gibbet.

On the second day Jennet, one of our housemaids, brought her back and told me that Keziah seemed to be possessed and was acting in an unusual way. I went to her and found her in a strange state. I put her to bed and told her she was to stay there. She remained there for a week. The weals on her thighs had become inflamed and as I couldn't think how to heal them I went to Mother Salter in the woods and asked her advice. She was pleased that I was looking after Keziah and gave me some lotions to put on the sore places and a concoction of herbs for Keziah to drink.

I nursed Keziah myself. It was something for me to do during that strange time. I think part of her trouble was that she could not face people. Ambrose was dead and she stood alone and as the perpetrator of that wicked hoax she was afraid to face the world.

She used to ramble in her talk sometimes as I sat by her bed. There was a great deal about Ambrose and the manner in which she had tempted him; she blamed herself; she was the wicked one.

"Oh, Damask," she said, "don't think too bad of me. It were as natural to me as breathing and there was no holding back. 'Tis like that with some of us . . . though 'twill not be with you maybe . . . nor with Mistress Kate. The men should beware of Mistress Kate . . . all fire on top and ice beneath . . . and them's the dangerous ones. And you, Mistress Damask, you'll be a good and faithful wife, I promise you, which is the best thing to be."

Then she talked about the boy. "He never looks at me, Damask . . . or when he does it's to despise me. He'll never forgive me for being his mother. He's dreamed dreams, that boy. He believed he was sent from Heaven. A Holy Child, he thought, and then he finds he's the result of a win between a wanton servant wench and a monk who broke his vows."

I begged her to be at peace. The past was over; she must start afresh.

"Mercy me," she said with a return of her old smile. "You talk like your father, Mistress Damask."

"There's no one I would rather talk like," I assured her.

I was a comfort to her strangely enough; and it was I who dressed her wounds with the ointments her grandmother had given me; I assigned her duties to another of the maids that she might rest in solitude until she could face the world.

She used to sit at her window and watch for a glimpse of Bruno. I believe he knew that she watched for him; but he never glanced up at her window.

Once I said to him: "Keziah watches for you. If you would look at her window and smile it would do her so much good."

He looked at me coldly. "She is a wicked woman," he said.

"She is your mother," I reminded him.

"I don't believe it."

His mouth was grim; his eyes cold. I saw then that he forced himself not to believe this. He dared not believe it. He had lived so long with the notion that he was apart from us all that it was more than he could endure to accept it as otherwise.

I said softly: "One must face the truth, Bruno."

"The truth! Is that what you call the words uttered by a wicked monk and a lecherous serving girl?"

I did not tell him that I had heard Ambrose talking to him a few moments before he had murdered Rolf Weaver.

"It's lies!" said Bruno almost hysterically. "Lies, lies, all lies."

In a way, I thought, he is like Keziah. She cannot face the world and he cannot face the truth.

How quickly one becomes accustomed to change. It was but a month since the last packhorse laden with Abbey treasure had departed and there we were adjusted to our new way of life.

The trees were in full leaf; the bracken plentiful; the shrubs green and bushy; the roses bloomed that year as never before and my mother was out in the garden through most of the day. Bruno had helped her make an herb garden because Ambrose had passed on his knowledge in this field. My mother was quite animated by this prospect and Bruno worked with her in a silence of which she did not seem to be aware.

Already weeds had started to grow in the Abbey gardens; no one interfered; they were unsure how such action would be regarded. Each day we had expected something to be done, but St. Bruno's seemed to have been forgotten. At the end of each day several beggars would be at our gates and a bench with forms had been set up in the garden and on my father's orders any beggar received a quart of beer and as many spice cakes as he could eat.

I sat one day in my mother's rose garden—a delightful spot with a wall surrounding it and reached through a wrought-iron gate and I said to myself: "It won't go on like this. This is a lull. Something will happen soon. Keziah could not stay in her bedroom; she would have to bestir herself. My father would return to a more normal life and not spend so much time in solitude and prayer. Someone would take over the Abbey. I had heard that the King made gifts of Abbey lands to those who had earned his favors. Oh, yes, it had to change."

And while I was brooding on these matters the gate clicked and Bruno and Kate came into the garden. I noticed that their fingers were interlaced. They were talking earnestly. Then they saw me.

"Here's Damask," said Kate unnecessarily. I noticed that her eyes were brilliant and her expression soft; and I was sad because with Kate, Bruno could be different from the way he could be with anyone else. I felt shut out of a magic circle of which I so longed to be a part.

"The roses are more beautiful this year," I said.

I sensed that they wanted to go away or for me to go; but I stood my ground.

"Come and sit down," I said. "It is very pleasant here."

To my surprise they obeyed me, and we sat Bruno between us. I said, "This reminds me of the old days in the Abbey grounds."

"It is not a bit like that," retorted Kate. "This is my aunt's rose garden, not Abbey land."

"I meant the three of us together."

"It's a long time ago," said Bruno.

I wanted to recapture the days when we were a trio of which I was a definite part.

I went on: "I shall never forget the day we went into the Abbey . . . the three of us and you showed us the jeweled Madonna."

A faint color had come into Bruno's cheeks. Kate was unusually silent. I guessed that they were, as I was, thinking of the moment when the great iron-studded door had opened and its creak had sounded loud enough to awaken the dead. I could smell the dampness, which had seemed to rise from those great flagged stones; I could feel the silence.

I said: "I've often wondered what happened to the jeweled Madonna. Those men must have taken her away and given her and all her jewels to the King."

"They did not take her," said Bruno. "There was a miracle."

We both turned to him and I knew that this was the first time he had spoken of the jeweled Madonna even to Kate.

"What happened?" asked Kate.

"When they went into the sacred chapel the Madonna was not there."

"Then where was she?" asked Kate.

"No one knew. She had disappeared. It was said she had gone back to heaven rather than let the robbers get her."

"I don't believe that," said Kate. "Someone hid her away before the men could get her."

"It was a miracle," replied Bruno.

"Miracles!" cried Kate. "I don't believe in miracles anymore."

Bruno had stood up, his face flushed and angry. Kate caught his hand but he flung her aside; and then he ran out of the rose garden. Kate ran after him.

"Bruno!" I heard her call imperiously. "Come back to me."

And I was left sitting there, with the realization that I could never be as close to him as Kate was and feeling lonely and sad because of it.

While I sat in the rose garden Simon Caseman came in. I thought he was looking for my mother and I told him I thought she was in the herb garden.

"But it was you I came to see, Mistress Damask," he said; and he sat beside me. He studied me so intently that I felt embarrassed under his gaze, especially as the recent encounter with Bruno and Kate had upset me. He went on: "Why, you are growing into a beauty."

"I do not believe that to be true."

"And modest withal."

"Not modest," I said. "If I thought I were a beauty I should not hesitate to admit it, for beauty is not a thing to take credit for since it is bestowed and not earned."

"And wise," he said. "I confess to be a little overawed in your presence. Your father constantly speaks of your erudition."

"You should take that as paternal pride. To a father his geese are swans."

"In this case I find myself in wholehearted agreement with the parent in question."

"I can only believe that you have lost your sense of judgment then. I fear for your performance in the courts."

"What a joy it is to talk with you, Mistress Damask."

"You are easily content, Master Caseman."

"There is one thing I would like to ask you, with your permission."

"That permission is given."

"You are no longer a child. Have you ever thought of giving your hand in marriage?"

"I suppose it is natural in all young women to think of eventual marriage."

"He to whom you gave your hand would be doubly favored. A beautiful and clever wife. What more could any man ask? He would be fortunate above all men."

"I have no doubt that any who asked my hand in marriage might well have his thoughts on my inheritance."

"My dear Mistress Damask, he would be too dazzled by your charms to think of such a matter."

"Or so dazzled by my inheritance that he might well be mistaken about my beauty and erudition, don't you think?"

"It would depend on the man. If he were, he deserves to be. . . ."

"Well? Hanged, drawn and quartered?"

"Worse than that. Rejected."

"I had no idea that you had such a talent for gallant speeches."

"If I have it is you who have inspired them."

"I wonder why."

"Do you? You, who are so clever, must have been aware of my intentions."

"Toward me?"

"Toward no one else."

"Master Caseman, is this a proposal?"

"It is. I should be the happiest of men if I might go to your father and tell him that you have consented to be my wife."

"Then I am afraid I cannot give you that pleasure."

I had risen. But my heart was pounding for I felt afraid; and I could not tell why this sudden desire to run should have come to me. I was here in my mother's peaceful rose garden with a man who was a member of our household, a friend of my father and one of whom he thought highly, and yet I experienced this sudden revulsion.

Simon Caseman had risen too. He stood beside me. He was not a big man—only two inches or so taller than I, and his face was very close to mine. His eyes were warm, alert and golden brown; his hair had a reddish tinge too; and the lines on his face made it appear to me, seen so close, like a fox's mask. I knew in that moment that I was afraid of him.

I turned to go but he caught my arm. His grip was firm as he said: "What have you in mind, Mistress Damask? Is it to marry someone else?"

I wished the color would not flame into my cheeks. I said: "I had not thought of marrying anyone."

"You do not plan to enter a convent?" His lips curled slightly. "That would be an unwise plan . . . at this time when so many of our convents have gone the way of our monasteries."

I withdrew my arm and said coldly: "I do not think I am of an age to consider marriage."

His hand lightly brushed the front of my gown. "Why, Mistress Damask, you are a woman already. You should not delay your enjoyments of womanhood, I do assure you. Pray do not reject me without consideration. I do verily believe that your father would not object to our union. I know that he wishes to see you under the protection of one whom he trusts. For these are troublous times in which we live."

"I shall make my own choice," I said.

And I walked out of the rose garden.

I was very shaken. I was not yet seventeen and I had already had two proposals of marriage whereas beautiful Kate, who was two years older, had not had one.

Or had she? But who could have proposed to Kate?

It was strange that I should have had this thought about Kate because a week or so after that scene in the rose garden Lord Remus called at the house.

We had known that he was coming because my father had settled some matter of law for him and as he was a very rich and powerful nobleman my mother was making a very special occasion of his visit.

All that day Clement had been working in the bakehouse; he had made pies with fancy crusts and there was one in the form of the Remus coat of arms. Clement was delighted with it because in the Abbey kitchen he had not had the opportunity of indulging in such frivolity. My mother was in her element for if there was anything she liked better than working in her garden it was preparing for visitors in the house. She took on a new authority. It was clear that she wished we entertained more.

Kate and I watched the arrival of the visitors from the window of her room. We were disappointed in Lord Remus who was fat and walked with a stick, wheezing as he made his way up the slope of the lawn from the privy steps. But he was very richly clad and quite clearly a man of great consequence.

Father led him into the hall where we were all waiting to greet the visitors. Mother first and Lord Remus was very gracious to her, then myself as the daughter of the house and the others, Rupert, Kate, Simon and Bruno. (I was delighted to see he was included.) My family, Father called us.

Kate swept a beautiful curtsy which she had been practicing all day; her long hair was caught up in a gold net and she looked beautiful.

That Lord Remus thought so was obvious for his eyes lingered on her, a fact of which no one was more aware than Kate.

It was a banquet that was put before our distinguished guest. There was fish—dace, barbel and chub all served in herbs of my mother's growing. Lord Remus congratulated her on her cook and she was delighted. Then there was sucking pig and beef and mutton followed by my mother's own brand of syllabub. There was ale and wine in plenty and I saw my mother's eyes gleam with satisfaction and I thought how easy it was for her to be happy in the moment; and how strange it was that such a short time ago we were living in terror of what would happen next and I could not get out of my mind the image of Brother Ambrose hanging from his gibbet at the Abbey's Gate.

Kate, who was seated opposite Lord Remus, asked him when he was last at Court and he replied that he was there but a week be-

fore. He talked of the Court and the King's dissatisfaction with
his state and how his temper was such that it was apt to flare up
if one were careless enough to rouse it.

"I'll warrant you, my lord, are the soul of tact," said Kate.

"My dear young lady, I have a desire to keep my head on my
shoulders, for that I consider is where it belongs."

Kate laughed a great deal and I saw my mother glance at her
and I thought afterward she will be reprimanded for her forward-
ness; but for the time that could pass, for Lord Remus did not
seem to object to it.

Lord Remus had drunk a great deal of the elderberry concoction which my mother admitted was particularly fine this year
and he was inclined to be talkative.

"The King needs a wife," he said. "He cannot be happy without
a wife, even when he is looking for a new wife. He must have a
wife."

Kate laughed a great deal and the rest of us smiled; I guessed
my parents were thinking uneasily of the servants.

"This time," said Lord Remus, "he is looking for a Princess from
the Continent, but some of the ladies are just a little reluctant."
He glanced at Kate. "Like me, young lady, they are anxious to keep
their heads and in view of what happened to the unfortunate
Anne Boleyn and even to Queen Katharine, the reluctance is un-
derstandable."

"It is like the Arabian nights," said Kate. "Perhaps if the King
could find a Queen who could continue to amuse him she could
continue to live."

"That is what the new Princess will have to aim for," said Lord
Remus. "I hear that the sister of the Duke of Cleves has the King's
attention. Master Holbein has painted a beautiful portrait of her
and the King declares himself to be enamored of the lady already."

"So the new Queen is chosen."

"That is what is being said at Court. Master Cromwell is eager
for the marriage. I never liked the man—a low fellow—but the
King finds him clever. It would be a good marriage for politics'
sake, so they say. I'll dareswear that very soon you will be seeing
another coronation."

"She will be the King's fourth wife," said Kate. "I should love to see her. I daresay she is very beautiful."

"Princesses are rarely as beautiful as they are made out to be," said Lord Remus. "I'll warrant those who lack royalty can often make up for it in beauty." He was smiling at Kate in somewhat bleary-eyed concentration. Our elderberries were very potent that year. They must have been or I am sure he would not have spoken so freely.

I think my father was rather relieved when the meal was over; then my mother led Lord Remus into the music room and she sang a very pleasant ditty to him which he applauded with delight and then Kate took her lute and sang.

She sang a love song and every now and then she would raise her eyes and smile in the direction of Lord Remus. Her long hair escaped from the gold net and fell about her shoulders; she pretended to throw it impatiently back but I knew her well enough to realize she was calling attention to it.

When Lord Remus left we all conducted him to the privy stairs and watched his barge sail up the river.

I noticed that Kate was laughing as though at some secret joke.

She came to my room that night. She had to talk to someone and she had always used me for this purpose.

She stretched out on my bed. She always did that while I was expected to occupy the window seat.

"Well," she said, "what thought you of my lord?"

"That he eats too much, drinks too much and laughs too much at his own jokes and not enough at other people's."

"I know so many to whom those words could apply."

"Which shows that my lord is so like many others that there is very little new one can say about him."

"One could say that he is rich; that he has a large estate in the country and a place at Court."

"All of which could make him very desirable in the eyes of scheming young women."

"There you speak sense, my child."

"Pray do not call me your child. I have had a proposal of marriage which is more than you have had."

She narrowed her eyes. "Master Caseman?"

I nodded.

"He doesn't want to marry you, Damask, so much as all this
. . . your lands, this house and everything that you will inherit
from your father."

"That is exactly what I implied."

"You are not so foolish after all."

"And no longer a child, since plus my inheritance I am considered marriageable."

"Lucky Damask! And what have I to recommend me? What but
my beauty and charm."

"Which seem to have their effects. Even gentlemen with a place
at Court and an estate in the country seem to be not unimpressed
by them."

"So you think he was impressed?"

"Without doubt. But were you wasting your talents?"

"Indeed not. He could make me his lady tomorrow an he wished
it. He has had two wives and buried them."

"By the faith," I said, "he is almost as much married as the King.
But, Kate, he is an old man."

"And I am a young woman without your inheritance. Your father will give me a dowry, I doubt not, but it will not be anything
to compare with what his darling daughter Damask will bring to
her husband."

"I would that there need not be this talk of marriage. It seems
to me to be a melancholy subject."

"Why so?"

I did not answer. I thought of the fox's mask which I had seen
on Simon Caseman's face and of Kate's planning to lure Lord
Remus into marriage because he had a high-sounding title, an
estate in the country and a place at Court.

"Marriage," I said, "should be for the young, those who love
not worldly goods and titles but each other."

"There speaks my romantic cousin," said Kate. "Who said you
had grown up? You are a child still. You are a dreamer. It so often
happens that those we love are not the ones we dare marry. So
let us be gay. Let us enjoy what we can while we may."

But she was no longer bantering; and there was a faraway look in her eyes which I did not then fully understand. That came later.

A change had come over Keziah. She had come out of that trance-like state and suddenly began to take on her old duties. Once or twice I heard her singing to herself. She had lost a certain amount of weight and I often noticed her gazing longingly at Bruno with an expression of intense longing which, if he was aware of it, he ignored. As far as I knew, he ignored her. I remonstrated with him over this. It seemed very cruel to me. But his eyes would flash angrily and to tell the truth I was so wretched when he was cool to me, that I avoided the subject.

He had changed a little too since the day when he had spoken of the jeweled Madonna. One of the servants told me that she had asked him to lay his hands on her and this he had done with the result that the violent rheumatics she had suffered in her legs had disappeared. They knew who he was, and the legend that he was indeed divine lived on. Clement in the bakehouse talked a great deal, I imagined. I wondered how he had ever observed rules of silence. The belief was beginning to spread throughout the household that Keziah and the monk had lied under torture and this was what Bruno wished.

My father told me that he was giving him a little time to grow accustomed to the great change in his circumstances before discussing with him the choice of a career. Bruno was well educated —indeed something of a scholar. Perhaps he would like to go into the church or the law. My father, I knew, would be willing for him to go to one of the universities if Bruno wished it. So far Bruno had discussed his future with no one; and he seemed only to care for the company of Kate and myself.

But I could not completely ignore his treatment of Keziah.

"You could be gentle with her," I protested. "Speak to her kindly."

"Why should I?" he asked.

"Because she is your mother and longs for a smile from you."

"She disgusts me, and she is *not* my mother."

"You are cruel to her, Bruno."

"Perhaps," he answered.

"I refuse to believe that she is my mother."

Poor Bruno. It was hard for him to bear. To have believed himself to be apart from us all, a miraculous creation, and to find that he was the son of a servingwoman. But there was cruelty in him. I saw that now, as clearly as I had seen the fox's mask on Simon Caseman's face.

I tried to talk to him about the future but he would not discuss it with me. I wondered whether he did with Kate for I knew that they were often together.

When Lord Remus paid us another visit Kate declared herself not in the least surprised. It was what she had expected, she said. He dined with us again and gave us more news of the Court. It seemed almost certain that the Cleves marriage would take place. The King was in excellent humor. He had walked up and down the nursery with young Prince Edward in his arms looking very pleased with the world. The Prince was a little pukey but his nurse, Mrs. Penn, guarded him like a dragon and wouldn't allow the slightest wind to blow on him. The King had not been in such good spirits since the day he had married Anne Boleyn.

But it was not so much the King and Court which interested Lord Remus. It was Kate. When he had left she came to my bedroom and lay on the bed giggling.

"Methinks the hook is well into his lordship's mouth," she said. "Soon we shall haul him in."

She was right. Within a week he was making a formal request to my father to pay court to Mistress Kate.

My father, so she told me, sent for her, and told her that Lord Remus was offering her marriage. He did not believe Kate would consider such a marriage, and she must not think that he would wish to force her into it.

"Force me, forsooth," she cried to me. "As if I hadn't angled for it! Think, Damask, a place at Court. I shall be there, right at the heart of things. I shall dance at Hampton and Greenwich. I shall ride at Windsor. Who knows, the King himself may look my way. I shall have jewels in plenty, fine gowns and servants to call my own."

"And all you have to do is take Lord Remus as your husband."

"I can do that, Damask."

"You don't love him, Kate."

"I love what he has to offer."

"You are mercenary."

"If it is mercenary to be wise then mercenary I am."

"So you will really marry this old man?"

"You will see, Damask."

Kate was betrothed. She wore a big emerald on her finger and another at her throat. Her moods were startling. She was feverishly gay and suddenly melancholy. Sometimes she hinted that she might not marry after all and at others she laughed the idea of not doing so to scorn.

Once I went into her room and found her lying facedown on her bed staring straight before her.

"Kate," I said, "you're not happy."

She studied the great emerald on her finger. "See how it glows, Damask. And it is just a beginning."

"But happiness is not to be found in the glow of an emerald, Kate."

"No? Tell me where then?"

"In the eyes of the one you love and who loves you."

She threw back her head and laughed. But I saw the tears were near.

I was angry with her. Why should she do this? I hated the thought of her going to that old man; and since I had listened to Keziah's ramblings images often forced themselves into my mind.

"Perhaps," I said angrily, "it is of no consequence. You are incapable of love."

"How dare you say that!"

"I dare," I said, "because you are ready to sell yourself for emeralds."

She was laughing again: "And rubies," she said, "and sapphires, diamonds, and a place at Court."

"It disgusts me."

"Virtuous Damask, who has no need to sell herself but whose inheritance will choose a husband for her."

But her smile was forced and her laughter brittle. I knew she was not as content as she wished me to believe.

* * *

Two months after Lord Remus first came to our house Kate and he were married. There was to be a grand celebration at the house and Clement and his scullions were working for days in the kitchens.

A disturbing thing happened on the night before the wedding. I went to Kate's room because I was anxious to have a word with her. She was not there.

As the house had retired, I sat there waiting for her, but she did not come. I was afraid that she had run away, and I wondered whether to raise the household, but something within me warned me against that. It was four of the clock when she came in; her hair was streaming about her.

"Damask," she cried, "what are you doing here?"

"I came here at midnight when the household retired to speak with you. I was anxious about you and you were not here. I thought of rousing the household."

"You have not told anyone I was missing from my bedchamber, I hope."

I shook my head. "No. I did not think you had run away on the eve of your wedding to the noble lord. Or if you had I thought that could wait until morning. Kate, where have you been?"

"You ask too many questions."

"Kate, you have been with a lover."

"Well, Mistress Prim. What have you to say to that?"

"Tomorrow is your wedding day."

"And tonight I am free. And pry as much as you like tonight, cousin, for tonight is your last chance to do so."

"You have forestalled your marriage vows."

Kate laughed so much I thought she would have hysterics.

"Oh, what a wiseacre you are! Your hand has been asked in marriage by Rupert and Simon. That makes you so knowledge-able. But there is one you do not mention. Bruno. What of Bruno?"

"What . . . of Bruno?" I asked slowly.

"You do not know Bruno," she said. "Who does? Think of him. A holy child and then to find he is the result of the sinful liaison between an erring monk and a serving girl whose life has been scarcely pure. Conceived on the Abbey grass . . . under a hedge. Oh, yes, surely they were discreet enough to take cover during the performance."

"Kate," I said, "what is the matter with you?"

"You do not know, Damask?" she said. "After all there is so little you know."

"I know that you do not love the man you are going to marry. You have sold yourself for emeralds and a place at Court."

"How dramatic we have become. How easy for you! Oh, yes, it *is* easy to say 'All for love' when you lose nothing by it."

"Where have you been tonight? Are you playing fair with Lord Remus?"

"I don't intend to satisfy your curiosity on that point. I think you are jealous of me, Damask. I have made my choice. I think it is a wise one. Tomorrow I shall go to Lord Remus and do what is expected of me."

I went to my room. I could not sleep. I had thought I had understood Kate. But who understands any other human being?

The next day the wedding took place in our house chapel. Lord Remus was led in between two young bachelors whom he had brought in his suite and each of them wore the customary bridelace on branches of green broom attached to their arms. Kate looked beautiful. The seamstresses had been working for weeks on her gown of brocade and cloth of silver; her hair hung loose about her shoulders. Rupert carried the silver bridecup before her as they went in procession to the chapel and I walked behind her as her attendant. And all members of the household followed with the musicians playing sweet music and some of the maids carrying the big bridecake.

The ceremony was performed and as the bridecup was handed around Simon Caseman, who was standing behind me, whispered: "Your turn next."

Bruno was with the party. He looked aloof and scornful and the day after Kate's wedding he disappeared as mysteriously as he had appeared in the Christmas crib.

"I always knew," said Clement, "that he was no ordinary being."

A Child Is Born

There was no trace of Bruno. Rumor was now certain that he was indeed the Holy Child, that Ambrose had lied under torture and had been killed for his blasphemy. As for Keziah there was evidence that she too had been submitted to torture. The wounds on her thighs would not heal and she had gone strange in the head since her "confession." People were always ready to believe the fantastic.

Clement was constantly talking of the miracle and how the Abbey had changed and that the Child had the gift of healing the sick.

Even my father believed the rumors.

"But if it were so," I said, "why had Bruno not been able to save the Abbey?"

"I can only think that he has been preserved for something even greater," answered my father.

I wanted to think so too. But most of all I wanted him to come back. I could not understand my feelings for him. I thought of him constantly. I remembered how we had talked together in the days when there had been an Abbey and how elated I had been when I had claimed his attention for a while. I was obsessed by him. I remembered certain allusions Kate had made. Once she had said that Bruno was more important to either of us than anyone else in the world. She was right—as far as I was concerned, though I was sure worldly magnificence meant more to her.

Strangely enough after Bruno's disappearance Keziah grew better. She mingled freely with the other servants and as they were afraid to speak of the strange affair of the child in the crib it was never mentioned.

I discovered that there was another reason for the change in Keziah.

She had been making butter in the dairy and came to me in my room. I was surprised to see her at that hour of the morning and she said: "It came to me, Mistress, all of a sudden that I should speak with you."

"What is it?" I asked.

She smiled and said quietly: "I'm with child, Mistress."

"No, Keziah!"

" 'Tis so, Mistress. I've known a week or more and I've had that happy feeling that comes with it. Or so 'twas always with me."

"It is wrong. You should not feel happy. You have no husband. What right have you to have a child?"

"The right that's given every woman, Mistress. And I can scarce wait to hold the little 'un in my arms. 'Twas always a child of my own I wanted. But there was always the voice within me that said no. You can't bring a bastard into the world, Keziah. You must go to your Granny."

"You should think of this before. . . ."

"One day you'll understand. There's no thinking before. 'Tis only after that you get to thinking. Three times I've been to Granny in the woods. And twice she has brought about that which I knew must be, though never wanted it. There was the first time. . . ." Her face puckered. She had been trying to convince herself that she and Ambrose had never had a child. "This time," she went on quickly, "I won't go to her. I want this child. 'Tis maybe the last I'll ever have for I am getting past the age for child-bearing. And this little 'un will be to me what I've never had before."

"Who is the father of this child?"

"Oh, there's no doubt of it, Mistress. It was him all right. It had to be. There couldn't be a shadow of doubt. This little one belongs to Rolf Weaver."

"Keziah! That man! That . . . murderer!"

"Nay, Mistress, 'twas the monk who were the murderer. My Rolf . . . he were the victim."

I was horrified. I stared at Keziah's expanding body. That man's seed! It was horrifying.

I said: "No, Keziah. In this case it is justified. You must go to your Granny."

Keziah said, "Hush you, Mistress. Would you murder my baby? I want this child as I never wanted a child before . . . and I've grieved for all of them. When I saw that boy my heart yearned for him. But he spurned me but when I knew that I carried this seed in my body it gave me comfort. I shall have this child."

There was a strange exalted look about her and she would not listen to anything I said.

I could not forget that man with the hair growing low on his brow; I could not forget what he had done to Keziah, to our lives.

I had thought that was the end of him when he had lain lifeless on the grass. It was a shock to know that he lived on in Keziah's body.

I missed Kate very much. Life had become dull as never before. I was aware of Simon's watchful eyes; I knew he believed he was going to make me change my mind.

My mother said to me: "You're growing up, Damask. It's time you married. It would give me and your father such pleasure to see our grandchildren. Now Kate is settled it will be your turn next."

My father was too close in thought to me to mention marriage again; but he would like to see me with a man to protect me. I had two to choose from—Rupert and Simon; I knew that no objection would be raised whomsoever I chose, although naturally they would prefer it to be Rupert, he being related. Neither of them had anything in great worldly possessions to offer me. Rupert had great skill with the land, Simon was gaining a reputation as a clever lawyer. Both of them would benefit by the wealth I should bring to them. Perhaps that was why I hesitated. I wanted to be chosen for myself, as Kate had been.

"I am of no great age yet," I told my mother.

"I married your father when I was sixteen," she told me. "I was in the schoolroom. I have never regretted it."

"But then you married Father."

"You've always idolized him," she said, snipping at the stalk of a rose. Whenever she talked I always felt that more than half her attention was on the flowers she was either planting, cutting or arranging.

Kate came to see us, full of exuberant excitement. Married life suited her. The adoring Remus could not take his eyes from her; and I could see that marriage had made her even more attractive. For one thing she was sumptuously clad; she had a damask gown and a kirtle of velvet; her feet were in velvet shoes with garnet buckles and there were new jewels sparkling at her throat.

She had been to Court. She had seen the King. He was magnificent—enormous, royal and terrifying. He bellowed his wishes and everyone obeyed without a second's hesitation. His temper was notoriously short, especially when his leg pained him. He sparkled with jewels and every square inch of flesh on his big body was royal. He had smiled on Kate; he had patted her hand. In fact if he had not been completely besotted by the young and giddy niece of Lord Norfolk who knew what might have happened? Kate was a little regretful but not much. It was a precarious existence, everyone realized, to be singled out for very special attention by the King. A pat of the hand and smile of appreciation were very welcome and by far more comfortable.

She was bubbling over with the joy of being the harbinger of exciting news.

He disliked Anne of Cleves so much that it was very likely Cromwell would lose his head for arranging the marriage, and it was said that the Duchess had no great liking for the King. It was said that there had been no consummation on the wedding night and the King was furious with Hans Holbein for making such a flattering picture of a plain woman for whom he could have no fancy. And there was Katharine Howard, fluttering her eyes at the King with a mixture of awed Oh-Your-Grace-can-you-really-be-glancing-*my*-way and a promise of all kinds of sexual excitements. She had secretive eyes and a certain wanton manner. It was said that Norfolk was pleased. One niece, Anne Boleyn, had come to grief soon after insisting on the crown; but the King was older now, his leg was a perpetual irritation and as Katharine was young and pliable it seemed possible that she might hold the King's attention; and if she could give him a son, who knew he might be satisfied. Though it was not even of such vital importance to get a son now that there was Prince Edward in the royal nursery.

So Kate rambled on of the glories of Windsor and hunting in the Great Park; of a ball at Greenwich and a banquet at Hampton.

"Do you remember how we used to sail past Hampton, Damask, and talk about the great Palace?"

"I remember it well," I told her. I should never forget the sight of the Cardinal sailing by our privy steps with the King.

Kate had more news for us. She was to have a child.

Lord Remus was delighted. He had not believed this possible but his beautiful clever Kate was capable of anything. He followed her with his eyes, marveling at her grace and beauty. Kate reveled in it; she laughed and flirted gaily with her husband and it was only to me that she talked freely.

She wanted to go to her old room, she said; and I went with her there. When we reached it, she shut the door, and the first thing she said was: "Damask, have you seen him? Has he ever come back?"

I didn't have to ask to whom she was referring. I said: "Of course he has not come back."

"He went because I married. He told me he would go right away and he would not come back until he was ready. What did he mean by that, Damask?"

"You knew him so much better than I."

"Yes, I did. I think, in his way, he loved me." She eyed me maliciously. "You are jealous, Damask. You always wanted him, didn't you? Don't deny it. I understand. It was a way he had. He was different from all others. You could never be sure whether he was a saint or a devil."

"I never thought that."

"No, you thought he was a saint, didn't you? You adored him too openly. You were no challenge to him as I was. He had to convince me. You were already won. So he loved me, but it wasn't good enough for me."

"You wanted riches. I know that full well."

"And see how happy I have made my husband. A child. He never thought to get that . . . at his time of life. He's so proud. My patience, how he struts! As for me, I'm a marvel, I'm as much a miracle to Remus as Bruno was to the monks of the Abbey. I rather enjoy being a miracle. That's why I understand Bruno so well. I feel for him. I understand his bitter disappointment."

"But you didn't love him well enough to marry him."

She smiled ruefully. "Imagine me, the wife of a poor man . . . if you can."

I agreed that I could not.

"You can't be happy," I said.

"I can always be happy when I get what I want," she retorted.

Keziah grew more and more strange. I spoke to my father about her.

"Poor woman," he said, "she is paying for her sins."

I was always touched by Father's attitude for I had never met anyone who could be as good as he was and yet have such sympathy for sinners.

One day one of the servants came to tell me that Keziah was missing. She had not slept in her bed that night. I wondered whether she had found another lover but I thought that could hardly be the case for she was now within a month or so of her confinement. I was alarmed and some instinct sent me to the witch's hut in the woods.

She was there.

Mother Salter bade me enter. I felt the shiver of apprehension I always felt in her house. It was a small cottage with one room in which was a short spiral staircase. This opened into the room above. It was overcrowded; there were cabalistic signs on the wall and bottles in which she kept her concoctions. There were jars of ointment on the shelves and from the beams there always hung bunches of drying herbs. The smell was peculiar; a mixture of herbs and something indefinable. A fire always seemed to be burning and a great sooty-sided caldron hung over it suspended on a chain. There were two seats on either side of the fireplace and whenever I had seen Mother Salter she was seated in one of them.

It took a great deal of courage to enter her house; the sickly did because they hoped to be cured; those who wanted a love potion came; as for myself I was so anxious about Keziah that I walked boldly in.

She pointed to one of the seats beside the fireplace and smiled at me. She was very old but her eyes were lively and young. They were small and dark, embedded in wrinkles, crafty and knowledgeable, rather like a monkey's.

I said, "I'm worried about Keziah."

She pointed upward.

My relief was obvious. "So she is here."

She smiled at me and nodded. "Her time is near," she said.

"So soon?"

"The babe is eager to get out into the world. She'll come before her time."

"It's to be a girl?"

Mother Salter did not answer. She knew such things and had often prophesied correctly the sex of a child.

"And Keziah?"

Mother Salter shook her head. "Her time is running out," she said.

"You can save her."

"Not if her time has come."

"It can't be," I cried. "*You* can do something."

She gave me a grin which was not pleasant to behold. There was something malevolent about it and it showed her blackened teeth. Then she stood up and beckoned to me. She started up the short spiral staircase. I followed.

I stepped straight into a room with a small latticed window. It was darkish but I recognized the figure on the pallet.

"Keziah," I said, and knelt beside it.

"It's the little 'un," she said. "It's Dammy."

"Yes, I'm here, Kezzie. You gave me a fright. I wondered what had happened to you."

"Nothing's going to happen to me again on this earth, little 'un."

"That's foolish talk," I said sharply. "You're going to be all right once . . . once this is over."

"He were going to kill me," she said. "This is his way of doing it. What a man he were! All that man going to the worms, where I shall soon be going."

"What talk is this!" I cried indignantly.

Mother Salter cackled. She was standing there like a vulture watching us.

"Keziah," I said, "come back to us. I'll look after you. I'll look after the baby. . . ."

Keziah seized my hand; hers was hot and burning. "You'll look after the child, Dammy? You'll look after my little baby? You've promised me."

"I promise you, Keziah, we will look after the child."

"She's to be brought up like a little lady. She must sit at the table where you used to sit with Mistress Kate and Master Rupert. That's what I want to see. I want her to be full of booklore, like my boy. But he never looked my way. He wouldn't have me for his mother. He wouldn't believe it. But I want her to have book learning. I want her to be a lady. I call her my little Honey. I remember it well . . . there he was standing over me and it had never happened that way before and through the window I smelt the honeysuckle . . . and that's when my baby was made. Honeysuckle, sweet and clinging. I call her my little Honey."

Then I knew that Keziah was part of my life and that if she were no longer there I should have lost that part; and perhaps, next to my father, Keziah when I was very young had been nearest to me, for my mother had never really been close.

Now she lay there with the beads of sweat clinging to the faint hairs about her lips; and the rosy color of her cheeks replaced by a network of tiny reddish lines. Something had gone out of her, that gaiety, that love of living. She was no longer in love with life and that could only mean she was preparing to leave it.

I said urgently: "Keziah, you're going to get well. You've got to. What shall I do without you?"

She said: "You'll do very well. You don't need me now . . . haven't for a long time."

I said, "The baby will need you. Your little Honey."

She grasped my hand firmly; hers was hot and dry. "You will, Mistress Damask. You'll take her. You'll look after her as though she was your little sister. Promise me, Damask."

I said: "I promise."

Wrekin the cat had come up. He pressed his body against my foot and purred. Mother Salter nodded.

"Swear it," she said. "Swear, my girl. I and Wrekin will be your witness."

I was silent, looking from the rather malevolent face of her whom we called the witch to the strangely altered one of Keziah on the bed. I sensed that it was a solemn moment. I was swearing to make a child my concern, the child of a serving girl and a man whom I had seen murdered and whom I could never regard as anything but as low as the beasts of the forest. Worse, because at least they killed from fear or from the need for food. He had found joy in torturing others; and I had rarely been so disgusted in my life as when I had witnessed Keziah's desire for this man. And I was promising to care for their child! But Keziah's dry hand was pressing mine. I saw the anguish in her eyes.

I bent over her and kissed her. And it was not fear of Mother Salter but love and pity for Keziah that made me say: "I swear."

It was a strange scene in that bedroom. Keziah dying and the old woman standing by yet showing no grief.

"You'll come to bless this night," she said to me. "If you keep your word. If you don't you'll come to curse it."

Keziah moved uneasily on the bed. She whimpered. Mother Salter said to me: "Be gone now. When the time comes you will know."

I came out of the cottage into the woods and ran all the way home.

I knew that I must tell my father of my promise. If I told my mother she would say: "Yes, the girl can come to us and she shall be brought up with the servants." Then she would forget about it and the child would become part of our household. There were children now in the servants' quarters for one or two of them had been got with child and my father would never turn away a deserted mother.

But this was different. I had promised that Keziah's child should be brought up in the house, sit at the schoolroom table. I knew I must keep my word.

I told my father what had happened. I said: "Keziah has been almost as a mother to me."

My father pressed my hand tenderly. He knew that my own mother while she had looked after my physical needs in an exemplary manner had perhaps sometimes been a little absentminded when absorbed by her garden.

"And," I went on, "this is Keziah's child. I know she is a servingwoman but this child who is about to be born will be the brother or sister of Bruno . . . if it is true that he is Keziah's son."

My father was silent and a look of pain crossed his face. We rarely mentioned what had happened at the Abbey. And the fact that Bruno had disappeared had deeply affected us all. My father was becoming convinced that the confession had been a false one and that Bruno was in fact a Messiah or at least a prophet.

I went on quickly: "I gave my word, Father. I must keep it."

"You are right," he said. "You must keep your word. But let Keziah bring her child here and tend it. Why should she not do that?"

"Because she will not be here. That was why they made me swear. Keziah . . . and Mother Salter . . . believe that Keziah will die."

"If this comes to pass," said my father, "then bring the child here."

"And she may be brought up as a child of the household?"

"You have promised this and you must keep your promise."

"Oh, Father, you are such a good man."

"Don't think too highly of me, Damask."

"But I do think it and I shall always do so. For, Father, I know how good you are—so much better than those who are supposed to be holy."

"No, no, you must not say these things. You cannot see into the hearts of people, Damask, and you should not judge unless you can. But let us walk down to the river where we can talk in peace. Do you not miss Kate?"

"I do, Father, and Keziah too. Everything seems to have changed. It has all become quiet."

"There is sometimes a quiet before a storm. Have you noticed that? We must always be prepared for what may happen next.

Who would have believed a few years ago that where our flourishing Abbey stood there should be almost a ruin? Yet the winds had been blowing that way for some time and we did not notice them."

"But now there is no Abbey and the King has found a new wife. Kate has said that already he has his eyes on a girl named Katharine Howard."

"Let us pray, Damask, that all goes well with this marriage because you have seen what disaster the King's marriage can bring to his people."

"It was the break with Rome. Surely that was one of the most important events which ever befell this country."

"I believe so, my child, and it has had far-reaching effects—and will doubtless have more. But when you talk to me of bringing Keziah's child into the household, I wonder when you will be bringing up your own."

"Father, are you still hankering after my marriage?"

"It would please me greatly, Damask, if before I died I saw you betrothed, with a good husband—one whom I could trust—to care for you, to give you children. I longed for sons and daughters and I have but one. And you are more precious to me than all the world, as you well know. But why should I not see my house peopled by children—the children you will bring me in my old age, Damask?"

"You make me feel that I must marry without delay to please you."

"As my desire to see you happy is even greater than that for grandchildren, it would be far from my wish. I long to see you married—but for my contentment you must be a happy wife and mother."

I pressed his arm gently. I am sure that if Rupert had asked me to marry him at that moment I should have agreed to do so because I wished to please my dear good father more than anything else on earth.

One of the serving girls brought a message for me. Mother Salter wished me to go to her.

When I arrived the old woman was seated as usual on the chimney seat, Wrekin at her feet, the sooty pot bubbling over the fire.

She rose and led the way up to the short spiral staircase. On
the bed lay a body under a sheet and on the sheet was a sprig of
rosemary. I gasped, and she nodded.

"It was as I said it would be," she murmured.

"Oh, my poor Keziah!" My voice trembled and she laid a hand
on my shoulder; her fingers were bony, her nails like claws.

I said: "And the child?"

She led the way downstairs. In a corner of the room was a crib
which I had not noticed when I came in. In it lay a living child. I
stared in wonder and Mother Salter gave me a little push toward
the crib.

"Take her up," she said. "She's yours."

"A little girl," I whispered.

"Didn't I tell you?"

I took up the child. It was unswaddled and wrapped in a shawl.
Her face was pink and crumpled looking; its very helplessness filled
me with pity that was close to love.

She took the child from me.

"Not yet," she said. "Not yet. I'll nurture her. When the time
comes, she'll be yours." She laid the child back in the crib and
turned to me. Her claws dug into my arm. "Don't forget your
promise."

I shook my head. Then I found that I was weeping. I was not
sure for what—for Keziah whose life was over, or for the baby
whose life was just beginning.

"She was young to die," I said.

"Her time had come."

"But it was too soon."

"She had a good life. She loved a frolic. She could never resist
a man. It had to be. Men were the meaning of life to her. It was
written that they would be the death of her too."

"That man . . . the father of her child . . . I loathed him."

"Yes, my fine lady," she said. "But how can any of us be sure
who fathers us?"

"I am sure," I said.

"Ah, yes, you, but who else can be? Keziah never knew who
her father was. Nor was her mother sure. My daughter was an-

other such as Keziah. They couldn't resist the men, you see, and they both died in childbirth. You're a fine lady and you'll make little Honeysuckle one too." She squeezed my arm. "You've got to, haven't you? Wouldn't dare do aught else, would you? Remember, you gave your word. And if you don't keep it, my fine young lady, you'll have the curse of dead Keziah on you forever and what's worse still, Mother Salter's."

"I've no intention of not keeping my promise. I want to. I long to have the child. My father has said that I may bring her up as my own if I so wish."

"And you must so wish. But not yet. . . . She's too young yet. I'll keep her with me until the time comes. Then she shall be yours." She had brought with her the sprig of rosemary which she pressed into my hand. "Remember," she said.

I left the witch's cottage mourning for Keziah, remembering so many scenes from my youth and at the same time I was thinking of the child and how happy I should be to have a baby to care for. I longed for children of my own. Perhaps, I thought, my father was right when he said I should marry.

The Shadow of the Ax

An imperious letter came from Kate, brought by one of Lord Remus's servants. We were at supper in the big hall where we took our meals at the long table at which places were always laid for any travelers who might call. There was usually someone—footsore and weary; they all knew of the benevolence of Lawyer Farland who had the reputation for never turning any away. Conversation at our table was usually interesting because as my father said it was stimulating to hear new views. In the kitchen there were always salted joints of pig hanging from the beams and Clement invariably had an assortment of pies to hand. Next to her garden my mother loved her stillroom and her kitchen. In fact one served the other. She dried her herbs and mixed them, experimenting with them, and was almost as excited by the result as she was by growing a new rose.

This was supper and it was six of the clock, and early summer, so the doors were wide open. As we sat at table one of the servants came in to say that there was a man at the gate who wished to see Father.

He rose at once and went out. He came back with a man whose clothes proclaimed him to be a priest. My father looked pleased; he always enjoyed giving hospitality but naturally to do so to some gave him more pleasure than to others.

The man was Amos Carmen and it appeared that he and my father had once known each other and the reunion gave them much pleasure. He did not take his place at the table where callers usually sat but a place was laid next to my father and the two of them talked together. They had at one time been together in

St. Bruno's and thought of taking up the monastic life. Amos had become a priest while my father's intention was to found a family.

When Amos began to talk about the changes in the Church I could see that my father was growing a little uneasy. Although those at the table might be trusted there were the servants to consider and it was so easy in these days to betray oneself. To imply by word or deed that one did not consider the King to be the Supreme Head of the Church could mean death. When my father changed the topic of conversation I think the newcomer realized what was happening for he immediately fell in with the new subject and we were discussing the uses of herbs on which he had complimented my mother because of the manner they had been used in the pies which were being served to us.

It was a change to see my mother animated. It was usually when we had horticulturists to dine with us that she sparkled.

"It's amazing," she was saying, "how little use is made of the flowers and herbs which grow in our meadows and hedgerows. They are there for anyone's taking and they can be so tasty. Primroses and marigolds make excellent garnish in pies and tarts."

"I can see, Madam," replied Amos with a smile, "that you are a past mistress at the art of cookery."

Mother dimpled rather prettily. She was far more susceptible to flattery about her flowers and her household than her looks; and she was still good looking.

Father said: "She is the best housewife in England. I'd defy any to deny it. Why, when Damask here is snuffling with a cold it seems nothing will cure her mother gives her juice of buttercup. Following the dose there is such an attack of sneezing that the head is cleared at once. And I remember how when I had blisters on my feet she cured that with . . . crowfoot, was it?"

"It was indeed," said Mother. "Oh, yes, there is a great deal to be learned from the roots and flowers and herbs."

And so we discussed the herbs which could ease pain or delight the palate and it was while we talked thus that the letters arrived from Kate.

How grand her servants were in their bright livery! Ours seemed humble in comparison. One of the letters was addressed to Father and Mother, the other to me.

We did not consider it polite to read them at table, which was a trial to me as I was burning with impatience to have Kate's news. The messenger was taken to the kitchens to be refreshed, although, said Father jocularly, one wondered whether such a fine-looking gentleman should be invited to sit at the head of the table.

The conversation continued concerning new plants and vegetables which my mother believed would shortly be introduced into the country. My mother was saying that like Queen Katharine she often longed for a salad, but unlike the Queen had been wont to do, she was in no position to send to Flanders or Holland that the proper ingredients might be acquired.

"And I believe," said Amos Carmen, "that there is talk of bringing in Flemish hops and planting them here."

"It is so," cried my mother. "I should verily like to see more and more such things coming into the country. There are so many edible roots like the carrot and the turnip. It is ridiculous that we cannot grow them here. But we shall. Do you remember the visitor we had from Flanders?" She turned to her husband.

He remembered well, he told her.

"He told us, you may also remember, that plans are afoot to bring these edible roots into the country. They would grow very well here, so why should we be deprived of them? How I should like to make a salad of these things and take it to the Queen. . . ."

She stopped for she remembered that Queen Katharine who had sent to the Low Countries for her salads was now dead. We were all silent. I was remembering how the King and Anne Boleyn had worn yellow as their "mourning" and had danced on the day of Queen Katharine's death. And now Anne herself was dead and Jane was dead and the news was that the King was mightily dissatisfied with his new Queen.

It seemed impossible to speak of any subject without coming back to that one which was in everybody's mind.

But what I wanted was to get away to read Kate's letter.

"I have written to your parents to tell them they must do nothing to prevent your coming to me. I need your company. There was never any state so uncomfortable, humiliating and dull, if it were not enlivened by bouts of misery, as having a child. I swear it shall never happen again. I want you to come and stay with me. Remus is agreeable. In fact he is eager. He is so delighted at the thought of the child and so proud of himself (at his age!) that he would willingly put up with any tantrum I care to throw and I assure you I throw them constantly. I have been thinking what I can do to relieve the tedium and the *misery* and I suddenly thought the answer is Damask. You are to come at once. You will stay until the child is born. Only a matter of weeks now. Make no excuses. If you don't come I shall never forgive you."

Father came to my room. He was holding Kate's letter in his hand.

"Ah," he said, "you know the gist of this, I'll warrant."

"Poor Kate," I said, "I think she was not meant to bear children."

"My dearest child, that is what every woman is meant to do."

"Every woman except Kate," I said. "Well, am I to go?"

"It is for you to say."

"So I have your permission?"

He nodded. He was looking at me in a quizzical, tender way. Afterward I wondered whether he had a premonition.

"I shall hate leaving you," I told him.

"The birds have to leave the nest at some time."

"It will not be for very long," I assured him.

The next day Amos Carmen left and I was busy making my preparations. It would be the first time I had been away from home. I looked wryly at my clothes. I guessed they would seem very homely in Kate's grand mansion.

We were to go by barge some ten miles upriver; and there we should be met by members of the Remus household. I should take two maids with me and Tom Skillen would be in charge of the barge. Then our baggage would be put onto pack mules and horses which would be waiting to take us to the Remus Castle.

I was so excited and eager to see Kate again. It was true that without her and Keziah—as she used to be in the old days—life was a little drab. Then there was Bruno whom in my heart I knew I missed more than any. I often wondered why. He had seemed so remote to me and I had often thought that it was only rarely that he remembered my existence. But I, no less than Kate, had felt this strong emotion for him—in Kate it was an imperious desire for his company; in me a kind of awed respect. Kate demanded it while I was glad when it came my way. I was eager for the crumbs which fell from the rich man's table while Kate was seated at it as if she were supping there.

The day before I was due to leave Amos Carmen came back to the house. I came upon him with Father. They were standing by the stone parapet near the river in earnest conversation.

"Ah," said my father. "Here is Damask. Come here, daughter."

I looked from one to the other; I knew at once that they had something on their minds and I cried anxiously: "What is it?"

My father said: "You may trust this girl with your life."

"Father," I cried, "why do you say that?"

"My child," he said, "we live in dangerous times. Tonight our guest will be on his way. When you are in the household of Lord Remus perhaps you should not mention that he visited us."

"No, Father," I said.

They were both smiling placidly, and I was so excited at the prospect of my visit to Kate that I forgot what their words might have implied.

The next day I set out. Father and Mother with Rupert and Simon Caseman came down to the privy stairs to wave me off. Mother asked me to take note of how the gardeners at Remus dealt with greenfly and what herbs they grew and to find out if there were any recipes of which she had not heard. Father held me against him and bade me come home soon and to remember that in Kate's house I was not at home and to guard well my tongue. Rupert asked me to come home soon and Simon Caseman looked at me with a strange light in his eye as though he were half exasperated with me, half amused. But he implied at the same time that his great desire was to make me his wife.

I waved to them from the barge and I sent up a silent prayer that all would be well until my return.

Tom Skillen had changed; he was more subdued now that he had lost Keziah; skillfully he took the barge upriver; we passed several craft and I beguiled the time by asking Tom Skillen if he knew to whom they belonged. When we passed Hampton, the great mansion which was growing more and more grand every week, I thought often as I always did of the King's sailing down the river with the Cardinal at his side.

Then I reflected how pleasant it would be to sail with the whole of the family on a barge like this which would carry us all miles away, right into the country where I believed people could be safe from the troubles which seemed to beset us all. I visualized a peaceful house, exactly like ours, but too far away to be involved in unhappy events.

Far away? But where was one safe? I remembered the men of Lincolnshire and Yorkshire who had risen against the reforms in the Church which the King and Thomas Cromwell had brought about. What had happened to them? I shuddered. I remembered the body of the monk outside the Abbey and that of Brother Ambrose, swinging on the gibbets. There was no peace anywhere. One could only pray that one was not caught up in danger. Had those men of Yorkshire and Lincolnshire known when they began their Pilgrimage of Grace that so many of them would end on a gibbet?

Death, Destruction, Murder. It was everywhere.

I prayed fervently that it would never come to that house by the river which had been my home. But as my father had often said: We lived in violent times and the disaster which befell anyone concerned us all. We were all involved. Death could point its finger at any one of us.

Was it so in the reign of the previous King? He had been a stern man and a miser; he had never been the people's idol as the present King had been. He was not a man of passion. As the grandson of Owen Tudor and Queen Catherine, widow of Henry V, his claim to the throne was somewhat dubious; and some said the marriage between the Queen and the Tudor had never in fact taken place. But to substantiate his claim he had married Elizabeth, eldest daughter of Edward IV—and thus by one stroke he had strengthened the royal stem and united the houses of York and Lancaster. A clever King—devious and unlovable, but he had made England rich. No doubt there had been dangers in his day, but there had never been so many pitfalls as at this time. There had never been so willful a man whose passions must be satisfied and his conscience placated all at the same time.

But enough of fear. I would think of Kate and her marriage and of my own, which I suppose could not be long delayed.

I had a choice—Rupert or Simon—and I knew it could never be Simon. Good as he was—a clever lawyer, said my father, an asset to his business and his household—he somehow repelled me. It would be Rupert, good kind Rupert, of whom I was fond. But his mildness made me feel indifferent toward him. I suppose like all girls I dreamed of a strong man.

Then I was thinking of Bruno. How little one knew of Bruno! It was never possible to get close to him. But ever since I had heard the story of the child found in the Christmas crib he had represented an ideal for me. His very strangeness attracted me as I am sure it had Kate. We believed then that he was aloof from us all and in our different ways we loved him.

This was why I could not contemplate marriage with Rupert with any enthusiasm. It was because deep within me I had this strange, rather exalted emotion for Bruno.

The two serving girls, Alice and Jennet, were giggling together. They had been in a state of excitement ever since they had known they were going to accompany me. I knew they believed that life in Kate's household would be far more exciting than in ours.

It was very pleasant on the river and in due course we arrived at that spot where we were to disembark and there were the servants in the unmistakable Remus livery waiting to help us and there were the pack mules to which our baggage was tied. We said good-bye to Tom Skillen and rode off in our little party and two hours' ride brought us to Remus Castle.

It was of a much earlier period than our residence which had been built by my grandfather. Its solid gray-granite walls confirmed the fact that they had stood for two hundred years and would doubtless stand for five hundred more. The sun glinting on the walls picked out sharp pieces of flint so that they shone like rose diamonds. I gazed up at the machicolations of the keep as we crossed the drawbridge over the moat. We passed through the gateway with its portcullis and were in a courtyard in which a fountain played; as we clattered over the cobbles I heard Kate's voice.

"Damask!" And I looked up and saw her at a window.

"So you're here at last," she cried. "You're to come straight to me. Pray bring up Mistress Farland without delay," she commanded.

A groom took my horse and a servant came out to conduct me into the castle. I said that I would first wish to go to my room that I might wash off the grime of my journey and I was led through a great hall up a stone staircase to a room which overlooked the courtyard. I guessed it was not far from Kate's. I asked that water be brought to me and the maid ran off to do my bidding.

I was soon to discover what an imperious mistress of the household Kate was.

She came to my room. "I told them to bring you to me without delay," she cried. "They shall hear of this."

"'Twas my orders that I first rid myself of some of the dirt of the roads."

"Oh, Damask, you have not changed a bit. How good it is to have you here! What do you think of Remus Castle?"

"It's magnificent," I said.

She grimaced.

"It is just what you always wanted, wasn't it? A castle, a place at Court—and you to flit twixt one and the other."

"And how much flitting dost think I do? Look at me!"

I looked at her and laughed. Elegant Kate, her body misshapen, her mouth discontented; nothing the satin gown edged with miniver could do could alter that.

"And soon to be a mother!" I cried.

"Not soon enough for me," grumbled Kate. "I dread the ordeal but I yearn for it to be over. But you are here and that is good. Here is your water so remove the dust at once. And is that your traveling gown? My poor Damask, we must do something about that."

"Your ladyship looks very grand, I swear."

"No need to swear," said Kate. "I'm well aware of how I look. I have been so ill, Damask, so sick. I would rather jump out of this window than go through the same again. And the worst is to come."

"Women are having babies every day, Kate."

"*I* am not. Nor shall there be another day."

"And how fares my lord?"

"He is at Court. Does that not make it even harder to bear? Though they say the King is in ill humor and it takes very little to bring a frown of displeasure. Heads are very insecurely balanced on shoulders these days."

"Then should you not be glad that yours is in a firm position?"

"Still the same old Damask, still counting your blessings. It *is* good to have you."

And she was certainly the same old Kate. She asked questions about what was happening at home and when we talked of Keziah she was a little sad.

"And it is that man's child," she said. "I wonder how she will grow up. Conceived in such a way . . . born of such parents." And she put her hands on her body and smiled.

Kate was impatient for my company. There was so much to talk of, she told me. If I had refused to come she would never have spoken to me again. When I said I would unpack my baggage she told me there was no need for that: a servant would do it. But I wished to do it myself, so I unpacked and showed her a little silk gown for her baby that had been made from the silk produced by my mother's silkworms. Kate was indifferent to it; she preferred a little charm bracelet I had brought and which had been put on my wrist by my parents when I had been born.

"When the child can no longer wear it, it must be given back to me."

"So that you can put it on your own child's wrist? Well, Damask, when is *that* to be?"

I flushed slightly in spite of my determination not to betray my feelings. "I have no idea," I said sharply.

"You'd best take Rupert, Damask. He will be a good kind husband—just the man for you. He will care for you and never cast eyes on another woman. He is young—not like my Remus. And although he is poor in worldly goods you have enough for both."

"Thank you for settling my future so easily."

"Poor Damask! Oh, let us be candid one with the other. You wanted Bruno. Are you mad, Damask? He would never have been the man for you."

"Nor for you either, it seemed."

"Sometimes I wish I had gone with him."

"Gone?" I demanded. "Gone where?"

"Oh, nothing," she replied. Then she hugged me and said: "I feel alive now you've come. This place stifles me. When I was at Court it was different. There's an excitement there, Damask, that you couldn't understand."

"I know I'm an ignorant country girl in your estimation—though may I draw your attention to the fact that my home is nearer London than yours—but I can certainly imagine how exciting it must be to wonder from one moment to another when you make some remark, perform some action, whether it will send you to the Tower, there to live—oh, most excitingly—awaiting the order for release or decapitation."

Kate laughed aloud. "Yes, it is good to have you here. Bless you, Damask, for coming."

"Thank you. I suppose your blessings are preferable to the curses I could have expected had I refused."

I felt my spirits rising. I suppose we belonged together in a way, and although I disapproved of almost everything Kate did, and she was contemptuous of me, although we sparred continuously, I felt alive when I was with her. I suppose because we had grown up together, she seemed like a part of myself.

We supped together that night alone in her room. She had a little table there on which she often took her meals.

"I dareswear you and your husband dine and sup here alone when he is in residence," I said.

She laughed again, her eyes flashing scornfully.

"You don't know Remus. What should we talk of, do you think? He is getting deaf too. I should throw a platter at him if I had to endure him alone. No, we eat in style when he is here. We use the hall which you noticed when you came—or perhaps you didn't. All Remus's relics of past wars—halberds, swords, armor—look at us while we eat; I at one end of the table—and by the grace of God —he at the other. Conversation is lively or dull depending on the guests. We often have people from the Court here—then it can be very amusing; but often it is dull country squires who talk endlessly of plowing their lands and salting their pigs until I feel I shall scream at them."

"I am sure Lord Remus finds you a most accommodating spouse."

"Well, at least I am providing him with a child."

"And he considers that the price he has to pay is worthwhile? You are"—I looked at her searchingly—"quite pleasant to the eye even in your present state of discontent. And you have doubtless renewed his youth by proving that he is still not too old to beget children."

She said quickly: "I said I was providing him with a child. I did not say it was of his begetting."

"Oh, Kate," I cried, "what do you mean?"

"There! I talk too much. But you don't count. I just like to tell the truth to you, Damask."

"So . . . you have deceived Remus. It is not his child. Then how can you pretend it is!"

"You have not yet learned much of men, Damask. It is easy to convince them that they have the power to do what they fancy themselves doing. Remus is so puffed up with pride at the thought of being a father that he is ready to forget it might have meant his playing the cuckold."

"Kate, you are shameless as you ever were."

"More so," she mocked. "You surely cannot expect me to improve with experience."

"I don't believe you."

"I am so glad," said Kate with a grimace. "My indiscretion is forgotten."

"And here you are about to undergo the greatest experience any woman can and you lie here puling about it."

"For two whole months I have lived in solitude—save for the guests who have come here. I have had to endure the solicitude of Remus. I have had to behave like a woman who yearns for her child."

"And in your heart you do."

"I don't think I was intended to be a mother, Damask. No. I

want to dance at Court. I want to hunt with the royal party. To return to the Castle or the Palace—we were at Windsor recently and there we danced and talked and watched mummers or the play, and there is a ball. That is the life. *Then* I can forget."

"What do you want to forget, Kate?"

"Oh," she cried, "I am talking too much once more."

The gardens at Remus were beautiful. My mother would have been delighted with them. I tried to remember details so that I could tell her about them when I returned home. There was one very favorite spot of mine—a garden with a pond in the center surrounded by a pleached alley; because it was summer the trees in this alley were thick with leaves. Kate and I used to like to sit by the pond and talk.

I was gratified that she had changed since I had come. The lines of discontent had disappeared from her mouth and she was constantly laughing—often at me, it was true, but in that tolerant, affectionate manner with which I was familiar.

It was in the pond garden that she talked to me of Bruno.

"I wonder where he went," she said. "Do you believe that he disappeared in a cloud and went back to heaven? Or do you think it was to London to make his fortune?"

"He did disappear," I mused. "He was found in the crib on that Christmas morning and Keziah did seem to lose her senses when she met Rolf Weaver. Her confession may have been false."

"What purpose was there in his coming?"

"St. Bruno's became rich after his arrival and it was due to him."

"But what happened when Cromwell's men came? Where were his miracles then?"

"Perhaps it was meant that they should have their way."

"Then what was the purpose of sending a Holy Child just to make St. Bruno's prosper for a few years so that greater riches could be diverted to the King's coffers? And what of the confessions of Keziah and the monk? Keziah could never have made up such a story. Why should she?"

"It may have been some devil prompting her."

"You have been visiting the witch in the woods."

"I did because of Honeysuckle."

"You are foolish, Damask. You have promised to take this child, you tell me. And your father agrees. You are a strange unworldly pair. The child of that beast and a wayward serving girl. And she is to be as your sister! What do you think will come of that?"

"I loved Keziah," I said. "She was a mother to me. And the child could be Bruno's sister. Have you thought of that?"

"If Keziah's stories are true they would be half-brother and sister, would they not?"

"The relationship is there."

"How like you, Damask. You fit events to truth as it pleases yourself. At one moment you want Bruno to be holy so he disappears up to heaven in a cloud; the next minute you want to make a reason for taking this child, so she is Bruno's half-sister. You see you are not logical. Your thinking is muddled. How much easier it would be if you had simple motives like mine."

"To get what you want from life and to make others pay for it."

"It's a good arrangement from the taker's point of view."

"It could never be a good arrangement—even if it worked."

"It's going to work for me," said Kate blandly.

Whatever topic we started with, Bruno would find a way into our conversation. Kate would soften a little when she spoke of him. She often recalled details of those days when we used to go through the ivy-covered door and find him waiting for us. I was sure that at times she believed that Bruno was something more than human.

"Do you think we shall ever knew the truth about Bruno, Kate?" I asked.

"Who ever knows the whole truth about anybody?" was her reply.

I dispatched a messenger to my father to tell him of my safe arrival. I said I would be coming home shortly after the baby was born. I knew that Kate would not wish me to go. I had an idea that she visualized keeping me there as a companion for herself. She told me once that she needed me.

"And since you don't altogether fancy Rupert I might arrange a grand marriage for you," she promised me.

"My father would expect me to go home."

"I am sure he is eager to see you married."

But with the baby due to arrive at any time we were both awaiting the signs so that our conversation was often of the imminent birth. I went through the layette which had been prepared for the child and Kate and I discussed the names of boys and girls which we thought would be suitable for the infant.

Kate liked to talk about the Court and the King's affairs and her recent adventures at Windsor made her feel that she was really very knowledgeable—particularly compared with a stay-at-home cousin.

The King's marriage was the great topic for we all knew that he was greatly dissatisfied with his bride.

"It is a most unfortunate affair," said Kate happily as we sat in the pond garden. I was stitching at a little garment I was making for the baby. Kate sat idly, her hands in her lap, watching me.

"Of course poor Anne of Cleves is a most unsuitable wife. The King would never have thought of taking her but for the state of affairs on the continent."

I begged to hear more. I had heard rumors but I liked listening to Kate's more racy version than those which had been vaguely alluded to at our dinner table.

"The King always hated the Emperor Charles and the King of France," Kate explained, "and the thought of their joining up together was quite alarming. They say that he believed they were plotting a mischief against him. So he wanted allies on the Continent. Cromwell believed that the Duke of Cleves would be that ally; so why not make a firm alliance through marriage with the Duke's sister?"

"And the lady was willing," I said. "Did she know what had happened to Queen Katharine and Queen Anne?"

"Surely the whole world knows! It was bruited about Europe as I believe no other affair ever has been. The King's Secret Matter was undoubtedly the world's most well-known scandal. Ladies were not too willing. There was Mary of Guise—and she a widow. Very comely, said those who knew her. The King fancied her but she refused him for the King of Scotland. That is something he will not readily forgive the Scots. And now he is angry with Master

Cromwell, because the lady of Cleves does not live up to his expectations. Remus saw the account which Cromwell's man sent him of the lady. It compared her beauty with that of other ladies as being like the golden sun to the silver moon. She was said to surpass them all. And Holbein the artist made a portrait of her but omitted to put in the pockmarks. Her face is pitted with them. They say that when he saw her the King was horrified and disgusted and naturally furious with those who had brought her to him."

"Poor woman!"

"She could not speak a word of English so she did not know what was being said about her."

"She must have sensed the cold reception."

"I was sorry for the King. I wondered whether he compared her with that other Anne. Do you remember her, Damask? How fascinating she was riding in her litter! Did you ever see anyone like her? So elegant . . . so attractive. . . . She was a real Queen. I shall never forget her."

"Nor I the day you blackmailed poor Tom Skillen into taking us up the river to see her pass by."

"How grateful you should be to me. But for my astuteness you would never have seen Queen Anne Boleyn. No, I shall never forget her. She was unforgettable. How could the King have let her go for the sake of Jane Seymour! That is something I have never been able to understand. Jane was so simple, so dull. . . . Compared with all that brilliance. . . ."

"Perhaps men sometimes tire of brilliance and fancy a little peace."

That made Kate laugh. "His Grace the King? Never! Well, he would have quickly tired of her had she lived, so, poor soul, perhaps it was as well she died. When I saw the new Queen at Shooters Hill whither we had ridden out with the King's party to greet her, I was mightily astonished. I had insisted on Remus's taking me, although he had feared I should not ride at that stage of my pregnancy. But I insisted and there she was. Damask, the pity of it. So plain! That dreadful skin and her clothes! If they had tried to make her look ugly they could not have succeeded better. She had some twelve or so ladies with her—all as ugly as she was. They are fat, these Flemings, and have no style. How different from the French. Anne Boleyn was Frenchified, was she not? Do you remember the way she held her head? And the King. He looked magnificent . . . although I will whisper to you that he no longer has that golden look he once had. His face is red and he is fat and his eyes have grown smaller and his mouth tighter . . . and when he frowns he is quite terrifying. But on this day he was in a coat somewhat like a dress—purple velvet, embroidered with gold thread and trimmed with gold lace. The sleeves were lined with cloth of gold and the coat was held together by buttons which were diamonds, rubies and pearls. His bonnet was a glitter. And his new Queen! She was in a gown of raised cloth of gold and on her head was a caul and over that a bonnet. How hideous are the Dutch fashions! To see them meet was most revealing. The people cheered and the King could not give vent to his real feeling, but those near him knew that the thunder was rumbling and those responsible for bringing Anne of Cleves to England trembled then and have been trembling ever since."

"Surely that was Cromwell."

"Cromwell, yes, and there are many who hate that man and will doubtless be pleased to see befall him that which has been the fate of many others."

"He is too powerful a man to suffer because the King does not like the look of a woman."

"Powerful men have fallen before. And they say that the King never loved Cromwell. He has accorded him scarce any dignity nor respect. 'Twas different with the Cardinal—yet look what became of him."

"It is dangerous to serve princes."

"You are not the first to have mentioned the fact," said Kate with a wry smile. "Do you know that after he had seen her for the first time the King was so incensed that he cried out: 'Whom shall men trust? I promise you that I see no such thing in her as hath been shown to me by her pictures or report. I love her not.'"

"Could he expect to love her on such a short meeting?"

"He meant he had no desire for her. And so long had he been without a wife that this was ominous. To tell the truth I believe he already had his eye on Katharine Howard and if this were so this would doubtless make Anne of Cleves seem even more repulsive than she might otherwise have been thought. Remus said that the King summoned Cromwell and demanded to be told how he could be released from the 'great Flanders mare.' Poor Cromwell, he is at his wits' end. But should we say 'Poor Cromwell'? Secretly I think not. Perhaps we are smiling a little because he is now himself in that danger in which he has placed so many. When we think of those days when his men came to St. Bruno's. . . ."

"He was but doing the King's bidding."

"Oh, a little more than that. He was the enemy of the monks. But for that man perhaps now Bruno would be living at the Abbey and you and I would be stealing through the secret door to have word with him. But that is all gone. It is as though it never was. And now it is Cromwell's turn to face the wrath of his sovereign."

"I pity any who must face that."

"Have you forgotten? Do you remember the monk who hung on the gibbet . . . how limp was his body! It made me shudder to look at him. And Brother Ambrose. . . ."

"Please don't talk of it, Kate. I'd rather forget."

"There's the difference in us. I'd rather remember now and say 'There, Cromwell, it is your turn now.' "

"But has it come to that? He has a great title bestowed on him, has he not?"

"Oh, yes, my Lord of Essex and Lord Chamberlain of England. Remus tells me that the King has bestowed thirty manors on him. Well, I suppose he deserved some to fall to him when one considered how many he has diverted to the King. But that was in April. It is now June. The summer skies are darkening for Master Cromwell and it is all due to this marriage."

"How knowledgeable you are."

"These are matters which are discussed at Court and sometimes here when people come from Court."

"And you find it dull?"

"Not such talk. Not such people. It is the country squires who bore me. Moreover I would wish to be at Court and not merely to listen to what goes on there when good fortune sends us a visitor."

"And what of Cromwell, Kate? What do they tell you of this man?"

"That the Cleves marriage has been a mistake from beginning to end. The King loves only attractive women and they procured for him a Flanders mare. The marriage was necessary, said Master Cromwell, because the King must placate the Duke of Cleves since the Emperor Charles of Austria and King François of France have put their heads together and have made an alliance which is surely to attack England. The German States could be brought to England's side because of the union with one of them and the unhappy King could see that he must do as his statesmen bid; and so against his inclination he married Anne of Cleves but declared that he could not bring himself to consummate the marriage." Kate began to laugh. "Imagine it! He went into the nuptial chamber but he had no inclination to go farther."

"I am sorry for her," I said.

"They say she was terrified. She feared that wishing to be rid of her he would trump up some charge against her. And now the Emperor Charles and King François have fallen out, and while this should be a matter for rejoicing, when the King knew what had happened he was furious, for it seemed he had married for no reason at all. He did not care now whether he had the support of the German States or not, for his two great enemies were even greater enemies of each other and while this state of affairs persisted he had nothing to fear. He demanded that Cromwell should extricate him. Cromwell does not know which way to turn. The clever man is caught in his own net."

"I wonder any man desires to go to Court. Look at the peace of this garden! How much more pleasant it is to watch the lilies on the pond and the bees in the lavender than to be concerned in the King's business."

"The rewards are great," said Kate.

"And to gain them one must risk one's head?"

"Damask, you are without ambition. You do not know how to live."

"But it is precisely what I would wish to do. It is you who think that there is some virtue in gambling with death."

"I would rather live boldly for a week than dully for twenty years. I am sure my way of life is more to be desired than yours."

"When we are old, we will remember this day and perhaps then we shall understand who is right."

We were silent for a while. Then she said that she thought her time would be sooner than she had believed possible.

"We must send for your husband," I said.

But she shook her head. "We shall do no such thing. I do not want him here, intruding on us."

She was adamant. I was a little alarmed. There was a feverishness about her. I kept thinking of Keziah lying in Mother Salter's cottage with the sprig of rosemary on the sheet.

Lord Remus came to the Castle. Kate was disappointed that he had returned so soon, but he told me that he must certainly be present when his child was born. There was no doubt that he adored Kate. I was surprised because she was not always gracious to him; but he reacted to her tantrums as though she were a favored child, as though everything she did must be accepted because she did it so charmingly.

But at least what he had to tell was of interest to Kate.

Kate had insisted that she was in no mood to entertain and we took our meals as before in her room. The difference was that Lord Remus was often with us. Kate would have preferred him to be absent but when he talked of the Court affairs she became animated and interested.

Because of his post in the King's household Lord Remus could talk knowledgeably of affairs and although I imagined that ordinarily he was a man of discretion Kate could worm anything out of him. She wanted to know the truth about Cromwell and therefore she had it.

"The man is in a frenzy of anxiety," Lord Remus told her. "He has been arrested at Westminster. I heard from my Lord Southampton, who was present, that he was taken completely off his guard. He came to the Council and as he entered the room the Captain of the Guard stepped forward with the words, 'Thomas

Cromwell, Earl of Essex, I arrest you in the name of the King on a charge of High Treason.' Southampton says he never saw a man so astonished and then afraid."

"How many times," cried Kate, "had Master Cromwell called for the arrest of men who were more innocent than he!"

"Be careful, Kate."

"What nonsense!" she retorted. "Do you think Damask will inform against me? And of what should she inform?"

"It is necessary to guard the tongue, my dear. We do not know who may be listening or how words may be distorted. We cannot trust our own servants these days."

"Tell us more," commanded Kate.

"The fellow was near hysteria. He threw his bonnet to the ground. He called on the members of the Council to support him. They knew he was no traitor, he said. But all were against him to a man. They have always hated the fellow. He went straight to the Tower and before the day was out the King's men were ransacking his houses. I have heard he had accumulated much treasure during his days of power and that the King's coffers will be much enriched by it."

"Master Cromwell will have a taste of what he was delighted to do to others. I can see them now at the Abbey. Those laden packhorses! All the riches and treasures of St. Bruno's."

Lord Remus again begged his wife to have a care and this time she was silent. I knew she was thinking of Bruno and the anguish he had suffered.

I said to Lord Remus: "How could this man who has worked for the King so suddenly become a traitor? Are not his fortunes linked with those of the King? Is he a traitor then because two Princes of Europe have become enemies when they were friends?"

Lord Remus looked at me gently. There was something very kind about him and he and I had become good friends. I think he liked the deference I always showed him, which I felt was due to his age and position, and in any case I was sorry for the manner in which Kate behaved toward him.

"Why, Damask," he answered, "the way to the King's favor is through good fortune and can any man expect good fortune to attend him all the days of his life? There are those who would say

that Thomas Cromwell has led a charmed life . . . until now.
They will tell you that Cromwell rose from humble stock to greatness. There again he resembled his master Wolsey. His father,
they say, was a blacksmith and a fuller and shearer of cloth, but
I have heard that he was a man of some small means having in
his possession a hostelry and brewhouse. Cromwell is a man of
great ability. Shrewd, cunning, but with little of those graces
which would have helped his progress at Court. He was well fitted
though to do the work the King gave him to do. But he was never
liked. The King was never affectionate toward him as he was
toward the Cardinal. While he used Cromwell he despised him.
It seems there is little chance for the man now."

"I wonder any man wishes to serve the King."

Lord Remus's eyes opened wide with fear. "It is the duty and
pleasure of us all to serve His Majesty," he said loudly. "And it is
wrong to show pity for those who . . . are traitors toward him."

I asked of what Cromwell had been accused. Was it bringing a
wife whom the King found repulsive? If he had brought a beauty
would he have been now living in peace in one of his many man-
sions?

"He is accused of secret dealing with the Germans. He has
failed in his foreign policy, for the alliance he made with the Duke
of Cleves is proved a nuisance to the King who wishes now to
conclude a treaty with Emperor Charles. Cromwell's policy has
brought no good to the country and in addition it has brought a
wife to the King of whom he wishes to be rid."

"It might so easily have gone the other way."

Lord Remus bent toward me and said: "There is little sympathy
for this man. His actions have not won the love of many. There
will be plenty who will not shed a tear when his head rolls—as
it surely must."

Then I thought of my father's saying that the tragedy of one
was the tragedy of us all; and I was very uneasy.

We were all very relieved when Kate's pains started and her
labor was not long. Trust Kate to be lucky.

Remus and I sat in the anteroom of her bedroom in deep sympathy with each other. He was very anxious and I tried to comfort

him. He told me all that Kate had meant to him, how life had changed for him since his marriage, how wonderful she was and how terrified he had been when she was at Court lest the King's eyes stray too often toward her. How grateful he was to Norfolk's niece, Katharine Howard, who was not nearly so beautiful as Kate (who was?) but had a straying wanton glance which had greatly beguiled the King so that he scarcely saw anyone else. He was sure that as soon as the King was free of his distasteful marriage, he would wish to make Katharine Howard his fifth Queen.

I shuddered and he said quietly, "You may well feel sorry for the poor child. She is so young, so unaware. I trust if it should ever come to a crown for her, fate will not be as unkind as it has been to her predecessors."

And by fate of course he meant the King.

I tried to make him talk about the affair to keep his mind off Kate, but even at such a time he was too much aware of the dangers to say overmuch.

Then before we dared hope to we heard the cry of a child and we rushed into the room—and there he was, a healthy boy.

Kate lay back in her bed—exhausted and pale, beautiful in a new way, ethereal and triumphant.

The midwife was chuckling.

"A fine boy, my lord. And what a pair of lungs!"

I saw the color flood Remus's face. I doubt whether he had ever known such a proud moment.

"And her ladyship?" he said.

"It's rarely been my luck to have such an easy birth, my lord."

He went to the bed and stood there looking down at her, his expression one of adoration.

Kate was too tired to talk; but she caught my eye and said my name.

"Congratulations, Kate," I said. "You have a fine boy."

I saw the smile curve her lips. It was one of triumph.

The child was named Carey which was a family name of the Remuses. Kate affected an indifference to him which I did not believe she really felt. She refused to feed him herself and a wet nurse came in—a plump rosy-cheeked girl who had enough milk and to spare for her own child when Carey had had his fill. Her name was Betsy and I said to Kate that it was a shameful thing that a country girl who had come as the child's wet nurse should show more affection for him than his own mother.

"He is too young for me yet," Kate excused herself. "When he grows older I shall be interested in him."

"Such maternal instincts!" I mocked.

"Maternal instincts are for such as you," retorted Kate, "who doubtless has not a soul above feeding and cleaning infants."

I loved the baby. I would nurse him whenever possible and young as he was I was sure he knew me. When he was crying I would rock him in his cradle and never fail to quieten him. Lord Remus used to smile at me.

"You should be a mother, Damask," he said.

I knew he was right. Being with little Carey made me long for a child of my own. I thought I would like to take the boy home with me, for I said to Kate it was time I went home.

She raised a storm of protests. Why did I constantly talk of going home? Wasn't I content to be with her? What did I want? I only had to ask and she would see that it was brought to me.

I said I wanted to be with my father. He was missing me. Kate must remember that I only came to be with her until she had her child.

"The baby will miss you," said Kate slyly. "How shall we keep him quiet when you are not there to rock the cradle?"

"He'd rather have his mother."

"No, he would not. He prefers you, which shows how clever he is. You're of much more use to him than I am."

"You are a strange woman, Kate," I said.

"Would you have me ordinary?"

"No. But I should like you to be more natural with the child."

"He is well cared for."

"He needs caresses and to be made aware of love."

"This boy will own all these lands. He's a very lucky baby. He'll soon grow out of the need for caresses and baby talk when he sees this grand estate."

"Then he will be like his mother."

"Which," said Kate, "is not such a bad thing to be."

So we bantered and enjoyed each other's company. I knew that she sought every pretext to keep me there and I was delighted that this should be so. As for myself I thought often of my father and were it not for him I should have been contented enough to stay. I guessed that he must have missed me sorely and now that Kate had her boy, I thought he would write urging me to come back; but his letters to me were accounts of home affairs and there was no urgent request for me to return.

I was a little piqued by this, which was foolish of me; I might have known there was a reason.

Little Carey was a month old. My mother wrote that she had heard that a fruit called the cherry had been brought into the country and had been planted in Kent. Could I please try to find out if this was so? And she had also heard that the King's gardener had introduced apricots into his gardens and they were prospering well. She would so like to hear if this was the case. Perhaps some of the people who visited Remus Castle and who came from the Court would be able to tell something about these exciting projects.

The people who came from the Court did not talk of apricots. There was about them all a furtive air; they lowered their voices when they talked but they could not deny themselves the pleasure of discussing the King's affairs.

The King was determined to rid himself of Anne of Cleves. Cromwell, who had made the marriage, was going to unmake it.

I thought of him often in his prison in the Tower—his fate was not unlike that of the great Cardinal, only his lacked the dignity. The Cardinal had had the King's affection and had died before the ignominy of the Tower and death there could overtake him. I was filled with pity for these men—even Cromwell—and no matter how much I remembered that terrible time when the Abbey had been defiled and violence and misery had prevailed, still I felt pity for the man who had climbed so high only to fall.

I heard now that Cromwell had been forced to reveal conversations which he had had with the King on the morning after the wedding night. During these conversations the King had made it perfectly clear that the marriage had not been consummated.

"Cromwell has admitted," so said one of our visitors, "that the

King told him he found the lady so far from his taste that nothing could induce him to consummate the marriage. If she were a maid when she came, so Cromwell assures us the King said to him, then His Majesty had left her as she was when she came, though as for her virginity, His Majesty was inclined to doubt that she was in possession of such a virtue when she arrived. Now Parliament will bring in a bill to declare that the marriage is null and void and that if a marriage has not been consummated this is a ground for divorce."

"How unfortunate are the King's wives," I said.

"I do not think the lady who will soon become the fifth would agree with this."

"Poor girl. She is very young, I hear."

"Aye, and the King is eager for her."

"Perhaps when he is married to her he will soften toward her and pardon Cromwell."

"That man has too many enemies. His doom is certain. The King never had any affection for him."

I shivered.

I shall never forget that July. The scent of roses filled the pond garden and the leaves were thick in the pleached alley. I used to carry the baby out to the seat in his wicker basket and sit him down at my feet while I stitched at some garment for him. Kate would join me. She was planning her next visit to Court.

"They say Katharine Howard is already the King's wife. I wonder how long she will last."

"Poor girl," I murmured.

"At least she will be a Queen, if only for a short time. I have heard it said that in the Duchess of Norfolk's household she was a very merry little lady at one time."

"The King would hardly wish for a somber one."

"Rather free with her smiles and other favors."

"'Tis always better to smile than frown—something which you might remember."

She laughed. "My mentor!" she murmured. "You always seem to know what is best for me. Why should you think that you are so much wiser than I?"

"Because I should be hard put to it to be less so."

"Oh, so now we are clever! Go on, clever Damask. I will sit with my hands folded and listen to your sermons."

We were silent for a while. There was no sound in the garden but the buzzing of the bees in the lavender.

Then she said: "How does it feel to die . . . to leave all this, I wonder."

I looked at her in a startled fashion and she went on: "How did Queen Anne feel in her prison in the Tower, knowing that her end was near. It is four years since she died, Damask, and in the month of May, the beauteous month when all nature is reborn . . . and *she* died. And now that man, who was no friend of hers, is also to die. She was brave. They say she walked most calmly to her death, that she was elegantly attired as always. She was scornful of her fate. That is how I would be. And think of the King, Damask. He heard the death gun booming from the Tower. 'The deed is done,' so they tell me he said. 'Uncouple the hounds and away.' And to Wolf Hall he went where Jane Seymour was waiting. But she did not long enjoy her crown."

"Poor soul," I said.

"Yet she died in her bed and not on a bloody scaffold."

"Perhaps it was better that she died thus than live to face a worse death."

"Death is death," said Kate. "Wherever it is met. But not all die as Anne died. I can picture her lifting her head high as she walked and as calmly laying it down to receive the blow from the executioner's sword. How different is Cromwell. He begs for his life, they say. He has sworn all that the King asks him to swear. He declares the King confided to him on the wedding night . . . because that is what the King wishes. He begged for mercy."

"And will it be granted?"

"Is the King ever merciful?"

"I wonder," I said.

We were interrupted in the garden by the arrival of a visitor. He came from Court and Kate went out to greet him. That day we dined in the great hall and Kate was animated and I thought that having a child had by no means impaired her beauty. Lord Remus could not take his eyes from her and I marveled at her power to win such devotion without making much effort to do so.

The talk was of the Court as Kate wished it to be.

The fall of Cromwell and the King's infatuation for Katharine Howard were the topics.

"My Lady of Cleves now passes her time most comfortably at Richmond Palace," our visitor told us. "Those who have seen her say that a great serenity has fallen upon her. She has many dresses and all of the latest fashion. She walks in the gardens and is most pleasant to all who approach her. The truth is that she has come through a trying ordeal. They say she was terrified when the King showed he would not have her and greatly feared that her head would roll in the dust as had that of Queen Anne Boleyn."

"What a merciful escape."

"It is not always judicious to cut off the heads of those who have powerful friends in Europe. Thomas Boleyn was an Englishman, and no powerful monarch. So Anne lost her head."

"It is small wonder that my lady Anne revels in her freedom," I said. "I can understand how she feels now. Free . . . with no anxiety! Free to enjoy the King's mercy."

"The King was merciful to Cromwell too" was the answer. "He gave him the ax in place of the gallows. As a lowborn man it should have been the gallows but the King was a little moved by his pleas for mercy and granted the block."

"And now he is no more."

I could not join in the laughter and merriment of that night when the mummers came into the hall and there was dancing to entertain our visitors. I kept on thinking of the feverish relief of Anne of Cleaves, the mercy shown to Thomas Cromwell—an ax to cut off his head instead of a rope to hang about his neck—and of the young girl who was blithely walking into danger as the King's fifth wife.

Kate came to my room that night.

"You brood too much, Damask," she told me; for she understood the trend of my thoughts although I had said nothing. "Does it not seem to you that by the very fact that we live in a world where death can come at any moment to anyone, we should cherish those moments we have of life?"

I thought that perhaps she was right. And a few days later Rupert came to Remus Castle.

* * *

Our visitor from Court had left and we were quiet again.

Intending to take little Carey into the rose garden and sit there and enjoy the peace of the place while I worked at my sewing I went to the nursery where I found Betsy in tears. Carey who had been well fed was sleeping and when I asked her what was wrong she told me that her sister's master, who had been good to her, had yesterday been drawn on a hurdle and taken to Smithfield to undergo the dreaded sentence of hanging, drawing and quartering. This barbaric custom of hanging a man and cutting him down when he was still alive to disembowel him was so horrifying that to hear of it sickened me; I tried to comfort Betsy and asked of what her sister's employer had been accused.

"He was not rightly sure," she told me. "But it was doubtless speaking against the King and the new law."

He did not rightly know meant that there had been no trial. What had happened to our country since the King had broken with the Church and ordinary humble folk must watch their words?

I could not think of how I could comfort Betsy so I took the baby and went out to the rose garden. Kate came there and sat beside me as I stitched. She too was somber for she had heard of the tragedy.

"He was hanged, drawn and quartered with three others as traitors," she told me, "while three more were burned as heretics. What a strange state of affairs. Those who were hanged, drawn and quartered were traitors because they spoke in favor of the Pope; those who were burned as heretics were studying the new religion and spoke against him. So those who are for Rome and those who are against Rome die together at the same hour at the same place."

"There is a simple explanation," I said. "The King has made it clear that there is to be but one change. The religion is the same —the Catholic Faith, but in place of the Pope as Supreme Head of the Church there is an Englishman, the King. To declare the Pope head of the church makes a man a traitor. But to study and practice the new doctrines set out by Martin Luther is heresy. Lowborn traitors are hanged, drawn and quartered; heretics are burned at the stake. That is how things stand in this country at this day."

"All men and women should take the greatest care not to dabble in these things."

"My father told me that Luther had said: That what the King of England wills must be for the English an article of faith—to disobey which means death."

"How do we know," said Kate soberly, "whether we are not at this moment talking treason?"

"Let us hope that only the birds and insects can hear."

"It was more comforting when there was the old law. Now it is so difficult to know whether or not one speaks treason."

"So one must be careful before whom one says one single word which can be considered treason. I'll dareswear Betsy's sister's master wished no harm to the King. It may well be that by talking of this man we could be accused of treason. Perhaps Betsy by shedding a tear for him is a traitor. It is a frightening thought."

"Let us talk of other things. I will show you the sapphire bracelet Remus has bought for me. That man is so proud to have a son. He says he is afraid to let it be known, for the King can be very envious of men who get healthy sons."

"Could it then be treason to have a son! The young Prince Edward is something of a weakling, I believe."

"How strange that my little Carey should be such a lusty animal while Edward with all the royal care and fuss is puny."

"Is it treason so to discuss the heir to the throne?"

"Treason is lurking round the corner always ready to creep up on one. If we talk of a ribbon—could that be treason? If my ribbons are of a prettier color than those of Queen Katharine Howard and I say so—could that be treason? Methinks, Damask, that we should guard our tongues and never speak at all except to say the sun is shining or it rains or like your mother discuss the merits of one rose against another. That is safety. But this is a matter of which we have talked often, and in spite of all I would rather go to Court and risk death than die of boredom here."

But the thought of treason had had a sobering effect on us both and neither of us was in the mood to banter.

It was the following morning when Rupert came.

As soon as he rode into the courtyard accompanied by his servant, I knew he had brought bad news. I ran out to him and embraced him.

He said: "Damask, oh, my dear Damask. . . ."

"Father?" I asked. "Is it Father?"

He nodded and I saw that he was trying to control his features that he might hide his grief.

"Quickly," I cried. "Tell me quickly. What is it?"

"Yesterday your father was taken to the Tower."

I stared at him in horror. I could not believe it.

"It's not true," I cried. "It can't be true. Why? What has he done?"

And even as I spoke our conversation of the last few days came back to my mind. How easy it was to be a traitor to the King. What could he have done to take him to the Tower, he who had never done anything to harm anyone in his life before?

"I must talk to you," said Rupert. "Where is Kate? Where is Lord Remus?"

Lord Remus was out with the hunt. Kate, having heard the sounds of arrival, joined us in the courtyard.

"Rupert," she cried. "Welcome, brother." Then she saw his face. "Ill news?" she cried, looking from one of us to the other.

"Father has been taken to the Tower," I said.

The color left her face; her great eyes looked stony. I had rarely seen Kate so moved. She turned to me, her lips quivering, and held out her hand. I grasped it and she pressed it firmly. She was reminding me then that she understood my suffering and that she was as my sister.

"Pray come in," said Kate. "Do not let us stand out here."

She slipped her arm through mine and we went into the great hall.

Kate said: "We cannot talk here." And she led us to an anteroom. There she bade Rupert sit down and me too; and seating herself she said: "Pray tell us all."

"It was yesterday while we were at dinner. The King's men came and arrested Uncle in the King's name."

"On what charge?" I cried.

"Treason," said Rupert.

"It could not be true."

Rupert looked at me sadly. "They took Amos Carmen too. They found his hiding place. They went straight to it as though someone had betrayed the fact that he was there."

"In our house?" I asked.

Rupert nodded. "After you left, Amos came back. He was being hunted. He had declared the Pope to be the true head of the Church and refused to sign the Act of Supremacy which as a priest he was required to do. He was going to escape to Spain because there was no hope for him here while the King lived; your father was helping him."

I covered my face with my hand. How could he have been so foolish! He had walked straight into danger. It was what I had always feared. That which had threatened us had at last caught up with us.

It was Kate who spoke. "What can we do to save him?"

Rupert shook his head.

"There must be something," I cried. "What will they do to him? That . . . which they have done to others?"

"It would be the ax for him," said Rupert as though to comfort me. "He is of gentle birth."

The ax! That greatly loved head to be severed by the executioner. That good life to be ended by a stroke! How could such things happen? Had these people never known what it was to love a father?

Kate said gently: "This is a terrible shock to Damask. We must take care of her, Rupert."

Rupert said: "That is what I am here to do."

"I must go to him," I said.

"You would not be allowed to see him," Rupert reminded me. "It is his wish that you should remain here with Kate."

"Remain here . . . when he is *there!* I shall do no such thing. I am coming home at once. I will find some way to see him. I will do something. I will not stand by and allow them to murder him."

"Damask . . . this is a great blow. I have broken it too roughly, too harshly. Here you are safe. You are away from the house. He did not wish you to come home while Amos was there. He would allow none of us to be involved. He declares again and again that he and he only is responsible for hiding Amos. He was not in the house, but you remember the little cottage in the nuttery. Uncle hid him there and himself took food to him. No one went to the loft above. Only garden tools were stored in the lower part, you remember. It seemed he was safe there. It would be folly to go back now. We do not know what will happen next."

"So they came while you were at dinner."

Rupert nodded.

"And he . . . how did he go?"

"Calmly, as you would expect. He said, 'No one here knows of this but myself.' And then they went out and took Amos. They have both been carried off to the Tower."

"And what can we do, Rupert?"

Rupert shook his head blankly. What was there to do? What could anyone do? What the King willed was an article of Faith— and Amos had broken the King's law and my father had helped him do this.

Kate, wondrously gentle for her, said: "I am going to take you to your room, Damask. You are going to lie down. I will bring a posset which will soothe you. You will sleep and then you will be better able to suffer this blow."

"Do you think I am going to sleep while he is in the Tower? Do you think I want possets? I am going back at once. I am going to find out what I can do. . . ."

Rupert said: "It's no good, Damask."

"You may stay here if you are afraid," I said, which was unkind and unfair too. "I shall not cower behind Lord Remus. I am going home. I am going to discover what can be done."

"*Nothing* can be done, Damask."

"Nothing. How do you know? What have you tried to do? I am going back at once."

Rupert said: "If you go I shall come with you."

"You should stay here, Rupert."

"Where you are I wish to be," he said.

"I will not have you risk anything for me. But I shall not stay here. I shall go back at once. There may be something I can do."

Rupert shook his head but Kate surprisingly came down on my side.

"If she wishes to go back, she must," she said.

"But it is dangerous," protested Rupert. "Who knows what will happen now?"

"What of my mother?" I asked.

"She is stunned by the blow."

I could imagine her, startled out of a world where she had lived shut away from events and the blight on her roses was by far the greatest tragedy she could envisage.

"And what is being done?" I asked.

"What can we do?" asked Rupert. "He was taken yesterday. He is in the Tower. They have allowed him to take a servant with him. Tom Skillen went. He came back for a blanket and some food. They allowed him to take them to him. So he is not being so badly treated as some."

I said firmly: "When can we start?"

"We could leave tomorrow," said Rupert. "It is too late today."

Kate said: "That is wise. You will go tomorrow. Rupert must rest. He has had a long journey."

I was silent, staring before me, visualizing it all. His calm acceptance when they came to take him; the barge would have taken him through the Traitors' Gate. And he would have been thanking God that Damask was not at home, that she had not been in the house at all while he had sheltered Amos. He would be saying, "Damask is safe." As if I wanted to be safe while he was in danger. Why had I gone? Why had I not been there? I would have done something, I promised myself. I would never have allowed them to take him. I thought of him in his dismal prison in the Tower. So many had exchanged their comfortable beds for a pallet on the cold stone floor—to await death.

But it could not come to that. It must not. There would be a way.

Kate was leading me to my room.

There was the night to be lived through before we left. I could not wait to start on the journey home. Remus had come in from the hunt, beaming and full of high spirits. The change in him when he heard the news was astounding. His skin turned a pale-yellow color and his jaw worked without his volition. I was looking at Fear. No man in these days cared to be connected with a traitor.

He recovered quickly, for he was remote from my father; all he had done was marry a cousin of his wife. Surely that could not be construed as treason? After all there had been no question of Lawyer Farland's treachery at that time. He had been a rich man, a respectable lawyer who had given good service to many of the King's close friends. Remus decided that he was safe and the fear passed. But I could see he was glad that I had decided to leave his house.

At dawn I was up, ready to leave. I was touched by Kate's solicitude. Never before had she shown her affection for me so clearly; she was deeply moved and she whispered to me: "Rupert will take care of you. Do as he wishes." Then she threw her arms about me and held me tightly for a second.

She stood at the gateway watching us ride away.

It grew lighter as we rowed upriver but I scarcely noticed the landscape as we passed. I was thinking of him; pictures kept coming in and out of my mind; I thought of his standing by the wall watching the barges go by, his arm about me. I heard his voice telling me that the tragedy of the Cardinal was the tragedy of us all. How prophetic were his words, for the Cardinal had fallen when the King broke with Rome and the reverberation of that break still echoed through the land and it was for this reason that my own father now lay in his dank and dismal prison awaiting death.

It was more than I could bear. I was in such despair that only my anger could rouse me from it. I would in my present mood have gone to the King himself and told him what a cruel and wicked thing this was to harm a good man who had done nothing but what he believed to be right.

There on the bank were the towers of Hampton Court. I shivered as we passed it. Work was still being done on it, I remembered inconsequentially. My father had mentioned only the last time we had passed that a great astronomical clock was being erected in one of the courtyards and that the lovers' knots with the King's and Jane Seymour's initials which had been put into the great hall were already out of date since there had been another Queen since and talk of yet another. The towers which had always seemed so enchanting to me, now seemed menacing.

How slowly Tom Skillen rowed, I thought impatiently. But it was not true that he did. Poor Tom, he also had changed from the carefree young man who had crept into Keziah's bedroom by night.

We had arrived. The barge was tied to the privy stairs and I scrambled out and ran across the lawns into the hall, where I found my mother. I threw myself into her arms and she kept repeating my name. Then she said: "You shouldn't have come. He didn't wish it."

"But I am here, Mother," I said. "No one could stop my coming."

Simon Caseman appeared. He stood a little apart from us, a woebegone expression on his face. He looked strong and powerful so I appealed to him.

"There must be something we can do," I said.

He took both my hands in his and kissed them. "We will never give up hope," he said.

"Is there some way of getting to him?" I asked.

"I am trying to find out. It may be possible for you to see him." I was so grateful that I pressed his hand warmly.

He said: "You may rely on me to explore every path."

"Oh, thank you. Thank you."

"My dearest child," said my mother tearfully. "You will be so worn out with the journey. Let me get something. I have heard that the juice of the pimpernel will raise the spirits when one is melancholy."

"Oh, Mother," I said, "nothing could raise my spirits except to see him come through the door a free man."

Simon had edged Rupert aside. Rupert had done his task in bringing me home and he could only now regard me with sorrowful eyes which told me how well he understood my pain and would willingly bear it for me. There was something very good about Rupert. He reminded me of my father.

"What can we *do?*" I demanded of Simon, for he seemed more capable than any.

He said: "I am going to one of the jailors. I know him well. I did a little business for him and he owes me something. It may well be that he could let us through so that you might see your father."

"If that could only be."

Simon pressed my shoulder. "Rest assured," he said, "that if this cannot be brought about it will be due to no lack of effort on my part."

"When?" I demanded.

"Stay here with your mother. Comfort her. Go into the gardens with her. Behave as though it were any day and this had not happened. Try please. It is the best. And I will get Tom to row me to a tavern I know and there I may well discover something. I will see if I can find my warder friend and I'll make him see that he can do no harm in allowing you and your father to see each other."

"Thank you," I murmured.

"You know," he said quietly, "that my greatest pleasure is to please you."

I was so grateful to him that I felt a little ashamed for not really liking him in the past. Rupert was good and kind, I knew, but he accepted disaster. Simon was ready to fight against it.

"First the pimpernel," said my mother.

Simon said: "Take it. It will do you good to do so and your mother good to prepare it. Try to sleep a little. Then go into the garden with your mother. Take the flower basket and gather roses. Rest assured I shall be back with news soon. You must get through the time till my return as best you can."

I thought how much he understood my grief and I warmed toward him still further. I allowed my mother to take me to her room and there she brought me the potion brewed from the juice of the pimpernel and what other ingredients I knew not.

She made me lie down and she sat by my bed and she talked of it, that terrible day when they had been at dinner—as they had so many times before and how they had been eating one of the mutton pies which Clement made so well, when the King's men came in. I could see it all so clearly. I might have been there. I could almost taste the mutton pie garnished with my mother's herbs; I could feel the terrible fear in my stomach and the dry constriction of my throat. And I saw his dear face so calm, so resigned. He would be as though he had almost known it must come.

And he would have gone with them quietly, sitting there in the barge while the oars dipped in the water and they came through the Traitors' Gate.

I slept for many hours. It was the pimpernel perhaps and other herbs which my mother had given me. I suppose she thought the only way in which I could forget my misery for a short while was in sleep.

To my joy the meeting was arranged. Simon came to my room and asked to be allowed in. He stood there smiling at me and as the light which came through leaden panes was not great it threw shadows and again I saw the fox's mask and was ashamed for thinking of it in the face of all his consideration for me.

"Tomorrow I shall take you to your father," he said.

The relief was great. I felt almost happy. Yet I knew that I must be stealthily let into his cell, that the meeting would be brief. Yet somehow I felt that by seeing him I could achieve something.

"How can I thank you?" I said.

He replied, "My reward is to do everything in my power to help you."

"You have my gratitude," I told him.

He bowed his head and taking my hand, raised it to his lips. Then he left me.

How I lived through the rest of that day and the night I cannot be sure. The next day I put on doublet and hose which belonged to Rupert. My hair betrayed me as a woman. Without a moment's hesitation I had seized it in my hand and cut it off. It was thick and I cut it to hang almost to my shoulders. Now with a cap set on it I might have been a boy.

When he saw me Simon stared. "Your beautiful hair!" he cried.

"Doubtless it will grow. And I could not look like a boy with it so I must needs cut it."

He nodded. Then he said: "You will soon be seventeen, Mistress Damask. You have made yourself look like a boy of twelve."

"So much the better," I replied, "for since you thought I should wear doublet and hose, you must believe I shall have a greater chance of seeing my father if I am believed to be a boy."

"So you would sacrifice your beautiful hair for a few brief moments with him."

"I would sacrifice my life," I said.

"I have always admired you, as I believe I have made you aware —but never so as at this moment."

And we went down the river together and I shall never forget seeing that grim gray fortress rise before us. How many, I wondered, had looked up at it knowing that somewhere within it lay a loved one? I had heard much of it—of the dungeons from which it was impossible to escape, the dark torture chambers; I had many times seen the great Keep and I knew the names of the many towers—the White Tower, the Salt Tower, the Bowyer Tower, the Constable Tower and the Bloody Tower in which, not so long before, the two little sons of King Edward IV had been murdered as they slept and their bodies buried, some said, under a secret stair in that very fortress. I had seen the church of St. Peter ad Vincula before which was Tower Green, the grass of which four years before had been stained by the blood of Queen Anne Boleyn, her brother and those men who were said to be her lovers.

And now my own beloved father might be destined to join the band of martyrs.

It was growing dark as we rowed upriver. Simon had said this was the best time to go. In the Lantern Turret lights burned. They were lighted at dusk and kept burning through the night to act as river signals. The river smelled dank and evil. We were now close to the stone walls.

At last we came to rest, the barge was tied to a stake and Simon helped me out.

His warder friend came out of the shadows.

"I'll wait here," said Simon.

The warder said: "Watch your step, boy." And I wondered whether he was pretending to think me a boy or knew who I was. My heart was beating wildly but not with fear. I could think of only one thing: I was going to see my father.

The warder thrust a lantern into my hand.

"Carry that," he said, "and say nothing."

The stone was damp and slippery. I had to watch my steps carefully. I followed him through a passage and we came to a door. He had a bunch of keys and using one of these he opened it. It was iron studded, and consequently heavy. It creaked as it opened. He carefully locked the door behind us.

"Keep close," he said.

I obeyed, and we went up a stone spiral staircase. We were in a stone-floored corridor. It was very cold. Here and there a lantern burned on the wall.

Before a heavy door the warder paused. He selected a key from his bunch and opened the door. For the moment I could scarcely see anything and then I gave a cry of joy for there he was. I put down the lantern and clung to him.

He said: "Damask. Oh, God, I am dreaming."

"No, Father. Did you think I would not come?" I seized his hand and kissed it fiercely.

The warder stepped outside the door and stood there; my father and I were alone in the cell.

In a broken voice he said: "Oh, Damask, you should not have come."

I knew that his joy in seeing me was as great as mine in seeing him, but that his fear for me was even greater.

I laid my cheek against his hand. "Do you think I would not have come? Do you think I would not do anything . . . anything. . . ."

"My beloved child," he said. Then: "Let me look at you." He took my face in his hands and said: "Your hair."

"I cut it off," I said. "I had to come here as a boy."

He held me against him. "Dearest child," he said, "there is much to say and little time to say it in. My thoughts are all for you and your mother. You will have to take care of her."

"You are coming back to us," I said fiercely.

"If I do not. . . ."

"No, don't say it. You are coming. I will consider nothing else. We will find some way. . . . How could you have done anything wrong? You who have been so good all your life. . . ."

"What is right for some of us is wrong in the eyes of others. That is the trouble in the world, Damask."

"This man . . . he had no right to come to you. . . . He had no right to ask you to hide him."

"He did not ask. I offered. Would you have me turn away a friend? But let us not talk of what is past. It is the future I think of. Constantly I think of you, my dearest child. It gives me great comfort. Do you remember our talks . . . our walks. . . ."

"Oh, Father, I cannot bear it."

"We must needs bear what God has decided we must."

"God! What has God to do with this? Why should wicked murderers prosper while saints are done to death? Why should they dance in their castles . . . a new wife every. . . ."

"Hush! What talk is this! Damask, I beg of you have a care. Do you want to please me? Do you want to bring me happiness?"

"Father, you know."

"Then listen to me. Go back home. Comfort your mother. Watch over her. When the time comes marry and have children. It can be the greatest joy. When you have little ones you will cease to mourn for your father. You will know it is the rule of life—the old pass on and make way for the young."

"We are going to take you back home, Father."

He stroked my hair.

"We shall find a way. We must. Do you think I can endure to be there without you! You have always been there. All my life I have looked to you. I never thought till now that there would come a time when you . . . would not . . . be there."

"My love," he said, "you distress yourself . . . and me."

"Let us be practical then. We shall try to get you out of here. Why should you not change clothes with me now. . . . You could go and I could stay here."

He laughed tenderly. "My dearest, do you think I would look like a boy? Do you think you could be mistaken for an old man? And do you think I would leave here one who is more dear to me than my own life? You talk wildly, child, but your talk pleases me. We have loved each other truly, we two."

The warder was at the door.

"You'll have to come away now. It's dangerous to stay longer."

"No," I cried, and clung to my father.

He put me from him gently. "Go now, Damask," he said. "I

shall remember as long as I live that you came to me, that you cut off your beautiful hair for the sake of a few brief moments."

"What is my hair compared with my love for you?"

"My child, I shall remember." Then he caught me to him and held me tightly. "Damask, take care. Watch your tongue. You must know we are in danger. Someone betrayed me. Someone could betray you. That is something I could not endure. If I know that you are safe and your mother is safe . . . I can be content. To be careful, to care for each other, to live in peace . . . that could be the greatest thing you could do for me."

"Come now," growled the warder.

One last embrace and there I was standing in the dank passage, that heavy door between him and me.

I was unaware of the journey to the barge. I only vaguely saw the rat that scuttled across our path. There was Tom Skillen waiting to help me into the barge.

And as we rode along the dark river, guided by the lights from the Lantern Turret, one thing my father had said kept recurring in my mind. "Someone betrayed me."

I did not see him again. They took him out on Tower Hill and that noble head was severed by the ax.

On the day it happened my mother, on Simon Caseman's advice and without my knowledge until afterward, gave me a draft which she had made with poppy juice. It sent me into a deep sleep from which I did not awaken until I was fatherless.

I rose from my bed, heavy eyed but heavier hearted; I went downstairs and found my mother seated in her room, her hands in her lap, staring blankly before her.

I knew then that she was a widow and I had lost the dearest and best of fathers forever.

For the next few days I went about in a kind of daze. When people spoke to me I did not hear. Rupert tried to comfort me; so did Simon Caseman.

"I'll take care of you for evermore," Rupert told me, and I did not realize until later that he was asking me to marry him.

Simon Caseman was more definite. I did not forget that he had arranged the meeting with my father. He had seen his execution and that of Amos Carmen, and he told of it.

"You would have been proud of your father, Damask," he said. "He walked out to his death calmly and without fear. He laid his head upon the block with a resignation which was the admiration of all who beheld it. But I will not speak of it. It is better not."

I was silent; my grief welling up within me. I had shed no tears. My mother said it would be better if I did.

Simon said: "His last thoughts were of you. I had a word with him. You were his great concern . . . you and your mother. He longed to see you in the care of a strong man. That was one of his greatest desires. Damask, I am here to take care of you. You need a strong arm to lean on; you need the love which only a husband can give you. Let us delay no longer. It would be his wish and remember, you are alone in a dangerous world. When a man is arraigned for treason who knows what is in store for his family? You need me to care for you, Damask, as I need you because I love you."

I looked at him and the old repellence came back. I fancied I saw the fox's mask and I drew away from him. Doubtless my expression betrayed my feelings.

"I would not marry for expediency," I said, "though, Simon, I am grateful to you for what you have done for me at this cruel time, but I could not marry you, for I do not love you and I would not marry where I did not love."

He turned and left me.

I forgot him; I could think of nothing but my loss.

Two days after my father's murder a strange thing happened. They had not told me, because they did not wish to grieve me, that Father's head had been placed on one of the poles which were stuck on London Bridge. He was well known in the city and this was meant to be a warning to all men who planned to disobey the orders of the King. It would be called the head of a traitor. There were other grizzly spectacles there and to have known that his was among them would have been too much to be borne. I remembered how five years before our neighbor, Sir Thomas More, had been beheaded and his head stuck on the bridge. His head had disappeared and rumor had it that his daughter Margaret Roper had gone by night and taken her father's head that it might no longer be exposed and be given decent burial.

Had I known that Father's head was there I should have planned to do what Margaret had done. I would have asked Simon Caseman to help me.

One of the servants brought the news to us that Father's head was no longer there. It had disappeared. He had seen for himself. One of the watermen had told him that there was consternation because at dawn the pole on which it had been placed was lying on the bridge and the head was gone.

They were all talking of Sir Thomas More, a man who would never be forgotten, for his goodness lived on in the minds of men and there were many who thought he was a saint. He had had a beloved daughter who it was said had taken his head; my father also had a beloved daughter.

I wished that I had done what Margaret did. I wished that I had gone stealthily by night and taken down that beloved head that I might give it decent burial.

But the mystery remained.

My father's head had disappeared.

The days were empty. I could not believe that only four had passed since that terrible time when my mother had made me drink poppy juice and I had slept while he went to his death.

I should have been there. But I knew he would have wished me to be unconscious during that dark hour. He would have approved my mother's action. I could think of nothing but my loss. I recalled so much of our life together. Everywhere in the house were memories of him.

It was the same in the garden. I wandered down to the river and sat on the wall watching the river craft and I thought as I had so many times of the day when the King and the Cardinal had passed.

I stayed there until it was dusk and my mother came out and said: "You will be ill if you go on like this."

I went back to the house with her, but I could not stay indoors and I wandered once more out into the garden and watched the first stars appear.

And then I heard my name called softly and turning, I saw that Rupert had joined me.

"Oh, Rupert," I said, "I feel none of us can ever be happy again."

"Pain cannot last forever," he said gently. "It will become less acute and there will be times in the future when you will forget."

"Never," I said fiercely.

"You are so young and he meant so much to you. But others could mean as much. Your husband . . . your children. . . ."

I shook my head impatiently and he went on: "I have something to tell you."

I thought that he was going to suggest marriage again and I wanted to leave him and go into the house, but his next words startled me.

"I have his head, Damask."

"What?"

"I knew that you would not wish it to remain there. So when it was dark I took Tom Skillen with me. I knew I could trust him. He waited in the boat and I took down the pole. . . . I have his head . . . for you."

I turned toward him and his arms were around me. He held me against him.

"Oh, Rupert," I said at length, "if you had been caught. . . ."

"I was not caught, Damask."

"You might have been. You risked great danger."

"Damask," he said, "I want you to know that I would risk everything I have for your sake."

I was silent and then I said: "Where is it?"

"It is in a box . . . hidden. I knew you would wish to give it decent burial."

I nodded. I said: "He once said that he would like to be buried in the Abbey burial ground."

"We will bury him there, Damask."

"Can we?"

"Why should we not? The place is deserted."

"Rupert! Only you and I must know. Only you and I will be the mourners at his funeral."

"It would be better so."

"Rupert, it is a comfort to me to know that he no longer is there . . . for people to look at him . . . perchance to mock, to shame him."

"Goodness is not shamed no matter how it is mocked."

I seized his hand and pressed it.

"When shall we bury him, Rupert?"

"Tonight," he said. "When the household is asleep. We will go to the Abbey burial grounds and there we will lay him to rest."

We went through the ivy-covered door. How eerie it looked by the faint light from the crescent moon. Rupert had brought a lantern and a spade.

"Don't be afraid," said Rupert, "there's no one here."

"Only the ghosts of those monks who have died miserably because they have been dispossessed."

"They would never harm us."

We made our way to the burial ground and I stood by holding the lantern while Rupert dug a grave.

I myself held the box which held that precious relic. Then together we prayed and called for a blessing on that great good man.

I shall never forget the sound of clods of earth falling on the box; and at that sound the tears started to my eyes.

I think from that moment I began to feel that I could face life again.

Each day I went to the monks' burial ground. I planted a rosemary on the grave. I used to kneel beside it and talk to my father as I had when he was alive. I asked for courage so that I could go on living my life without him.

The Stepfather

A week after that night when we had buried my father's head Kate came and declared her intention to take me back to Remus Castle.

I said I would stay where I was for I wanted to visit the spot where my father's head was buried.

But Kate was determined.

"You are coming back with me," she declared. "Young Carey misses you. Betsy says she has not had one peaceful night since you left."

At length I was persuaded and I left with Kate for Remus.

Kate swore that little Carey was happy now that I had returned, but I said he was far too young for that; but I did find comfort in the child. Kate took great pains to please me. She coaxed me into showing some interest in the gowns she had had made for her. She insisted that I admire the jewelry Remus gave her.

She was going to Court soon. Though she complained the Court had become dull.

"The King," she said, "finds great pleasure in his new wife and makes excuses to be alone with her. This takes a great burden off his courtiers but means there is less entertainment; and he's in a good mood too, except when the ulcer on his leg is painful, but the Queen knows how to comfort him. She is young and very pretty but I have heard she has had some experience in offering comfort before her marriage."

But I could not bear to talk of the King. I regarded him as my father's murderer and I was filled with a hatred toward him which had it been known would have doubtless meant a sojourn in the Tower for me and my head on a pike over London Bridge.

There was a certain amount of talk too about the new laws against heretics. A heretic was one who did not accept the King as Supreme Head of the Church, be he Papist or anti-Papist.

"It's a very simple rule," said Kate. "The King is right whatever he does. Whatever he says is the truth and all those who contradict are traitors. It's all one has to remember."

And I was sure that there had never been a time so fraught with danger as these in which we lived.

In Remus Castle we seemed away from the world. I did love the baby and I began to believe that he had special feeling for me. It was true that if he were bawling lustily, which he often did, and I picked him up he would stop and something like a smile would touch his features. Kate was proud of the child in an offhand sort of way. She left him to the nurses but because I was interested in him and wanted him often with me, she saw more of him than she would otherwise have done.

His christening in the castle chapel was a grand affair and as many people from Court were present, I made the acquaintance of Dukes and Earls who before had been merely names to me. Their conversation was chiefly about the King and the new Queen. It was amazing how people could not prevent themselves discussing subjects which they knew could be dangerous. They reminded me of moths flying to a candle.

The Queen, it seemed, had a definite charm which enthralled the King. She was not pretty by any means, she lacked the elegance of Queen Anne Boleyn, but the King had not been so delighted with any of his wives as he was with Katharine Howard— apart from Anne Boleyn before their marriage perhaps. The new Queen had a way with her, I gathered. She was good-natured, easygoing, sensuous—just what an old man needed to revive his youth and that, it seemed, was what Katharine Howard was doing for King Henry. As for the last Queen, Anne of Cleves, she was thoroughly enjoying her life at Richmond Palace and delighted to call herself the King's sister as she congratulated herself on her lucky escape.

There was, it was true, an insurrection on Yorkshire, when men rose to protest against the new Supreme Head of the Church, but that was quickly suppressed and the requisite amount of blood shed to ensure that the people understood what happened to those who opposed the King.

But now that the King had found a wife who pleased him so much that he did not want to change her, life seemed to have become more peaceful.

Six weeks had passed since my father's death and then one day Lord Remus came out to the pond garden while Kate and I sat there with the baby in his basket and said: "I have grave news for you, Damask."

My heart pounded in fear; but even then I wondered what else could happen that could seem of any real importance to me.

Lord Remus was frowning. He did not seem to know how to begin.

"Damask," he said, "you must know that when a man is judged a traitor and is executed there are occasions when his worldly possessions are confiscated by the King who may take them for himself or divert them to someone he considers is deserving of them."

"You are telling me," I said, "that the King has not only robbed my father of his head but has taken his estates as well."

"That is what I understand, Damask."

"So . . . I am homeless."

"It is not quite as desperate as that. A certain amount of leniency has been shown in your father's case." He added with a cynicism which he did not seem to realize, "It is not as though his estates were so very large . . . by the King's standards, that is."

"Please tell me what has happened."

Lord Remus hesitated. He coughed. "It's a little delicate," he said, "but I have been asked to break this to you and so must I. You should not think that your father's house will no longer be your home. Simon Caseman has made that clear. There is always to be a home for you there."

"Simon Caseman!" I cried. "What is this to him?"

"The King's officers have decided to bestow your father's house on him."

"But why?"

"He has lived with your family. He has been your father's right-hand man in business."

"But . . . if it is decided to take my father's estate from those to whom it belongs . . . my mother and myself . . . why not to Rupert who is related to us?"

Lord Remus looked uneasy. "My dear Damask, to leave it to a relative would not be to confiscate it from the family. The King wishes to reward Simon Caseman and this is his way of doing it."

"Why should the King wish to reward Simon Caseman? He has worked with my father. I should have thought he might have been suspect since he lived in that house of iniquity."

"There has been an investigation of the case. Simon Caseman has said that he is eager to marry. . . ."

"No," I cried. "That can't be."

Lord Remus went on as though I had not spoken. "He is eager to marry your mother and this will solve a difficulty. Neither you nor your mother will be homeless although, in accordance with his right, the King has deprived your father and his heirs of their possessions."

I stared at him. "My *mother* to marry Simon Caseman?"

"In a reasonable time . . . not immediately. It seems a good arrangement."

I could not believe it. It seemed incredible to me. My mother to marry this man who but a short time ago had been pleading with me to marry him.

It was like a nightmare; and then the light began to dawn on me. I saw his face in my mind—the fox's mask exaggerated and I heard my father's voice: "Someone in the house has betrayed me."

Kate came bursting into my room.

"I wondered where you were. I couldn't imagine why you didn't come down. What's the matter?"

I said, "I have just heard that our house now belongs to Simon Caseman and that he is going to marry my mother."

"Remus told me," she said.

"Oh, Kate, do you realize what this means? He planned it. The King wished to reward him. For what? Mayhap for informing against my father and Amos Carmen?"

Kate stared at me in disbelief.

"You can't mean that."

"Something within me tells me that it could be true."

"Then he would be your father's murderer."

"If I could be sure of that I would kill him."

"No, Damask, it can't be."

"It fits, Kate. He asked me to marry him. He has asked me several times. Does he love me? No, he wanted my inheritance."

"That may be so, but a man is not a murderer for wishing to make a good marriage."

"I refused, and he took this opportunity of betraying my father."

"How can you know that?"

"Because someone in the house betrayed him and who but Simon Caseman?"

"You jump to conclusions."

"You forget he will have my father's estates. That is what he always wanted. That was why he asked me to marry him. Oh, I knew it was the fox's mask I saw there on his face."

"Fox's mask. What nonsense is this?"

"I saw it on his face. When his face is in shadow it is there. His eyes are tawny like a fox's. He is a sly fox who came in to rob the hen roost."

"Do you feel all right, Damask? This has all been too much for you."

"And I have lost my senses!" I cried. "That's what you think. But did you know that my mother is going to marry him?"

"Remus has just told me it is so."

Kate stared at me incredulously.

"I must go home at once," I said.

When I arrived at the house it seemed very quiet. I was not expected so there was no one to greet me. The house seemed different. Of course it was different. It was a house in mourning. It had a new master now.

I went up to my mother's stillroom. She was there and when she saw me she flushed as red as the reddest of her roses. She knew that I was aware of what she was preparing to do and I was glad to see that she could show some shame.

"I have heard, Madam," I said.

She nodded and sat down on a chair. She waved her hand in front of her face like a fan. She was now quite pale and was implying that she was about to faint. I thought how like her it was to faint in a crisis. It had been her way out of a difficult situation more than once. I forgot that she was my mother. I despised her in that moment because Simon Caseman was so hateful to me and now that I was home the enormity of my father's loss was brought back afresh.

I said: "So you are going out of mourning for your murdered husband and putting on wedding garments ready for your next."

"Damask," she said, "you must try to understand."

"I understand too well," I said.

Her hands fluttered helplessly. "We should have been homeless. It seemed the only thing to do."

"You think he chose *you* for his wife?"

"You see, Damask, he has the estates now and it is the best thing for us all, that was why he chose me. . . ."

"You mistake me. I know very well why that man chose you. I am surprised that my noble father should ever have married a woman who could forget and forgive his murder when his body is scarcely cold, and be ready to dance at her wedding."

"It will not be a grand affair, Damask. A quiet wedding, we thought."

I laughed scornfully. She would never understand anything but her garden and her herbs and how to make her pastry light. I felt a sudden pity for her—poor helpless woman, who had never really made a decision for herself.

"Simon Caseman," I said. "You can consider him . . . after you have been Father's wife!"

"Your father is dead."

I turned away to hide my emotion.

"Oh, Damask," she went on. "I know how close you two were. He cared more for you than for me. It was always Damask. . . ."

"He was the best of husbands as well as fathers," I said fiercely.

"He was a good man, I know."

"And so you have decided to put this adventurer in his place."

"I don't think you have realized what is happening, Damask. Your father's estates are confiscated."

"And passed to Simon Caseman. Why, do you think? Why?"

"Because he was your father's right-hand man. They have worked together. This is his home too. And he will marry me and we can go on as in the old way."

"As in the old way! When *he* is not here. I would to God we could go on in the old way. Do you think it will be the same with your new master? Mother, I know a daughter should not say this, but I will. You are a fool."

"I think your grief has upset you so much that you do not know what you say."

"I know this, that Simon Caseman came into this house with the express purpose of making it his. Did you know that he has asked me to marry him . . . many times. So devoted he was. So chivalrous! He thought to get possession of the place through me. I was not so susceptible to his charm as you are. I said, no, I would never marry you. So he casts about for other ways. Who else is there? There is my mother. But she has a husband. Let us get rid of him and marry the accommodating widow."

"Damask. Damask, what are you saying?"

"I am saying that I am very suspicious of a man who asks the daughter to marry him and when she refuses and the mother is in a position to give him what he seeks, promptly decides to take her."

"My child, be careful. Do not say such things. They are wild. They are impossible. But they could mean disaster for you."

"To speak against the King's man, yes. I'll dareswear you are right."

"All wise men are the King's men. You should know that."

"So my father was unwise?" Whenever I mentioned his name words seemed to choke me. My emotion gave my mother the advantage. She came to me and laid a hand on my shoulder.

"Listen to me, Damask," she said, "this terrible thing has happened to us. Your father hid that priest in the nuttery cottage. In doing so he risked his life, our estates and our future. I know that he was a saintly man, but saints who endanger their lives and those of their family are not acting wisely. What would become of us, Damask, if I do not make this marriage? We should be thrown out onto the roads as beggars or onto the mercy of our relations. I daresay Remus would help us. But when I marry Simon we shall continue to live here. It will be as before. . . ."

"It will never be as before," I said. "*He* is gone."

"My child, you have to grow away from this. Some are taken . . . in that way. How do any of us know where we shall be tomorrow? I thought of the house and everything here. I thought of you and the home . . . and Simon will be a good husband to me."

I said: "You are older than he is."

"It is of no moment."

"How could I stay here and see that man in my father's place?"

"You will become accustomed to it. Simon is a good man of business. He has prospered and he will continue to do so. The choice is stay here and live in comfort or go out penniless into the world and starve or live on the bounty of relations. Simon has come to me with his offer of marriage. I have accepted it."

"You want this marriage," I said. "When you speak of it there is a gleam of pleasure in your eyes."

"I was never a woman who wished to stand alone. Simon has promised to look after me. There are women who must have a husband. I am one. Simon and I understand each other. Your father and I had little to say to each other. He was always buried in a book or teaching you. I could never understand him when he quoted in his Greek or was it Latin?"

"You make excuses," I said. "You are eager for this marriage. I see it. You are ten years or more older than he. And he is marrying you for the estate!"

"The estate is his without me."

"But he wants it as it was. He wants a woman to look after the household as you do. He does not want it said that he turned the family from the home to beg in the streets. He wants to have power over us. Can't you see?"

"You imagine this, Damask."

"And who informed against Father?" I asked.

"There were many who could have done it."

"The servants, who would lose a good master by it?" I demanded.

"There are others who could have done it."

"His wife," I asked, "who fancied a young man in her bed?"

"Damask!"

I was sorry at once. "Oh, Mother," I said, "I cannot bear it. He has gone forever. I shall never see his dear face again, never hear his voice. . . ."

I covered my face with my hands and she was holding me in her arms. "My child," she said, "my baby. I understand. You are upset. You and he were as one. I used to feel shut out. You never had much time for me, did you? I understand. Try to accept this, daughter. Try to see that we have to go on and this is a way."

I felt limp and exhausted by my emotion. I allowed her to take me to my room and tuck me in. She brought me a potion. She had just devised it, she said. There was pimpernel to make me feel happy and thyme to give me pleasant dreams and there was an ashen branch to lay on my pillow for it was said to drive away evil spirits—those who put cruel thoughts into the mind.

I let her soothe me and, worn out with emotion, I slept.

When I awoke I was refreshed. I thought of my mother, helpless like her shrubs in the gale, blown this way and that by circumstances which were too much for her. I could not blame her. I knew her character well. She was a good housekeeper; she wanted to live in peace; my father had had little in common with her for she had never been educated beyond learning to read and write; she could never follow his reasoning. He had determined to educate me and he had often said that education was not learning the fruit and flowers of other men in order to repeat them and make a show of erudition; its purpose must be to set the mind in motion that it might produce flowers and fruit of its own.

I must not blame her.

And she was right. I had now to fend for myself. I would have to make some plan, for I did not believe I could continue to live under this roof and see that man in my father's place. I had been wrong to voice my suspicions of him, for I must admit they were but suspicions. Could he really have been responsible for my father's betrayal? Perhaps he was merely the jackal who waited for the moment to come in after the kill.

I must be fair. What had he done? He had asked me to marry him and I had refused. My father had been murdered and his estates given to Simon. Why? I must be reasonable. I must be logical. Could it in truth be because he was my father's betrayer? I could not be sure and because I was not sure I must not accuse him. I would find out though. And meanwhile must I live on his bounty?

I dreaded meeting him but I could not avoid him for long. I came from my room and found him in the hall. He watched me as I walked down the stairs.

"Welcome home, Damask," he said.

I stared blankly at him.

"It is good to have you back," he went on.

"I suppose you are expecting me to congratulate you on your forthcoming marriage."

"No, I was not expecting that. You take it hardly, I know."

"The murdered husband is scarcely cold in his grave."

"My dear Damask, you have been infected by those Greek tragedies on which you set such store. Now I am going to ask you to take care. I would not have you in disgrace. Curb your tongue, I beg of you. You could be in dire trouble so easily. I am going to take care of you now. I shall be your stepfather. . . ."

I laughed. "It was not quite the role you at first chose for yourself!"

"I think you understand my feelings for you."

"Which were conveniently transferred to my mother."

"Your mother and I are scarcely young romantic people."

"I believe she is some years older than you."

"It is not a great deal."

"So convenient! Although had she been thirty years older I am sure you would have found that no obstacle."

"My poor sad Damask!"

"I am not your possession yet."

"I am devoted to you and to your mother," he said. "These estates have been bestowed on me. I could not take them from you. So this marriage seems to be the best solution."

"You could always hand them back."

"I do not think that would be allowed. I am doing what I think is best for us all."

"And if I had agreed to marry you, what then?"

I saw the flicker of his eyes; the marking of the fox mask was clearer for a moment.

"You know my feelings for you." He had taken a step toward me.

I held him off.

"Do not forget that you are an affianced bridegroom," I said sharply. I looked at him steadily. "Tell me, who betrayed my father?" I added.

He clenched his fists together. "I would I knew," he said.

"*Someone* betrayed him," I said. "I shall not allow it to be forgotten. I shall never rest until I discover who it was."

He held out his hand to me. I stared down at it.

"I want to make a bargain with you," he said. "We shall both try to find that man who took the happiness from the household and brought about the death of the best man on earth."

The tears started up in my eyes and he looked at me with tenderness, so that I was sorry momentarily that I had suspected him.

I turned and ran from him back to my room. I could not go down to the hall to eat. My mother sent up a leg of chicken for me and a slice of the crusty cob loaf which I used to love. I could eat nothing; and when finally I slept, for I believe she had laced my wine with one of her potions, I dreamed of Simon Caseman. He had the face of a fox and in my dream I believed him to be an evil man.

I was torn by my doubts. My mother and Simon were kind to me. She gave me potions and ordered that the foods I had once enjoyed should be prepared for me. He was tolerant and never forced his company on me; sometimes I found his eyes on me and as mine met his he would assume a tender expression, as though he was now regarding me as a cherished daughter.

I thought, I cannot endure this.

Their wedding was to be a quiet one, for it was such a short time since my father's death; but the entire household was now accepting Simon Caseman as the master.

I could not rouse myself. I thought, I cannot continue in this way. Soon I must make a decision. But at this time I was too stunned to do anything but let time wash over me while I lay listless believing that in due course my grief would be subdued and some notion would come to me as to how I could make something of my life.

At times I thought of going to Kate. Yet I did not wish to throw myself on the bounty of Lord Remus. I did know that since my father's arraignment Kate's husband was made a little uneasy by my presence. Kate however would imperiously overrule that if I had wished to go. There was another thing. Every evening at dusk I went through the ivy-covered door into the Abbey burial ground and visited my father's grave. The rosemary I had planted was growing well. I often thought how frightened I once would have been to wend my way at dusk past the Abbey walls—empty and ghostly in the evening shadows—and to go among the graves of long-dead monks. But because his dear head was there, I knew no fear, for a belief had grown up within me that the dead protect those whom they especially loved and I certainly felt that my father was protecting me.

I lived for my visits to his grave; and when I went to the Abbey I would remember those days when Kate and I had crept through the secret door to be with Bruno. He was never far from my thoughts and I longed to see him again.

I pondered on my feeling for Bruno. It took my mind off my present uneasy situation. I compared the emotion he could rouse in me with my love for my father. I had known my father as well, I think, as it is possible for one person to know another. I was aware of his beliefs, for he had talked to me so openly; I knew before he told me what his opinions would be on almost any problem. Losing him was like losing a part of myself. But Bruno? What did I know of Bruno? Very little. I had never understood him. Bruno seemed to have built a wall about himself. One could never be sure of what he was thinking. I suppose that having for years believed himself to be a superhuman being who had been sent into the world for some special purpose, to have been certain that he was holy, must surely have had an effect on him. Then the confession of Keziah and Ambrose and all the violence which attended it, the dissolution of St. Bruno's Abbey . . . what would that have done to him? He had given little indication except that he rejected the confession of those who claimed to be his parents. There was the same aloofness about him. He would never betray himself completely to anyone. Sometimes he had seemed as though he did not belong to this world, yet his arrogance, his frustrated anger were essentially worldly. I remembered Brother John's explaining how the Child had been caught stealing cakes from the kitchen and lying when accused.

How lost and bewildered I was during those weeks!

Rupert was bewildered too. He did not know what the future held for him. He had loved the land. I had seen him come in from my father's fields as animated as he had ever been, because they had succeeded in gathering in the harvest before the storms came. The workers were fond of him. He was a good master to them; and he understood everything that he asked them to do. He would pick up a flail and thresh corn in the barn with the most humble of his workmen; I had seen him winnowing, shaking the flat fan-shaped basket in the wind; most of all I remembered his going out in the snow at lambing time to rescue young lambs and how he himself would nurse them and feed them. Sowing and reaping, growing the foods which supplied the household and selling the surplus, this had been Rupert's occupation and he could imagine no other.

Once when I was coming back from visiting the Abbey burial grounds I heard a voice call me. It was Rupert's.

"Damask," he cried, catching up with me, "you should not be out at this hour."

"I will go out when I will," I replied impatiently.

"It is unsafe, Damask. There are robbers about."

"I have no fear of them."

"But it is dangerous."

I turned impatiently away and he said: "Damask, don't go yet. I would like to talk to you."

"Then talk," I said.

"I think often of the future. What will become of us all?"

"For that we must needs wait and see."

"There will be changes. We have a new master of the household now."

"He has made little changes so far, but doubtless that will come, after the marriage."

"Then what, Damask? I have worked for your father for many years. He had promised me that part of the lands which I cultivated should one day be mine. He hoped of course that you and I would marry." He was a little wistful.

I said quickly: "He realized that marriages can only be made by two people—the two who are to become husband and wife.

He would have been the first to say that they must both agree wholeheartedly."

"And you do not feel that you could marry me?"

"I could not think of marriage. It is far from my mind."

"I will tell you something. Lord Remus owns several estates and Kate swears that she will insist on his giving me a place of my own."

"Then you have no need to be anxious about your future."

"If you shared it, we could go from here together."

I shook my head. He sighed and insisted: "Your father wished it."

"He only wished for my happiness," I said.

"I would make you as happy as it is possible for you to be now that you have lost him. I would live solely for you. I would care for you, cherish you."

"I know it," I said.

"Marry me, Damask. Let us go from here. You would be safer than you are now, because those who are related to a man who has been accused of treason are in constant danger. One careless word . . . even a look could incriminate you. As my wife, you could lose your identity as your father's daughter."

I turned on him angrily. "Do you think I want that? I am more proud of it than anything that has ever happened to me."

I turned and ran from him up to my room. I shut myself in and I wept. My tears were mingled sorrow and anger. Would I never get over my loss? And how dared Rupert suggest that I would ever wish to hide the fact that I was my father's daughter. I considered Rupert then. He was good; he was kind; he had meant no harm. I went to my window and looked out toward the Abbey. I could just make out the gray tower. I thought of the burial ground—how ghostly it would look now with the faint moonlight shining on the tombstones above the graves of long-dead monks.

There was talk now that the Abbey was haunted. One of the farm workers and his wife returning home at dusk declared they had seen a monk emerge from the Abbey wall. The monk had appeared to pass through the stones; he had stood for a while, and they had been so frightened that they had run.

It was natural, was the verdict. How many of the monks had

died because of what had happened? Think of those two who had hung in chains at the Abbey's Gate. There was he who had sought to escape to London with some of the Abbey treasures and had been caught and hanged; there was Brother Ambrose who had murdered Rolf Weaver. There was the Abbot who had died of a broken heart. Wasn't it natural that such men should be unable to rest in their graves and come back to haunt the place where they had lived and suffered?

People were afraid to go near the Abbey after dark. Even in daylight they liked to have a companion.

Strangely enough this had no effect on me. I could not feel afraid and I continued to visit my father's grave.

My mother had become Simon Caseman's wife. Now that the wedding was over I was aware of a change creeping over the household. It was subtle at first but none the less there. The servants were made aware of a different rule in the house. Simon was not going to be the lenient master my father had been. He walked with a certain swagger; the servants must always call him Master. The men must never forget to touch their forelocks and the maids must make sure they curtsied almost to the ground. He watched the household accounts with care. He dismissed a few of the servants as being unnecessary. Beggars would no longer be sure of food and wine; he ordered that travelers should not be encouraged to regard us as a kind of hostelry. Not that we had had many such since my father's death; knowing that he had been arraigned and condemned, people were afraid to come near us. But now that there was a new master they might come, so Simon Caseman gave the order that they were not to be encouraged.

My mother had become a little nervous, I noticed. She was very eager to please him. She agreed with everything he said; and what disgusted me was that she had a kind of adoration for him and this, when I considered her lack of appreciation of my father, angered me.

I was certainly beginning to feel things more strongly which was, I suppose, a sign that I was growing away from my grief.

One day I discovered lettering on the wrought-iron gates of the house. This was CASEMAN'S COURT. Before the house had had no name. It was simply known as Lawyer Farland's House. The resentment when I saw those letters affected me like a physical pain.

He was the master. He wanted us all to know that. He wanted us all to know that we lived on his bounty. My mother must present her household accounts to him—something she had never done to my father. She was an excellent and thrifty housewife but I noticed that she was always nervous on Fridays, the day she must produce her accounts.

Rupert's position had changed. He was no longer treated like a member of the family. He was a workman, though a superior one. He was not allowed to make his own decisions.

I alone was not subjected to this treatment. If I wished not to join them for meals I did not and I was not called to order for this. I was not expected to do anything in the house. I often found his eyes fixed on me in a strange kind of way. I was suspicious of him, disliking him. I was constantly looking for the fox's mask on his face; it seemed to have become more apparent; his eyes were sharper, more tawny. I was very wary of him and I hated him and the changes he was making in our house, for these very changes reminded me more and more of the old days and my dear father.

Less than two months after the marriage my mother told me that she was going to have a child. I was horrified, although I suppose it was natural enough. She was thirty-six years of age, young enough to bear a child; but the fact that she should so soon be fruitful seemed to me an insult to my father and I was disgusted. How she had changed. She seemed to me simpering and foolish, pretending to be as a young wife might have been with her first child.

Simon Caseman was delighted. He seemed to regard it as a personal triumph. He knew that my father had longed for a family and he had only been able to get one girl who lived; whereas he, married but two months, had already given evidence of his virility.

I knew now that I wanted to go away and I decided I would write to Kate and ask if I might stay with her for a while.

Simon cornered me one day in the garden and he said: "Why, Damask, I see so little of you. I might think that you deliberately avoid me."

"You might well think it," I said.

"Have I offended you in some way?"

"In many ways," I replied.

"I am sorry."

"You appear to be far from that."

"Damask, we must accept circumstances, you know, even when they go against us. You know that I have always been fond of you."

"I know that you offered me marriage."

"And you are a little hurt that I married another."

"Not on my own account—only on that other's."

"She seems well content."

"She is perhaps easily content."

"I'll venture to say that she was never more content than now."

"You venture too far."

"It does me good to speak to you."

"I don't reap a like benefit," I retorted.

"I am sorry that I have taken that which should be yours."

"You lie, sir. You are very happy to have what you always wanted."

"I did not get all that I wanted."

"Did you not? It is a fair house; the land is good. And you do not talk like a good husband?"

"I hear that you wish to go to your cousin."

"Don't tell me that you propose forbidding me to do so."

"I would not presume to do that."

"I am glad because it would have been useless."

"Let us be good friends, Damask," he said. "I want to tell you that you are welcome here as long as you care to stay."

"It is a very gracious gesture to allow me to remain as a guest in my own house."

"You know that it is mine."

"I know you took it."

"It was bestowed on me."

"Why on you? Could you tell me that? It is a question on which I have long pondered."

"You can guess, can you not? Because I was capable of managing it. It had been my home for some years. I was ready to marry the widow of the previous owner which would relieve the family hardship considerably. It seemed a good arrangement."

"For you, yes." I walked off and left him.

* * *

Rupert asked me to walk with him in the nuttery. It used to be a favorite place of mine but since the hut in which my father had hidden Amos Carmen was there, it had become too painful a reminder of all that had happened.

He slipped his arm through mine. "Damask," he said, "I must talk to you very seriously."

"Yes, Rupert."

"I am going away. Lord Remus has offered me a farm. I shall manage it and in a short time it will be my own. Kate has prevailed on him."

"Her marriage was a great blessing not only to her but to you."

"Damask, you are growing bitter."

"Circumstances change us all, doubtless."

"There is still much that is good in life."

"I see little at this time."

"Well, it is a dark period through which we are passing. But it won't always be so. The world we knew has gone. It is for us to build a new life."

"You may well do that with your new farm. You will go away from here and forget us."

"I shall never forget you. But my surroundings will be different. The problems of the present will, I know, impose themselves on the past."

"It is easy for you."

"I loved your father, Damask, and I love you."

"I was his daughter. Do you think your love can be compared with mine?"

"Still it was love."

I took his hand and pressed it. "I shall never forget what you risked to bring his head to me," I said. The tears were on my cheeks and he drew me to him and kissed them gently.

Suddenly I knew that if I could not find the great ecstasy I had dreamed of with Rupert, at least I could find comfort. I could leave this house. It would mean a great deal to me not to see my mother and Simon Caseman together. To leave this house . . . I had never thought to do it. I had dreamed of myself growing old in it, my children playing in these gardens as I had done; my father delighting in his grandchildren. That dream could never become a reality. But Rupert was offering me consolation. He was telling me that although I should mourn my father forever, I could start to make a new life for myself.

He said: "The farm is not far from here. Between these lands and Remus's estate—not far from Hampton. I shall be between you and Kate. We can meet often . . . if you decided not to come altogether. But I hope you will because I know, Damask, that I can look after you."

"Rupert," I answered emotionally, "you are a good man. How I wish that I could love you as a husband should be loved."

"It would come, Damask. In time it would come."

I shook my head. "And if it did not? You would be cheated, Rupert."

"You could never cheat anyone."

"Perhaps you do not know me, for I sometimes feel I do not know myself. To leave here. . . . Oh, Rupert, I had never thought of it. I visit my father's grave . . . frequently."

"I know and I do not care for you to be wandering about the Abbey grounds alone."

"You fear that there is some evil lurking there?"

"I fear desperate men might be lurking there."

"Monks perhaps returning to their old home, or the spirits of murdered men?"

"I fear for you to go there. Damask, we could remove your father's remains. We could take them with us. We could make a sanctuary in our new home and there you could have that precious box with you always. You could make a shrine to his memory."

"Oh, Rupert," I cried, "I think you understand me as no one ever did . . . since Father."

"Then come with me, Damask. Come away from this house which is no longer your home, come away from a situation which has become distasteful to you."

It seemed that I must. Yet I hesitated. It was not as I had always thought it should be. Was life always to be a compromise? I thought of Kate's marrying Lord Remus for what he could give her. Should I be doing the same if I married Rupert? Lord Remus gave Kate jewels, riches, a place at Court, and I had despised her for her mercenary motives. But if I married Rupert because he could take me away from a situation which had become intolerable to me was I not in like case?

"I am so unsure," I said. "I do not know what I should do. Be patient with me, Rupert."

He pressed my hand gently. I could sense his elation. I knew he would always be patient.

"Think on it," he said. "You know I would not wish you to do anything which was distasteful to you. Remember too that it was his wish."

I did remember it and it weighed greatly with me.

And that night I lay in my room and thought that I would marry Rupert, and I was ashamed because at one time I had believed he would have married me for the fortune I could bring him.

Now I was without that fortune and he still wished to marry me. I had misjudged him.

This made me feel very tender toward him.

Yet I could still not make up my mind.

I was sitting in my mother's walled rose garden thinking about the future when Simon Caseman came in.

He took the seat beside me.

"By my faith," he said, "you are more beautiful with your hair half grown than you were when it reached past your waist."

"As I was never very beautiful that need not be a great deal."

"Your verbal darts ever amuse me."

"I am pleased you can be so easily amused. It must be a blessing in this drab world."

"Oh, come, stepdaughter, are you not unduly morbid?"

"Considering what has befallen me this last year, most certainly not."

"I should like to see you happier."

"The only thing that could make me happier would be to see my father walk into this garden alive and well, happy and secure from . . . traitors."

"We are none of us secure from traitors, Damask. We have to remember that we live on the very edge of a volcano which can erupt and destroy us at any moment. If we are wise we take what we can get and do our best to enjoy it while we can."

"I see you put your policy into action. You are enjoying what you have taken."

"Most willingly would I have shared it with you."

He moved closer to me and I drew away with some alarm.

"Foolish Damask," he said. "I would have made you mistress of this place."

"It was what my father intended—that I should in due course come into my own."

"He would have wished to see you mistress of it, yes. You have been foolish. And one day you will see how foolish. I shall be a very rich man one day, Damask."

"Do you see your way clear to acquiring more lands?"

He pretended not to see the significance of the question.

He went on as though talking to himself. "The Abbey is going to ruin. It cannot always be so. Imagine what could be done there. The lands are rich. They will not lie idle forever. It will be bestowed on someone who will cultivate it, possibly build a fine mansion. There are enough bricks there to build a castle."

"Caseman Castle!" I mocked. "It sounds even grander than Caseman Court."

"You have ideas, Damask. Caseman Castle!"

"And you have ambitions. Not content with a court you must have a castle as well."

"There is no end to my ambitions, Damask."

"But they are not always realized—even in your case."

His eyes smoldered as they looked into mine.

"That can only be decided at the very end," he said.

I was afraid of him in that moment. I thought: I must get away. It is unsafe here. I will marry Rupert. It is the only way.

Marry for security, for safety, for a hope of forgetting? I was as mercenary as Kate.

"You gained this house through some service in an influential quarter," I said. "You are doubtless looking around to find means of doing a similar service, the reward of which would be the Abbey and all its lands."

He looked at me, laughing; but I knew I had put into words the ideas fermenting in his head.

I stood up. "You are a very ambitious man," I said.

"Ambitious men frequently get what they set their hearts on."

"No one can ever achieve the impossible," I retorted over my shoulder as I hurried away.

That night I had a great desire to see my father's grave. I waited until the household was sleeping, then I crept quietly out of the house. The moon was shining brightly and how beautiful the country looked—vague, mysterious in that cool pale light.

I slipped through the ivy-covered door into the grounds. I sped across the grass and paused for a while to look at the gray walls of the Abbey. Suddenly I was startled by the hoot of an owl; I looked up at the roof—half open now to the sky—and I thought of this historic Abbey's falling into Simon Caseman's hands.

I went along to the burial ground and wending my way among the tombstones, I knelt by the grave in which lay my father's head. The rosemary was flourishing. I took a little sprig of it and slipped it into my gown.

"As if I needed rosemary to remember you, dear Father," I murmured. And I went on: "Give me courage to live without you. Show me what I must do."

I looked about me almost expecting to see him materialize beside me, so sure was I that he was close.

It was hard to go on living in the house which now belonged to a man whom some instinct forced me to mistrust, and Kate would have delighted to have me with her. But she would try to find a husband for me, I was sure, and I did not wish for that. If I had wanted a husband I would marry Rupert of whom I was fond and whom I trusted. Then my thoughts went to Bruno as they constantly did, and I wondered afresh whether that confession of Keziah's had been wrung from her and that she had dared not deny it. I thought of her tied to the bed and that evil man bending over her. Had she screamed words which he put into her mouth? And had the monk supported her story because torture impelled him to? How could one be sure what was truth when people were threatened with unendurable agony until they confessed what their tormentors asked of them? How many men at this moment were being racked in that grim gray fortress along the river? How many were suffering the torture of the thumb-

screws, the rack and the scavenger's daughter, that dread machine
of which I had heard, shaped like a woman and covered with iron
spikes which as a man was squeezed into an embrace, penetrated
his body, puncturing heart and lungs.

The times were cruel. Simon Caseman was right in one way.
We should enjoy what we could while we could.

I fancied that it was my father's spirit which comforted me.
And I rose from my knees and left the burial ground filled with
that peace and lack of fear which always astonished me on these
occasions.

I was on the edge of the burial ground and the Abbey was in
sight when I saw the figure of a monk gliding across the grass.
Was this the ghost of some departed monk who could not rest
and had risen from the grave to haunt the scene of his tragedy?

I stood very still. Strangely enough I was not really frightened.
Years ago Kate would invent gruesome tales of ghosts who rose
from the tomb to come back to haunt those who had wronged
them; and I would lie in my bed trembling with fear. Sometimes
I had begged of her not to talk of ghosts when it grew dark—which
of course always provoked her to do so. But now I was surprised
by the calm within me. I was not so much frightened as curious.

The figure had crossed to the Abbey wall. I expected it to disappear through it but it did no such thing. It pushed open a door
and passed into the Abbey.

All was silence. Then I heard the owl again. Something
prompted me to cross the grass to go to the door through which
the monk had passed. On this impulse I did so; I pushed the door
which opened easily. The cold dankness of the Abbey rushed to
greet me. I half stepped inside but for some reason which I could
not understand my hair seemed to rise up from my head and I
was afraid.

I believed in that moment that the special power which pro-
tected me in the burial ground and which came from my father's
spirit could not follow me beyond those gray walls.

I had an overwhelming desire to run away. I sped across the
grass as fast as I could and let myself out through the ivy-covered
door.

The fear left me then. I walked home.

I had corroborated the opinion of the farmer and his wife and those others who said they had seen a figure near the Abbey.

So the Abbey was haunted.

My mother was now noticeably larger and happily making preparations for the birth of her child. She decorated the cradle which had been mine and which had been put away for eighteen years. She had polished it and cleaned it and I had seen her rocking it with a faraway look in her eyes as though she was already imagining the baby there.

We heard little news of the Court for we did not have visitors now; Kate did not write. She had never really been a letter writer. It was only when anything was wrong or she wanted something that it would have occurred to her to take up a pen.

I would have written to her but I did not wish to write of Caseman Court. And in any case there was little to say.

The King, it was said, was happy in his marriage and the Queen accompanied him everywhere. She was gay and good-natured and it was said that people only had to ask for a favor and she would be ready to grant it. Moreover she was not one to forget her old friends. She was kindhearted too and did her best to reconcile the King to the little Elizabeth, daughter of Anne Boleyn, who had been the present Queen's cousin.

I had no doubt that Kate would have plenty of scandal to relate about Court affairs, but Kate was far away and because the King was at last happy with a wife we were lulled into a sense of security.

There was a reminder of the terrible things that could overtake us when the Countess of Salisbury was executed. She had had no fair trial but she was suspected of being on the side of the rebels in the Northern uprising—at least this was said to be her crime. Her royal blood was doubtless the true reason. As the grand-daughter of George Plantagenet, the Duke of Clarence, himself brother of Edward IV and therefore in closer line to the throne than the Tudors whose claim had never been very firm, she had always been considered to be a menace and this pretext to be rid of her was too good to be missed. The old lady—she was nearly seventy years of age—had suffered greatly from the cold of her prison cell and the young Queen, feeling great pity for her, had smuggled in warm clothing that at least she might know that comfort. But nothing could save her. Her royal blood must flow to keep the throne safe for our tyrant King.

I remember well the day she died. It was Maytime. Why did so many have to leave this earth when it was at its most beautiful? She walked out to the block but refused to lay her head on it for, she declared to the watching crowd, she was no traitor and if the headman would have her head he must win it.

We heard she was dragged by her hair to the block and there so butchered that the ax wounded her arms and shoulders several times before her head was struck off.

How glad I was that I had not seen it.

A few days later I heard that the Abbey had been bestowed.

My mother had got the news from one of the servants who had had it from one of the watermen who had paused at the privy stairs while she was feeding the peacocks to shout the news to her.

My mother announced it while we were at dinner and I shall never forget the look on Simon Caseman's face.

"It's a lie!" he cried, for once robbed of his calm.

"Oh, is it?" said my mother, always ready to agree.

"Where had you this news?" he demanded.

Then she told him.

"It could not be true," he said; and I knew that he was imagining himself master of that place.

But it seemed that it was true. That week there were workmen putting back the lead on the roof. Simon went over there to talk to them, and when he came back he was pale with fury.

The workmen had been instructed to repair the roof; others were there cleaning the place.

They did not know on whom it had been bestowed. They merely had their orders to make it ready for habitation.

Part II

The Owner of the Abbey

It was June and the weather had turned hot. I had never seen so many bees at work on the clover, and the pimpernel made an edge of scarlet around our cornfields. Down by the river the nettles bloomed in profusion. My mother would be gathering them soon to make some potion. I believe she was happy. It amazed me that she could so soon recover from my father's death. The fact that a new life was stirring within her might have been responsible for this; but I had grown farther from her though I had never really been close.

I was thinking that soon they would be cutting the hay, and that this would be the last time Rupert would supervise that activity. He would leave us after harvest and I would have to make up my mind whether I was going with him. The workmen were apprehensive; they had trusted and relied on Rupert. I wondered idly whether people worked better through fear or love. Then I fell to thinking of haymaking in the good days before the King broke with Rome and we had not thought State affairs could so disrupt our house. Everyone used to be called in to work in the fields and the greatest fear in those days was that the weather might break before the crop was carried in. Father himself used to join us and I would come out with my mother to bring refreshment to workers in the fields so that little time should be lost.

I had almost made up my mind to go with Rupert for it was clear that I could not remain under Simon Caseman's roof. Kate had written urging me to come to Remus Castle and I thought that perhaps I should go to her for there I could discuss my future. She would urge me to marry Rupert. I knew that she still thought I would in time come to see the reason of this. Once she had plans for making a grand marriage for me. This was hardly likely now that I had no dowry. Nor did I care for that.

It was twilight—the end of a lovely summer's day. The night was calm and still for the slight breeze of the day had disappeared.

As I sat at my window one of the servants came by. She looked up at me and said: "I have a message for you, Mistress Damask. 'Twas from a gentleman who would have word with you."

"What gentleman?"

"Well, Mistress, he would not say. He said to tell you that if you would go to the ivy-covered gate he would be there and you would know who had sent the message."

I could scarcely hide my excitement. Who could have sent such a message but Bruno? Who else knew of the ivy-covered door?

I said: "Thank you, Jennet," as calmly as I could, and as soon as she had gone I went to my room, changed my gown and arranged my hair in its most becoming fashion. I took a cloak and wrapped it around me and I went at once to the door in the Abbey wall.

Bruno was there. His eyes were alight with a kind of triumph which could only be because I had come. He took my hands and kissed them. He seemed different from ever before.

"So you have come back!" I cried.

"And you are pleased?"

"It is not necessary for me to tell you what you know already."

"I knew you would be happy to see me. Damask, you are different. Are you happier now?"

"Yes," I replied, because it was true. In this moment I was happier because he was back. "What happened? Where did you go? Why did you leave us so mysteriously?"

"It was necessary," he said.

"To leave us . . . without a word of explanation."

"Yes," he replied. "And since I went you have lost your father."

"It was terrible, Bruno."

"I know. But I am back now. I shall stop you grieving. You can be happy again now I'm back."

He held my hand firmly in his; with the other he opened the door and we went through into the Abbey grounds.

I drew back. "It has been bestowed now, Bruno."

"I know it."

"We should be trespassing."

"You have trespassed many times before."

"It's true."

"And now you are with me. It was always believed by the monks that I should become their Abbot."

"Terrible things have happened to us both."

"Perhaps it was necessary. There has to be a testing time for us all."

"There is so much I want to ask you. Where have you been? Have you come back to stay? Where are you living? It is not the same with us now. Our house belongs to Simon Caseman."

He turned to me and smiling gently, touched my face. "I know all this, Damask. I know all."

"Do you know who has taken the Abbey?"

"Yes," he said, "I know that too."

"Some rich nobleman, I'll swear. It will seem so strange. But it is better so mayhap than that it should fall into further decay."

"It is better so," said Bruno.

"Where are you taking me?"

"Into the Abbey."

"It is said to be haunted. People have seen a ghostly figure . . . a monk. I have seen him myself."

"*You*, Damask?"

"Yes. When I came to my father's grave." I told him how Rupert had brought my father's head to me and how we had buried it.

"You are not affianced to Rupert?" he asked quickly.

"No, but mayhap I will be soon."

"You do not love Rupert."

"Yes, I love Rupert. . . ."

"As a husband?"

"No, but I think we need each other."

"You will not be afraid to go into the Abbey with me?" I hesitated and he went on: "You remember you and Kate once came in."

"I was very frightened then."

"Because you knew you were doing wrong. You should never have looked at the sacred chapel. You should never have seen the jeweled Madonna. But now, she has disappeared, and the sacred chapel is empty."

"I would be afraid to go in now, Bruno."

He gripped my arm. "You do not think any harm could come to you when you were with me?"

I did not answer for all the time we were drawing closer toward those gray walls.

He turned suddenly and I saw his face stern in the moonlight. "Damask," he said, "do you believe that I am not as other men?"

"But. . . ." I could hear Keziah's voice then, that confession of hers. "He threatened me and I told him what should never be told. . . . I was with child by the monk. . . ."

"I want you to know the truth," he went on. "It is important to me that you should. Lies were told. People tell lies under torture. The woman Keziah lied; the monk lied. The world is full of lies —but one must not attach too much blame to the liars when they lie under stress. They have never learned to master their bodies. Physical torture will make a liar of many a great man who yearns to speak only the truth. I tell you this: I *know* I am not as other men. I came into the world . . . not as they would have you believe. I *know* it, Damask. And if you are to be with me . . . you must know it too. You must believe it. You must believe in me."

He looked strange and beautiful in the moonlight—godlike—different from anyone else I had ever known and I loved him, so I said as meekly as my mother might to Simon Caseman: "I believe you, Bruno."

"So you are not afraid to go into the Abbey with me?"

"Not with you."

He pushed open the door through which I had seen the ghostly figure pass, and we were in the silence of the Abbey.

The coldness struck me at once after the warm air outside; it rose through the soles of my shoes from the stone floor and I shivered.

"There is nothing to fear while you are with me," Bruno assured me.

But I could not forget Keziah's coming back after that terrible night at the inn with Rolf Weaver and although I wanted to believe as Bruno desired me to, I could not in my heart accept the fact that Keziah could have made up such a story.

But I was with Bruno and happy as I had not been since my father's death and I sensed that he had asked me to come tonight because he had something of great importance to say to me.

He had found a lantern which he had lighted and he said he would take me to the Abbot's lodging. It was a strange, eerie exploration and during it I expected us to be confronted by the ghostly monk. Bruno showed me a fine vaulted hall and the many rooms where the Abbot had his dwelling. It was clear that the workmen had been there and this house was in the process of being turned into a residence of some magnificence. We left the Abbot's lodging and Bruno showed me the refectory, a plain stone building with strong buttresses, where the monks had sat for two hundred years under the raftered oak roof.

Very soon, I thought, the man on whom the Abbey was bestowed would be living here, and Bruno was taking a last look while he could still do so. He led me through the cloisters; he took me to the cells of the monks; he showed me the bakehouse where he had once sat with Brother Clement. I reminded him of what I had heard of his stealing cakes hot from the oven.

"They like to tell these tales of me," said Bruno.

That night he showed me so much that I had never seen before. I wondered why but I guessed later. I saw the monks' parlor and dorter; I saw the infirmaries, the Brothers' kitchen, the cloisters, the monks' frater. And all by the light of the lantern and the moon.

"You see," said Bruno to me, "this is a world of its own, but now a shattered world. Why should it not be born again?"

"What will he on whom it has been bestowed do with so much?" I asked. "He will have a very fine manor house from the Abbot's lodging, but there is so much else besides."

"There is more—much more. And beneath it all a labyrinth of tunnels and cellars. But they are dangerous and you should not visit those."

He took me then to the church. Although this had been robbed of its valuable ornaments and thieves had stolen the gold and silver thread from the vestments, little damage had been done to the church itself. I stared up at the high vaulted roof supported by the massive stone buttress. The stained-glass windows were intact. They represented the story of the Crucifixion. Now the shrouded moonlight reflecting the brilliant blues and reds cast an uncanny light on the scene.

Bruno drew me to a curtain which hung to the right of the altar and pulled this aside. We were in a small chapel and I knew instinctively that this was the Lady Chapel in which eighteen years before Brother Thomas had placed the crib he had fashioned and on the following Christmas morning the Abbot had come and discovered a living child in it.

Holding my hand firmly in his, Bruno drew me into the Chapel.

"It was here they found me," he said, "and I have brought you here because there is something I wish to say to you and I wish to say it here. I have chosen you to share my life."

"Bruno," I cried, "are you asking me to marry you?"

"That is so."

"Then you love me! You truly love *me?*"

"As you love me," he answered.

"Oh, Bruno . . . I did not know. I never thought that you loved me enough for that."

"What if I offered you a life of poverty?"

"Do you think I would care for that?"

"But you have been brought up in plenty. It is true now you have lost your inheritance but you could marry comfortably. Rupert will be able to offer you a good home."

"Do you think I wish to marry for a good home?"

"You should consider well. Could you live a hermit's life in a cave, in a hut? Could you suffer cold in winter? Could you wander the countryside with sometimes no roof but the sky?"

"I would go anywhere with the one I loved."

"And you love me, Damask. You always did."

"Yes," I agreed, for it was true. I *had* always loved him, in a strange, compulsive way which was due to the fact that I had seen him always as different from other men.

"Then you would come with me . . . no matter what hardship you had to endure?"

"Yes," I said, "I would come with you."

He embraced me then. His lips warm with passion were on my own.

"You would love me, obey me and bear me children?"

"Gladly," I cried.

"Did you not always know that I was the one for you?"

"Always, but I did not think you cared for me."

"You thought it was Kate," he said. "Foolish Damask."

"Yes, I thought it was Kate. She is so brilliant, so beautiful . . . and I. . . ."

"You are my chosen one," he said.

"I feel as though I have stepped into a dream."

"A happy dream, Damask?"

"Happy," I replied, "as I never thought to be again."

"Then we will plight our troth here . . . in this chapel where years ago they found me. That is fitting. That is what I wish. Damask, consider. A life of hardship. Can you face it . . . for love?"

"Gladly," I replied earnestly. "And I rejoice that you have nothing to offer me. I want to show you how much I love you."

Again he touched my face gently. "You please me, Damask," he said. "Oh, how you please me. Here on this altar we will make our vows. Damask, swear to love me, and I will swear to cherish you."

"I swear," I said.

We left the chapel and came out into the night air. We crossed the patch of grass where we were wont to sit when we were children.

"This is our wedding night," he said.

"But there has been no marriage ceremony."

"When you plighted your troth to me in the chapel we were as one."

"Bruno," I said, "you were always different from everyone else. That is why I have always loved you, but if we are to be married I shall have to tell my mother. There will be a ceremony. . . ."

"That will be for later. You belong to me now. You trust me. You believe in me. It must be so or you would not be my chosen one or I yours. You have said you love me enough to give up everything—a life of easy comfort, yet you do not know what hardship is. Are you sure, Damask? It is not yet too late."

"I am sure. I will cook for you, work for you. . . ."

"And believe in me," he added.

"I will be everything you wish," I promised. "I shall be happier with you in a cottage than in a castle."

"It must be so. You *must* trust me, believe in me, work with me and for me."

"So shall I, with all my heart."

"This is our wedding night," he said again.

I understood his meaning and drew back. I was a virgin. I had been brought up to believe that this was a state which should not be surrendered until marriage—but this *was* marriage, he had said, and I must not expect life with Bruno to be as it would with other men.

"You are thinking that I plan to seduce you and leave you?" he said sadly. "So you doubt me after all."

"No."

"But you do. You hesitate. I thought you were brave. I believed you when you said you trusted me. Perhaps I was mistaken. Perhaps you should go back to the house. . . . Perhaps we should say good-bye."

He kissed me then with a passion I had not dreamed of.

I said: "Bruno, you are different tonight. What has happened?"

"Tonight I am your lover," he replied.

"And I am ignorant of love . . . this kind of love. I will do anything you ask of me, but. . . ."

"Love has many facets. It is like the diamond in the Madonna's crown. Do you remember it, Damask? It shone with a pale light and a fiery light—it was red, blue, yellow . . . all the colors of the spectrum. . . . But it was the same diamond."

As he spoke his hands moved over my body and I was never more aware of the strange nature of the fascination he had for me. I was conscious of his power over me but I was not sure whether my feelings for him were love as others had experienced it. It was not what I felt for Rupert or my father. Nor was his love for me like Rupert's. I sensed in Bruno a need to subdue me and in myself an urgent desire to be subdued.

I could believe in that moment that he was different from all other men. Perhaps every girl feels this of her lover. I did not mean merely that he possessed all the perfections. I felt in that moment that there was some godlike quality about him and that no matter what the consequences I must obey him.

My will dissolved I was willing and eager to cast aside everything that I had been taught, to throw aside my respect of that chastity which must be surrendered only to my husband. But Bruno *was* my husband.

I had convinced myself. Bruno knew it. I heard his low laugh of triumph.

"Oh, Damask," I heard him say. "You are the one for me. You love me, do you not . . . utterly, completely . . . so that you are ready to give up all for me?"

I heard myself answer: "Yes, Bruno. I do."

And that was my wedding night; there on our bed of bracken we were as one.

Nothing, I knew, could ever be the same again; and even in these moments of passion I could not rid myself of the thought that I was taking part in some sacrificial ceremony.

It was early morning when I crept into the house, bemused and disheveled. We had walked back to the house together, our arms about each other, and Bruno had stood waving until I disappeared inside.

I was in a state of exultation and wonderment after my experience and I could think of nothing else. Life had become a glorious adventure. I had reached a peak of happiness and for the time I did not want to look back or look forward; I wanted to remain poised as though on my mountaintop, to savor all that had happened, to remember our whispered words, our need of each other, to recall the moments of perfect union.

Bruno seemed to me like a god. That sense of power which had always been apparent was magnified.

There is no one like him in the whole world, I thought. And he loves me. I am his and he is mine forever.

I had come across the hall and as I was about to mount the stairs I was aware of a movement. A figure appeared. I was looking up at Simon Caseman. In the dim light his face looked chalky; the fox's mask stood out clearly, his eyes were narrowed.

"So," he said quietly but venomously, "you creep out at night like other sluts." His hand darted forward and I thought he was going to strike me, but he had plucked a leaf from my sleeve. "You could have chosen a more comfortable bed," he added.

I attempted to walk past him but he barred my way.

"I am your guardian, your stepfather. I want an explanation of this wanton behavior."

"What if I don't propose to give it?"

"Do you think I shall allow this? Do you think you can deceive me? You betray yourself. I know what has happened. Nothing was ever more clear to me."

"It is my own affair."

"And do you expect me to feed and clothe your bastards when they come along?"

I was suddenly so angry that I brought up a hand to strike him. He caught my arm before I could do so and he brought his face close to mine. "You slut!" he cried. "You. . . ."

"Do you wish to wake the household?"

"It would be good to do so that they might know what sort you are. Whore! Doxy! Any man's for the asking!"

"I proved I was not that to you."

"By God," he said, "I will teach you. . . ."

I could see the lust in his eyes and it frightened me.

"If you do not release me," I said, "I shall awaken the whole household. It would be well for my mother to know the kind of man she has married."

"A man who is doing his duty by her daughter?" he asked, but I could see that I had alarmed him. He knew my sharp tongue and he feared it.

He stood back a few paces. "I am your stepfather," he said. "I have a responsibility toward you. It is my duty to take charge of you."

"As you took charge of my father's possessions?"

"You ungrateful slut! Where would you have been if I had not allowed you to stay here? If I had not come here. . . ."

The words slipped out: "Perhaps my father would be free now."

He was taken aback, and I thought: I believe it's true. I believe he betrayed him.

Loathing for him swept over me. He was about to speak but he changed his mind. It was as though he were trying to pretend he had not understood the significance of my words.

There was a silence while we looked at each other. I knew my suspicion of him showed in my face; in his a certain hatred mingling with his lust.

He said: "I have tried to be a father to you."

"When you were rejected as a husband!"

"I was fond of you, Damask."

"You were fond of my inheritance . . . that which is now yours and should have been mine."

"It fell to me when your father . . . lost it. How fortunate for you that it came to me and not to some stranger. Think what would have happened to you and your mother if I had not been here to take care of you."

"I am thinking of what would have happened if my father had never taken you into his office. I am thinking of what would have happened if he had never given you a home here."

"You would have lost a good friend."

"It is we ourselves who decide the value of our friends."

"You are a wicked, ungrateful girl." He was recovering from the shock of my veiled accusation. "Good God," he cried. "I have the feelings of a father toward you. I have tried to cherish you. I have thought highly of you and I find that you are but a willing wench who will surrender her virtue for the sake of frolic in the grass when all decent folk are in their beds."

In sudden fury I slapped him across the ear and this time he was too late to prevent me. I hated him not so much because his crude words and sly hints were besmirching my exalted experience, but because I felt more sure than I ever had that he was the man who had informed against my father. If I had been entirely convinced I would have wanted to kill him.

The strength of my blow sent him reeling against the banister. He fell down two or three steps. I heard him groan as I hurried up the stairs and went along to my room.

I sat in a chair and watched the sunrise. I lived through the night—my union with the man I loved; my encounter with the man I hated. Sacred and profane! I thought.

I sat there dreaming and it occurred to me that there was one quality they had in common! A love of power.

I dozed a little and dreamed of them and in my dreams I was lying with Bruno on the grass; he was bending over me and suddenly his face changed to that of Simon Caseman. Love and lust —so close in a way and yet so far apart.

It was dawn. A fresh day. I was full of excitement, wondering what it would bring forth.

In the morning my mother came to me.

"Your father has sprained his ankle," she said. "He fell on the stairs last night."

"How did he do that?" I asked.

"He slipped. He will keep to his chamber today. In fact I have insisted that he rest."

She looked important. For once she was insisting; but I guessed that he had chosen to stay in his room because he did not wish to see me.

"I must see that the fomentations are put on," she said. "There is nothing like them for easing a sprain. Alternate hot and cold. Dear me. I thank God I have my chamomile lotion ready. That will ease the pain; and I think I shall give him a little poppy juice. Sleep is always good."

I said: "The man has merely sprained his ankle, Mother. You talk as though he is sickening for the plague."

"Don't say such things," she scolded, looking over her shoulder.

And I marveled that this man should have brought a happiness to her which my saintly father had failed to give her.

I wanted to be alone to dream of my future. What next, I asked myself? Shall I see him again tonight? Will he send a messenger for me? The day seemed long and irksome. Every time I heard a step on the stair I hoped it would be one of the maids come to tell me that Bruno was waiting for me.

That afternoon my mother came to my room. I felt sick with disappointment. I had thought the step on the stair was that of one of the maids bringing a message from Bruno.

My mother looked excited.

"The new people are at the Abbey. Oh, dear, your stepfather is not going to be pleased. He always hoped nothing would come of it. I do hope they will be good neighbors. It is pleasant to have good neighbors. I wonder if the lady of the house is interested in gardens. There is so much land there. I believe she could be very successful."

"A rival, Mother, perhaps," I said. "Shall you like it if she produces better roses than yours?"

"I am always ready to learn improvements. I do wonder what they will do there. All those useless buildings. I suppose they will pull them down and do some rebuilding. That was what your stepfather planned to do."

"And now he will have to abandon his plans and we shall have him nursing a grievance as well as a sprained ankle."

"You are always so ungrateful to him, Damask. I don't know what has happened to you lately."

She went on talking about the Abbey. She was very disappointed by my assumed lack of interest.

I waited to hear from him. There were so many questions I would have asked him. A terrible fear had come to me. What if I should never see him again? I had had the impression that our vows and even our lovemaking had been a kind of ritual. I had had the impression that all the time he was trying to prove to me the fact that he was no ordinary human being. Even when he spoke of love it was in a mysterious fashion. It occurred to me then that he *needed* to believe himself to be apart. He was proud, I know, and the fact that Keziah had claimed him as her son humiliated him so deeply that he refused to accept it.

I was trying to attach human motives to his actions. But was he after all superhuman?

I was alternately exultant and apprehensive. I kept to my room. I did not wish to see Rupert nor my stepfather. As for my mother, her chatter irritated me. I could only long for Bruno to come to me.

It was three days after that night when Bruno and I had made our vows, Simon Caseman had remained in his room ever since

nursing his ankle, which I suspected was not as incapacitating as
he made it out to be.

I was in my room when one of the maids came out and told
me that there was a visitor in the winter parlor. My mother was
there and had sent for me to join them.

I was unprepared for what was waiting me.

As I reached the winter parlor my mother came to the door.
Her face was a study of perplexity.

"The new owner of the Abbey is here," she stuttered.

I went in. Bruno rose from his chair to greet me.

Events had taken such a strange turn that I felt I could believe
anything, however fantastic. Bruno, the child of the Abbey, turned
adrift into poverty, who only a few nights previously had asked
me to share a life of hardship with him, was the owner of the
Abbey!

At first I thought it was some joke. How could it be possible?

As I stood facing him in the winter parlor I said something like
this. He smiled at me then.

"Is it true then that you doubt me, Damask?" he had said reproachfully.

And I knew that he meant doubt his ability to rise above all
other men, doubt his special powers.

Fortunately my mother's inborn habits and her insistence on
the correct manner in which to receive guests got the better of all
else. She would ring for her elderberry wine to be brought.

And while we drank it Bruno told us of his good fortune, of
how he had prospered in London; how he had gone to France on
the King's business and because he had executed that business
with an especial skill he had been in a position to acquire the
Abbey.

From anyone else it would have sounded incredible but his
presence, his assurance and that air which was unlike anyone else's
insisted on our belief.

I could see that my mother did not doubt it at all.

"And all that land . . . all those buildings that make up the
Abbey," she said.

"I have plans," he answered, smiling.

"And the gardens?"

"Yes, there will be gardens."

"You will live there alone?"

"I am planning to marry. It is one of the reasons I have called on you today."

He was smiling at me and my heart was lifted. All the misery of the past fell away from me then.

"I have come to ask you for Damask's hand in marriage."

"But this is all so . . . unexpected. I must consult my husband."

"There is no need," I said. "Bruno and I had already decided to marry."

"You . . . you *knew* . . . ," stammered my mother.

"I knew that he would ask my hand and I had already made up my mind to accept him."

I held out my hand; he took it. It seemed symbolic. Then I saw the look of pride in his eyes; he held his head high. He was so clearly delighted by the effect this had on us. And why had he not told me on that night that he was the new owner of the Abbey? Clearly because he had wanted to be sure that it was for himself that I would marry him. It was his pride—his human pride. And I was glad.

He was so proud now that momentarily I was reminded of the peacocks strutting on the lawn. There was no divinity in such an attitude surely, I thought tenderly.

It was a human attitude and it pleased me for that reason. I wanted him to be human. I did not want a saint or a miracle man. That's what I would teach him. I wanted a husband whom I could love and care for, who was not all-powerful, who needed me.

There was so much to learn, so many explanations to hear, but for that moment in the winter parlor, I was happy as I had never thought to be again.

It was the only topic of conversation. Bruno, the child who had been discovered in the Christmas crib, was the new owner of the Abbey.

Of course, said the wiseacres, it was another miracle. They had never trusted Keziah. She had been made to confess under torture.

It had seemed strange that the Abbey had had to be dissolved but the divine purpose was rarely other than mysterious. Now they would see . . . what they would see. He, who had clearly been intended to rule the Abbey, was back, and it all had a seemingly natural appearance which was often the way of miracles.

Bruno was lighthearted. Here was another side to his nature. He had never been like this in the old days.

He made plans. He was going to build from the stones of the Abbey a mighty mansion. Like the phoenix of old a new Abbey would arise to replace the old one.

I lived a fantastic existence during those months. Bruno wanted the wedding to take place immediately.

My mother was shocked. A wedding must be prepared for. What of my dowry? What of the formalities to which well-brought-up people must submit?"

"I want no dowry," said Bruno. "I want only Damask."

The effect on Simon Caseman was what I would have expected. At first he was angry. He had lost the Abbey on which he had set his heart; and that he had lost it to Bruno, the penniless waif, the bastard of a serving girl and a monk was impossible for him to believe at first.

"It's a hoax," he declared. "We shall find that he is deceiving us. How could it be possible?"

"People say," said my mother timidly, "that with him everything is possible."

"It's a trick!" insisted Simon.

But when he had to accept the fact that it was indeed true a smoldering silence was his response. When he learned that I was to marry Bruno he said nothing but I knew that he was far from unmoved; and if I had not been in such a state of bliss I might have been apprehensive, for I was certain that he was a dangerous man.

Rupert was bewildered. "It seems so incredible, Damask," he said.

I repeated what Bruno had told us about finding good fortune in London and pleasing the King.

"It's impossible," said Rupert. "Such a thing could not possibly happen in such a short time. Even Thomas Wolsey, whose rise was phenomenal, did not succeed like that."

"Bruno is not like ordinary people."

"I don't like it, Damask. It smacks of witchcraft."

"Oh, no, Rupert! We just have to accept that Bruno is different from the rest of us."

"Damask, are you truly happy?"

"As I never believed it possible to be after my father died."

Rupert did not answer. He was very unhappy, I know. His dream that he and I should one day marry was shattered; but it was more than that. His nature was such that while he saw his own plans for his future life in ruins he could still be apprehensive for that which I had chosen.

As soon as the harvest was over he would go to the Remus estate. Then I supposed I should see very little of him.

It has always surprised me how when something becomes a fact —however mysteriously it happens, however fantastic it is—in a short time people grow accustomed to it and cease to regard it with wonder.

So it was with the return of Bruno and his acquisition of the Abbey.

Bruno had taken the name of Kingsman. It had not occurred to me before that he had no surname. I suppose he should have had that of Keziah but he refused to take it. He told me why he was called Kingsman. When he had gone to France on the King's service His Majesty had been so delighted with him on his return that he had granted him an audience and asked his name. Bruno had told him that he did not know his parents and that he had had no need of a name until that moment. He had decided to call himself the King's man. This delighted the King who had greatly approved, and had increased his favor with His Majesty and had made the way to acquiring the Abbey easy.

"There is so much I want to know," I said.

"You will know in time," Bruno replied.

He was eager to show me the Abbey. "Your new home," he called it, and together we wandered through that vast estate.

"There are bricks here in plenty," said Bruno, "to build us as fine a mansion as you could wish."

"Will that not be costly?"

"There is one thing you will have to learn, Damask. Never apply the same standards to me as you must to other men."

"You talk as though you have endless wealth."

He pressed my hand. "Much will be revealed to you."

"Now you talk like a prophet."

He smiled and the look of pride was on his face.

We would leave the church tower, he said, which was particularly fine and Norman; we would leave the Lady Chapel too because a house of this size would need its chapel; but the lay brothers' dorter, their infirmary and kitchens would be demolished. The monks' dorter and refectory would in time be the servants' quarters. He had grand plans. We should see great changes during the next months. I should help him plan our new establishment.

"You will marry a rich man after all, Damask," he said. "And you believed, did you not, that you were to marry a poor one?"

"Why did you tell me this? Why did you think it necessary to test me?"

"I wanted to be sure that you wished to come to me . . . for myself only."

"And you—who know so much—did not know that I would do that!"

"In truth I never doubted you. I knew . . . because I know these things. But I wanted to hear you say it. I wanted you to know yourself."

"None knows me better, Bruno."

"Perhaps I do."

He was smiling enigmatically now—the mystic.

I insisted on his giving me details of his rise to fortune.

He hesitated but finally he told me, and his story was, as Rupert had pointed out, incredible.

When it was known that Rolf Weaver was in the Abbey and that his purpose was to make an inventory of the treasures there and divert them from St. Bruno's Abbey to the King, there had been time to secret some of the jewelry into hiding places in the tunnels and cellars. The Abbot died and because of the scandal created by Ambrose and Keziah it was known there would be no compensation for anyone there. All the monks would be turned adrift to fend for themselves. Brother Valerian had therefore given each monk a few jewels which would perhaps give him a start so that he might not die of starvation and have to suffer the indignity of begging. Had this been discovered death would have been the reward of those who had jewels in their possession but the desperate nature of their situation made them ready to take that risk.

As I knew, Bruno had come to our house for a while. There he had kept the jewels secreted on his person and later he had left us to go into London. He had reason to believe that Brother Valerian had given him jewels of some special value; he knew too that several monks had been discovered selling jewels from abbeys and monasteries and had been condemned to death for this, so he delayed before selling and came to our house that he might have somewhere to live during that waiting period. He then tried the smallest of the jewels in his possession and this realized enough money to take him abroad. He had decided to go to France, Italy or the Low Countries and there sell the remainder of the jewels in his possession.

He had when in London made the acquaintance of one of the King's most important ministers who, aware of who he was and being convinced that the confession of Keziah and Ambrose had been wrung from them by torture, befriended him; and hearing that he was going abroad suggested that he might take a message to an important minister who served the Emperor Charles.

This Bruno had done so successfully that he was brought to the King's notice and the King had received him and thanked him personally for the service rendered. Now that he was growing older and he suffered so acutely from the abscess in his leg, the King had grown more interested in booklore and the erudition of Bruno had attracted him. They had even enjoyed a very pleasant discourse on theology and Bruno, being well versed in the King's own book which had years ago earned for him the title of Defender of the Faith, the King found the conversation very agreeable.

Bruno disposed of more jewels advantageously and was able to live like a man of some means, so no surprise was shown when he let it be known that he was interested in acquiring an estate and that Abbey lands would suit him very well.

St. Bruno's had not yet an owner and was available to someone who could pay what was necessary.

"So," he finished, "that is why I am here and the mansion which will arise from the ashes of the old Abbey will be my home, your home and that of our children."

It was a strange story and had it been anyone but Bruno, would have been hard to believe; but when told it I was ready to accept the fact that with him—who was different from other mortals—nothing was too strange to be true.

There was the excitement of wedding preparations. My mother was ready to forget everything in her desire to do all that was necessary.

That I was to live near by delighted her; that I was to marry a man of great wealth—for so it seemed—pleased her too. She had been secretly worried about my dowry.

Now there was the bridecake to be made and my dress to be planned, she was in a fever of excitement—so much so that she did not even notice the glowering looks of her husband.

Clement was determined to excel himself. He and Eugene had already spoken to Bruno. As soon as the wedding was over they wanted to come to the Abbey. We should need masters of our bake and brew houses. And who knew the Abbey's better than they?

To be back would be glorious for them both; Clement was a man who could settle in anywhere, but Eugene had suffered nostalgia. To be back, to serve their young master. I overheard them as they discussed it. "It's a miracle," whispered Eugene.

"And what do you expect but miracles with that one?" answered Clement.

Kate and Lord Remus came to Caseman Court for the wedding.

On the first day of their arrival Kate was up in my room—the door shutting us in—she stretched on my bed and I in the window seat as in the old days.

"You, Damask!" she cried. "*You* to marry Bruno! I can't believe it."

"Why be so incredulous? You have come to a wedding, yet you are surprised to find there is to be a bridegroom."

"That bridegroom!" she said. "And to think of it! He is rich. Is he as rich as Remus? To buy the Abbey! How is it *possible?*"

"You know Bruno is not as other men. When he wants something he takes it."

"Not always," she contradicted.

"You must admit he has the Abbey. He always wanted it. In the old days he believed he would be the Abbot. Now he owns it."

"But how could he have bought it? It must have been presented to him. Some have been given abbeys for good service. What service could Bruno have rendered the King?"

"He went on a mission to France."

"What does Bruno know of missions to France?"

"You don't know Bruno."

"I don't know Bruno! I know more of Bruno than you will ever know."

"I suppose you would know my husband better than I."

"You can be a simpleton at times, Damask."

"And you are so wise."

It was like the old days. But there was something different about Kate. She did not like my marriage.

I took her over to see the Abbey and walked on that spot where we used to play. Bruno joined us there.

"Now," said Kate, "we are three grown-up people. What a lot has happened since we played as children here."

"You have become Lady Remus," said Bruno.

"And a mother," she answered. "And you have become the owner of this great Abbey."

"That surprises you, does it not?"

"Greatly."

"Damask was less surprised."

"Why, Bruno," I said, "I was astounded."

But he went on: "Damask does not care for worldly possessions as you do, Kate. What do you think now of the penniless boy who took shelter in your home?"

"I think," said Kate, "that he was sly. He had jewels in his possession, it seems, on which he founded his fortune. He should not have kept that to himself."

They were regarding each other intently and I said: "That is all in the past."

Bruno turned to me. "And our future, Damask . . . yours and mine . . . is here in this place. Together we will build the finest house that ever was seen and even Remus Castle will seem insignificant beside it."

"I like not these comparisons," I said. "Let us show Kate what we intend to build onto the Abbot's Lodging."

He was delighted; and once again I was aware of that burning pride as he showed Kate his domain.

We were married almost immediately. It was a ceremony slightly less grand than Kate's had been. But I had my bridal gown which had been made by my mother's seamstresses with herself supervising them; my bridecake was, I think, finer because Clement had made it so. And Eugene had worked hard that the bridecup might compare with that drunk at royal weddings.

There was dancing and revelry in the hall and later we were conducted to the Abbey with a party of the guests, and we were alone in our new home.

Wife and Mother

How strange, how wonderful to wake up next morning in the bedroom which had been the Abbot's. I lay looking up at the vaulted ceiling and tried to think clearly of all that had happened to me during the last few weeks. I certainly could not have imagined anything like this.

Bruno was awake and I said to him: "Does it not show how wonderful life can be when you consider what has happened to me?"

I had quickly learned that this was the sort of thing he loved to hear. I would never forget how he had kept secret the fact that he was a rich man because he was so anxious to be taken for himself and I felt tender toward him on account of this. I understood him well. He had believed himself to be apart from the rest of the world, a very special being and because that rude awakening had humiliated him more than he could endure he needed constant reassurance. He should have it. I would give it to him; and in time he would be able to face the fact that I loved him none the less because of his birth. I would assure him that it was far more commendable for a man without spiritual advantages to achieve what he had done, than it would have been for one who had special powers.

But that was for later.

We talked of this wonderful thing and he promised me more and more wonder. He was eager to go over the Abbey with me, to explain what he would have and for me to offer ideas. We would build our home together, he said.

That morning I discovered that he had engaged several servants and apart from a very few they were men and all of a kind. Although there was no physical resemblance to Clement and Eugene they reminded me of them. Then I asked myself if I thought these people resembled monks because we were in an old abbey.

I said to Bruno: "They remind me of Clement and Eugene."

"It is because they were at one time monks. When they were turned out they were lost and bewildered. Now that they have heard the Abbey is occupied, and by whom, they have come back. They wish to work here."

I was uneasy. "They must remember it is no longer a monastery."

"They know full well that the King has dissolved the monasteries."

"Is it wise. . . ."

He laughed at me. "You must leave such matters to me. We are going to have a rich estate and rich estates need many workers. These men know the Abbey. They have implored me to give them work here on the land they know and have known all their lives. I could not say no to them. Besides they will work well for me."

"I understand that. But. . . ."

"I do assure you, Damask, this place now is very different from what it was under the Abbot."

"I think, Bruno," I answered, "we shall have to consider our actions with care. Everyone should. How can we know what new laws will be in force?"

He turned to me then and his face was radiant. "Here you will be in our own little world. Leave your fears to me, Damask."

He looked so tall and handsome, so godlike, so calm, that I felt I could safely forget any little apprehension I might have left. And that impression stayed with me when he took me into the old scriptorium and I found yet another stranger there.

Here was indeed the monkly countenance. The skin of this man was like old parchment, the eyes embedded in wrinkles alert yet calm, the high cheekbones with the flesh stretched tightly across them, the thin mouth all suggested the scholar and stoic. I knew before Bruno introduced him as Valerian that here was yet another of the monks of the Abbey.

"There are still some of the old manuscripts which were not

destroyed by the vandals," said Bruno. "Valerian hid them away.
Now he is here to bring them out to sort them and to compile
our library."

Yes, even on that first morning I was disturbed. But I forgot as
we explored the Abbey.

"The church tower must stay," said Bruno. "And how could we
demolish the church?"

We went to look at it. It had been built, like so many, in the
form of a crucifix and was impressive indeed for the height from
the floor to the highest point of the vaulted ceiling was some fifty
feet. As I stood there I could fancy I heard the chanting of the
monks. My footsteps sounded noisy as I walked across the flagged
floor to the five altars each dedicated to a saint—the center one
to Saint Bruno who had founded the Abbey, as that other Saint
Bruno had founded the Carthusians; and there was the screen
beyond which was the Sanctuary where any who were persecuted
could find refuge.

"How could one deliberately demolish such a place?" I asked.

Bruno smiled at me. "We understand each other," he said. "We
will leave the church."

Then we went out and studied the many buildings which would
be taken down to make our mansion.

"It will be a great labor," said Bruno, "a great and inspiring
one."

"And we will build together like birds building a nest."

"A nest!" cried Bruno laughing at me. "All this glory to be compared with a straw and mud!"

"A nest to a bird is a home, as this will be to us," I said indignantly.

And he laughed and kissed me; and I thought exultantly, we
are just the same as any young married couple—in love with each
other and the future.

He took me into the monks' dorter and frater. In the frater was
a long refectory table and benches and at each end of the room
was a stone spiral staircase leading to numerous cell-like rooms in
the doors of which were grilles through which one could see inside; and each appeared to be exactly like the others. There were
pallets on the floors and crucifixes on the walls, for those who had

come to rob the place had not considered these worth taking away.

"Our mansion will not be in the least modern. We must keep the architecture to this ancient Norman style," said Bruno.

"It must necessarily be so for we shall be using the old stone and some of these places are too interesting to change."

He agreed. He would not wish to change the scriptorium; and the brewhouse and bakehouse could not be improved on. At the moment we had very few servants but we should need more. He intended to make profitable use of the farm and the mill.

"In the old days," he told me, "these guesthouses were often full. I should not wish weary travelers to be turned away, and perhaps in time St. Bruno's Abbey will become the Sanctuary it once was."

"And you will be the Abbot. What of me? Abbots cannot have wives, you know."

"I shall do as I please."

"I am certain of that," I replied lightly.

We went to the fishponds. There were three of them, the first flowing into the second, the second into the third.

"There used to be enough fish to feed the whole population of the Abbey and to sell," said Bruno. "I hope it will be the same now."

"You will have your Abbey, I can see."

"I shall have the sort of community I wish for and none shall say me nay."

"But in these days one must show a little care."

"How you harp on care." He was faintly exasperated. "You are safe with me."

"I know, Bruno. As if I were afraid!"

But I did feel uneasy.

I told him of the night Rupert and I had buried my father's head.

"I wish that I had been the one to bring it to you."

"It was a risk," I said. "I am thankful that Rupert was not discovered."

"He is in love with you," said Bruno.

"Yes."

"But you were ready to face hardship with me, little knowing that you were coming to this!"

"It would have made no difference, Bruno," I said. "No difference at all."

They were strange days. There was so much to do, so much to talk of, so much to explore.

We did not leave our little world during those days. As long as Bruno was with me I was happy. I was eager to run my own household. Should I have a stillroom to compare with my mother's, a garden like hers?

I would rather be with Bruno, listening to his plans. We often talked of the children we would have, and I gleaned that Bruno greatly desired to have a son.

We were so close at such times of the day and close indeed at night; it was only when I would see that fanatical gleam in his eyes that I felt him moving away from me. Sometimes I think he sensed a certain disbelief but was determined to dispel it, to force me to accept what he wished me to; and this made me uneasy for I knew myself well enough to be sure that I could not be made to accept what I did not believe.

But that was not for the moment.

We were happy, discovering each other. We had passion, the ecstasy we shared at night beneath the Abbot's vaulted ceiling; and we had a great plan; we were going to make a home.

Just over a week after my wedding day when I was settling into my new home and no longer awoke with a sense of wonder and had to tell myself this had really happened, a messenger came from Caseman Court to say that my mother was in childbirth and asking for me. I hastily donned a cloak and walked to my old home. Would she have sent for me, I asked myself, if all had been going well?

Poor Mother, I thought, who had been so unworthy of my beloved father and married almost before he was cold in his grave. So many memories from my childhood kept crowding into my mind as I made my way back to her: the tenderness she had bestowed on me; those days when I had gathered wild flowers for her and she had shown me how to arrange them; the excitement when roses like the musk had been introduced into the country. Now they all seemed endearing.

I reached the gate where the bold brass letters CASEMAN COURT stood out arrogantly. I crossed the lawn where the gorgeous peacock, followed by the drab peahen, strutted on the grass and I was reminded poignantly of the days when I had fed them pulse, and Father had laughed to watch and asked me if I did not think there was something entirely stupid about the peacock and was he not an example to all of us not to be overproud of the gifts which only God could give us?

The servants looked at me curiously when I came into the hall. I could imagine the gossip there must be about what was going on at the Abbey. We must be careful, I thought apprehensively.

I demanded: "How is my mother?"

"It's a hard birth, Mistress," said one of the maids with a curtsy.

I ran up the stairs; as I reached the gallery Simon Caseman came out of a room.

"So you came," he said.

"Of course I came. What is happening?"

"She has given birth to a boy but that is not all."

"You mean . . . it is not going as it should?"

"I think there is another child. The first is healthy. It will live."

"I was thinking of my mother."

"It is an ordeal for her. She has had such anxieties lately." He looked at me reproachfully. "She has worried about your strange marriage."

"There was no need. But I do understand her fears. When she announced her marriage to me, I was uneasy for her."

The midwife called out something and we went into the room where my mother lay.

"Two little boys," said the midwife. "And for the life of me I can't tell one from the other."

"Two!" cried Simon, and I sensed his exultation.

"And their mother?" I asked.

"'Tas been a trying time for her. But she'll pull through. Exhausted she were but she opened her eyes and said, 'A boy!' And, poor soul, that was what she wanted. I said to her, 'Not one boy, my dear lady, that wasn't enough for you. You've got two of them

—and for twins I've never seen such big 'uns. 'Twas small wonder they made such a to-do about coming out."

"May I see my mother?" I asked.

"Bless you, Mistress, it's what she wants. She's asked for you time and time again."

I went into the room. My mother lay back on her pillows, her hair disordered. On her face was a smile of triumphant woman.

"Mother," I said kneeling by the bed, "you have given birth to healthy twins."

She nodded and smiled.

"You should rest now," I said.

She smiled at me, then her expression changed. "Damask, are you happy?"

"Yes, Mother."

A shadow passed across her face. "It was all so strange. I never knew the like. Your father was distressed."

"My father is in heaven, Mother," I said. "And I believe that he rejoices in my marriage."

"Your stepfather is uneasy. He fears all may not be as it should."

"Tell him to keep his fears for his own affairs, Mother." Then because I saw that the conflict between us hurt her, I went on quickly: "You should be content now that you have two little boys to care for. You will, however, not be able to spend so much time in your garden."

She smiled. Pleasant normal conversation—that was what she wanted. If anything was inclined to worry her she preferred to thrust it to one side.

When I came out of her room Simon Caseman was waiting for me.

"I wish to have a word with you before you leave, Damask."

I followed him into the room which had been my father's study. Many times had we sat there looking out over the lawns to the river. Many subjects had we discussed. I felt a pang of nostalgia for the old days and a longing to be able to talk to him again. I would have discussed my misgivings with him; I could even have talked with him of Bruno.

"I want to know what is happening at the Abbey," Simon Caseman said. "I heard strange rumors."

"What rumors are these?" I hoped my voice did not betray the alarm I felt.

"That some of the monks have returned."

I said cautiously, "Clement and Eugene, who worked for my father, have places in our household."

"Monks!" he said, his eyes narrowing. "And others too. All monks."

"The lands are extensive," I said. "There is the farm which of course must be productive. If there are one or two monks there it is because there are many seeking work."

"I trust," he said, "that you are not becoming involved in lawlessness."

"I do not understand you."

"St. Bruno's was disbanded. It would be unwise to found it again even if it is under the name of Kingsman."

"Many abbeys have become as manor houses since the King and his ministers have bestowed them, I take it you have no objection to that?"

"Providing those on whom they have been bestowed do not break the law."

I felt certain in that moment that he had betrayed my father and I hated him.

I blatantly tormented him. "Owners of such abbeys as ours must of course make full use of all they have to offer. I had no idea how large it was and how much was contained in it. We have our farm, our mill, and fishponds in which are hundreds of fish. There is great wealth in the Abbey. We must make sure that full use is made of it."

I could see the lights of envy in his eyes. His lips tightened. "Take care, Damask. There is so much that is strange going on, I fear. You may be walking into danger."

"You fear! Nay, you hope."

"Now I understand you not."

"You wanted to add the Abbey to your possessions. You told me so. You were too late. It is ours."

"You misunderstand me. Have I not always been good to you? Did I not allow you to make your home here?"

"My home was already made."

"You are determined to plague me. You always have. Desist, Damask. It is better so. If you had been my friend. . . ."

"I don't understand what that term implies."

"I offered you marriage."

"And quickly consoled yourself with my mother."

"I did it to keep a roof over your heads."

"You are so considerate."

"Do not goad me too much—you and that husband of yours. If it is true that you are gathering the monks together there, you should beware. I know that Clement and Eugene are not the only ones you have there."

"Those two came from this house, remember. You accuse us of harboring monks, what of yourself? Did they not work for you? Take care that you are not proved guilty of that of which you accuse us. My husband has good friends at Court. He has even been honored by the King."

With that I bowed and left him. I knew that he was staring after me with that look of mingled anger and desire which I knew so well. He would never forgive me for refusing him and marrying Bruno, any more than he would forgive Bruno for gaining the Abbey which he had so desired.

His words kept ringing in my ears: "Beware."

Without consulting Bruno I engaged two serving girls. They were sisters of two of the servants at Caseman Court who had been reckoning on going to my mother, but when I asked them to come to the Abbey they readily accepted.

I explained to Bruno that it made us seem a more normal household, which amused him.

A few weeks after their arrival one of them—Mary—came to me, her eyes round with awe. She had been to Mother Salter's in the woods; she blushed a little, so I guessed it was for a love potion—and Mother Salter had sent a message for me. She wished to see me without delay.

That morning I called at the old woman's cottage. The fire was burning as I had seen it before; the blackened pot was simmering. The black cat sprang up on the seat beside her and watched me with its yellow eyes.

"Be seated," said Mother Salter, and I sat in the fireside alcove opposite her. She stirred what was in the pot and said: "The time has come, Mistress, for you to keep your promise. You have a fine house now. An Abbey no less. You are ready to take the child."

She rose and drew aside a curtain—lying on a pallet was a child asleep. I calculated that she must be almost two years old for she was the daughter of Keziah and Rolf Weaver whom I had promised to care for.

So much had happened since I had made that promise that I had forgotten it. Now it gave me a few qualms of uneasiness. When I had promised to take the child my father had been alive; he had agreed that she might come to our house.

Mother Salter sensed my uneasiness. "You cannot go back on your pledge to a dying woman," she said.

"Circumstances have changed since I made that pledge."

"But your pledge remains."

The child opened her eyes. She was beautiful. Her eyes were a deep blue, the color of violets, her lashes thick and black as her hair.

"Take her up," commanded Mother Salter.

The child smiled at me and held out her arms. When I took her she placed her arms about my neck as Mother Salter commanded her to do. "Honeysuckle child," said the witch, "behold your mother."

The child looked wonderingly into my face. I had never seen such a beautiful creature.

"There," said Mother Salter, "remember your vow. Woe to those who break their promises to the dead."

I took the child and carried her out of the witch's cottage and I took her to the Abbey.

"What child is this?" demanded Bruno.

"I have brought her to live here," I replied. "She will be as our own."

"By God," he cried. "You do strange things, Damask. Why do

you bring a child like that into our household? Ere long you will have a child of your own, I trust."

"I pledged myself to take her. Then it was easy. My father was alive. I told him of my pledge and he said I must keep it."

"But why make such a pledge?"

"It was to a dying woman."

He shrugged his shoulders. "The servants will care for her."

"I have promised to treat her as my own."

"For whom should you have made such a promise?"

"Bruno," I said, "it was to Keziah on her deathbed."

"Keziah!" His face darkened with anger. "Keziah." He said the name as though there was something obscene about it. "That creature's child! Here!"

Oh, Bruno, I thought, are you not that creature's child? But it was for that reason of course that he felt so angry.

"Listen to me," I said. "Keziah was dying and she asked me to care for this child. I promised. I will not go back on my word."

"And if I will not have the child here?"

"You will not be so cruel."

"You do not know me yet, Damask."

I stared at him. Now he was different from ever before. The angry passion distorted his face. It was as though a mischievous boy had drawn a mask over that irresistible perfection of features which had so enchanted me. Bruno looked almost evil in his hatred of Keziah's innocent child.

As usual when I was alarmed my tongue was at its sharpest. "It seems I have something to learn which will not be pleasing to me," I cried.

"You will take the child back where she belongs," he said.

"Her place is here."

"Here! In *my* Abbey!"

"Her place is with me. If this is my home, it is hers."

"Take her back without delay whence you found her."

"To her grandmother—Mother Salter's cottage in the woods?"

Oh, God, I thought, she may well be your grandmother too.

I wished that I could shut out the thoughts which came to me. It was because this beautiful innocent little girl was his half-sister that he could not bear to have her in his house. Where was the godlike quality I had so much admired? It was replaced by a vile human passion—Pride! I sensed fear too. I knew Bruno in that moment better than I ever had before and I sensed that he was afraid. I had believed I could love him in his weakness even as in his strength; but my feelings had changed for him in those moments. My adoration had gone; yet in its place was a deep maternal tenderness.

I wanted to take him in my arms and say: "Let us be happy. Let us forget that you must be above all other men. We have each other; we have most miraculously this wonderful Abbey!" (Yet when I thought of that I was uneasy for I realized then that I did not entirely believe his glib explanation of how he had come into possession of it.) "We have the future. Let us build our Abbey into a sanctuary for ourselves and those in need. Let us bring up our children in a good life and let this little one be our first."

"I had thought you would do anything to please me," he said.

"You know it is my great desire to please you."

"And yet you do this. . . . Such a short time we have been married and you go against my wishes."

"Because I made a pledge . . . a sacred pledge to a dying woman. You must see that I cannot break my word."

"Take the child back to whoever has cared for her so far."

"That is her grandmother, Mrs. Salter. She has threatened me with curses if I do not take the child. But I will have to keep her, though not from fear but because I gave my word and I intend to keep it."

He was silent for a few moments. Then he said: "I see that you made this rash promise. It was unwise. It was foolish. Keep the child out of my way. I do not wish to see her."

He turned away and I looked after him sadly. I was unhappy. I wished that I were like my mother—placid and uncritical. But I could not stop my thoughts. I could not prevent myself from knowing that he was afraid to offend the witch of the woods.

There was a rift between us now. Nothing would ever be the same again. Bruno was aware that he had allowed the mask to slip for a moment and had shown me something of the man beneath it. The child had done this. She had forced him to show himself vengeful and, worse still, afraid; and it was inevitable that our relationship must change from that moment. We were together less frequently. The child took up a great deal of my time. She was intelligent, quick and mischievous, and each day I was startled by her incredible beauty. She sensed Bruno's antagonism though they had scarcely seen each other since her arrival. In her mind I was sure he was regarded as some sort of ogre.

She would toddle around after me so that it was not easy for me not to be with her; I sensed that she was always a little uneasy if I were not present because her eyes would light up with a relieved pleasure when she saw me, which was very endearing.

Naturally the coming of a child had changed the household. It had been a very unusual one before but now it became more normal. Bruno consulted me about the building which had started and behaved as though there had never been the disagreement between us, but I realized that as the time passed he would have to see a great deal of Honey and it was no use trying to hide her from him.

He seemed to realize this and to accept the inevitability of the child's presence. I was glad of this although the antagonism between them was apparent. In Bruno it showed in a feigned indifference but the child was too young to hide her feelings; she ran from him and when he was near kept close to my side.

So it remained an uneasy situation; but each day I loved the child more. I loved Bruno too, but differently. I found a strange sort of pity creeping into my emotions.

My mother announced that the christening of her twins was to take place and Kate wrote that she would be present, leaving Carey with his nurses and Remus to his business affairs. She would stay at Caseman Court of course, but her first call would be at the Abbey to see the bride.

Within a few days she had arrived and true to her word came at once to the Abbey. She looked as elegant as ever in her fine velvet gown and beautiful too, flushed with the October wind which had caught little tendrils of hair escaping from under her headdress.

She came into the hall of the Abbot's Lodging and looked about her. I was on the landing at the top of the first flight of stairs and saw her a few seconds before she was aware of me.

"Kate," I cried. "You are more beautiful than ever!"

She grimaced. "I was fit to die of boredom. Even the Court has become deadly dull. I have much to tell you, Damask. But first there is so much I wish to know."

She looked at the great hall with its beautiful open timber roof, its molded arches and its carved pendants and corbels.

"So this was the old Abbot's Lodging. Very fine. I'll swear it compares favorably with Remus Castle. But what does it all mean?" She caught my hand and looked at the ring on my finger. "*You,* Damask. *You.*"

"Why should you seem so surprised?"

"That he should marry at all. It had to be one of us, of course. And I was already married to Remus, so there *was* only you. But this mansion . . . how did he acquire it? He who was so poor. How did the Abbey fall into his hands?"

"It was a miracle," I said.

Her eyes were wide; she looked at me searchingly. "Another miracle?" she asked. "Impossible! We were deluded about the first, weren't we? Do you know, Damask, I don't think I believe in miracles."

"You were always irreverent."

She gazed up at the carvings in the spandrels. "But it's beautiful. And this is your home now! Why did you not write and tell me what was happening? Why did you keep it to yourself? You should have warned me."

"There was no time."

"Well, I wish to hear everything now. *This* your home, Damask. Our old Abbey your home. Do you know they are saying, Damask, that the Abbey is becoming what it once was?"

"I know there are rumors."

"Never mind rumors. Let us be together and talk. There is so much to tell."

I took her up the great staircase with its beautifully carved balustrade to the solar where I had been sitting doing a piece of needlework—in fact making a dress for Honey—when she arrived.

Although it was October the afternoon sun streamed into the long room and I led her to the window where I had been seated.

"Do you need refreshment, Kate?" I asked.

"Your mother's stillroom provided all I needed. How proud she is of her twins. Where is your husband?"

"He is very occupied during the day. There is so much to be done here. We did not know the Abbey in the old days, Kate. I was astonished when I realized its spaciousness. There is going to be a great deal of work if we are to make it flourish as it did in the days of. . . ."

She was watching me closely. "But it must not flourish as an abbey, must it?"

"Indeed it is no abbey in the sense that St. Bruno's was. But there is the farm and the mill and the land has to be prepared for next year's harvests." I was talking because I was afraid of what questions she would ask me if I stopped. I said, "There will be the hay to be cut and baled; the corn; the animals. . . ."

"Pray do not render me accounts of the laborers' duties for I have not come to hear that."

"But you must understand that there is much work to be done . . . we shall need many men if we are to make this place prosper."

"And Bruno? Where is he?"

"I believe him to be somewhere in the Abbey. Perhaps he is talking about the farmlands, or the mill, or like as not he is in the scriptorium with Valerian."

"What did he say when he knew I was coming?"

"Very little."

"Don't be maddening, Damask. What effect did it have on him?"

"What conceit! Do you think it is such an important event because you at last deign to visit us?"

"I should have thought it worthy of some comment."

"He does not easily betray himself."

This she conceded.

I asked how Carey was. Had he grown?

"It is a natural function for children to grow. Carey is normal in every way."

"I long to see him."

"You shall. I will bring him to the Abbey." She was looking at me searchingly. "What banal questions we ask each other! And you have this child here—Keziah's child!" She looked at me searchingly. "Is that wise?"

"I had pledged myself."

"And Damask would always keep her word. And Bruno? What does he feel? His marriage not more than a few weeks old—and already a child!"

"He accepts the fact that I must keep my word. And I love the child."

"You would. The eternal mother! That is you, Damask. And are you happy?"

"I am happy."

"You always adored Bruno . . . blatantly. But then you were always so honest. You could never hide your feelings, could you?"

I avoided her eyes. "I don't think you were indifferent to him."

"But you carried off the prize. Clever Damask."

"I was not clever. It just happened."

"You mean that he returned and asked you to marry him?"

"I do mean that."

"And he said I will lay the rich Abbey at your feet. I will give you riches and jewels. . . ."

I laughed. "You were always obsessed by riches, Kate. I remember when we were young you always said you would marry a Duke. I'm surprised that you settled for a mere Baron."

"In the battle of life one takes an opportunity when it comes if it is reasonably good. To let it pass might mean to miss it altogether. There were not many noble visitors at your father's house, were there? Remus seemed a very worthy object of my attention."

"Is he as doting as ever?"

"He dotes," said Kate. "And of course he is eternally grateful for the boy. But it is of you that I wish to talk . . . *you*, Damask. So much has happened here—more than has been happening in my little circle. Your mother producing twins and your strange marriage. That is what interests me."

"I think you know what happened. Bruno came back and asked me to marry him. There had been a great deal of talk about the new owner of the Abbey. No one knew who it was. I agreed to marry Bruno—then he revealed to me who he was and that by a miracle he had acquired the Abbey."

"It's a fantastic story and I never wholly believe fantastic stories."

"Are you suggesting that I am lying to you, Kate?"

"Not you, Damask. But you must admit it is so very strange. So he asked you to marry him and only after did he reveal that the Abbey would be your home. What a secretive bridegroom! I'll dareswear you promised to share a life of poverty with him."

"I had thought that was what it would be."

She nodded slowly.

"Bruno is a proud man."

"He has much of which to be proud."

"Is not Pride a sin—one of the seven deadlies I had always been led to believe?"

"Oh, come, *you* are being censorious now, Kate. Bruno has a natural dignity."

"That was not quite what I meant." Her face darkened momentarily and then she shrugged her shoulders. "Show me the Abbey, Damask," she said. "I should enjoy seeing it. First this house. This solar is beautiful. I shall imagine you here when I am back at my gloomy old castle."

"So the castle has become gloomy? I thought you were very proud of such a fine old place."

"It is a castle merely—inhabited by the Remus family since the days of the first Edward. It could not be compared with an abbey, could it now?"

"I should have thought so and to its advantage."

"Now, Damask, you are at your old trick. You are teaching me to count my blessings. You were always something of a preacher. What do you think of the new religion? Did you know that many are probing into it? And it is against the law of course, which makes it so exciting. I believe it to be a simpler religion. Imagine the services in English! So easy for people to understand which is good in a way and yet so much of the dignity departs. It is so much more impressive when you are in doubt as to what it is all about."

"You still flit from subject to subject in the same inconsequential manner. What has religion to do with architecture?"

"It seemed to me that everything in this world is connected with everything else. There! You are thoughtful. Have I said something profound? Perhaps I am becoming clever. You and Bruno were the clever ones, were you not? How you used to madden me when you put on that superior manner and tried to carry the subject beyond me. But I could always get the better of you both. I haven't changed, Damask, and I doubt that you and Bruno have either."

"Why should any of us wish to get the better of each other?"

"Perhaps because some of us have what the other wants. But no matter. Where is Bruno? Manners demand that he should be here to greet me."

"You forget your visit was unexpected."

"He knew that I was coming to Caseman Court, did he not?"

"And do you expect him to be waiting here on the chance that you will come?"

She shook her head. "I would never expect that from Bruno. Come, show me your beautiful dwelling."

I led her across the solar into my own little sitting room.

"It's charming," she cried. She gazed up at the ceiling with its carved wooden ribs and gesso ornamentation and the decorations of the frieze. "That was done not very long ago," she declared. "It is quite modern. I'll warrant the old Abbot had it refurbished after the first miracle when the Abbey grew rich. So he owes that to Bruno. It is surprising how much so many owe to Bruno."

I took her from room to room. She expressed admiration for all she saw but I fancied it was tinged with envy. The gallery enchanted her. It was bare at the moment for tapestries and precious ornaments had been torn from the walls by Rolf Weaver and his men; but they had not harmed the window seats and the one beautiful oriel window which looked out on the cloister and the monks' frater.

At the end of the gallery was a small chapel on either side of the door of which were panels each decorated with an effigy of Saint Bruno.

"They lived well, these monks," said Kate with a smile. "And how lucky you are that it should have been *you* whom Bruno brought to this wonderful place."

As we made a tour of the Abbey she constantly exclaimed with admiration at so much; I knew that she found the place which had dominated our imaginations when we were children to be entirely fascinating and that she envied me. She climbed the monks' night stairs; she opened the door of one of the monk's cells and stood there looking around her. "How quiet it is!" she cried. "How cold. How ghostly."

She was thinking, she said, of all the pent-up emotion which had been suffered in this place. "Look at that pallet," she cried. "Imagine the thoughts of men who have occupied that! They shut themselves off from the world and how often during the night would they have longed for something they had left behind. Is it living, Damask, to shut oneself away from temptation, from life? What a strange place an abbey is." She looked through one of the slitlike windows in the monks' dorter. "You will be frightened here at night, Damask. Who knows, you may see the ghosts of long-dead monks flitting through the cloisters? Do you think people who have lived and suffered return to the scene of their tragedies? Think how many tragedies there must have been in this place!"

She was envious. She wanted the Abbey and I understood her so well—always she had sought to take what she wanted.

I almost wished that I had not shown her all that was here. There was such potential riches. In time if allowed to develop it I could see that the owner of such a place could be enormously rich and powerful; and was that not what Kate had always wanted to be? I knew in my heart that she had a special feeling for Bruno. He had dominated our childhood. That aloofness, that difference which his origins had created made him stand apart from all others so that he had that indefinable quality, a near divinity; and in our hearts perhaps neither of us was sure whether there had in truth been a miracle in the Christmas crib on that long-ago Christmas morning.

I understood her so well, my worldly Kate; and I loved her none the less for this. I knew her strength and her weakness and both were great. We had been rivals for Bruno. I had known that all the time even when we were children playing on the grass of the forbidden territory.

What was she feeling now? I know she compared the Abbey

with Remus Castle: was she comparing my husband with hers?

In the scriptorium when they came face to face, Kate was like a flower when the sun comes out after rain. Her eyes shone and her cheeks glowed like my mother's damask roses so that I felt like a country wench beside a Court beauty.

"We have been admiring your Abbey," she told him.

He too had changed. I saw the gleam in his eyes. Pride in his Abbey—and more than that an immense satisfaction because Kate could be shown what he possessed.

"And what do you think of it?" he said.

"Magnificent. So you have become a landowner! And such land. Who would have thought it possible? It is a miracle."

"A miracle," he repeated. "And you are well, Kate?"

"I am well, Bruno."

He had scarcely glanced at me. He had indeed changed toward me since the coming of Honey. Kate, as she always had, dominated the scene. A vivid memory came to me of her turning somersaults on the Abbey grass diverting his attention from me to herself. It was rather like that now. She was trying to hold him with her glowing beauty; it was as though she were saying: Compare me with your plain little Damask.

"So you are visiting us. . . ."

"I have come for the christening of the Caseman babies and to see Damask and *you*. . . ." She lingered on the last word.

"And you have found many changes?"

"What changes in the Abbey! They are talking of nothing else throughout the countryside."

"So you came to see for yourself. And how do you find it?"

"Even more wonderful than I had thought to."

She was looking at him eagerly, calling attention to herself. I knew her well. She had no scruples.

How affected was he? What was he remembering?

"My son is not with me," she said. "But one day I will bring him to show him to you."

"I shall want to see him," he said.

I put in: "We will choose a time when Bruno has the time to spare."

"Tomorrow I must come again," said Kate. "My stay here may

not be of long duration and there is so much we have to talk about. I want to hear your plans for this wonderful place. Damask has been showing me. I had no idea that there was so much . . . only having seen it from the gatehouse and as tall gray walls, and of course what I saw when I came through the ivy-covered door."

He was watching her intently. I wondered what he was thinking.

We returned to the Abbot's Lodging and all the time he talked to her earnestly of the great plans he had for the Abbey.

"There will not be a larger estate for miles round," he said with pride. "Once it is in order, once the farms are producing . . . you will see."

"Oh, yes," said Kate, "I shall see. And deeply shall I envy you from my castle keep."

The next day the twins were christened in the chapel at Caseman Court. I had never seen my mother so happy. Simon Caseman was a proud father too.

The boys were named Peter and Paul, and Paul bawled lustily throughout the proceedings, a fact which made my mother delight in his show of manhood while at the same time Peter's docility showed her what a good child he was.

The following day Kate again visited the Abbey. We went to the solarium and indulged in her favorite occupation of gossiping.

Remus, it seemed, had taken on a new lease of life since his marriage and the birth of his son. She seemed a little rueful about this which I found shocking. She laughed at me.

"Rich widows," she said, "are *so* attractive."

"Is it your next ambition to become one?"

"Hush. Why, if Remus died in his sleep from an overdose of poppy juice I should be suspected of having administered it."

"Don't talk of such things even in a jest."

"Still the same old Damask. Afraid. Always looking over your shoulder for the informer."

"There have been informers in my life once. They shattered it."

She laid her hand over mine. "My poor poor Damask. How well I know! Your good faithful heart was broken for a time. How glad I am that it has healed! And now you are so lucky. . . . I

am sorry I recalled that sad time. And I did not mean to suggest
that I would be rid of Remus. He is a good husband and it is sometimes better to have an aging one than a young one. He is so grateful, poor Remus; and I verily believe that if I were to take it into
my head to adventure a little—he would not take it amiss."

"I hope you do not . . . adventure . . . as you call it."

"That is a matter on which I propose to keep you in doubt. And
I do not see why if Remus were ready to turn a blind eye you
should show a censorious one. But talking of wayward wives,
I must tell you the latest Court scandal. It concerns the Queen.
Are you listening?"

"I am all ears."

"I fear our dear little Queen may well be in trouble. Cruel men
and women are closing in on her and she, poor soul, is in no position to oppose them."

"This marriage surely is a happy one."

"It was. How amusing to see the King's Majesty in the role of
uxorious husband. She is such a charming little creature. By no
means beautiful. Though the cousin of Anne Boleyn, she is completely without elegance. Poor little Katharine Howard. She reminds me of Keziah in a way. She is the sort who could never say
no to a man and it seems that she has said yes very frequently."

"Tell me what has happened. I have heard nothing."

"You soon will for I believe all that her enemies would wish has
been proved against the Queen."

"The poor child," I murmured. "For she is little more."

"She is a little older than you and a little younger than I, which
I am ready to agree is young to leave this life."

"It has not come to that."

"If all that is rumored is proved against her she may well be
walking out to Tower Hill as her fascinating cousin did some six
years ago."

"Can the King have had so many wives in such a short time?"

"Indeed he can. Was there not sly Jane to follow Anne who
followed Spanish Katharine? Of course his marriage to her lasted
twenty years and for all that time he remained married to one
wife; and then Anne of Cleves who was not at all to his liking.

She was the fortunate one. She now enjoys life mightily at Richmond, I believe; and now pretty little Katharine Howard."

"With whom he is so happy."

"With whom he *was* happy. Poor Katharine, rumor has it that she learned a loose way of life in the dormitory she shared with the other girls of her grandmother's household—some lowborn and little more than servants—and that as young as thirteen she had taken a lover. These unscrupulous women found the corrupting of this nobly born young girl's morals an amusing occupation. It is said that young Katharine had soon formed an immoral association with a musician and that was but a beginning. Afterward she went through a form of marriage with a young man named Francis Dereham. Thus she was no virgin when she married the King although I'll swear she professed to be."

"Her grandmother is surely the Dowager Duchess of Norfolk?"

"Of a surety she is, and little care she took of her fascinating granddaughter. Poor Katharine! Daughter of a younger son, she was of little account until the King singled her out for notice. Then my Lord Norfolk begins to appreciate his niece, just as he did with that other niece, Anne Boleyn. But you remember how he deserted her when she needed support. I'll swear the fellow is now preparing to desert Katharine."

"Is Katharine in danger?"

"Unlike Anne, she is really a little fool, Damask. Oh, how differently I should have managed my affairs had I been in her place!"

"Queen Anne could not have managed her affairs with any great skill for they led her to Tower Hill and the executioner's sword."

"True enough," admitted Kate. "But this is different. Anne could not get a boy and the King was obsessed with the need for a boy."

I thought of Bruno then. I believed he was obsessed by the desire for a boy. At least, I thought ironically, he could not cut off my head if I failed to provide one.

"He was also enamored of Jane Seymour," went on Kate. "This is why Anne lost her head—through circumstances outside her control. It is not quite the same with Queen Katharine Howard. She was loose in her morals, they say; she had several lovers and allowed this to be known by the unscrupulous people of her grandmother's household. I am told that several of them acquired places in her Court because they asked for them with veiled threats and she was perforce obliged to give them to them."

"And all this has been brought to the King's ears? I was of the opinion that he loved her dearly and if this is so surely he will forgive what she did before he married her."

"You live in a backwater, Damask. You do not know what goes on. Do you not realize that this country is split by a great religious conflict? Have you ever heard of a man called Martin Luther?"

"Of course I have," I said hotly. "I fancy that my father and I have had more discourse on theology in one week than you ever had in your life. And Bruno and I talk of these matters too."

"I know your discourse. You would argue the rights and wrongs. I mean not that. This is politics. There is fast growing in this country two great parties—those who support the Catholic Church and those who would reform it. Did you know that Anne Boleyn was growing very interested in the reformed ideas? This brought her many enemies from the Catholic side. Of course, they had always detested her because of the divorce. How big a part they played in bringing about her downfall we shall not know, but depend upon it they played a part. Now our little Queen Katharine cares not for religion. She merely wishes to be happy and gay and to keep her royal husband so. But she comes from the Norfolk family—the Duke, her uncle, is a leader of the Catholic party. Cannot you see that those of Reformed party are determined to bring her down? She would not dabble in politics. She would not understand what it is all about. So . . . they will delve into her past; they will discover that she has lain carnally with several men and may have called herself married to one of them. We are going to see fearful happenings at Court. You may depend upon it, Damask."

"We must pray for her."

"Forget not that the Reformed party prays for her destruction. So many prayers coming from Catholics! So many from those who wish for reforms. And all to the same God. How can they all be answered, Damask?"

I said: "I shall pray for the Queen, not for any form of religion.

She is only about our age, Kate. It is tragic. Is she going to lose her head?"

"The Reformed party is beside itself with anxiety. It fears she may not, for the King dotes so much upon her."

"If this is true the King will never let her go."

"I am told that that is what she believes. But she has some powerful minds against her. Archbishop Cranmer has examined her, they say, and methinks he will not be a very good friend to her."

After that conversation I could not get the poor little Queen out of my mind. I pictured her agony as she recalled the fate of her cousin Anne Boleyn, and she would lack the reasoning and mental powers of that Queen. Poor uneducated little Katharine Howard, who had had the misfortune to be attractive enough to catch the King's fancy!

Then I ceased to think of her because the miraculous event had come to pass. Before Kate left us to return to Remus Castle I knew that I was with child.

When I told Bruno he was overcome by joy. The difference which had arisen between us over the arrival of Honey was swept away. This was what he had longed for. A child—a son of his own.

This paternal pride was indeed a human quality, and it delighted me. And what pleasure we had in talking of the child we would have.

At this time I was able to bring Honey into our little circle. He rarely spoke to her and his indifference was hurtful, but at least she was allowed to be in our company. She accepted that and if he ignored her she did the same to him; but I was pleased that she no longer seemed afraid of him, and she did not cower close to me when he was present.

We had added to our household considerably; during the weeks after Kate's departure several men arrived at the Abbey to offer their services for the great amount of work that would in due course have to be done out of doors. I had engaged new servants. I had a housekeeper now, a Mrs. Crimp, who, I was delighted to say, took a great interest in Honey.

I had a suspicion that some of the men who presented themselves for work were familiar with the Abbey and had worked there before. Some of them might have been lay brothers. There was danger in this but to be in Bruno's presence was to share to a certain extent his confidence in himself; and the fact was I was obsessed by the thought of my child and longing for its arrival.

For Honey I had a deep protective love but I knew that nothing could compare with the emotion which my own child would arouse in me.

I was shut in a little world of my own. Vaguely I listened to the news from Court. Those men who had been the Queen's lovers in the past were being questioned in the Tower. Sometimes, when on the river, I would look at the gray fortress and a brief vision of bloodstained torture chambers would flash into my mind. In the past I would perhaps have brooded on that, recalling my father's sojourn in that dreaded place. But always the exaltation engendered by the presence of the child would overcome all other feelings.

I used to say to myself: But the King loves her. He does not wish to be rid of her. He will not let her die.

Travelers called at the Abbey for one of the guesthouses had been thrown open as it had been in the old days. They told stories of the King's great distress when he had heard of the scandals about his wife. It was particularly hard to bear because immediately before the news had been broken to him he had told his confessor, the Bishop of Lincoln, that he was so delighted to have found matrimonial bliss at last that he wished him to arrange a thanksgiving to God for giving him such a loving and virtuous Queen.

We heard also that when the poor little Queen was told of what she had been accused her fears sent her into a frenzy, and knowing that the King was at prayers in the little chapel at the end of the long gallery in Hampton Court she had run down this, screaming hysterically while her attendants who had been ordered to keep her under restraint captured her and forced her to return to her apartments.

A brooding sense of disaster was in the air. The King was all powerful. He stood between the two factions—Papists and anti-Papists—and in his eyes they could both be traitors, because those who did not accept the religion set out by him were enemies who should be punished by death. He made it clear that nothing was changed, but the head of the Church—the King instead of the Pope. He hated the Pope no less than he hated Martin Luther.

But for me there was nothing of any great importance but the gestation of my child. I shut my eyes to the fact that the atmosphere in the Abbey was changing each day, and that since I had become pregnant I was treated with the awed respect which I had noticed was accorded to Bruno.

When my mother heard of my condition she was overjoyed. She came to the Abbey bringing herbs and some of her concoctions. I would visit her and we talked together as women do. We were closer now than we had ever been.

I admired the twins—Peter and Paul—two well-formed, lusty little boys. She doted on them, and could scarcely bear them out of her sight. They had even lured her from her garden. Constantly she discussed their tempers, their intelligence and their beauty. She refused to swaddle them because they protested lustily when she did so and she liked to see them kick their little limbs.

I began to enjoy our chats. She had so much advice to offer and I knew that it was good. The midwife who had attended her she fancied was the best in the neighborhood and she was going to insist that she attended me when my time came.

She made little garments for my baby when I knew she would rather have been stitching for her adored twins.

I took to visiting her often for we had become not so much mother and daughter but two women discussing the subject nearest to our hearts. She confided to me that she hoped to have more children but even if she did not she considered herself singularly blessed to have had her two little boys and both healthy.

One day though a tinge of alarm touched me.

I was in her sewing room when beneath the material on which she was working I discovered a book. It was so unlike my mother to read anything that I was surprised and even more so when I picked it up. I opened it and glanced through it and as I did so I felt my heart begin to beat very quickly. There clearly enough were set out the arguments and the tenets of the new religion. I hastily shut the book as my mother approached but I could not forget it.

At length I said: "Mother, what is this book you are reading?"

"Oh," she said with a grimace, "it is very dull, but I am struggling through it to please your stepfather."

"He wishes you to read it?"

"He insists."

"Mother, I do not think you should leave such a book where any might pick it up."

"Why should I not? It is but a book."

"It is what it contains. It is a plea for the reformed religion."

"Oh, is it?" she said.

"To please me be more careful."

She patted my hand. "You are just like your father," she said. "You are one to make something from nothing. Now look at this. Already Master Paul is growing out of it. The rate that child grows astonishes me!"

I was thinking: So Simon Caseman is dabbling with the reformed religion!

I thought of the Abbey where a community life alarmingly similar to the old was gradually, perhaps subtly, but certainly being built up.

It occurred to me then that Simon Caseman, for harboring such a book in his house, and Bruno, for installing monks in his newly acquired Abbey, could both be deemed traitors.

A short while ago I would have gone home and argued the matter with Bruno. I might even have gone so far as to caution Simon Caseman, but strangely enough the matters seemed of secondary importance for I had just begun to feel the movement of my child and I forgot all else.

I was like my mother, shut into a little world in which the miracle of creation absorbed me.

Perhaps all pregnant women are so.

Christmas was almost upon us and I had decorated Honey's little room with holly and ivy and told her the Christmas story.

In those December days preceding Christmas there had been a great deal of talk about the King's matter. Even my mother mentioned it. There was great sympathy for the Queen who it was said was in a state of hysteria and had been ever since her accusation. Many believed that this was an implication of her guilt.

"And if she had taken a lover, poor soul," I said to my mother as we sat over our sewing, "is that so very wrong?"

"Outside the bonds of matrimony!" cried my mother, aghast.

"She believed herself married to Dereham."

"Then she deserves death for marrying the King."

"Life is cruel for a woman," I said.

My mother pursed her lips virtuously. "Not if she is a dutiful wife."

"Poor little Katharine Howard! She is so young to die."

But my mother was not really moved by the young girl's fate. It occurred to me that in a world where death came frequently the value of life was not really great.

It was just before Christmas that Francis Dereham and Thomas Culpepper were executed. Culpepper was beheaded but Dereham, because he was not of noble birth, suffered the barbarous hanging and quartering, the traitor's death.

I thought of them all that day—poor young men, whose crime had been to love the Queen.

At that time we thought these deaths would be enough and that the King so loved Katharine Howard that we were sure he would pardon her. Alas it was not to be so. The Queen had too many enemies. As a Howard she was a Catholic and many of the King's ministers did not wish to see a Catholic influence on the King.

Her fate was sealed when the King's ministers, before he could prevent them, circulated the story of her misconduct abroad and after this the King's own honor being involved he could scarcely with dignity take her back.

François Premier sent condolences. He was shocked by the "great displeasures, troubles and inquietations which his good brother had recently had by the naughty demeanor of her, lately reputed for Queen."

Distressed, wounded and humiliated (this last a state calculated to arouse his anger against the cause of it) the King did not intervene to save Katharine and on a bleak February day the

King's fifth wife walked out to Tower Hill where but six years before her cousin Anne Boleyn had met a similar fate.

A hush was on the land on that terrible day. Five Queens—two divorced, one died in childbirth (and who knew what her fate would have been had she lived?) and two beheaded.

The people were beginning to wonder what monster this was who sat on their throne; and when they saw him, as they did occasionally on public occasions, and in place of the handsome golden boy who thirty years before had been romantically in love with his Spanish wife, was a portly bloated figure—purple of complexion, tight-mouthed, eyes peering through slits in that unsightly countenance, a suppurating ulcer on his leg, they lowered their eyes but they dared do no other than shout "Long live the King."

They remembered that whatever else he was, he was their all-powerful ruler.

My baby was due in June. The larger I grew the more impatient I became. One of the men who had come to the Abbey and who I suspected used to help Brother Ambrose in the old days had made a little garden for me at the back of the Abbot's Lodging. My mother had advised and sent me plants and I grew quite fond of it. Here I would sit with my sewing and watch Honey at play. Now over two years old, she was a lively child; I had told her that she would soon have a companion and she used to ask every day how much longer it would be before it arrived.

My mother had advice to offer every time we met. She had become a frequent visitor to the Abbey. I wondered whether she would notice that some of the workers were onetime monks, and mention this to Simon. I remembered the book I had seen in my mother's room. If Simon was flirting with the new religion he might do us some harm. Besides, I had a feeling that he would not forgive me for refusing him and for taking the Abbey and Bruno. But as he too was acting outside the King's law, he would have to walk very warily himself.

My mother, however, noticed nothing strange; she would only comment on the manner in which I was carrying the child and impress upon me that the moment I felt the first signs I was to send a messenger to Caseman Court. She would at once send for the midwife and come herself. That was only if we should have miscalculated the time. If we had been right then the midwife would be in residence days before the expected event.

It was April—two months before my child was due—when I became aware of a change in Bruno. He was often absentminded. Sometimes when I spoke to him he did not answer.

I said to him: "Bruno, all this rebuilding must be very costly. Are you perchance anxious about the expense?"

He looked at me in a startled fashion.

"What gave you that notion?"

"You seem preoccupied."

He frowned. "Mayhap I am anxious about you."

"About me? But I am well."

"Having a child is a trying time."

"You must not fear. Everything will be all right."

"I shall be glad when our son is born."

"I'm afraid when you say 'our son' in that way. What if we should have a daughter?"

"My firstborn must be a son," he said, and what I thought of as his prophet's face was very apparent. "It will be so," he continued firmly.

He convinced me then, as he could at times, that he had special powers.

I smiled complacently. Son or daughter I should love either. But if Bruno cared so intensely that it should be a son then I hoped so too.

"I am glad there is no need to worry about money. You must be exceedingly rich. I know this place cannot be producing much so far."

"I beg you, Damask, leave these matters to me."

"I would not have you worried. Mayhap we could postpone some of this building until the farm and the mill begin to show a profit."

He laughed and the fanatical gleam was in his eyes.

"Doubt not that *I* can do all that I set out to do."

He came over to me and kissed my brow.

"As for you, Damask, all I ask of you is to give me my son."

"It cannot be too soon for me," I assured him.

It was a few nights later. I awoke suddenly and found that Bruno was not beside me.

It was well past midnight and I wondered whether he had gone over to the scriptorium. He was often there with Valerian and it occurred to me that he might be going over accounts. Deep in my mind the thought persisted that he was concerned about money.

I rose from my bed and went quietly into Honey's room; she was sleeping peacefully. Then I went to the bedchamber I shared with Bruno and going to the window looked out. There was no light in the scriptorium, so Bruno could not be there.

I sat down on the window seat looking out at those buildings—the cloisters, the gray walls, all that I could see of the Abbey. I wondered whether the old Abbot had ever sat on this very window seat, sleepless perhaps, looking out on his domain. I looked across to the tall tower of the Abbey church and beyond it I could see the first of the fishponds; moonlight touched its waters with a silver light.

My child moved within me and happily I placed my hand reassuringly on it.

"Soon now, my little one," I murmured, "and never was a child awaited with such joy."

I was dreaming of my child though I refused to think of it as a boy; although I knew that Bruno did and so did others in the Abbey. There was no one in this place who did not await with awe and reverence the birth of my child. I could well understand how Queen Anne Boleyn had felt when she was with child. It had been so important for her to produce a boy. I wondered what her feelings had been when the Lady Elizabeth was born. And later when she had given birth to a stillborn boy!

My thoughts were interrupted suddenly for clearly in the moonlight I saw a figure gliding across the sward. I thought at first it was the ghost for the figure was wearing the robes of a monk of St. Bruno's and over his head was a cowl which concealed his face. This was the ghost I had seen when I visited my father's grave.

I stood up, my hands on my body as though to calm the child.

The figure was coming from the direction of the tunnels and making its way toward the scriptorium.

It turned suddenly and looked toward the monks' dorter and as it did so, the cowl fell back from his head and I saw that it was Bruno.

He hastily pulled up the cowl and went toward the scriptorium; later I saw the light of a lantern there.

I went back to bed. I was puzzled. I could understand his going to the scriptorium in the night if some detail had occurred to him, but from whence had he come and why should he have worn the garb of a monk? I felt certain then that the ghost who had reputedly haunted the Abbey was Bruno.

I went back to bed and lay there pondering. I must have slept for when I awoke it was time almost for rising and Bruno was beside me.

I made a sudden decision to say nothing of the matter and this decision in itself was an indication of the changing relationship between us.

It was less than a week later when Bruno came into my sitting room where I was reading to Honey and said he had something to say to me.

He said: "Damask, I have to go away for a short while."

"Away?" I cried. "But where?"

"It is necessary for me to travel to the Continent."

"For what purpose?"

A faint irritation crossed his features. "A matter of business."

"Abbey business?"

He said patiently: "You will realize that the development of these Abbey lands goes on apace."

"I notice," I replied, "that it grows more like the old community every day."

"What can you know of the old community, Damask? You were never here. You saw everything from the outside."

"There are several of the old monks here," I said, "and they regard you as their Abbot."

"They look on me as their master, which I am. I have given these men work as I might give work to any laborers."

"The difference being that they have worked here before. They have tilled the soil and baked the bread and caught the fish . . . and lived the life of solitude. What is the difference in what they were doing now and doing then?"

"A great difference," said Bruno, a trifle impatiently. "Then this was a monastic order—something of which you are entirely ignorant. Now it is a manor house. It happens to have features of a monastery because it was once an abbey. I do beg of you not to interfere in what does not concern you."

"I must always speak what is in my mind and always shall." I was getting excited and feared it would be bad for the child, so I went on meekly: "You were telling me that you were going abroad."

"Yes, I am not sure how long I shall be away. It may be several weeks, maybe longer."

"Where are you going, Bruno?"

"To France . . . to the Low Countries perhaps. You have nothing to fear. You will be well looked after here."

"I am not afraid for myself," I said. "There is no question of that. Why are you going?"

"There are business matters to which I have to attend."

"Abbey business?"

He was clearly impatient with my persistence. "My dear Damask, this is a costly enterprise. If we are to continue we must make it a profitable one. There are certain edible roots which are commonly used on the Continent and very palatable they are and good to eat. I am going to learn of these. There are carrots and turnips which have not been grown in this country. I wish to learn of how to produce them and perhaps to bring some back with me. Hops for making beer are grown a great deal in Holland. To discover such matters it is necessary for me to go and see for myself."

It seemed reasonable, but I thought of his prowling about at night and I wondered why he had thought it advisable to wear a monk's robes. He must have been impersonating a ghost. It could only mean that if he were seen not only did he not wish to be recognized but he wanted anyone who saw him to be afraid.

It was mysterious. If Honey had not been there I should have been unable to restrain my curiosity and asked for an explanation. But this was not the moment.

Later I considered it again. The more I knew of Bruno, the more I realized I did not know. There were times when he was like a stranger to me. He showed so clearly that he resented my curiosity, and the relationship between us was changing quickly.

In a few days he had left.

One day during Bruno's absence, Rupert came riding over to the Abbey. I called a groom to take his horse and then conducted him to the solar and sent for wine. Honey came in and Rupert picked her up and swung her in his arms. There was immediate friendship between them.

"Is everything well?" he asked me anxiously.

I told him I was very well. He savored Eugene's wine and said it was good.

I told him Eugene had come to us when he left Caseman Court.

"Why, it is as though the Abbey is reborn," he commented.

"It is very different," I contradicted quickly. "This is merely a manor house, but as we have so many buildings and the land so we must needs make use of them. We plan to develop the farm. Indeed we must for it is necessary for us to make the place profitable."

Rupert said he would like to ride around our farmlands before he left and I said I would accompany him.

I asked how he was faring and he told me he was pleased with his land. He had a pleasant though small manor house and his benevolent brother-in-law had given him the place, which was very likely due to the importuning of Kate.

"It is of course not as grand as Remus Castle nor St. Bruno's Abbey, but it serves me well."

He looked at me wistfully and I said briskly: "Rupert, you should take a wife."

"I am in no mind to," he answered.

"Do you have good servants?"

"Indeed, yes. They serve me well."

"Then perhaps the need is not so urgent. But you would like to have children. You would make a good father . . . and a good husband too I doubt not."

"I think," he answered looking at me steadily, "that I shall remain a bachelor all the days of my life."

I could not meet his eye then. I knew that he was telling me that since I had declined to take him no one else would do.

He will change, I promised myself. When he grows older he will marry. I wanted him to, because I was fond of him and when I contemplated the joys of having children I wanted him to know that too.

After he had eaten of Clement's tansy cake I mounted my horse and together we rode out to the farmlands. He examined them carefully. Abbey land was invariably good land, he said. We would have a very prosperous farm there in a few years.

I had told him that Bruno was on the Continent studying the new edible roots which were being brought into England. He knew of them and said that he hoped to grow them too. The English were now delighted in what was known as the salad and which had been popular on the Continent for some years. Queen Katharine of Aragon had been very partial to a salad, but she had always had to send to Holland for it. Now we should grow them here and if the King's next Queen fancied a salad she could have one from an English garden.

When it was clear that we could not possibly be overheard he brought his horse close to mine and said quietly: "I have been a little concerned, Damask."

"Why so?" I asked.

"It was something Simon Caseman said."

"I have always distrusted that man. What did he say?"

"He referred to your husband as the Abbot and said that there was little difference in the Abbey as it is now and as it was ten years ago."

"What did he mean by that?"

"I understand that several of the monks have returned."

"They work on the farm at the mill and about the place."

"It could be dangerous, Damask."

"We are doing nothing against the law."

"I am sure you are not, but there are these rumors because sev-

eral of the monks who were here have come back and are working as before."

"But we are doing nothing wrong," I insisted.

"You must not only keep within the King's law but *appear* to
do so. I do not like it that Simon Caseman should be talking."

"He is malicious because he wanted the Abbey for himself."

"Damask, if you should need me at any time, you know I shall
be there."

"Thank you, Rupert. You have always been good to me."

After he had gone I continued to think of him. If I could have
loved him instead of Bruno, life would have been less compli-
cated. But one cannot love where it would be wise to do so, for
love and wisdom do not go hand in hand.

I had no regrets, I assured myself. But I liked to remember that
Rupert was my staunch friend.

At last the month of June was with us. Bruno had recently returned from the Continent. He had little to say about his visit
and I found myself scarcely curious because the baby's arrival was
imminent.

My mother came almost every day. When she had satisfied herself that my condition could give no cause for alarm she turned
her attention to the state of the little garden James had made for
me. James was a man of about thirty. Whether he had been a
monk, or a lay brother, I had never asked. I felt it was wiser to
know nothing. In any case his knowledge of plants was good and
my roses almost rivaled those of my mother.

She and I sat there and talked of babies; she recalled some of
the mannerisms I had shown in my infancy but her talk was chiefly
of Paul and Peter. She was knotting a shawl for my baby as she
talked and her fingers moved busily. It occurred to me that she
was a great deal more content than she used to be in the old days
and I marveled at this. It seemed strange that anyone could find
Simon Caseman a more satisfactory husband than my father, but
that was what she appeared to have done.

She was telling me that she had been to see the midwife who
assured her that everything concerning me appeared to be going

well and a normal birth was expected. She had arranged that as soon as my first pains started she was to be sent for.

I felt a sudden rush of affection for her.

"I never really knew how much you cared for me," I said.

She turned quite pink and said: "Nonsense! Were you not my own child?"

Then I fell to musing that what had been the great tragedy of my youth had to her in a way been an escape, and how strange life was when nothing seemed to be wholly bad, nothing wholly good.

A few days later my pains did start, but by that time, due to my mother's care, the midwife was already installed at the Abbey.

My labor was not prolonged and for me the joy of knowing that my baby would soon be in my arms exceeded any discomfort. It was necessarily an agonizing experience but I had so longed for my baby that I could endure it as I suppose martyrs do torture and death.

At last it was over and when I heard the cry of my child my heart leaped with joy.

I saw my mother—for once authoritative—and the midwife and Bruno.

"My baby . . . ," I began.

My mother was beaming. "A beautiful healthy baby."

I held out my arms.

"Later, Damask. In a very short time you shall see your lovely little girl."

A girl! I felt the tears in my eyes. I believed then that I had wanted a girl.

I noticed Bruno then. He had not spoken. He would want to see his daughter.

But there was the child; they laid her in my arms and I thought: "This is the happiest moment of my life."

I had known that Bruno had been convinced that the child would be a boy but I had not thought he could be so bitterly disappointed.

He scarcely looked at the child. As for myself, I could not bear her out of my sight. During those first nights I would sometimes awake from a hazy dream in which she was no longer with me. I would leap up calling for the nurse. "My baby. Where is my baby?"

I would have to be assured that she was sleeping peacefully in her cot.

The christening ceremony was simple—not the solemn occasion which would have been accorded to a boy. Bruno seemed scarcely interested. He was still nursing his disappointment in the child's sex.

I thought: I will make up for his indifference, my darling child. I shall love you so much that you will miss nothing.

She was named Catherine—a version of Kate's name and that of the two Queens. I called her my little Cat. She was an ugly baby, said the midwife, and whispered the consolation that it was always those who were born ugly who became the real beauties.

I was sure she was right for my little Cat grew prettier every day.

The Passing of an Age

All through that year I was so absorbed with my child that I gave
little thought to what was going on in the Abbey. There were great
changes of course and this was Bruno's first harvest. Activity was
everywhere. From the old barns came the sound of the threshing.
Some of the animals had to be slaughtered that November and
salted to provide food for the winter. I was but vaguely aware of
all this because my entire thoughts were concentrated on my
baby. If she sneezed I would send for my mother and she would
come with many possets and lotions; and she would reassure
me with her laughter, telling me that she had been the same when
I was a baby.

"All these anxieties come with the first," she told me. "Wait
until you have your second. You will not be half as fearful."

My baby flourished. She was the joy of my life. I marveled at
her tiny hands and feet; her eyes were blue and wondering; when
she first smiled at me my heart filled with an overflowing love
and I cared for nothing that had gone before since it had brought
me my child.

The world outside began to intrude on the little paradise I
shared with my baby.

There was a letter from Kate.

"I am coming to see you. I must have a glimpse of my . . . what is
she? Cousin of some sort, I suppose."

I smiled. How typical of Kate to think of the child's connection
with her!

"According to you she is the most wonderful child who ever existed but a mother's testimonial is rarely accurate. So I must come and see this model of perfection for myself. Remus is going to Scotland on the King's business. So while he is away, why should I not visit St. Bruno's Abbey?"

I was delighted as always at the prospect of seeing Kate, but a little uneasy for she had a penetrating eye and she was particularly interested in the relationship between Bruno and myself, which had not grown closer since Catherine's birth. Moreover I was perfectly content with my child.

Kate arrived in due course, full of vitality and as beautiful as ever.

"How convenient that we should not be too far away!" she announced. "What if I had married a Scottish lord? It would not have been so easy for us to meet." She scrutinized me. "Damask! The Mother! It suits you, Damask. You are more plump. Quite the matron. No, scarcely that. But different. And where is this paragon who is named after me?"

"I call her my little Cat," I said fondly.

She admired the baby. "Yes, a little beauty. Well, Cat, what do you think of Cousin Kate?"

My baby gave Kate that beautiful smile and Kate bent over and kissed her.

"There, sweetheart," she said, "we are to be good friends."

I could see that she was not so much interested in the child as intensely curious about the state of affairs between Bruno and myself. She talked openly about Remus. She was patronizing in a tolerant way, but she was certainly grateful for the life of luxury which she owed to him.

Carey came with her—a lovely boy nearly two years old, curious, mischievous and with a look of Kate.

He was interested in little Cat and would stand by her cot gazing at her. She liked him too, it seemed. And there was of course Honey whom I had been particularly careful not to neglect since the arrival of my baby. I wanted them to grow up as sisters but I suppose it was inevitable that she should be a little jealous, for try as I might I could not entirely hide my absorption with my own child.

I washed and fed Catherine myself but I would make sure to always have Honey by to help. "She is only little, Honey," I would say. "Not a big girl like you. She has much to learn."

That cheered her a little.

"She is your little sister," I said; and I thought then that if Keziah's story was true Honey was in fact my baby's aunt.

But now Kate was with us and life naturally changed. She was curious about everything that was going on in the Abbey. She watched it with a sort of envy which told me that she was imagining herself here in my place.

When Bruno joined us I was aware of her feelings for him. His feelings for her were more guarded, but I knew that he was not indifferent to her.

She was of course knowledgeable about what was going on at Court and loved to show off her superiority in that respect.

The King was looking for a new wife.

"Poor man, he is so unlucky with his wives! And now no woman is very anxious for the greatest honor in the land. Girls tremble when the King casts a lascivious eye in their direction. They are inclined to say Anne Boleyn's famous remark in reverse as it were, 'Nay, Sire, your wife I cannot be. I would liefer be your mistress.'"

"I pity the poor woman he chooses next," I said.

"She will be a woman who has married before, you may be sure of it. This new statute would terrify an unmarried girl. You know it has now been declared high treason for anyone not a virgin to marry the King. Parents are afraid to send their young daughters to Court."

"Perhaps he will not marry at all for he is no longer young."

"He is nearly fifty years of age, and overweight. He has an ulcer on his leg which is quite offensive. But he is a King withal and his courtiers wait upon his smiles and scurry from his frowns. So he has great attraction left."

"Is power more important than handsome looks and youth?" I asked.

"Power is the very essence of masculine charm, I do assure you.

I could never love the most beautiful cowherd in the world but I might easily feel affection for an aging King."

"How cynical you have become!"

"I have not become so. Come now, you know I have always been so."

"Well, pray do not cast your eyes upon the King for strange as it may seem I should suffer a pang or two of sorrow if your head was severed from your shoulders."

"It has always been firmly planted thereon and there I intend it to remain. My dear cousin, what pleasure it gives me to be with you! Forget you not that I am married to Remus and unless he meets a gory end in Scotland, which is not unlikely since he carries arms there for the King and the battles have been fierce, I am in no position to take another husband."

"Oh, Kate, do not talk so!"

"You are still the same sentimental Damask. Nay, have no fear for me. I shall know how to take care of myself if I should become a widow."

"I had no idea that it was in order to fight that Lord Remus was in Scotland."

"The young mother sees not beyond her nest. Did you not know that our King, having lost his wife to the executioner's ax, has turned his attention—temporarily—to other matters? He wished to be proclaimed King of Scotland. So, Remus in the company of His Grace of Norfolk has now marched over the border. I hear that the Scots have been thoroughly routed and I do believe that His Majesty the King is preparing to join his forces there. So you see, my Remus, between His Grace of Norfolk—uncle of two Queens—and the King himself, will be in the best of company. As I am, for I do declare, my sweet Damask, that little gives me as much pleasure as my discourse with you."

And so we talked of matters at Court and we went over the past and recalled incidents from our childhood as one does with those who have shared it.

She was very content to leave Carey with the children and I saw less of my little daughter during Kate's stay than I had since her birth. But much as I enjoyed Kate's company I longed to assure myself continually that my child was not in some danger.

Kate might laugh at me as my mother did but I could not help this. The child was dearer to me than anything on earth.

We dined at eleven in the morning and supped at six o'clock. Meals were taken in the big hall and all came to table. It meant very little opportunity of intimate conversation. I sat on one side of Bruno, Kate on the other and often I would catch her eyes sparkling with a mischief of which I could not quite understand. I could not discover their feelings toward each other. Kate's was light and bantering; he was inclined to be quiet, but he was watchful of her, I know.

Clement excelled himself during Kate's visit. There were big joints of beef and mutton succulently cooked; there were enormous pies and he often decorated these with the Remus coat of arms in honor of Kate. There was bacon, fowls, butter and cheese in plenty. And Bruno was anxious for us to try the carrots and turnips which he had recently brought in and which were fast becoming very popular.

There was often talk about the work of the farm and those whose duty it was to fish and prepare what they caught for our table or to sell it would talk of the day's catch in their places below the salt cellar.

Kate listened attentively and occasionally she would banter with Bruno or with me.

The children did not join us, none of them being old enough.

Sometimes when I was in my nursery Kate would wander around the Abbey grounds.

Once she came back and said: "Damask, what is happening here? This is becoming more like a monastery and Bruno is like the King of his domain. I doubt there is another such community in England at this time. What do you know of Bruno?"

"I don't understand you, Kate."

"You should know him. He is your husband."

"Of course I know him." Even as I spoke I knew I lied.

"What is he like . . . as a husband?"

"He is a busy man. There is much to do."

"Is he affectionate, kind, Damask? How passionately does he love you?"

"You are too full of questions."

"I want to know, Damask. He wanted a son, did he not? How was he when he found he had a daughter?" She laughed almost triumphantly and I hated her in that moment because I felt she was pleased because I had had a daughter and not the son for which Bruno longed.

"He wanted a son. True he wanted a son. What man does not? He was a little disappointed."

"Only a little? Parents are generally pleased with what they get. Not Kings though . . . and those who are Kings. Poor Anne Boleyn! She lost her head because she could not give the King a son."

"She lost her head because the King preferred another woman."

"If she had had a son he would never have rid himself of her. Sly little Jane and her ambitious uncles would have to have been content for her to hold sway as mistress instead of wife. Still, it is a lesson, is it not? It is dangerous to sport with Princes."

Later she talked of the days when we had discovered Bruno and all met together in the Abbey grounds.

"Everything that happens to us has its effect," said Kate. "What we are today is due to what happened to us then. We three started weaving a pattern. We shall go on with it for the rest of our lives."

"You mean Bruno, you and me?"

"You know very well I mean just that. We shall always be involved with each other. We will be like fruit on a tree . . . first the buds, then the fruit and when our time comes we shall drop off one by one. But we shall always be on the same branch, Damask. Remember that."

I did remember it after she had gone, and I wondered what she and Bruno said to each other when they met and I was not present. I wondered what passed between them.

But it did not seem of any great importance. I was absorbed by my child.

That December the King marched up to Scotland and defeated the Scots at Solway Moss. We did not talk very much about the war. Scotland seemed far away. But for his services to the Crown the King presented Lord Remus with an estate on the border with the result that he remained there for some months so that Kate came to visit us once more.

I knew that she had left us most reluctantly. The Abbey fascinated her still as it had when we were children. She would wander off alone and I believe she often went to that spot where we all used to meet. She was not sentimental, she insisted, it was merely a pleasant spot and it was rather amusing to recall old times.

I saw her once or twice with Bruno. I wondered if he talked to her of his plans and I wondered whether she warned him of making the place too similar to what it had been in the old days.

She said that I had become too much the housewife, the fussy mother, my thoughts straying to the nursery when she wished to discuss something serious with me. I pointed out that her notion of serious talk was generally gossip. This she conceded but added that gossip was at the very roots of great events. I should know that by now.

It was June again—Catherine's first birthday. Clement made a cake for her and we had a little ceremony in the nursery. I suppose Carey and Honey enjoyed it more than Catherine, but she was such a bright child and her eyes were round with wonder as she watched the other children.

Kate refused to come to the celebration; so did Bruno. I felt resentful toward them both for this; but Kate snapped her fingers. So at the party were myself and their nurses; Clement and Eugene who adored the children joined us and played games to the amusement of the young people. Clement was very good at crawling around the floor like a dog carrying them on his back while he barked realistically.

I laughed so much to see them.

Kate was full of Court gossip as usual, for the King had found his new wife.

"Poor lady!" cried Kate. "They say she is somewhat reluctant. She adores Thomas Seymour. What a man! Uncle of the young Prince Edward and . . . irresistible. But the King has cast his eyes in her direction and so Master Thomas for all his buccaneering ways must needs retreat and Lady Katharine Latimer—another Kate, you see, how his Grace seems to love the Kates, albeit briefly—though retiring and reluctant has no choice when the royal finger points to her and says, 'You are the next.' "

And so it was, for within a few weeks the King married Katha-

rine Parr. Kate was disappointed that the wedding, although celebrated openly, was to take place in Hampton Court which
meant of course that she would not be invited to attend.

"How different from his marriages to those other English
ladies, Anne Boleyn and Katharine Howard. They, poor ladies,
were married secretly and in haste. There is no need to hasten
over this."

"I wonder how she feels," I said. "How would one feel if one's
predecessors had either been disposed of or died at one's bridegroom's command?"

"I heard she was most reluctant. But she is no giddy girl. She
nursed two husbands so doubtless is ready to nurse a third."

I thought about the Queen a great deal. I mentioned her in
my prayers. I trusted that she would meet a better fate than the
other wives of the King. I had no desire to go to Court as Kate
had. I said to her that I would rather not have known the poor
ladies who had suffered.

By August I discovered I was pregnant again.

Bruno was delighted. I had failed to give him a boy in my first
attempt but I had shown that I was fruitful and would do so now.

The thought of having another child delighted me, and that
state of euphoria overcame me again. I was scarcely aware of anything else. I discussed children with my mother once more. I
brought out the small garments which Catherine had worn when
a baby. I thought of little but my child.

It was almost Christmas again. I had already told the little girls
that they would in due course have a brother or sister to join them
in their nursery. I thought that Honey looked a little sullen at the
time.

Then she said: "I don't want it."

"Oh, come, Honey," I said. "You will love it. A dear little baby—
imagine."

"I don't want it," she declared. "I don't want Cat here. I want
only Honey . . . like it was."

Jealousy was something I had always feared and had sought to
avoid. I tried to make much of her, to show that it made no
difference.

She asked whom I loved best; herself, Catherine or the new one which was coming.

I replied that I loved them all the same.

"You don't!" she cried. "You don't."

I was quite disturbed about her. It was true, of course. I was fond of her. But how could I help loving my own child more dearly?

The day after that conversation Honey was missing. I was full of remorse, accusing myself of betraying the fact in some way that she was less important to me than she had been. I must find her quickly. This was not easy. I searched the house, then I called in Clement. She had always been his special favorite and I thought he might know of some secret hiding place of hers.

He was concerned. His first thoughts were for the fishponds. He took off the great white apron he wore and his hands still floury he ran as fast as he could to the ponds.

Fortunately two of the fishers were there. They said they had been there all the morning and they would surely have seen the child if she had come that way.

We were greatly relieved. By this time Eugene had joined us; there were also the children's nurses and Clement thought it would be better if we split up and made two or three search parties. So this we did. I went with one of the young nursemaids, a girl of fourteen named Luce.

I suddenly thought of the tunnels. I had never explored the tunnels. Many of them were blocked and Bruno had expressed a wish that no one should attempt to penetrate them as he feared they might be dangerous. When he was a boy there had been a collapse of earth in some of them; and one monk had been buried alive there.

I thought of this as I ran toward the tunnels and imagined little Honey hurt because she thought she had been displaced by my own little girl and for this reason running away or going to some forbidden place.

I had told her that she was not to go near the tunnels or the fishponds, but when children wish to call attention to themselves or are unhappy because of some imagined slight I was well aware that the first thing they do is disobey.

I called: "Honey! Honey!"

There was no answer.

"She would surely not enter the tunnels," said the nurse. "She would be afraid."

I was not sure.

To reach the tunnel it was necessary to descend a stone stairway; and this I proceeded to do. The young nursemaid stood at the top of the stairs, too frightened to descend, but I was too anxious about Honey to be afraid.

I called her name as I went. Having come in from the bright sunshine I could see nothing for a while. And then suddenly from below a dark figure loomed up out of the gloom. I felt a cold shiver run down my spine. I took a step forward, the step was not there and I fell down two or three steps and landed on the dank soil.

The dark figure bent over me. I screamed.

A voice said: "Damask!"

It was Bruno who stood over me and I could sense his anger. "What are you doing here?"

"I . . . I fell."

"I know that. You came here in the dark! For what purpose?"

"Honey is lost," I said. He helped me to my feet. I was shaking.

He said: "Are you all right?" There was anxiety in his voice and I thought resentfully: It is not for me, it is for the child.

I replied shakily: "Yes, I am all right. Have you seen Honey? She is lost."

He was impatient.

"I have asked you not to enter these tunnels."

"I never have before. It was because the child might have wandered down."

"She is not here. I should have seen her if she had been."

He took me by the arm and together we mounted the stairway. When we reached the top he studied me intently. Then he said: "Never go down there again. It is unsafe."

I said: "What of you, Bruno?"

"I know those tunnels. I knew them as a boy. I should know what to avoid and how to take care."

I was too concerned about Honey to question this at the time, but it would come back to me later.

He left us abruptly and the nursemaid and I went back to the house. Honey was still not found.

I was getting frantic when a young boy from one of the shepherds' dwellings came with a message.

Honey was at Mother Salter's cottage. Would I go to bring her home as soon as I could?

I lost no time but went immediately to the cottage in the woods.

The fire was burning as I had seen it many times before and above it was the soot-black pot. On one side of the fire sat Mother Salter; she did not seem to have altered since I had first seen her, and on the other fireside seat sat Honey. There were smudges on her face and her gown was dirty. I gave a cry of joy and ran to her. I would have embraced her but she held aloof. I was aware of Mother Salter's watching eyes.

"Honey!" I cried. "Where have you been? I have been so frightened."

"Did you think you had lost me?"

"Oh, Honey. I was afraid something dreadful had happened to you."

"You wouldn't care. You have Catty and the new one coming."

I said: "Oh, Honey, do not think that means I can bear to part with you."

She was still half sullen. "You *can* bear it," she said. "You like Catty best."

"Honey, I love you both."

"The child does not think so." It was Mother Salter speaking in her low croaking voice.

"She is wrong. I have been frantic with anxiety."

"Take her then. It would be well to love her."

"Come, Honey," I said, "you want to come home, don't you? You don't want to stay here?"

She looked around the room and I could see that she was fascinated by what she saw. "Wrekin likes me."

"Spot and Pudding like you," I said, naming two of our dogs.

She nodded with pleasure. I had taken her hand and she did not resist. She continued to gaze around the room and because she had not learned to disguise her feelings I could see she was comparing it with her comfortable nursery at the Abbey. She wanted to come home but did not wish me to have too easy a victory. I knew Honey. She was a possessive, jealous little creature. For some time she had had me to herself and deeply she resented sharing me.

"It is the same with all elder children," I said to Mother Salter.

"Take care of this child," she replied. "Take the utmost care."

"I have always done so."

"It would be well for you that you do."

"There is no need for threats. I love Honey. It was a common enough sort of jealousy. How did she come here?"

"I watch over this child. She ran away and was lost in the wood. I knew it and sent a boy to find her. He brought her to me."

Her eyes were veiled; her mouth was smiling but her eyes were cold.

"I should know if she lacked aught," she went on.

"Then you know how well cared for she is."

"Take the child back. She is tired. She will know to come to me if she is in need."

"She will never be in need while I am here to care for her."

As we left the cottage I gripped Honey's hand tightly.

"Never, never run away again," I said.

"I won't if you love me best . . . better than Cat . . . better than the new one."

"I can't love you better, Honey. There is not all that love in the world. I can love you as well."

"I don't want the new one. I told Granny Salter I didn't want the new one."

"But there will be three of you. Three is better than two."

"No," she said firmly. "One's best."

I took her home and washed the grime from her, gave her milk and a great slice of cob bread freshly baked for her by Clement with a big *H* on it. This delighted her and she was happy again.

But when she was in bed I was seized by gripping pains and that night I miscarried.

My mother, hearing what happened, had come over at once bringing the midwife with her.

"It would have been a little boy," said the midwife. I did not entirely believe her; she was one of those lugubrious women who liked a tragedy to be of the first magnitude. She knew that we had wanted a boy.

It was great good fortune, she implied, that I had survived at all and it was in fact due to her great skill. I was confined to my bed for a week and during this time I had time to think. I could not forget Bruno's face when he knew what had happened. The precious child lost! Surely the King himself had not looked more thunderous when he had stood over his sad Queen's bed. I even imagined I saw hatred in his face then.

I thought a good deal about Bruno. I recalled seeing him at night from my window. He had been coming from the tunnels then. And why should he have been in the tunnels on that day when I had gone to look for Honey? If there was a danger of the earth collapsing it could do so at any time, and it was no safer for him than for anyone else.

By April of the following year I knew that I was again with child. The change in Bruno when he knew this was astonishing. Passionately he wanted children and yet when they arrived he was indifferent to them . . . at least he was to Catherine. Honey of course he had always resented. If my child was a boy how would he be? Would he try to take him from me?

Sometimes I would grow oddly apprehensive.

What did I know of this strange man who was my husband? What had I ever known? During those years when he had lived in the Abbey—the child who had been sent to them from heaven for some purpose—his character had been formed. Then rudely he had been awakened to the truth; and now it seemed he would spend his life proving that he was indeed apart from other men.

I felt I understood him; and for this reason I could feel tender toward him; but I was beginning to see how happy we might have been. This rebuilding of our little world was a fascinating project. We were giving work to many people and the neighborhood was becoming prosperous again; people were now beginning to look to the Abbey almost as they had in the old days. What happy use-

ful lives we could have led if Bruno had not been possessed by a
need to prove himself superhuman.

I saw less of him during my pregnancy. He worked as though
in a frenzy. We had moved from the Abbot's Lodging to the
monks' frater while the lodging was being rebuilt. Bruno had de-
signed the house in the old Norman style, like a castle.

There was something eerie about the monks' quarters. There
was no room large enough for us to share and we occupied separate bedchambers. Honey and Catherine had one of the cells for
theirs; they could have had separate ones—there were enough
cells, heaven knew—but I feared they might be frightened. I myself used to fancy I could hear slow stealthy footsteps in the
night and often coming up the winding staircase I would think I
saw a ghostly shape. It was imagination of course; but I used to
lie awake and think of the monks who had lived in this place for
two hundred years and wondered what they had thought as they
lay in their cells at night. I grew fanciful as women will when pregnant and I asked myself whether when people died they left something behind them for those who came after. I thought more often
than before during that period of the terrible day when Rolf
Weaver had come; and I could imagine the terror of the monks
when they knew that he and his men were in the Abbey.

Sometimes I would get up in the night and look through the
grille in the door at the children, just to make sure that they were
safe. I should be glad when we could move back to our completed
house. But when I was with child what happened outside my little world was of a minor importance. I was the kind of woman
who was first a mother; even my feelings for Bruno were maternal.
Perhaps if this had not been so I might have been more aware
of what was happening about me.

There was a change in Caseman Court.

I did not visit the house often because I did not wish to see
Simon Caseman, but there was little that was subtle about my
mother and she dropped scraps of information. She told me that
some of the ornaments that used to be in the chapel had been
sold; and she let out once that there was a copy of Tyndale's translation of the Bible in a secret place in the chapel.

If Simon Caseman was embracing the doctrines of the Re-

formed Church, he was in as great a danger as I feared Bruno
might be in bringing back monks to the Abbey. I used to argue
with myself as I might have done with my father. Of what importance was it in what manner one worshiped God as long as one
obeyed the tenets of Christianity, which I believed were summed
up in the simple injunction to love one's neighbor?

It was a strange summer; through the long days the sound of
workmen laying bricks could be heard. I saw less and less of
Bruno, and I often thought that while the men built up the walls
of our grandiose castle he was fast building a wall between us
which was becoming so high that it threatened to shut him off
from me altogether.

Occasionally I heard news from outside. The King had been
declared by Parliament King of England, France and Ireland, Defender of the Faith and Supreme Head of the Churches of England and Ireland. That he had become war-minded and carried
the war into France meant little to me. There was rejoicing when
we heard on one September day that he had taken Boulogne and
had actually marched into the town at the head of his troops in
spite of the sickness of his body. Prayers were said in churches
throughout the country and Archbishop Cranmer, who leaned
toward the Reformed religion, pointed out to the King that if
people could pray in English they would understand for what they
prayed and their prayers would be more fervent. Simple people
wishing well to the King would not understand for what they
prayed in Latin. The King saw the point of this and allowed the
Archbishop to compose a few prayers in English and these were
said in all churches.

I could imagine the jubilation at Caseman Court. It was the
reverse in our household. Even Clement was slightly downcast.

Had I not been so absorbed in my children I might have been
more aware of the growing conflict in a country when it could be
so definitely felt between two houses.

Then we heard that the Dauphin of France had brought an
army against the King, and recaptured Boulogne, and the King
and his men were forced to retire to that old English possession
of Calais so that there had been little point in the venture.

"It might have been a different story," I had heard Clement say.

"If Master Cranmer had not tried to bring in his Reformed notions. God was clearly displeased."

In the old days my father would have discussed the changes with me. We would have considered the virtues of the old and new Church. Doubtless we would have defied the law and had a copy of Tyndale's Bible in the house. I knew that there was one in Caseman Court. I trusted it would not be discovered because I knew what this could mean to my mother and the twins. For Simon Caseman I could feel no concern.

As my time grew near I began to feel wretchedly ill.

November was a dark and dreary month and I was not looking forward to spending Christmas in the monks' quarters. I watched the transformation of the Abbot's Lodging and it seemed to me that each day it grew more and more like Remus Castle—but grander in every way.

Then one day two months before my time my child was born —a stillborn boy.

I did not know of this until a week later. I myself had come near to death.

Bruno wrote to Kate asking her to nurse me. Lord Remus was now in Calais with the forces there who were protecting the town for the King. Kate came without delay.

She was shocked to see me. "Why, you've changed, Damask," she said. "You've grown thinner and sharper of face. You have grown up. You look as though you have passed through experiences which have changed the Damask I used to know."

"I have lost two children," I said.

"Many women lose children," she said.

"Perhaps it changes them all."

"If they are as you. You are the eternal mother. Damask, has it struck you how different we all are, and how each of us has distinct characteristics?"

"You mean all people?"

"I mean us . . . the four of us . . . those of us on that branch I told you of before. There were four of us . . . you, myself, Rupert and Bruno . . . all children together."

"Bruno was not one of us."

"Oh, yes, he was. Not under our roof but he was part of our quartet. You are the eternal mother; I the wanton; Rupert the good steady influence."

She paused. "And Bruno?"

"Bruno is the mystery. What do you know of Bruno? I should love to discover."

"I seem to know him less and less."

"That is how it is with mysteries. The deeper one penetrates the maze the more lost one becomes. You should not have become involved in this particular mystery. You feel too keenly. You should have married Rupert. Did I not always tell you so?"

"How could you know what I should do?"

"Because in some things I am more learned than you, Damask. I lack your knowledge of Greek and Latin but I know of other things which are more important. You have been very ill. When I heard I was distraught as never before. There! What do you think of that?"

"Dear Kate."

"No, I am not your dear Kate. I am a designing woman, as you well know. Nothing changes me. Now I shall cheer you . . . not with possets and herb drinks. I leave that to your mother. I shall enliven you with my incessant chatter."

"I am glad to see you. Lying here I have been passing through the strangest fantasies. I have imagined that I am trapped in a monastery."

Kate grimaced. "That is easy to understand. Whatever made you choose this place for your lying-in?"

"We had to move out of the Lodging for the rebuilding."

"But you have such a vast estate. Why not choose something more fitting than these dreary cells? They give me the creeps."

"I have dreamed that I have been a prisoner here . . . that Rolf Weaver's men were here . . . that someone was trying to kill me."

"Now that I am here you will get well."

"Bruno is so strange."

"Does he not love you?"

"He does not love as other people do."

"Bruno loves passionately . . . himself."

"How should you know?"

"I know that he has great spiritual pride. So he will build a great castle; he will have a son to follow him. He will be lord of his enclosed world. He will restore the Abbey."

"No!"

"Not yet. In time perhaps."

"It would be treason."

"Kings do not live forever. But our conversation grows dangerous, and speaking of Kings, before Remus set out for Calais he was most graciously received by the Queen."

"Tell me of her."

"A kind and calm lady, with a different sort of beauty from that of the English ladies who had previously caught the King's fancy. Such an excellent nurse she is. I have heard that none can dress his leg as she can. She has a deft and gentle touch and if any other do it he will scream with pain and throw the nearest stool at them ere they have time to retreat. But she dabbles with the Reformed religion."

"Kate, how many people are dabbling with it, think you?"

"More and more each day. And I will tell you that the King's sixth wife has recently been in danger of losing her head through it."

"But I thought she was such a good nurse to him."

"Doubtless that saved her. Bishop Gardiner has been working against her. You have heard of Anne Askew?"

I had assuredly heard of Anne Askew who had declared herself publicly in favor of the Reformed ideas and for this had been sent to the Tower. She had been racked cruelly and finally consigned to the flames.

"It is known," went on Kate, "that while Anne Askew lay in prison the Queen sent her food and warm clothing."

"An act of mercy," I said.

"To be construed by those who upheld the old faith as an act of treason. It is said that the King's wife has come within hours of losing her head."

I often wondered how Kate was so conversant with Court gossip. But she told her stories of the Court with such verisimilitude that one completely believed her.

She made me see the serious-minded Queen who was so interested in the new ideas that she even talked of them to the King. She made me see cruel Wriothesley, the King's Lord Chancellor, who had determined to bring her to the block. I could hear his insinuating voice asking the King if the Queen had so far forgotten her place as to seek to teach the King religion. And the poor Queen's ignorance of what was happening until the King had signed the order to commit her to the Tower.

But the King was weary of hunting for a new wife. It was true the Queen had not given him a son; but she was a good nurse and if she were a headless corpse who would dress his leg? And the Queen, suddenly being aware of imminent danger, had used all her wits to extricate herself. She had become ill with anxiety but recovering in time she had told the King that she would never learn from any except God and himself.

As she had when a child, Kate assumed the parts of the people in her stories. Now she struck an attitude; she strutted—she would have made a good mummer. She seemed to grow large and royal; she narrowed her eyes and tightened her lips and she was the King.

"And he said to her—for I have it from one who overhears—'Not so, by Saint Mary. You have become a doctor, wife, to instruct us and not to be instructed of us, as oftentime we have seen.'

"At this," went on Kate, "the Queen trembled, because she saw the hand of Wriothesley in this and the ax very close and turned toward her."

Kate was the Queen now. " 'Indeed if Your Majesty have so conceived then my meaning has been mistaken, for I have always held it preposterous for a woman to instruct her lord; and if I have ever presumed to differ from Your Highness on religion it was partly to obtain information and sometimes because I perceived that in talking you were able to pass off the pain and weariness of your present infirmity.'

"With which clever reply His Majesty was pleased and he said, 'And is it so, sweetheart. Then we are perfect friends.'

"And when they came to arrest her they found her in loving discourse with them in the gardens, at which His Majesty vented his fury on them. So you see the King's sixth Queen came very near to losing her head and we might well be asking ourselves who the seventh was to be."

I shivered. "How near queens are to death," I said.

"How near we all are to death," replied Kate.

Kate left us soon after that, and I was surprised when a messenger brought me a letter from her in which she told me she was expecting a child.

"Remus is beside himself with glee," she wrote. "As for myself I am less gleeful. I deplore the long unwieldy months almost as much as the painful and humiliating climax. How I wish there were some other way of getting children. How much more dignified if one could buy them as one buys a castle or a manor house—and choose the one one wants. Would that not be more civilized than this animal process?"

I confess to a twinge of envy. I thought with burning resentment of my boy who had been allowed to die, how much I wanted him. And Kate was to have another child although she was never meant to be a mother.

During the next months I devoted myself to the little girls. I tried not to mourn for my lost child. I watched the gradual growth of our castle and I was amazed that Bruno should have had such wealth as to be able to create such a place.

When I asked him about it he showed great displeasure. He had changed toward me. The disappointment over the loss of the boy was intense and he made no secret of it. I could not help thinking of poor Anne Boleyn when she had failed to produce a boy. Then I remembered that Kate had referred to Bruno as a King.

Where was that young and passionate boy who had wooed me? I sometimes wondered whether that had been a part he had played for some purpose. Purpose! That was it. There was some purpose behind everything that had happened since his return.

My mother was a frequent visitor, for since I did not go to Caseman Court she must come to me.

"Your stepfather marvels at the magnificence of this new

place you are building. Your husband must be a man of boundless wealth, he says."

"It is not so," I said quickly. "You know the Abbey was bestowed on him. We have the material we need. We are using bricks from the lay quarters, so it is not so very costly."

"Your stepfather says that there is a movement in the country to bring back some of the monasteries, and that monks are getting together again and living together as they did before. Your stepfather thinks this is a highly dangerous way of living."

"So much is dangerous, Mother. It is dangerous to concern oneself with the new ideas."

"Why cannot people be sensible and live for their families?" she said irritably.

I agreed with her.

She would bring the twins with her and the children would all play together while we watched them fondly and laughed at their antics. I saw what Kate meant. My mother and I were of a kind after all—the eternal mothers, as Kate would say.

In due course Kate's son was born. She wrote:

"He is a healthy, lusty boy. Remus is as proud as a peacock."

When I told Bruno I saw the faint color touch the marble of his skin.

"A boy!" he said. "Some women get boys."

It was a reproach and I cried out: "Was it my fault that my child was born dead? Do you think I rejoiced in that?"

"You are hysterical," he said coldly.

I felt envious of Kate and my heart was filled with a burning resentment because my boy had died, while Kate, who was never meant to be a mother, had hers.

She wanted me to go to the christening.

"Bring the children," she wrote. "Carey does nothing but plague me to produce Honey and Catherine. He has thought up all kinds of new ways of teasing them."

Bruno made no attempt to prevent my going to Remus Castle as in due course I set out with the two little girls.

Kate's child was christened Nicholas.

"After the saint," she said.

After a while Kate shortened his name to Colas.

Before I went back to the Abbey news reached us that the King was dead. Oddly enough I was deeply affected. The King had been on the throne for as long as I could remember; my mind kept returning to that day when my father had been seated on the wall with his arm supporting me as I watched the King and Cardinal pass by. Then the King had been a golden young man, not yet a monster; and the Cardinal, long since dead, had traveled down the river with him to Hampton. Since then he had brought about the death of two wives and the wretchedness of at least two others. And now he himself was dead.

I was on my way back to the Abbey when I saw the funeral procession passing from Westminster to Windsor. The hearse with its eighty tapers, each one of them two feet in length, and the banners of the saints beaten in gold on damask and the canopy of silver tissue fringed with black and gold silk, were very impressive. It was the passing of an age. I wondered what augered for the future. I thought of my father's being taken from his beloved home to a cold prison in the Tower and I could hear the cries of those who by this King had been condemned to the flames or the even worse fate of hanging and quartering. We had lived long under a tyrant. Surely we must hope for a brighter future.

We had a new King—Edward who was but ten years old, too young to govern, but he had a powerful and ambitious pair of uncles.

I reached the Abbey. It seemed to rise over me menacingly and I felt little confidence in the future.

The Quiet Years

There was consternation in the Abbey. James, one of the fishermen who had gone into the City to sell the surplus of fish which had been salted down, came back with the news that he had seen images taken from churches and being burned in the streets. He had joined a crowd in the Chepe and had listened to ominous conversation.

"This is the end of the Papists. They'll be hanging them from their churches ere long."

The new King was leaning toward the Reformed ideas and he was surrounded by those who shared his views—and perhaps had formed them. In his chapel prayers were said in English, and it would no longer be an offense to have a translation of the Bible in one's possession.

My mother visited us with the first spring flowers from her garden.

"The King is gone, God rest his soul," she said, "and it would seem to be the beginning of a new and glorious reign."

I knew that she was repeating what she had heard and I guessed that Simon Caseman was one who was not displeased with the turn of events.

I was uneasy though. Bruno would have to be careful. If the new religion was in favor, those in authority would frown on a community such as Bruno was attempting to build up, and although he might try to give an impression that he was merely the head of a large country estate, he would assuredly be under suspicion.

Because the King was too young to rule, his uncle, the Earl of

Hereford, was made protector. He was immediately created Earl of Somerset and became the most powerful man in the country. He was ambitious and eager to carry on the war in which the late King had interested himself and less than six months after the death of Henry VIII he was marching up to Scotland. Remus was with him and actually took part in the famous battle of Pinkie Cleugh, a costly victory for the Protector.

It brought the war home to us too—in the past it had all seemed too far away to concern us much—for at Pinkie Remus was killed.

Kate wrote of her dear brave Remus but it was not in her nature to mourn or to feign grief which she did not feel. She was now rich and free, so I guessed that she would not repine for long.

Our castle was now complete. I called it castle, although it still bore the name of St. Bruno's Abbey, for with its gray stone walls and Gothic style it had a medieval aspect. The Abbot's Lodging had been completely swallowed up in this magnificent structure. It had been built in the form of a square closely resembling Remus Castle with circular towers at the four corners. There were two flanking towers at the gateway with oiletts as seen in Norman structures and which were meant for arrows—something of an anachronism in our day, but Bruno had said that since we were building with old stones which had been used two hundred years before when the Abbey was built we must use them in the manner in which they were intended.

Some of the outbuildings should be built in modern style perhaps; but he was not yet concerned with those.

The parapets were embattled so that the vast and impressive building had the aspect of a fortress.

Although the exterior was that of a medieval fortress, the interior possessed all the luxury and elegance which I imagined could be found in places like Hampton Court.

Each tower had four stories and on each floor was a hexagonal chamber. These towers were like little houses in themselves and it would be possible to live in them quite apart from the rest of the household. Bruno took one of these as his own and spent a great deal of time there. The highest room was a bedchamber and since we moved into the new dwelling I saw very little of him.

Some of the old rooms had been left, but so much had been added that it was easy to lose oneself in the place.

There was a great banqueting hall and for this Bruno was seeking fine tapestries. He went to Flanders to find them and they were hung on the walls; at the end of the hall was a dais on which a small dining table was placed which would be for Bruno and his honored guests while the rest of the household would eat from the big table.

When I saw this place I could not understand why Bruno had reconstructed it. Sometimes I thought he wished to live like a great lord; and at others I wondered whether he was trying to establish a monastic order.

He gave a great reception when we went to live in the castle and many of our neighbors were invited; Simon Caseman came with my mother; Kate came too.

The great hall was decorated with leaves and flowers from our gardens, and it was indeed a grand occasion.

I stood with Bruno and received our guests and I had rarely seen him as excited as he was on that occasion.

I sat at the dais on his right hand, Kate was on his left and Simon Caseman and my mother were there. Bruno told me to invite some of the rich men whom my father had known and I had done this. They had all come eager to see if the rumors they had heard of the rebuilding of the Abbey were true.

There was feasting for Clement had excelled himself. I had never seen such an array of pies and tarts and great joints of mutton and beef. There was sucking pigs and boars' heads and fish of all kinds. My mother was in a state of wonder, tasting this and that and trying to guess what had given certain flavors.

There was dancing afterward. Bruno and I opened the ball and later I found myself partnered by Simon Caseman.

"I had no notion," he said, "that you had married such a rich man. Why I am but a pauper in comparison."

"If it galls you it is better not to make comparisons."

Bruno danced with Kate and I wondered what they talked of.

A strange thing happened during the ball, because suddenly a black-clad figure was noticed in our midst—an old woman in a long cloak, her head concealed by a hood.

The guests fell back and stared at her for they were sure, as I was, that she was some harbinger of evil.

Bruno strode over to her.

"I had no invitation to the ball," she said with a hoarse chuckle.

"I know you not," replied Bruno.

"Then you should, my son," was her answer.

I recognized her then as Mother Salter, so I went to her and said: "You are welcome. May I offer you refreshment?"

I saw her yellow fangs as she smiled at me.

And I thought: She has every right to be here; she is the grandmother of Bruno and Honey.

"I come in two minds to bless or curse this house."

"You could not curse it," I said.

She laughed again.

Then she lifted her hands and muttered something.

"Blessing or curse," she said. "You will discover which."

Then I called for wine for I was filled with a terrible premonition of evil, and I remembered in that moment that after Honey had been lost in the woods I had lost my baby.

She drank the wine; and then walked around the hall, the guests falling back as she passed. When she came to the door she said again: "Blessing or curse. That you will discover." And with that went out.

There was a hushed silence; and then everyone began to talk at once.

It was some sort of entertainment, they said. It was a mummer dressed up as a witch.

But there were some who recognized Mother Salter, the witch of the woods.

Some months after our grand ball Honey caught a chill. It was nothing much but I was always uneasy when either of the children were not well. I had made a nursery for them next to the room which had been mine and Bruno's bedchamber and was now more often mine alone, for he had lived more often in his tower. Honey had a persistent cough which was apt to wake her. I kept a bottle of cough mixture by her bed which my mother had made

and which was always effective and as soon as she started to cough
I would be in her room with it.

On this cold January night she started to cough. I was out of
bed and into the children's room. Catherine was sleeping peacefully in her cot. Honey, now big enough for a pallet, gave me that
intensely loving look when I appeared.

I said: "Now, my pet, we will soon stop that nasty old cough."

I gave her the draft, propped up pillows and put my arm
around her as she lay sleepily and happily against me.

I think she was almost pleased to have a cough so that she could
have my special attention.

"Cat's fast asleep," she whispered delightedly.

"We mustn't wake her," I whispered.

"No, don't let's wake her. This is nice."

"Yes. Are you cozy?"

She nestled against me. I looked down at her; the thick lashes
making an enchanting semicircle against the pallor of her skin,
her thick dark hair falling about her shoulders. She was going to
be our beauty. Catherine was vivacious, careless, lighthearted;
Honey was intense and passionate. If she were displeased and it
was usually through her jealousy of Catherine that she was, she
would be sullen for days, whereas Catherine would fly into a storm
of rage and a few moments later she would have forgotten her
grievance. They were completely unalike. Catherine was pretty—
her lashes were light brown tipped with gold; her hair was brown
with light streaks in it; her skin delicately tinted. Catherine was
enchanting, more lovable, less demanding, but Honey was the
beauty. She disturbed me even now because of her continual
watchfulness lest I should show I cared more for Catherine than
I did for her. I was the center of her world. If she were proud of
some achievement, I was to be told first; for me she gathered flowers—often those from my own garden. She watched me continually
and she wanted me to remember always that she was my girl and
that she had come to me before Catherine.

I assured myself that she would grow out of this. At the moment she was but a child. Yet she was seven years old—an age they
say when character is developed. I had given them lessons from
the time Honey was four, remembering my father's maxim that

a child cannot be taught too young. They must read as soon as it is possible for them to do so, my father had said, for thus a world is open to them which would otherwise be shut. I was in agreement with this and I was determined that my girls should be scholars if they had a tendency to be so, and if not at least educated ladies. Later I should arrange for Valerian to teach them. I had already spoken to him of this and he was delighted with the idea. He was a very good teacher. All this I thought as Honey and I exchanged whispers and finally she was quiet so I knew that she slept. Gently I removed my arm and crept back to my own room.

It was a moonlit night and still thinking of the children I went to a window and looked out. The sight of the Abbey buildings never failed to excite me and I could never become accustomed to living in such a place. I fell to thinking of the strangeness of my life and how different I had imagined it would be in the days when my father was alive. I thought of the strangeness of my husband and when I tried to dissect my feelings for him I could not do so. I had begun to suspect that I did not wish to because I was afraid of what I should find. He was a stranger to me in so many ways. Our closeness had always been a physical closeness. We could be lovers still. Was it because we were both young and felt the need of such contact? From his thoughts I often felt completely shut out; and I wondered whether he did from me—or whether he considered such a matter at all. I had disappointed him because I had not produced a son. We were always hoping that I should do so.

Then suddenly I began to think of Rupert and the tenderness he showed to me whenever we met, and I admitted that was something I missed in Bruno. Had he ever been tender?

I had felt tender toward him on those occasions when I believed that he needed me; and he did need me. In what ways? He needed to *prove* something.

I switched my thoughts away because I was fearful that I might make some discovery.

And then I saw a figure emerge into the moonlight. Bruno—again coming from the tunnels. I watched him make his way to the tower. I saw him enter. I watched and then I saw the light of lantern at his window.

It was the second time I had seen him coming from the tunnels in the night. I wondered why. It could only be because he did not wish anyone to know that he was there.

I returned to my bed. I wondered whether he would join me.

He did not. And in the morning he told me that it was necessary for him to take another trip on the Continent. This time he wanted to buy more tapestry for the walls of some of our rooms.

It occurred to me later that when I had seen him during the night on that other occasion he had almost immediately gone abroad afterward.

I wondered whether there was any significance in this. It was typical of our relationship that I did not feel it was possible to ask him.

My mother came visiting over to the Abbey, her basket full of lotions and unguents.

"My dear daughter," she cried, "watch over the children. One of our men has come in from the city with a tale that he saw a man dying in the Chepe. He saw another on one of the barges at the Westminster stairs. The sweat is with us."

I was alarmed for the children. I dosed them with my mother's remedies and forbade them to leave the house, but how could I be sure that someone had not brought the dreaded sweat into the Abbey?

Honey, sensing my fear, showed a terrified delight; she clung to me as though she were afraid that I was going to be snatched from her. Catherine was scornful and tried to slip away when she could. I chided her and she was penitent but I knew she would forget the warning the very next minute.

Kate came to the rescue.

"I hear the sweat is raging in London. You are too near for my comfort. You must bring the children to Remus. Here you will be safe from the evil."

I was delighted and prepared to set out for Remus Castle.

Widowhood suited Kate. She was rich and although so far no one had sought her hand—the death of her husband being too recent—there were one or two who were biding their time though they would not wait long, for the late King's speedy marriage to Jane Seymour before Anne Boleyn was cold in her grave had set a fashion.

Lord Remus had never been an exacting husband and had always been ready to indulge his wife, but now Kate was the mistress and master of the house and determined to enjoy her new position.

She had gowns of velvets and silks and I had never seen such puffing and ruching of sleeves before.

"You know nothing of Court fashions," she told me contemptuously.

Carey was now Lord Remus; he was a very important young gentleman. Someone had told him that he must take care of his mother—ironically, I thought, for no woman could care for herself as well as Kate; but Carey took it seriously. He could ride well, and was learning to shoot in the archery courtyard; he had a falcon which he was learning to use. Every time I saw him he seemed a little more grown up. He was some months younger than Honey, and a year or so older than Catherine; but he was cock of the walk in his own farmyard, I noticed.

Catherine quarreled with him incessantly; but he and Honey were good friends. I began to think that Honey showed a preference for him because he and Catherine were such enemies.

Kate was already making plans for the future. The Court, she said, had become nonexistent since the death of King Henry. How could a boy of eleven years or so hold a Court! The Protector Somerset was of course the real King and his brother Lord High Admiral Thomas Seymour was perhaps a little envious of him.

"Tom Seymour has hopes of the Lady Elizabeth," Kate told me. "You can see where that is leading."

"She could never be Queen of England," I said. "There is Mary before her, and would the old King not have both considered to be illegitimate to suit his own purposes?"

"Poor Edward is a sickly child. It's to be doubted whether he will ever beget children."

"I daresay they will marry him off as soon as possible."

"He is devoted to his cousin, Jane Grey. I think he would be delighted to take her."

"Which would be a satisfactory match since she herself has some pretensions to the throne."

"Have you thought that it could be a Protestant match, Damask, and what that could mean to the country? I would rather see someone gay on the throne. Jane is a prim little thing, so I have heard. Rather like you were, I imagine. So good with her Latin and Greek. Quite the little scholar."

Days had always passed cozily at Remus and now it had become a kind of oasis for me. There were no problems and I realized how relieved I was to leave the Abbey for a while.

Kate, restless because she was confined to the house in supposed mourning for her husband, planning the entertainments she would give at the Castle when that period was over, parading in her velvet gowns with only me and the occasional visitor to admire her, found the best method of passing the time in talking to me.

She enjoyed going over the past and she remembered more incidents from our childhood than I had believed she would. I remembered, yes, but then I was more introspective than she. So it was surprising to discover that these little incidents which had appeared too insignificant to mean much to her had somehow remained stored in her mind.

She frankly admitted that she had always intended to get what she could from life.

"And you must concede, Damask, that I have got a great deal. Life has been kinder to me than to you, yet you have been a better woman than I. You loved your father and you suffered deeply when you lost him. You thought I did not know how deeply but I did, Damask, and while I was sad for you I thought how foolish it was to love one person so much that to lose him can be such a tragedy. I would never love like that . . . except myself of course."

"There is great joy in loving, too, Kate," I said. "I remember so many happy times with my father. I would not have missed those for anything in the world."

"The more happiness you had the greater was your grief. People like you pay for the happiness they get."

"But not you?"

"I am too clever for that," retorted Kate. "I am sufficient for myself. I make myself dependent on no one."

"Have you never loved?"

"In my fashion. I am fond of you. I am fond of Carey and young Colas. You are my family and I am happy to have you round me. But this complete and utter devotion—it is not for me."

We talked of Bruno and what he had done at the Abbey, and what he proposed doing.

"Bruno is a fanatic," she said. "He is the sort of man who will end up at the stake."

"Don't say that, Kate," I said quickly.

"Why? You know it to be true. He is the strangest man I have ever known. Sometimes he almost made me believe that he was indeed sent from heaven for some purpose. Did you feel that, Damask?"

"I am not sure. I may have felt it."

"But no longer do?"

I was silent.

"Ah," she accused. "I see you do not. But he believes it, Damask. He must believe it."

"Why must he? If it were proved. . . ."

"He must. He dare not do otherwise. I know your husband well, Damask."

"So you have told me before."

"I understand him as you cannot. We are of a kind in a way. You are too normal, Damask. I know you well."

"You always did believe you knew everything."

"Not everything but a great deal. How he must have suffered when Keziah and the monk betrayed their secret. I pitied him then because I understood him so well."

"We never speak of it," I said.

"No. You dare not. Don't speak of it. You see what he is trying to do, Damask. To prove himself. I think I might be the same. But I do not have to prove myself. I am beautiful, desirable. You see how I took Remus. I would take any man I wanted. I know I can; they know it; there is no need to prove it. But Bruno has to *prove* to himself that he is superhuman. That is what he is doing. But how is he doing it? How is it possible for one who had nothing

. . . who was turned from his secluded life into the world, to become so wealthy that he can do all that Bruno is doing now? I doubt Remus could have afforded such a vast expenditure."

"It worries me at times."

"I doubt it not."

"Somehow it has all become fantastic . . . like a dream. Before I married Bruno there was a reason for everything. Now I often feel as though I am groping in the dark."

"I have a feeling, Damask, that you will grope for a long time and that perhaps it is better so. The darkness is a protection. Who knows what you might see in the blinding light of truth."

"I would always wish for the truth."

"Mayhap not if you knew it."

There were many such conversations with Kate, and I often came from them with the notion that she knew something and was holding it back. These talks stimulated me as they did her. I too liked to watch the children at their games. I devised entertainments for them; and I gave a party for them and some children of the neighborhood. We danced country dances and played guessing games and it was the best of good fun.

Kate never joined in but she sometimes liked to watch.

She called me the eternal mother.

"I'm never going to be able to placate Carey," she said, "when you and the girls depart."

My mother wrote that the twins were well and the sweat was abating; but I still stayed on.

Kate invited guests to Remus and those were exciting days when we watched from the keep while they rode under the portcullis and into the courtyard.

There would be interesting conversation at dinner and we learned that the Queen Dowager, Katharine Parr, had married Thomas Seymour, with whom she had long been in love.

Kate was amused. "Of course he wanted the Princess Elizabeth but she was too dangerous so he took Queen Katharine instead. A King's widow instead of a Princess who thinks she might have a claim to the throne! Anne Boleyn's daughter." She was pensive, thinking of the glittering, elegant woman whom she had so admired.

Kate giggled over the scandals of the Dower House where the Queen and Seymour lived, for the young Elizabeth was under the Queen's care and there were rumors of a far from innocent relationship between the Princess and Seymour.

On the day when the Queen Dowager died in childbed I returned to the Abbey.

There followed what I thought of afterward as the quiet years. There were changes but they were so gradual that I scarcely noticed them. There were many workers on the Abbey estate now and always great activity on the farm for more workers had joined us. More building had been done. There had even been extensions to our mansion. Bruno never seemed to be satisfied with it. Tapestries adorned many of our rooms. Now and then Bruno made trips abroad and often returned with treasures.

Honey was now eleven and she had lost none of her beauty. Catherine, more than two years younger, was more vivacious and independent. They were both bright and intelligent children and I was proud of them. Valerian had now taken over the control of their studies and each day they took lessons in the scriptorium. It was a disappointment to me that I had no other child. My mother, who imagined that she was learned in such things, said that perhaps I desired one too passionately. She was always concocting potions for me but nothing happened. Sometimes I had the notion that Mother Salter had indeed put a curse on me because she had feared I did not care sufficiently for Honey.

I often visited Kate and she came now and then to the Abbey. She had not married although she had been betrothed twice, but had decided against marriage before the ceremony was performed. She told me that she liked her freedom and since she was rich she had no need to marry for what she called the usual reasons.

The children now looked forward to their reunions. Catherine and Carey quarreled a good deal. Honey was aloof; she always seemed much older than Carey. Little Colas was always ignored by the others and only allowed to play with them if he took the minor parts in games—the usual fate of the youngest.

Sometimes the twins came to us, but my mother liked best for me to take the children to Caseman Court. On several occasions she talked to me of the Reformed religion. She would like to see me embrace it. I asked her why.

"Oh, it's all in the books," she said.

I smiled at her. One faith was as good as another to her. She would be ready to follow her husband in all ways.

We seemed to have passed into a different era. The young King was as different from his father as a king could be. The times had changed. It was no longer dangerous to show an interest in the Reformed faith. King Edward himself was interested in it; so were those who surrounded him. The Princess Mary, who was the next in succession to the King, would be very different, for she was fiercely Catholic; but it would only be if the King were to die without heirs that she would have a chance of ascending the throne.

He was sickly, it was true, but they would marry him young and according to Kate he had already chosen the little Lady Jane Grey, a choice greatly approved by those who wished to see the Reformed faith flourish.

Rumors came to us over those years but they did not seem of such significance as they had when the old King was alive.

The Lord High Admiral, Thomas Seymour, had lost his head; and sometime later his brother Somerset had followed him to the scaffold.

Politics! I thought. They were so dangerous and devious and the man in high favor one day was he whose head rolled in the straw the next.

But lightly these things seemed to touch us at this time.

Now that the Seymour brothers were dead the Duke of Northumberland was in control and he had married his son Lord Guildford Dudley to the little Jane Grey.

"He had a purpose," Kate said, during one of my stays at Remus. "If the King were to die Northumberland would try to make Jane Queen for that would mean that Guildford Dudley, Northumberland's son, were King—or as near as makes no difference."

"And what of the Princess Mary? Would she stand aside to see Jane Grey Queen of England?"

"It is to be hoped that the King will go on living, for if he did not there could be war in England."

"A war between the supporters of Jane and those of Mary would be a war between those of the old faith and the new."

"We must pray for the King's good health for that is to pray for peace," said Kate.

I did not know it but the quiet years were coming to an end.

The Abbey flourished. The old guesthouses were occupied by workers; and in the midst of this activity was the castlelike residence known as St. Bruno's Abbey. We were supplying corn to the surrounding districts; our wool was bringing in big prices. We had more animals than we needed for our own consumption and these were slain and salted down and sold.

I had discovered that no less than twenty of our workers were men who had been attached to the Abbey before the dissolution —some monks, some lay brothers. It seemed inevitable that they should band together and remember the customs of the old days.

The church was intact. It was used at night. Frequently I saw from my window after the household had retired, men making their way there. I believed they celebrated the Mass as they had in the Abbot's day.

Rupert had extended his lands; he visited us now and then and when he came Bruno took a certain pleasure in conducting him around our estate. There was no envy in Rupert; he admired everything and seemed genuinely pleased to see such prosperity.

One day he rode over. It was during one of Bruno's trips to the Continent and I knew as soon as I saw him that something had happened. Strangely enough the first thing I thought of was: He has come to tell me that he is about to marry. I was surprised at the feeling of depression that gave me.

It was not that I had a dog-in-the-manger attitude toward him; but I had come to regard him as very important in my life, and I suddenly realized what comfort the devotion he had shown me for so long had meant to me. Sometimes when I had been deeply perplexed I had thought of his existence, a close neighbor, someone to whom I could turn in trouble—always there, always delighted to be called on.

If he married, he would remain so—but I knew it would be different. I used to tell myself perhaps overemphatically how pleasant it would be if he married and had children. Some of the happiest times were when I had all the children at the Abbey—my own two girls, Kate's two boys and my mother's twins. I loved to hear their noisy games and sometimes join in. Kate watched me with cynical amusement, but these were some of the happiest hours of my life at that time.

I faced the fact now that my marriage was not what I had dreamed of. I looked around and wondered whose was. Kate's and Remus's—my parents, my mother's with Simon Caseman? I verily believed that my mother was the happiest wife I knew. But I had Catherine and I must be grateful to the union which had brought me her.

I took Rupert into my winter parlor and sent for wine and the cakes we served with it. Clement always had a batch fresh from the oven.

"You have news, I can see," I said.

He looked at me earnestly. "Damask," he said, "how much do you know of what is going on?"

"Here, you mean? In the Abbey?"

"Here and in the country."

"Here. Well, I live here. I know they are always busy producing something and we would seem to be prospering. In the country? Well, Kate keeps me informed, you know, and I hear many rumors. Travelers are constantly bringing news. The last I heard was that the poor King was very ill with the smallpox and measles and although he recovered it has left him with consumption."

"It will be a miracle if he lasts out the year."

"Then it will be a new Queen. It *will* be a Queen, won't it? Queen Mary, I suppose."

"There is always danger in the air when a monarch dies at such an age as to leave no heirs of his body."

"Is this what concerns you, Rupert?"

"*You* concern me," he answered.

I averted my eyes. I did not want a declaration of his devotion which I knew full well existed. It would have been an embarrassment to us both. I think I realized then that I loved Rupert. Oh, it was no wild searing passion. It was not like that which I had felt and could still feel for Bruno. Rupert had not that strange beauty which Bruno possessed; there was no mystery surrounding Rupert. He was just a good man. I loved him differently from the manner in which I loved Bruno. It was as though love were a fruit to be divided into half—one half gave passion and excitement, the other enduring love and security. I could see that what I longed for was both.

My thoughts were running on and I wanted to know what anxiety had brought Rupert here.

"There are rumors about this place," said Rupert. "You are unaware of this. The last to hear rumors are those whom they most concern. As yet they are whispers but many people are watching St. Bruno's Abbey. There is a mystery surrounding this place."

"It is prosperous because we have worked hard here."

"I want you to be on your guard, Damask. If there should be danger, stop for nothing. Take the girls and ride over to me. If need be I could hide you."

"The children are in danger?"

"When a house is in danger all the inmates could well be."

"What is this danger, which has suddenly loomed up?"

"It is not sudden, Damask, it has been there for a long time. Ever since Bruno came back and took the Abbey it has been said that the place is being re-formed. . . . It is known that many of the monks have returned. Talk to Bruno. There should be no assemblies . . . no private services . . . no monkly practices. It is inevitable that people will say that the monastery has been re-formed in defiance of the law."

I said: "The King is sick, is he not? I hear that the Lady Mary when she is Queen may well restore the monasteries."

"It would not be possible, but she would certainly not frown on those who practiced the monastic way of life. Remember though, Damask, she is not Queen, and in some quarters it is said she never will be."

"She is the heir to the throne."

"Is she? Was not her mother's marriage to King Henry declared to be no marriage? In which case she is a bastard."

"The King is not dead and we should not be talking of his death. Would that not be construed as treason?"

"We wish him no ill. We wish him long life. But if we must talk dangerously then so we must, for you could well be in danger. Lord Northumberland has just married his son to the Lady Jane Grey. For what purpose think you? Edward supports the Reformed faith; so doth Lady Jane. If Lady Jane became Queen with Lord Guildford Dudley as her consort the Reformed religion would prevail and those who were suspected of Papistry and living the monastic life would be regarded as enemies of the state."

"Rupert, it is good of you so to concern yourself for us."

"No, not good, for there is nothing I can do to stop myself."

"But how could this be? Who would accept the Lady Jane as Queen? Who now believes that the late King's marriage to Katharine of Aragon was no marriage? We know full well that it was declared so that he might marry Anne Boleyn and for this he had to break with the Church, which is where all our troubles started."

"Forget not Guildford Dudley's powerful father. Northumberland could bring force of arms to support the claims of his daughter-in-law."

"But he could not succeed, for surely Mary has the true claim."

"How much will true claims count against a force of arms? Who do you think is the most powerful man in our country today? It is not the King. He is but a child in the hands of Northumberland, and if Northumberland succeeds in putting Jane Grey on the throne the danger you are now in would not be diminished, I do assure you. But *I* think of now. There are enemies of St. Bruno's Abbey very close to you, Damask."

"I believe you are thinking of my mother's husband."

"He is an ambitious man. From humble beginnings he has become the owner of your father's house. He has done you a great wrong and people who do wrong very often bear great resentment against those whom they wrong."

"You think that he would wish to take revenge on me for the wrong he did me? You believe then, Rupert, that he was in truth the man who betrayed my father?"

"I think it likely. He profited much. He could only have been in his present position through marriage with you and you made it clear, did you not, that that was out of the question?"

"You know so much, Rupert."

"I have concerned myself closely with all that touches you."

"What should I do now?"

"Warn your husband. Beg him to stop these men who were once monks and lay brothers assembling together. It would be better if he sent them away."

"To where could he send them?"

"He could separate them. Perhaps I would take one or two. Kate could have more at Remus . . . anything rather than that it should be seen that a community of men who were once monks still live at St. Bruno's Abbey."

"I will speak to him on his return, Rupert."

He was very anxious but that satisfied him a little.

I sent for the girls and I was so proud of them. Honey was now thirteen years old and a real beauty; she had outgrown that acute jealousy of Catherine; and Catherine was of course my precious darling, my own child, and I loved her as I had not loved any since my father. My feelings for Bruno I set apart—I knew it now for a bemused fascination. It could have grown into overwhelming love, perhaps greater than anything, but I had for some time now realized that was not to be so.

Rupert was a favorite of the girls. They liked to visit his farm; it was he who had taught them to ride and they felt they had more freedom on his farm than they had at the Abbey. Bruno's indifference to Catherine and his resentment of Honey was noticed by the girls. They accepted it as children do and did not seek to change it. But I often thought that to Rupert they gave some of the love that might have been their father's. He was something between a highly favored uncle and father.

They chattered away, asking about the animals on his farm, some of which had been given names by them.

They embraced him warmly when he went and his eyes warned me: Do not forget our conversation. The danger is here. It could flare up at any moment.

Bruno returned in good spirits. He was always in an exultant mood after his visits to the Continent.

"Did you do good business?" I asked him.

He assured me that he had.

"What did you bring home this time? Anything new? My mother always wants to know what new flowers and vegetables have been produced in other countries."

He said he had brought a fine tapestry which would hang in the hall.

When we were alone in our bedchamber that night I told him of Rupert's visit and the warning he had given me.

"Rupert!" cried Bruno scathingly. "What is he hinting at?"

"He is truly concerned. We *are* in danger. I sense it."

He looked at me impatiently. "Have I not told you that you should trust me in all things? You doubt my ability to manage my affairs." He went to the window and looked out. He turned to me. "All this," he said, "is mine. I have rebuilt it. It rises like the phoenix out of the ashes. *I* did this and you doubt my ability to manage my affairs!"

"I don't doubt for one moment, but it often happens that some are more aware of danger than others. And there is danger in the air."

"Danger?"

"Many of the old monks and lay brothers are here. They are living a life which is very close to that which they led in the monastery."

"Well?"

"It has been noticed."

He laughed. "You have always sought to bring me down. You have always resented the fact that I am not as other men. Understand now, that I am not as other men. By God, do you believe that any other could have come to this place, taken it in the first place, and raised it up to what it is now if there had not been some superior power within him?"

I said: "It is certainly very mysterious."

"Mysterious! Is that all you have to say of it?"

"How did you acquire the Abbey, Bruno?"

"I have told you."

"But. . . ."

"But you do not believe me. You have ever tried to throw doubts on all that I have told you. I should never have chosen you."

Truly he frightened me. I thought: There is a madness in him! And I was ever afraid of the mad.

I cried: "So, you made one mistake. Your judgment was wrong. You chose me and you should never have done so."

He turned to me suddenly. I was sitting up in bed and he gripped my arm. It was a painful grip but I did not cry out; I met the blazing fanatical light in his eye with what I believed was calm good sense.

Then I said, "It *was* a mistake, was it not?"

"It need not have been. At that time it was not a mistake. You trusted me then."

"Yes, I trusted you then. And I believed that we should build a wonderful life together. But you deceived me from the start, did you not? You told me you were poor and humble."

"Humble . . . when was I ever humble?"

"You are right. Never were you humble. And the test you put me to, that was arrogant, was it not? You did not woo me as any other man would have done. You must feign poverty lest you fear I marry you for your estates."

He released my arm with an impatient gesture.

"You are hysterical. Rupert has been frightening you and although you have no faith nor truth in me you are very ready to believe him."

"I believe him because what he says makes sense. The Reformed party is in power. The King is a Protestant. Northumberland is a Protestant and they rule the country. Have we not seen the tragedy that can come to those who do not conform to the doctrines laid down by our rulers?"

"And you think *I* would be ruled by these inferior people?"

"Have a care what you say, Bruno. Who knows what may be heard and reported? It is clear to me that you would be ruled by none but your own overweening pride . . . your desire to prove that you are not as other men."

"And am I? Have you forgotten my coming?"

I thought of Keziah on that memorable night and her terror because she had betrayed that which should never have been betrayed; I thought of Brother Ambrose walking across the grass with Bruno and Rolf Weaver coming upon them, taunting. Bruno had seen that. He had seen his father kill the man who had taunted him. Yes, he had seen it and shut his eyes to it because he would not believe Keziah and Ambrose spoke the truth. He could not have it because if it did the image which he had created of himself would be destroyed. In this lies madness, I thought.

"I forget nothing," I said.

"It would be well that you remember."

He stood there beside the bed—tall and straight with the pallor of his face like marble, a contrast to those startlingly violet eyes which were so like Honey's. I thought: He is as beautiful as a god! And I felt that overwhelming tenderness take possession of me and I could not say to him: Bruno, you are living a lie because you are afraid to face the truth.

He began to speak. "I . . . I alone came back to the Abbey, did I not? It was lost and I regained it. How was it done?"

"Bruno, please tell me truthfully. How was it done?"

"It was a miracle. It was the second miracle at St. Bruno's."

I turned wearily away. There was no reasoning with him.

A New Reign

That happened in that momentous year of 1553. My thirtieth birthday was three months away. Thirty! It was not really old but in my thirty years I had seen events take place which had shattered the peace not only of my own household but of the entire country, I had suffered deep sorrow and known some happiness; and at this stage of my life I had reached a conclusion that I had made one of the greatest mistakes a woman can make in marrying a man who can never give her the rich fulfillment she craved. I had my daughters—my own Catherine and my adopted Honey; they were at that time my life; and when I thought of Rupert's warning and the dangers which beset us, it was of my children I thought, not of myself nor what might befall my husband and his Abbey.

The religious conflict was the main question of the day. Even my mother did not escape it.

When I visited her as I did not as often as I should have wished to, for I always feared to come face to face with her husband, or when she visited me she would chatter of her twins and their mischief, which seemed a source of great delight to her, her garden, her stillroom, her remedies. Only rarely would she refer to the new religion.

"You should study the new opinions, Damask," she said. "They are the views of the King and it is good for us all to follow him."

"Mother," I replied, "I cannot say, 'This is the right and that the wrong,' for it seems to me that there is much to be said for both sides."

"Nonsense," said my mother briskly, "how could wrong be

right and right wrong? It must either be one or the other. And this is the right, I do assure you."

"Having been assured by your husband?"

"He has studied these matters."

"Others have studied them. There are clever people on both sides. You must know that."

"It is easy for these people to be mistaken and your stepfather has given a *great* deal of time to it."

I smiled at her indulgently. How try to explain to her! But the fact that she was aware of these matters showed how firmly they must have a hold in my old home.

It was a June night—there was a full moon and I sat at my window and thought of what Rupert had said of our dangers and I wondered whether Bruno would join me that night when I saw dark figures moving toward the church. I knew what this meant. They were going to Mass. Bruno would be with them.

I shivered a little. They knew that if this were known they would be in danger, and yet they continued to act in this way. Perhaps they believed that Bruno with his supernatural powers could save them from any disaster which might threaten them. Some of the ex-monks were simple, I thought. Clement for one had clearly convinced himself that there was no truth in Keziah and Ambrose's story. Bruno had that power to convince people in the face of facts. The only one with whom he could not succeed was myself.

Clement was happy working in the bakehouse. He would sing Latin chants as he worked. It was clear to me that he almost believed that he had never left the Abbey.

The figures had disappeared into the church and I sat for some time thinking of the significance of this when suddenly I saw another figure. It was not one of the monks this time. I stared for the man who was making his way stealthily toward the church had a look of Simon Caseman.

Impulsively I put a cloak about my nightdress and ran downstairs.

I sped across the grass past the monks' dorter to the porch of the church. I went in. A figure moved forward. I had not been mistaken. It was Simon Caseman.

"What are you doing here?" I demanded.

"You may well ask." His eyes were alight with excitement. I had never seen the fox's mask so clearly.

"Trespassing!"

"In a good cause."

"You have no right to be here."

"Yes, every right."

"In whose name?"

"In the name of the King."

"You speak fine words."

"I speak the truth. What is going on in there? This has become a monastery once more. It was dissolved but here it is again."

"Do you not know, Simon Caseman, that many abbey lands have been bestowed?"

"I know it well. There is, mayhap, always a reason for such bestowals."

"A very good reason, and one which is the concern only of the bestower and the bestowed."

"That I agree, but when the place is used to break the King's law. . . ."

"The King's law has not been broken here."

"Not when that which has been abolished is slyly brought back."

"There are many workmen here, Simon Caseman."

"There are monks, too. They who have been dispossessed by the Crown now reinstate themselves against the laws of the land."

"What is happening here?" A voice cool, curt and authoritative was demanding. Bruno had come into the porch. From the church came the sound of chanting.

"This is happening," replied Simon Caseman. "I have witnessed that which could send you to the gallows. Rest assured I shall do my duty."

"Your duty is to go back to your house and live quietly there— although you do not deserve to, having taken that which would never have been bestowed on you but for ill justice."

"Do not talk of justice, I pray you. What is happening in this place? How is it that you have rebuilt it as you have? Do you think I do not know? Do you think you can draw the wool over my eyes with your talk of miracles? Miracles forsooth! It is clear indeed from what quarter came your wealth."

I saw that Bruno had turned pale. He was very uneasy.

"Yes," cried Simon Caseman, "I know full well. Where does the money come from to build a fine Abbey to gather together your monks and lay brothers? Where indeed. From the enemies of England. From Spain and Rome, that is where the money comes from."

"You lie!" cried Bruno.

"Then if it is a lie, where? Answer that, Bruno Kingsman. *Saint* Bruno . . . answer that. From whence came the money to rebuild the Abbey, eh? To start everything in motion, eh? Are you going to tell me it comes from the profit of the farm? I would not believe you. Great riches have been showered on this place and I am asking you whence they came. That is all I want to know."

The singing in the church had ceased. I saw the figures of the men within the church hovering not far from the porch.

"Lie to me if you wish!" cried Simon Caseman, his face working with passion. "You won't deceive me. I know. I have always known. The money came from Spain and Rome. It comes from our country's enemies. It comes from those who would bring the Pope back as Supreme Head of the Church against the laws of this land."

"You lie," cried Bruno.

"Then where, eh? Whence came the money to build this place? How much has been spent on it? Who has such money . . . apart from His Majesty the King and the richest families in the land? Tell us this, Bruno, *Saint* Bruno . . . weaver of miracles, tell us! Did it come from on high? Was it poured into your coffers from heaven?"

"Yes," answered Bruno soberly.

Simon Caseman burst into loud laughter. "You would call it from heaven since it comes from Spain. I and many with me would call it treason."

There was a hush in the porch at the mention of that dreaded word.

Then Bruno said: "Get you gone from here. We have no need of your kind."

"Indeed you have not. You would not find me breaking the

law of the land. This is meant to be the beginning of the restoration of the monasteries. I know there are such schemes afoot. They come from Rome and Spain . . . where your masters are. Think not that I shall allow this treason to continue."

Bruno went back into the church. I drew back into the shadows and Simon Caseman walked past me. I had never seen such a look of set determination in his face. I thought: Tomorrow he will inform on us. Perhaps by tomorrow night Bruno will be in the Tower.

Then my thoughts went to the girls and I wondered what would become of them.

I ran after Simon Caseman.

He heard my footsteps and turned slowly.

"So?" he said.

"What are you going to do?"

"My duty."

"I believe it will not be the first time you have informed."

He pretended to misunderstand. "It may not be the last, mayhap. I am a dutiful man."

"Particularly when there is much to be gained."

"Gained? What should I gain?"

"Revenge."

"You are dramatic, my dear Damask." His eyes surveyed me and I remembered that I had only my nightgown under my cloak.

I felt very frightened and that made me reckless, I suppose.

"Is revenge as satisfying as a fine house which you had no hope of attaining while my father was alive?"

"What has that to do with this?"

"A similar situation. You did your gainful duty once before, did you not?"

He was silent, taken aback; and I was certain then that I stood face to face with my father's murderer for that is what his betrayer would always be to me.

"I know," I said, "that you informed against my father. You murderer."

"Is this the way to talk to one who has your life in his hands?"

"I would not think that life worth having if I were not true to myself."

"You are a firebrand, Damask. You always were. What a reckless little fool! You might have had so much. But you chose him. . . . Is he a man or is he an idol? We shall soon see. He should hang well."

"You have made up your mind to inform against him as you did against my father."

"Your father?"

"Don't try to deceive me further, Simon Caseman. My father took you into his house. You had nothing of your own. All you had was envy, greed, and a sad lack of principles. You had selfishness, wickedness, ingratitude. . . ."

"In fact I was a very sinful fellow."

"For once you have spoken the truth. You are my father's murderer, Simon Caseman. You wanted his possessions."

"I wanted his daughter, I admit. And the fact is that even when she rants and raves I still do."

"How dare you!"

"As you dare, my reckless beauty. Here is the man who can have you all carried off to the Tower before another day has passed . . . and you dare abuse him."

"I would abuse you with my dying breath. Have you ever loved a father?"

"I never knew mine so that was beyond me."

"I loved my father. I loved him dearly. I saw him in his prison in the Tower. He was taken from there to his place of execution and his head was cut off. *You* cut off that head, Simon Caseman. Do you think I shall ever forgive you for that?"

"Your father was a fool. He should never have harbored the priest. He knew he was breaking the law. People who break the law must expect sudden and violent death. To give a priest shelter, to set up an abbey which has been dispossessed . . . these acts are breaking the King's laws and punishable by death. You would do well to remember that while you rant, however prettily, to one who could do you much good or as you wish so much harm."

"Not content with being my father's murderer you would murder us all. You want this Abbey, do you not? Is this the price you are asking?"

"Don't be so foolish, Damask. I would not harm you. Are you
not my own stepdaughter?"

"To my deepest shame I am."

"And one for whom, for all her waywardness and unkindness
to me, I have ever felt great warmth of heart."

"Have you ever felt that for any?"

"For you, you know."

"Are you suggesting that you wished to marry me for reasons
other than that I was my father's heir?"

"You are not your father's heir now, Damask. You are in acute
danger. Tomorrow you will wait for the arrival of the King's men.
You were not there when they took your father. This time it will
be your husband for whom they come unless. . . ."

"Unless what?"

"I would do a great deal for you, Damask."

"Then go away and hang yourself."

He laughed. "That is asking a little too much for if I were dead
how could I enjoy your company? No, Damask, you will have to be
more pleasant to me . . . if you wish to go on living in comfort
on your Spanish gold."

"I fail to understand you."

He took a step nearer to me. "I think you understand very
well. If you were to come to me in a friendly fashion I might be
persuaded to suspend my judgment on what has taken place tonight."

"I will ask my mother's advice," I said caustically.

"Oh, Damask, were you not unwise? Just think if you had not
been, your father would be alive today."

I turned away and started toward the house.

He called after me: "I shall give you twenty-four hours. Think
about it. You could have saved your father. Now is the time to
save your family."

Bruno was coming out of the church followed by several of the
monks.

Simon Caseman broke into a run and I hurried into the house
trembling.

*　*　*

Bruno did not come to our bedchamber that night. I spent most of it in the window seat waiting for his return. I wanted to find out whether indeed he had received money from Spain or Rome. It seemed to me the only explanation. I wondered it had not occurred to me before. Of course it was the answer. He had received money to rebuild the Abbey, and what more plausible than that he should have been chosen to do this.

Simon Caseman's words kept repeating themselves in my mind. I was responsible for my father's death. If I had married Simon Caseman he would not have informed on him because through me he would have had the house. But I would not marry him and so my father had to die. And now he had put another proposition to me. If I would go to him—and I knew what he meant by that—I could buy his silence.

I shivered at the prospect confronting us.

At least though we were safe for twenty-four hours.

Why did not Bruno come to me and comfort me? How characteristic of him was this. He allowed me to share nothing and the reason was that he knew I did not believe in him.

In the morning I went into the tower where he had his private quarters. He was working placidly at his books.

"Bruno," I cried, "I should have thought you would have had something to say to me."

He looked surprised.

"You can't have forgotten last night's scene?"

"Your stepfather is not worth a moment's thought."

I replied sharply: "He was responsible for my father's death. He is now threatening to bring about yours and many of those dependent on you."

"And you think he will succeed?"

"He succeeded with my father."

"Your father acted foolishly."

"Not as foolishly as you. You blatantly break the law. At least he did it in secret."

He smiled and lifted his head, and he looked so beautiful that I could have wept because all was not well between us.

"I tell you that there is no need to fear."

"No need to fear? When that man is our enemy and has witnessed what he did last night and moreover threatened to expose you?"

"He will do nothing."

"How can you be sure?"

"Because I know."

"He has threatened to expose you."

"You believe everyone but me. You imply that you do not think me capable of defending everything I have built up."

"With Spanish gold?" I asked.

"You see, you believe him."

"But it seems obvious now. Where could you have found so much money?"

His eyes glowed with an inner fire. "He asked if heaven opened its coffers for me. And the answer is yes. It was a miracle. It was for this purpose that I came to the crib on Christmas morning. Men and women have uttered calumnies concerning me. And you, the one whom I chose, believed them rather than me. But this I swear. The money with which I am rebuilding this Abbey did not come from Spain. It came from heaven. And if you say that could only be a miracle, I answer: So be it. I tell you that man cannot harm me. But you do not believe me."

"If you swear to me that you are not in the pay of the Spaniards. . . ."

"I do not beg you to believe me. I merely tell you that he will not betray us. It may be that in due course you will have a little faith in me."

With that he left me.

Twenty-four hours grace. I knew Simon Caseman well enough to believe that he would carry out his threat. He was an acquisitive and vengeful man. He could not believe that I would fall in with his monstrous suggestion. He enjoyed tormenting me, making clear to me how much I and my family were in his power. Moreover he lusted not only for me but for the Abbey, and I knew that to gain that was his main purpose.

It was no use remonstrating with Bruno though what he could do to save himself I could not imagine. I had no doubt that not only had Simon Caseman seen with his own eyes what was going on in the Abbey but he would have witnesses.

It occurred to me that I might take the girls and go to Kate. Would that save them? Would it involve Kate?

The tension was so unbearable that it left me numb; I felt as though I could only wait for what would happen next. I tried to act normally and went along to the bakehouse as I often did in the mornings to consult Clement about the food for the day. He had been present in the church last night.

I was surprised for he did not seem unduly perturbed.

"Clement," I said, "what will become of us all, think you?"

"We shall be safe," he answered complacently.

"You think those were idle threats?"

Clement raised his eyes to the ceiling. "Bruno will save us from evil."

"How can that be?"

"His ways are miraculous."

There was a complacency about the man which astonished me. He did not seem to realize that he could be dragged to a place of execution, hanged, cut down while still alive and barbarously tortured. Had he not heard of the monks of the Charterhouse? What had they done but deny the supremacy of the King as Head of the Church. His actions would be considered as treasonable!

"You heard what that man said last night, Clement. You were there."

"I was there. But Bruno spoke to us afterward. He said there was no need to fear."

"What can he do to save us?"

"That is for him and God."

They believe he is divine, I thought. Oh, what a rude awakening they would have on the morrow!

The sudden vision of kind simple Clement, who had carried my children on his back and had surreptitiously slipped them tidbits from his oven, being tortured was more than I could endure.

"Clement," I said, "you could get away. There is still time."

He looked at me in astonishment. "This is my life," he said.

Then he smiled at me almost pityingly. "You have no faith. But fear not. All will be well."

What faith *they* had in Bruno. During that day I realized what had been happening over the years. Bruno was not only refounding the Abbey, he was building up that image of himself which had been his before the coming of Rolf Weaver.

That day everything was as usual. No one but myself seemed to be aware of the threat which was hanging over us.

My mother called in the afternoon. I wondered whether Simon Caseman had confided in her and she had come to warn me. He could scarcely have told her of his suggestion to me.

She had brought the usual basket of good things—her newest wine, a new form of tansy cake she had made, her own special brand of marchpane.

She kissed me and said that I was not looking well. Her anxious eyes scrutinized me and I knew that she was wondering, as she did every time we met, whether or not I was with child.

I quickly gathered that she knew nothing of her husband's discovery for she was too frank to have been able to hide it, but she did talk to me about the merits of the Reformed religion.

"And it is true, Damask," she said, "that our King is of the Reformed faith. Poor lad, he is sick. They say that he never recovered from that bout of the smallpox. Some would say he was lucky to survive that at all." She became very confidential. "I have heard it said that he cannot live long, poor boy."

"Mother," I said, "has it occurred to you that if the King died, which I hope he will not, the Lady Mary could be Queen; and if she were, might there not be a return to Rome?"

"Impossible!" cried my mother, growing pale at the thought.

"Yet it is not an impossibility, Mother. Should we not be cautious about proclaiming our views until we are sure?"

"If you know the true faith, Damask, how can you deny it?"

"But what is the true faith? Why cannot we accept the simple rules of Christ? Why must it be so important that we worship in this way or that?"

"I am not sure, Damask, but I think you may be speaking treason."

"Treason one day, Mother, is loyalty the next." I was suddenly afraid for her, because she was so simple. She did not love a faith but a husband; she would have taken whatever he offered her. She proclaimed her beliefs in the Reformed faith because her husband had adopted them. Yet she could die for those beliefs as others had before her.

I embraced her suddenly.

"My dear child, you are affectionate today."

"How should I know whether I shall be in a position to be so tomorrow?"

"My word, we are gloomy! What ails you, Damask? You are not sickening for something? I will give you a little draft which contains thyme. That will give you pleasant dreams and tomorrow you will wake up in love with all the world."

Tomorrow? I thought. What will tomorrow bring?

But I must not alarm my mother. She was happy for today. Let her remain so. My father had once said that, living in such times as ours, we should take no thought for the morrow; we should savor each hour and if it contained pleasure, enjoy that to the full.

I could not in any case speak to her of my anxieties. How could I tell her that the man she had married and on whom she doted as though he were some prophet from heaven was threatening to destroy us and had offered me security if I became his mistress?

The day seemed long. I could settle to nothing. I went to the scriptorium as I sometimes did and listened to the girls at their lessons. What will become of them? I asked myself; and I wished, as my father had wished for me, that they were securely married and living somewhere far removed from the stresses caused by men's clashes of opinion.

At dinner we sat at the family table on the dais and the rest of the household at the large one in the hall, and although when a sound was heard from without I was aware of furtive looks in the direction of the door and I knew some of the company were attacked by acute apprehension and some trembled in their seats, there was no outward indication of alarm and confident looks were cast in Bruno's direction.

It was just as we were about to leave the table that a messenger did arrive.

I shall never forget the awful consternation which filled that
hall. I rose to my feet. I had taken the hand of Catherine who was
seated next to me. Her startled gaze was turned toward me. I
thought: Oh, God, it has come. What will become of us all?

Bruno had risen too but he showed no apprehension. Calmly
he left his place and went forward to greet the messenger.

"Welcome," he said.

"I bring ill news," said the messenger. "The King is dead."

I could sense the breaking of the tension; it was as though everyone present gave a long-drawn-out "Ah." The King was dead.
Who could say what would happen next? The Lady Mary was in
line for the throne. The Abbey was saved.

I saw Bruno's complacent smile. I saw the look of wonder in
the faces of those who had been with him in the church last night.

He had promised them a miracle—for only a miracle could save
the Abbey from Simon Caseman's treachery. And this was their
miracle. The death of the King; the end of the Protestant rule. The
Catholic Princess awaiting to mount the throne.

Momentarily he caught my eye. I saw the triumph there; the
enormous pride which I was beginning to think no one ever possessed in such strength as he did.

And immediately I thought: He knew all the time. He knew
the King was dead. He knew that if Simon Caseman's accusation
against him was going to succeed he should have brought it
months ago. He arranged for the messenger to bring the news at
a time when it would create the greatest effect. I was beginning
to know well this man whom I had married.

There was no thought in anyone's mind now but what was
going to happen next.

When I heard that Edward had died two days before the fact
was made known I was certain that Bruno had known of this and
for this reason he had flouted Simon Caseman and decided to
impress his followers by his miracle.

I was building up such a cynical view of my husband that I began to wonder whether I hated him.

But he was less complacent when the news came that the Duke
of Northumberland had persuaded the King to set aside his two

sisters, Mary and Elizabeth, on the grounds of their illegitimacy, and to declare his cousin Lady Jane Grey the true heir to the throne; but Mary had too much support for this to be accepted and immediately a Catholic faction began to form about her and the country was divided. Families were divided. The only aspect which made me rejoice was the fact that we had a respite. The affairs of the country were so much more important than those of a single abbey and no one was going to arrest people who, were Mary to come to the throne, would be considered true and loyal subjects while those who arrested them would be the traitors.

The country was in a ferment of excitement.

My mother came over to the Abbey trembling and apprehensive. Simon had gone to Northumberland to offer his services in the support of Jane Grey, whom my mother called the true Queen.

I knew why Simon had gone. It was imperative to him that Jane Grey become the Queen of England that the Reformed faith might be preserved. He had come down too far on its side to withdraw. I suspected him of expediency but I was not entirely sure that this was all his motive. He had adopted the Reformed faith when it was not safe to do so and the greatest villains could be very firm in their views when it came to religion.

"She is a virtuous woman, Queen Jane," said my mother. "She has lived a life of piety."

"I believe the same can be said of those whom many call Queen Mary."

"She is no Queen. Her father's marriage was invalid," cried my mother. "Was her mother not first the bride of King Henry's brother, Arthur?"

"There are many who will support her," I said.

"They will be the Papists," my mother said bitterly.

"It is a strange thing, Mother," I said, "but many Englishmen will be ready to support whomsoever they call the true Queen whatever their religion. I believe that to be so. And Mary has a great claim and after her Elizabeth."

"Bastards!" cried my mother, almost in tears, which showed me that she was afraid that Queen Jane's chances of holding the throne might not be good.

"Hush, Mother, do not become embroiled. It would go ill for you if any heard you call one who may well soon be our Queen by that name."

"She never shall be," said my mother fiercely.

The next day she came over to tell me that a vintner's boy had been deprived of his ears because he had declared in the Chepe that Queen Jane was not the true Queen and had shouted for Queen Mary.

"You see," said my mother firmly, "what happens to those who would deny the truth."

There were many rumors. We heard that Jane was reluctant to take the crown. She was but a child—sixteen years old—not much older than Honey and this had been forced upon her by ambitious men. I felt sorry for poor Jane because the Princess Mary's case was growing stronger every day. She was after all the daughter of King Henry VIII whereas Jane was only the granddaughter of his sister.

In the city people whispered together, afraid to voice an opinion openly, but I sensed that the majority of people were against Queen Jane, partly because they loathed her father-in-law Northumberland and were in no mood to accept his dominance but chiefly because they knew that Mary was the true heir to the throne.

This was in fact a division between the new Protestants and the old Catholics and the Reformed religion being so new had not yet taken a firm hold of the people.

Mary had fled to Norfolk and found thousands rallying to her cause. She was proclaimed Queen in Norwich. She crossed the border into Suffolk and set up her standard at Framlingham Castle.

Each day we waited for news. When Ridley, the Bishop of London, preached in favor of Queen Jane my mother was delighted.

"'Twill all come right," she said. "Such a sweet good girl she is!"

But a few days later the Earls of Pembroke and Arundel were proclaiming Mary Queen of England at Paul's Cross and we realized then that the nine days' reign was at an end. Poor little Jane could not stand out against the might of right. Mary was the true heiress of England; poor pathetic Jane was cast out.

I went to see my mother because I guessed she would be very anxious.

"What is happening?" she cried, distraught. "What can people be thinking of? The Queen has the favor of the Bishop of London. Who can gainsay that?"

"Many," I said, and I was filled with anxiety for her. "You will have to be very careful now. Do not talk freely to the servants. Heaven knows what this is going to mean." Then I realized that, as I with my family had moved into a certain security, my mother and hers had come close to danger.

I took the books Simon had instructed her to read and hid them.

"You should not keep them here. We are about to begin a reign of the sternest Catholic rule. You must live very quietly for a while. It must not be remembered that you support Queen Jane."

It was difficult to feign an indifference to the fate of Queen Jane. It seemed one must either support or reject. There was no middle way. I was sorry for the young girl, who had been such a reluctant Queen, knowing full well that she had no right to the title. I trusted she would be forgiven and not have to suffer for the ambition of others; but I could not help but rejoice that my home had been saved by her downfall.

Her sad little story was reaching its tragic climax. Nine days after Jane's accession to the throne Mary was proclaimed Queen of England.

Simon Caseman had returned unostentatiously to the house before that day, and was trying to pretend now that he had been away on business and had not gone to London to support Queen Jane. He was as ready as any to shout "Long live Queen Mary." At least he was wise in that.

I hoped he would continue to be so.

It quickly became apparent that the comparatively peaceful years of Edward's reign were over.

Before the month was out Lady Jane and her husband, Lord Guildford Dudley, were committed to the Tower of London.

Kate came to the Abbey from Remus, bringing Carey and Colas with her.

She was excited as always by great events. She wanted us to ride out to Wanstead to see the new Queen come to her capital and the young people joined her in the clamor to go.

I was glad to get away from the Abbey and we all rode out—myself and Kate with two of the men of our household to guard us and Carey, Honey, Catherine and Colas.

Kate was excited because the Princess Elizabeth was going to meet her sister at Wanstead and accompany her into London. Indeed everyone was gay and excited. It seemed incredible that such a short time ago I had had such fears. But even now I could not get out of my mind the thought of my mother at Caseman Court and I was wondering how she was feeling since her husband had lost what he had hoped for and if his Lutheran tendency were known would be in the kind of danger which had threatened my household such a short while ago.

I could not help noticing the admiring glances that came the way of my girls. Kate of course would always dominate any scene by that incomparable charm and now that she had poise and a certain look of experience to add to it, it had in no way diminished. But Honey was a beauty—in her way even more so than Kate. She was of course a child as yet but ready to burst into womanhood, and in her russet-colored velvet riding suit and her jaunty little feathered hat I thought she was one of the loveliest creatures I had ever seen. As for Catherine, in a similar hat but of dark-green velvet, she sparkled with the love of life—in contrast to the rather brooding silence of Honey, so that what she lacked in actual beauty she made up for by her vital personality. And Carey, what a handsome boy he was—with a look of Kate and not unlike my girls either. As for eight-year-old Colas, the baby of the group, he was determined to enjoy every moment. They might well all have been sisters and brothers. Catherine and Carey sparred continuously and we had to reprove them once or twice, telling Carey to remember not to speak to a lady as he spoke to Catherine, and Catherine to be less provoking.

And at Wanstead we saw the Queen's meeting with her sister Elizabeth. It was a historic moment, I thought—the daughters of Katharine of Aragon and Anne Boleyn meeting at Wanstead.

I'll swear that more eyes were on the Princess Elizabeth than on the Queen. That red-haired young woman of twenty reminded me in some ways of my own Catherine. She was no beauty but possessed of vitality and charm which was in great contrast to the silent manners of the new Queen.

Mary was dressed in violet-colored velvet which did nothing to enhance her aging looks, for she was thirty-seven years old. But the cheers were loyal and when the sisters kissed they rang out even louder.

The sisters left Wanstead and rode toward the city. We joined in the press of people with our servants closing around us to ensure that we were given passage. I made the girls ride on either side of me, and so we came through the city portal at Aldgate and into London. Our young people chattered excitedly all the time. It was wonderful to see the streamers hanging from the windows and there were many groups of children to sing songs praising the new Queen; and in the Minories all the crafts of the city were represented in their appropriate costumes.

We followed all the way down to the Tower; on the river gaily decked crafts seemed to prance with delight and sweet music could be heard everywhere as the guns boomed a salute.

I wondered whether from some window in the Tower the Queen of nine days looked out on all this rejoicing and wondered what her fate would be. Of one thing there could be no doubt. London was welcoming the new Queen and heralding in the new reign.

Catherine said suddenly: "What a pity that Peter and Paul did not come with us. How they would have loved the procession."

I shivered, and wondered how my mother was taking the news of the acclamation of a new queen while she who had reigned so briefly was awaiting her fate with dread.

Kate stayed with us for a while at the Abbey. She talked continually of the changing world. Under the last reign the Reformed faith had been the favored one; this was a return to Catholicism, and those who had been in high places during the last reign now found themselves out of favor.

Everyone was afraid to speak freely. It was seen how quickly one could fall out of favor and it was inevitable that after such a clash between two queens and two religions the blood should flow. Edward was buried at Westminster and the Queen had a solemn service performed for him in her private chapel with all the rites and ceremonies of the Church of Rome.

A few days later the Duke of Northumberland was beheaded.

Kate stayed for the coronation, which was in October, and we saw the Queen carried in her litter which was covered with cloth of silver and drawn by six white horses. Her gown was of blue velvet edged with ermine and she wore a caul of gold network on her head; it was set with pearls and precious stones.

I glanced at Kate and wondered if she remembered that other Queen whom we had seen years ago when Tom Skillen had been blackmailed by Kate into rowing us to Greenwich. How different that elegant radiant Anne from this aging, tired woman!

Kate whispered that the caul must be weighty with all those stones; and indeed the poor Queen looked as though it made her head ache.

And in an open chariot decorated with crimson velvet rode that other Queen's daughter—the young Elizabeth—and with her was her stepmother Anne of Cleves—the only one of Henry's poor sad queens to survive to that day.

It was a great pageant, but I wondered, and I am sure many did on that day, what lay in store for us all.

Of course I had known that a new reign would mean changes; for us at the Abbey it was as though we had a narrow escape from disaster. I was glad Simon Caseman remained subdued. He was wise in that he went about his estate neither condemning the new Queen nor praising her. Either would have been to call unwelcome attention to himself. An increased complacency was apparent in Bruno. He was regarded with an even greater wonder than before and I gathered from Clement that it was believed he had brought about another miracle which had saved the Abbey. It was the third. The first had been when he had come in the form of a baby in the crib and because of this the Abbey which had been in decline began to prosper; then he had returned to the Abbey after it had been disbanded and, lo, many had found it possible to return; and now when an enemy had threatened to destroy what he had built up, by a miracle the King had died in the nick of time and a new Catholic Queen was on the throne.

Bruno had done this—Bruno the miracle worker.

The first change was an act which abolished the Reformed liturgy, that which Edward and his Parliament had declared had been inspired by the Holy Ghost, and revived the old form which had been used in the days of Henry VIII. This was of greater significance than at first appeared because it was a pointer.

At the beginning of the following year we heard that there was to be a marriage between Mary and Philip of Spain, that most fanatical of Catholics.

There was an outcry about this and I knew that it gave great hope to those who wished to see the Reformed Church established. Mary was popular; she was the rightful heir; but the people of England had no desire to be dominated by Spain. The Parliament raised its voice to ask the Queen not to marry a foreigner, but this appeared to be of no avail.

I rarely went to Caseman Court. I was afraid of meeting Simon Caseman, but my mother and the twins were constant visitors to the Abbey.

Peter and Paul, so alike that one could not tell the difference between them, were about the same age as Carey and the children were almost as of one family. My mother had some time before asked that the twins should share my daughters' tutors and this had been arranged, and when Kate stayed with us Carey would join them in the scriptorium. I regretted that neither of my girls shone in the schoolroom. They were bright without being clever. Carey excelled far more at outdoor pursuits rather than lessons; Peter was the cleverest of the children; though this was not discovered for some time and both were thought to be clever children until it was discovered that Peter did most of Paul's bookwork for him and was always ready with a whispered answer for his twin. Paul was the sportsman and could rival Carey in outdoor pastimes. It always seemed to me that the twins had the shared attributes of one very accomplished person.

My mother doted on them; so did their father. He might be grasping, avaricious and of an unpleasant character, but he certainly loved his sons.

I often thought how happy we all might have been together, but for the covetousness of Simon and the overwhelming pride of Bruno. If Bruno could have been a normal husband and father and Simon could have forgotten that others had what he wanted, if we could have settled down and accepted what we had and made the most of it, how different everything could have been. There were outside events of course, and these could strike in such a devastating manner that, in my opinion, families should stand firmly together as a bulwark against them, and not allow themselves to be fraught with internal conflicts.

My mother's naïveté often gave me an insight into what might be happening at Caseman Court and it alarmed me.

When there was talk of the Queen's marriage my mother could not hide a certain exhilaration, and I could tell at once that she hoped that the Queen would be overthrown. I knew that she was voicing her husband's feelings for she would consider it her duty to share his opinions.

"Marriage with Spain," she said, as she and I sat in my garden together. "Why, we shall be a subject of that country! Do Englishmen want that?"

"I doubt not," I said, "that if the Queen married Philip of Spain there would be all sorts of conditions to prevent Spain's getting a hold on the country."

"When a woman marries she is influenced by her husband."

I smiled at my mother. "Mother," I said, "all women don't make as dutiful wives as you do."

She was a little uncertain what I meant by that but she went on: "We should have the Inquisition here. Can you guess what that means? No one would be safe. Any one of us could be carried off to face a tribunal. Have you any idea what it is like to live under the Inquisition in Spain?"

"It is terrible. I hate persecution in any form."

My mother dropped the shirt she was embroidering for Peter or Paul. She gripped my arm. "Then, my dear Damask, we must prevent its ever coming to these shores."

"I am sure the people will never tolerate it here."

"If this Spanish marriage takes place who can say what will happen? If we are a dominion of Spain, they will be here with their thumbscrews and their instruments of torture."

"They are already here, Mother, and were before the Queen thought of marrying a foreigner. I shudder sometimes when I pass the Tower and think of Father—and of the dungeons and the torture chambers in which so many people's beloved sons and husbands have suffered. Women too. . . . Have you forgotten Anne Askew?"

"She was a martyr."

"A martyr indeed."

"A saint," said my mother fervently.

"And would have been equally so had she been of any other faith."

My mother was silent for a while and then she leaned toward me.

"This reign cannot last," she said. "I have reasons for knowing this. I worry about you, Damask . . . you and the children."

"Mother, I worry about you and the twins."

"Yes," she said. "It's strange that religion should be the cause. I can't see why everyone cannot see the true way."

"Your way, Mother? Or that of your husband perhaps?"

"I have seen the truth," she said, "and I believe that you live dangerously. I should like to see *you* with us, Damask. So would your stepfather. He always speaks kindly of you."

I smiled cynically. "That is indeed good of him, Mother."

"Oh, he is a good man. A man of principles."

Oh, God, I thought, do you not know that he murdered my father?

"He thinks that you resent his taking your father's place."

"No one could take his place," I cried fiercely.

"I mean, my dear, because we married. Some daughters are like that . . . sons too. But you should remember that he has made me very happy."

I wanted to shout the truth at her. He murdered my father; he asked me to marry him; he has tried to make an infamous bargain with me; he has asked for my virtue as a price for my safety. And this is the man of whom you, my mother, think so highly.

But of course I said nothing. She was so innocent. She must go on in her blissful ignorance.

"You should try to be a little more reasonable, Damask."

I smiled rather sardonically and she smiled.

"Think about it," she went on, "think what the Spanish marriage would mean. Queen Jane is still a prisoner in the Tower. There are still many who would be ready to proclaim her Queen and even those who feel that she has no rightful claim can look to the Princess Elizabeth."

"But, Mother, how could the Princess come before Queen Mary?"

"The King proved his marriage to the Queen's mother was no true marriage."

"He proved it to himself," I said. "Mother, do you not think that simples and herbs and flowers and embroidery are of greater interest than these weighty matters?"

"Well," she conceded, "these weighty matters are for men."

"Then would it not be better . . . and safer . . . for women to keep to those things in which without doubt they excel?"

She nodded smiling. "All the same, I worry about you," she said. "I wish Bruno had bought a pleasant country mansion. An Abbey is suspect . . . particularly when. . . ."

"Oh, Mother, when religion and politics sway this way and that, the treason of yesterday becomes the loyalty of today. Let us all take care. And let us remember that the enemies of Rome are those who are in danger today, although tomorrow it may be different."

"Tomorrow," said my mother, brightening. "That will come."

It was small wonder that she disturbed me.

In the bakehouse Clement was kneading dough; the sleeves of his shirt were rolled up to his elbows and he seemed to caress the mixture as he worked.

Catherine was sitting on the high stool watching him, her lovely face bright with interest. She had always had some enthusiasms for as long as I could remember. They faded quickly but they were nevertheless intense while they lasted; Honey was more constant.

"Go on, Clement," she commanded; and I heard him say as I entered: "The Abbot had called us and we stood round the crib and there in it was the living child."

She turned as I entered.

"Here comes our mistress," said Clement, "to give me orders for the day. Mistress, I am trying a little burdock and purple orchis in the potage today. It gives a mightily pleasant flavor. I shall await your verdict."

"Mother," said Catherine, "Clement has been telling me the story. Was it not wonderful! It is like something from the Bible. Moses in the bulrushes. I always loved that story and now to know this. . . ."

I looked at her animated face and I was not sure what I wanted to say to her. She was so thrilled by the thought that her father was some sort of saint or messiah and even though I was convinced that this was false and I wanted my daughter to accept the virtues of truth, the alternative to the mystery story was not something which I could tell to my daughter. Catherine had always had to know everything once her interest was aroused. She knew more of the histories of the people who lived around us than any other member of the household. Now I saw that I was in a quandary which had been certain to arise sooner or later. She either had to accept her father as this superior being or learn the sordid story of his birth. For the moment I thought it better for her to accept the legend, but I wished it had not been so.

I discussed the food that was to be prepared that day and said: "Come, Catherine, it will soon be time you were at your lessons and I wish you to gather some flowers for me and arrange them."

"Oh, Mother, I *hate* arranging flowers. You know I can't do it."

"All the more reason that you should learn. It is one of the necessary accomplishments of a housewife."

"I don't think I shall be a housewife. I'll stay here all my life and become a nun and I'll have a convent of my own. An abbess I suppose I'd be."

"My dear child, it is not long ago that monasteries and convents were dissolved by order of the King."

"Ah, but that was in the old days, Mother. We have a new Queen now—a good, virtuous Queen. Doubtless she would wish to see the return of these institutions."

"You are a child, Cat," I said not without a twinge of alarm. "For God's sake do not get embroiled in these matters yet."

"Dear Mother, how vehement you are! I have always suspected you of being somewhat irreligious." She kissed me in that endearing way of hers. "Not that I didn't love you for it. I used to be frightened by all this . . . and all the people who looked like monks. I was afraid to go near some of the old buildings. Do you remember how I used to cling to your hand or your skirts? I used to think nothing can harm me while Mother is here, but she will always look after me."

"My darling, I always would."

"I knew, dearest Mother. You are so . . . as a mother should be. He is different, of course. He is wonderful. Clement has been telling me what it was like in the Abbey when he came. They did not know how to look after a baby and although they knew he was no ordinary baby as Clement says, he came in the shape of one and therefore was half mortal."

"Clement talks too much."

"It is all so *interesting*. There is so much I want to know."

"Confine your interests to your lessons for a while," I said.

She laughed with that high-pitched, infectious laughter which I so loved to hear. "Dear Mother. *Dearest* Mother. You are so practical . . . always. . . . So different from. . . . No wonder Aunt Kate laughs at you."

"So I am the butt for your amusement?"

She kissed the tip of my nose. "Which is a good thing to be and we all love you for it. Why, Mother, what would we do without you?"

"Now," I said, well pleased, "you will just have time to gather your flowers and arrange them before you go to the scriptorium. And do not be late. I have already had complaints of your unpunctuality."

She ran off and I looked after her with that love which was so intense that it was like suffering a pain.

After that I often found her in the bakehouse where Clement would tell her stories of her father's childhood. She discovered facts which I had never known. Each day she became more and more interested. Bruno had noticed it and he warmed toward her. At last he was taking an interest in his daughter.

One day I went into the schoolroom and heard Catherine and Honey quarreling.

"You are easily duped, Cat. You always believe what you want to. That is no way to learn what is true. I don't believe it. I don't like him. I never did. I believe he is cruel to . . . our mother."

Catherine spat out: "It is because he is not your father. You are jealous."

"Jealous! I tell you I am glad. I would have any man for my father rather than him."

I paused at the door and did not go in. Instead I crept silently away.

I thought a great deal about that conversation. It was inevitable of course now that they were growing up that they should form their own opinions. When they had been little I had kept them away from him, knowing that there was no time in his life for young children. I did wonder whether it would have been different if Catherine had been a boy.

I considered them now—Catherine was nearly twelve years old, Honey fourteen—almost a woman, Honey, for she had developed earlier than most. There was a certain touch of Keziah's voluptuousness about her and her beauty had by no means diminished. Those startling violet black-lashed eyes alone would have made her a beauty.

But she was not as easy to know as Catherine, who was all effervescence, her feelings close to the surface, tears and anger coming quickly and as quickly dispersing. Catherine showed her affection with a quick hug or a kiss; she could laugh derisively at one's failings and then show a quick penitence if she thought she had inflicted a wound. How different was Honey! I was aware that I must be careful with Honey and I always had been, taking the utmost pains to show that I loved her equally with Catherine. For me she had, I was fully aware, a deep and passionate devotion. It gratified me and at the same time alarmed me a little, for one could never be quite sure of Honey. How her name belied her! She was wild and passionate.

It was disturbing now that they were growing up and devel-

oping such distinct personalities; and the more adoration Catherine showed for Bruno the more loathing Honey seemed to feel;
and because they were young neither of them could cloak their
feelings; and as Bruno realized his daughter's growing appreciation and interest in him, so he was aware of Honey's intensify-
ing repulsion.

I decided that I would speak to Honey about it and I asked her
to walk with me one morning around the garden and pick flowers
with me. I was growing like my mother, I thought, in that I had
become so domesticated; but I never had a great interest in these
things and when I did my flowers my thoughts would be far away
with what was happening at Court, for instance, and what effect
any change there might have on our lives.

"Honey," I said, "Catherine talks to you often of her father."

"She talks of nothing else nowadays. Sometimes I think that
Catherine is not very intelligent."

"My dear Honey," I replied, in what Catherine called my un-
naturally virtuous voice, "is it unintelligent for a daughter to admire her father?"

"Yes," retorted Honey, "if he is not admirable."

"My dear child, you must not talk so. It is . . . ungrateful and
unbecoming."

"Should I be grateful to him?"

"You have lived your life under his roof."

"I prefer to think it has been under yours."

"He provided it."

"He never wanted me here. It was only because you insisted
that I was allowed to stay. I know so much. I go to my grandmother
in the woods."

"Does she speak of these things?"

"She is a wise woman, Mother, and she speaks sometimes in
riddles as wise people do. I wonder why. Is it because they are
afraid that if they speak clearly we might learn as much as they
know?"

"That could be a reason."

"My grandmother has told me some truths. She says it is well
for me to know of certain matters. I often think how different life
might have been for me but for you."

"My darling Honey, you have been a joy and a comfort to me."

"I shall always endeavor to be that," she answered fervently.

"My blessed child, you are my own daughter, remember."

"But by adoption. Tell me about my mother."

"Does not your grandmother tell you?"

"I would like you to tell me for people see others in different ways."

"She was gay and in a way beautiful . . . though you are more so."

"Am I like her then?"

"No, not in your ways."

"She was not married to my father. He came to disband the Abbey. What was he like?"

"I saw little of him," I said evasively.

"And my mother fell in love with him and I was born."

I nodded. So she had in a way and I could not tell Honey the horrible truth.

"I am *his* sister," she said. "My grandmother told me. She said: 'You are both my grandchildren.' And when I heard it I could not believe it. My grandmother says it is why he hates me. He would rather not have to see me."

"He does not believe it, because he will not accept the fact that your mother was his."

"He believes himself to be divine." She laughed. "Do divine people care so much that people shall adore them?"

"He believes he has a great mission in life. He has given homes to these people here."

"He never gives without counting what will come back to him in return. That is not true giving."

She was too discerning, my Honey.

"You should try to understand him."

"Understanding does not increase my respect for him. Perhaps I understand too well, as might be expected since we came of the same mother."

"Honey, I would like you to forget that. I think of myself as your mother. Could you not try to do the same?"

She turned to me and I saw the blazing devotion in her eyes.

"My darling child," I said. "You cannot know how much you mean to me."

"If I could have a wish," she told me, "it would be that I were truly your daughter and Catherine was my own mother's."

"Nay, I would have you both my daughters."

"I would liefer be the only one."

Yes, Honey gives me twinges of alarm. Her hate would be as fierce as her love.

There could not be peace for long. My mother had come over to tell me that Simon Caseman had gone away "on business." She was anxious, I could see, and I wondered what this business entailed.

Simon Caseman was clever. He had not come out openly on the side of Queen Jane but I was sure that had she succeeded in holding the Crown he would have supported her wholeheartedly. Now I wondered whether there was some fresh conspiracy afoot.

I was soon to discover. Sir Thomas Wyatt was leading a rebellion against Queen Mary.

My mother came hurrying over to the Abbey with the news that the Queen was in the Palace of Whitehall and Sir Thomas Wyatt's men were marching on the city. The Queen was in despair.

"She knows that this is the end of her reign." My mother's voice rang out triumphantly.

I said: "Where is your husband?" She smiled secretly.

"I worry about you, Damask," she said almost immediately. "I want you to bring the girls and come over to Caseman Court. When Sir Thomas Wyatt is triumphant I would not have you here."

"And if Sir Thomas does not triumph?"

"You will see."

"Mother," I said, "where is your husband?"

"He has business to do," she answered.

"Business?" I asked. "With Sir Thomas Wyatt?"

She did not answer and I did not press her to because I was afraid.

I said: "Sir Thomas would set Queen Jane or the Princess Elizabeth on the throne. And do you think that if he did so the people would stand by and let the rightful Queen be thrust aside?"

"I wish you would come with me to Caseman Court" was her answer.

But my mother was disappointed for on the cold February day which followed that when my mother had implored me to take care, the rebel forces marched in London and there was fighting in the streets of the capital. I heard that the Queen was intrepid and it was she who had to comfort her weeping ladies. Later I discovered how near Wyatt had come to success, and might have done so but when cornered in Fleet Street, surrounded and cut off from his fighting forces, he had given himself up believing the battle to be lost.

My mother was indeed distraught and knowing that Simon was not at Caseman Court I went over to see her.

"What has gone wrong?" she cried. "Why does the Papist woman always succeed?"

"Perhaps," I answered, "because she is the true Queen."

Shortly after that Jane, the Queen of nine days, was executed with her husband. That was a sad day for even those who were fanatically Papist were well aware that the innocent young girl of sixteen had been enemy to none; she had not desired the Crown which had been forced upon her by an ambitious father-in-law and husband; yet she had been led blindfolded to the dock and that fair head had been severed from her shoulders.

The Princess Elizabeth was implicated in the rebellion; and indeed it was said that the object of it was meant to place her, not Jane, on the throne.

Bruno said: "She is a wily woman and greedy for the throne. It is a pity that they did not take her head instead of Jane's."

"Poor Elizabeth," I remonstrated. "She is so young."

"She is twenty years of age—old enough for ambition. The Queen should not allow her to live."

But the Queen did allow her to live for Sir Thomas Wyatt, who that April laid his head on the block, declared with his last breath that the Princess Elizabeth was innocent of any conspiracy against her sister.

Simon Caseman had returned to Caseman Court. I wondered what part he had played in the Wyatt rebellion.

It was a marvelous thing that he could be involved and extricate himself before the involvement became an embarrassment. I was convinced that what he wanted was to see the end of Mary's reign, to prevent this return to Rome which was threatened and to see a Protestant ruler set up in the Queen's place.

The obvious choice was Elizabeth.

It was Bruno's belief that Elizabeth took her religion as she took her politics—from expediency. The Queen was Catholic and her proposed marriage to a Spaniard was unpopular; if Elizabeth were going to stand in contrast to her sister she must support the Protestant faith. And that was why she did so.

She had become important. People were looking to her more and more. There were many of Mary's supporters who would have liked to have her head; but the Queen was not vindictive. Some said she remembered the days of Elizabeth's childhood when she, Mary, had had a fondness for an engaging little sister.

And so although Queen Mary had placed herself firmly on the throne and strong men and factions surrounded her with the purpose and intention of keeping her there, there were uneasy moments. And the thoughts and hopes of many men and women were turned to the daughter of Anne Boleyn.

My mother came to the Abbey with the usual baskets full of good things. She had a story to tell. She had the twins with her for they seized the opportunity to come to the Abbey whenever they could and they carried her baskets for her.

The girls came to see what she had brought and to listen to her news.

"My word," she said, settling down, "there are goings-on in the city."

"Tell us, Grandmother," commanded Catherine.

"Well, my dear, 'tis a haunted house in Aldersgate Street, though maybe it is not haunted. It may well be that it is an angel of God abiding there. Who can say?"

"Do get on," cried Catherine. "Oh, Grandmother, you are so maddening. You keep us in suspense always with your stories."

"She will tell it in good time," I said. "Don't harass her."

"Good time," cried Catherine. "What is good time? *Now* is good time in my opinion."

"And who is wasting time now?" asked Honey.

"You!" cried Catherine. "Now, Grandmother."

"It's a voice that came from the bricks," said Peter. "I heard it. Didn't you, Paul?"

Paul agreed with his brother as he agreed in everything.

"What sort of a voice?" insisted Catherine.

"Well, if you had let me explain from the beginning," said my mother, "you would know by now."

"Which is perfectly true," I added.

"Well, tell us," cried Catherine.

"There is a voice which comes from the bricks of this house. And when the people cry, 'God save Queen Mary,' it says nothing."

"How can it be a voice if nothing is said?" demanded Catherine.

"What an impatient child she is," said my mother frowning. "You do not wait to hear. Now when the crowd shouts, 'God save the Lady Elizabeth,' the voice says, 'So be it.'"

"Who is it then?" asked Honey.

"That is the mystery. There is no one in the house. Yet the voice comes."

"There must be someone," I said.

"There is no one. The house is empty. And when the crowds shout, 'What is the Mass?' the voice answers, 'Idolatry.'"

Catherine had flushed scarlet. "It is some wicked person who is tricking people."

"It's a voice," said my mother, "and no one there. A voice without a body. Is that not a marvelous thing?"

"If it talked sense it would be," said Catherine.

"Sense! Who is to question the divine word?"

"I do," said Catherine. "It is only divine for Protestants. To the people of the true faith it is . . . heresy."

"Be silent, Cat," I said. "You are disrespectful to your grandmother."

"Is it disrespectful then to tell the truth?"

"Truth to one perhaps is not truth to another."

"How can that be? The truth must always stand."

I said wearily: "I will not have these conflicts in the house. Is it not bad enough that they persist in the country?"

Catherine persisted: "I must say what I feel."

"You must learn to curb your tongue and show a proper respect where it is due."

"Respect!" said Catherine. "My father would say. . . ."

I said: "I will have no more of this."

Catherine flung out of the room. "It is a pretty pass," she muttered, "when one must pretend to agree with wicked lies . . . just to please people."

"My word," said my mother, "there goes a fierce little Papist."

I noticed that Honey was smiling, as she always did when there was a difference between myself and Catherine.

With such frictions in the family, I wondered how one could hope for harmony in the world.

Catherine was triumphant when an investigation of the house revealed a young woman, named Elizabeth Croft, who had been secreted into a hole in the wall that she might answer the questions which were put to her and incite the people against the Queen and her Spanish marriage.

"There is your voice," cried Catherine and hurried over to Caseman Court to tell my mother.

"She was so discountenanced, I couldn't help laughing," she told me when she came back.

"You should have had more compassion," I told her.

"Compassion on such a bigot!"

"And you, my dear, do you perhaps suffer from the same complaint?"

"But I am in favor of the true religion."

"As I said, a bigot, Catherine. I do not wish you to become involved in these matters."

"I talk of them with my father . . . now." Her eyes were shining. "It is wonderful to have discovered him. All these years I have been at fault."

"He took no notice of you."

"Of course he did not when I was young and stupid. It is different now."

"I do beg of you to be careful."

She flew at me and hugged me. "Dearest Mother, you must know that I am grown up . . . almost."

"But not quite," I reminded her.

Peter came in to tell us that Elizabeth Croft was in the pillory for playing her part in the hoax.

"Poor girl," I said. "I hope she does not pay for this with her head."

I thought then: A common price to be asked. And when I considered the religious conflict which seemed to have intensified rather than to have diminished now that we had a firmly Catholic Queen I continued in my apprehension and promised myself that if it must be there in the outside world it should be curbed in the family.

That July Prince Philip of Spain landed in England and the Queen traveled to Winchester where they were married.

We saw their entry to the capital. They crossed London Bridge on horseback and I was struck by the wan look of the Queen and the pathetically adoring manner which she displayed toward her pale-faced, thin-lipped bridegroom. She was nearly ten years older than he and I felt sorry for her.

The marriage was very unpopular but when the people saw the treasure which Philip had brought with him they cheered. Ninety-nine chests were needed to carry it and these chests were filled with gold and silver bullion. This accompanied the royal couple on their journey to the Tower and at least that met with the people's approval. It was more loudly cheered than the bride and groom, but even in spite of this there were murmurings in the crowd.

Now we indeed saw the changes in the land. Under the Queen's father life had been dangerous. He had been a tyrant who had been wont to demand a man's head should he give offense; yet in that King's day life had seemed colorful. There had been constant drama at Court where the King had changed his wives frequently; this Queen remained constant to her husband; she doted on him; but the solemnity of Spain had already taken possession of the Court.

There was something else. The laws of Spain were being brought into the country. We heard a great talk about the true church which was the Holy Church of Rome and the word "heretic" was constantly used.

And then the fires of Smithfield began to burn.

Often from the gardens we would see the pall of smoke, and when the wind blew westward would smell it; we would shiver and fancy we heard the shrieks of the dying.

The Queen had been given a new name. It was Bloody Mary.

It was on a cold February day in the year 1555 when they took Simon Caseman.

The first I heard was when Peter and Paul came running over to the Abbey. At first I could not understand what had happened. They were incoherent.

"They came . . . they looked everywhere. . . ."

"They have taken books away with them. . . ."

"They tied up their barge by the privy steps. . . ."

I said, "Peter, Paul, tell me from the beginning. What is this?"

I think I guessed very quickly. After all it was not uncommon. And I had long known that Simon Caseman was flirting with the new faith.

Paul started to cry suddenly. "They have taken our father," he said.

"Where is your mother?"

"She is just sitting there . . . staring. She doesn't speak. Come quickly, Damask. Please come with us."

I hurried over to the house. I went into the hall where the table was set for a meal and I thought: It was to this hall they came to take my father. . . . Simon Caseman brought them to take him . . . and now they have come for Simon Caseman.

My mother was seated at the table. She looked as though she were dazed. I knelt beside her and took her cold hand in mine.

"Mother," I said, "I am here."

She spoke then. "Is it Damask? My girl Damask?"

"Yes, Mother, I am here."

"They came and took him," she said.

"Yes, I know."

"Why should they take him? *Why—*"

"Perhaps he will come back," I said, knowing full well that he would not. Had not the twins said they had found books and taken them away? He was doomed as a heretic.

"Mother," I said, "you should lie down. I will get you one of your potions. If you could sleep a little . . . perhaps when you awoke. . . ."

"He will come back?"

"Perhaps he will. Perhaps they have taken him for questioning." She clutched at my arm.

"That's it," she said. "They've taken him to question him on some matter. He will come back. He is a good man, Damask."

"Mother," I said, "let me help you to your bed."

The twins watched me as though I were possessed of some power to soothe her. How I wished I had been! For the first time in my life I should have been happy then to see Simon Caseman walk in.

"What harm had he done?" she demanded.

"Let us hope he will soon be back to tell you all about it."

She allowed me to help her to bed and I sent for that soothing draft; and I thought: Twice in her life a husband has been taken from her; and twice in the name of religion.

When she was sleeping I returned to the Abbey. I met Bruno as I came into the hall.

I said: "I have come from my mother. She is distracted with grief."

"So they have taken him," he said; and a smile played about his lips.

"You know!" I cried.

He nodded, smiling secretly.

I cried out: "You . . . arranged it. You informed against him."

"He is a heretic," he replied.

"He is my mother's husband."

"Have you forgotten that one night he would have done the same to me?"

"It is revenge then," I said.

"It is justice."

"Oh, God!" I cried. "It will be Smithfield for him."

"The heretic's reward."

I covered my face with my hands because I could not bear to go on looking into Bruno's.

"So much grief for your father's murderer!"

I turned and ran to my room.

The girls came to me.

"Mother, is it true then?" cried Catherine, her face working with emotion. "They have taken him. What will they do to him? What are they doing now?"

"He will die," said Honey. "He will die at the stake."

Catherine's face puckered. "They can't do it, can they? They can't . . . to him! He is your stepfather."

"That fact will not deter them," I said sadly.

Catherine cried: "And they will burn him to death simply because he believes God should be worshiped in a certain way? I know he is a heretic and heretics are wicked, but to burn him. . . ."

"To death," said Honey somberly.

They were too young to know of such horrors. I said: "It may be that it will not happen. I am going to bring the twins over here. You will be very kind to them. You will remember that it is their father. . . ."

They nodded.

Then I went back to my old home to look after my mother.

I sat with her and we tried to talk of other things: of her garden, of her stillroom. But all the time her ears were alert for the sound of a barge at the privy stairs, for the voice which I knew she would never hear again.

It was no use. We must talk of him, because it was of him that she was thinking. She told me how good he had always been to her; how happy had been her years with him.

"He was the perfect husband," she told me; and I thought of that good man, my father, and asked myself if she had mourned him like this, although I knew the answer to that.

"He was so clever," she said. "He wanted to know what people were writing . . . what people were thinking."

Ah, poor Simon Caseman, he should have known that one must not display interest even where our rulers had decided that we should not.

"They should have kept Queen Jane on the throne. This wouldn't have happened then."

No, Mother, I thought, not to you. But to others. Perhaps to Bruno.

Then I remembered that it was Bruno who had brought this about. He had done to Simon Caseman what Simon had tried to do to him.

I thought: I shall remember it forever. I had loathed the man but it sickened me to think that he had been betrayed by my husband.

The day had come. My mother wanted to go to Hampton Court, there to see the Queen and beg her to pardon her husband.

He was a heretic, proved to be a heretic, and so I heard would not diverge from his opinions. A strange man—so much that was evil in him and yet my mother thought him the perfect husband and he remained true to his belief in face of death.

I quieted my mother that day with her poppy juice and she slept.

I went out into the garden and looked toward the city. A pall of smoke was drifting down the river. The Smithfield fires were burning.

Then I went in and sat by my mother's bed that I might be there to comfort her when she awakened.

Death of a Witch

A year had passed since Simon Caseman suffered the heretic's death. My mother seemed to have aged ten years. Caseman Court had been returned to its rightful owner—myself—for as the wife of a good Catholic who had defied the reign of heretics and in some measure reformed the old Abbey, I was in high favor.

I did not tell my mother that the house had been returned to me. Her grief was too great for her to be concerned with such matters. She went on living there. It was a sad and sorry household.

Rupert was often there; he had offered to help with the estate and this he had done. I saw him frequently and his gentleness to my mother moved me deeply.

I loved Rupert. It was no wild passion—just a gentle enduring affection. Since the betrayal of Simon Caseman I had felt a kind of revulsion toward Bruno. He knew this and hated me for it. Honey was right when she said he wanted admiration all the time. I would say he wanted adoration.

In spite of her shock over Simon Caseman's death Catherine's devotion toward her father had intensified. They were often together and I believe that Bruno found pleasure in turning her from me. I was hurt that my years of love and devotion could be so easily undermined. But she was bemused by him, as others had been before her, and still were. God knows I could understand that. Was I not once as bemused as any?

Honey watched Catherine's growing devotion to her father and her estrangement from me with a satisfaction which could only alarm me.

The times were sickeningly melancholy; but never before had there been such discord in my own family circle.

I was turning more and more to my old home, where my mother was always glad to see me. Rupert was often there and we would all three sit together finding some consolation in talking of the old days.

It was a terrible year. I remember when Archbishop Cranmer was burned at the stake on a bitter March day in front of Baliol College in Oxford. They said that he held out his right hand first to meet the flames because it was with that hand that he signed a document recanting his beliefs.

Ninety-four people were burned that year—forty-five of them women; and there were even four children.

I found it difficult to go about my ordinary affairs. Whenever I went out of doors I seemed to smell the Smithfield fires. I dreamed of Simon Caseman writhing in agony, and I could not help remembering that Bruno had sent him to that fate.

Kate wrote from Remus. Carey would soon be sixteen years of age and she wanted to give a ball to celebrate his birthday.

The young people were excited. We lived in melancholy times and it was wise no doubt to get away from the news of arrests and dire consequences for a while; and Kate was the one to arrange such an occasion.

Honey, Catherine and I traveled to Remus with the twins and a few servants. Bruno refused the invitation and my mother preferred to stay at home; and as our barge took us downriver farther away from Smithfield and the Tower I felt my spirits rising a little.

I was amused by Catherine who could not hide her excitement at the prospect of the ball and at the same time wondered whether she ought not to have stayed behind to be with her father. The dress I had had made for her was of golden-colored velvet from Italy. The bodice was stiffened and the front opened to show a beautifully embroidered brocade kirtle—also from Italy. Honey's dress was similar but of blue velvet. Honey was nearly seventeen years old, Catherine fifteen. I thought with a pang: They are growing up. Soon it will be a case of finding husbands for them.

It was pleasant to be with Kate again. Even though she was past thirty, she was no less attractive than she had been at seventeen. I often wondered why she had not married again. It was certainly not due to a devotion to Remus.

She entertained a good deal in Remus Castle. Now her guests would be Catholic families. Kate was too wise to be embroiled in politics; she was one who would sway with the wind.

As soon as we arrived she carried me off for a private talk, and her first words were to compliment me on the looks of the girls.

"It should not be difficult to find husbands for them. They are an attractive pair. Catherine should have a good dowry. What of Honey?"

"I shall see that she is adequately provided for."

"Ah, yes, Caseman Court is yours now." A shadow crossed her face. "A bad business. How is your mother?"

"She has aged ten years. She works in her garden. Thank God she has that. Oh, Kate, what a melancholy country this has become!"

"It was more gay, was it not, under Henry when we were girls? I have a feeling, though, that this will not last. The Queen is a sick woman." She lowered her voice. "One must be careful how one speaks. Poor woman! She has brought misery to thousands."

"Is it the Queen? Or is it her ministers?"

"Ah, there you have it. She is a fanatic surrounded by fanatics."

"These burnings at the stake. There was never such horror here before."

"You forget those who were hanged, drawn, and quartered."

"There are those too and in addition that fearsome pall of smoke that seems to hang forever over Smithfield. I wonder what is coming to us all."

"There is the great consolation that it cannot last. It is the Spanish influence. These burnings of which you speak have been a feature of Spanish life since Torquemada and Isabella revived the Inquisition in Spain. If the Spaniards should get a hold on England it would be the same story here."

"God forbid!"

"Have a care, Damask. It is better to speak only of these things to those whom you trust—and whom can one trust?"

"All this in the name of religion!" I cried.

"In the name of envy, malice and covetousness perhaps. Many men go to their death sent by someone who covets an estate, a woman—or even desires revenge. Who sent Simon Caseman to his death, think you?" I was silent and she went on: "Bruno? Such a short time ago *he* threatened Bruno."

"Only a lucky chance prevented Bruno's being taken, I am sure."

"A miracle?" she said mockingly. "With Bruno there must always be miracles."

We were silent for a while and then she went on: "It will not last, Damask. It is said that the Queen cannot live long. She is the most unhappy woman in England. Her husband does not love her. She is distasteful to him, they say. He prefers to roam far from her and they say he is happier spending a night in an inn with the landlord's daughter than with her. I have heard some of our servants singing a rhyme which would no doubt cost them their lives if they were overheard in some quarters. I'll whisper it to you:

'The baker's daughter in her russet gown
Better than Queen Mary without her crown.'

There. But is it true? He is a strange, cold man, and we shall never understand these Spaniards."

"I am sorry for her but I deplore this sorry state into which we have fallen. It seems one is a heretic if one as much as discusses a new idea."

"Ah, we have a hint—and only a hint—what religious persecution can mean. But there is a growing resentment in the people. It might well be that if Wyatt had waited a few years . . . if he had risen *now* he might have had enough support to put Elizabeth on the throne."

"You think life would be different under her?"

"Who can say? She is young. She is clever. How many times do you think she has come within an inch of losing her head? The Queen has a softness for her sister though. She would rather remove her from the succession by giving birth to a child."

"Can she do this?"

"You will have heard of those supposed pregnancies which were not pregnancies at all. Poor woman. She suffers from dropsy, they say, and so great is her desire to bear a child that she believes she is about to do so. Imagine her grief when she discovers it is a false pregnancy."

"Poor lady. It is no great good fortune to be a Queen."

"It is no great good fortune to be any of us in this age," said Kate with a laugh. "Unless of course you are as clever as I am. Tomorrow at the ball you will meet good Catholic families most fervently loyal to the Queen and those who, like myself, reserve their judgment. They are the wise ones. They are poised . . . watchful of events and ready to leap to the appropriate side a moment before the rest of the country realizes what is happening. The wise ones are like me. They take their religion mildly; they are not fanatical or fervent . . . calmly swaying with the wind. Remember this, my dear Damask, and you will enjoy my ball."

The ballroom of the castle was decorated with leaves and flowers and the musicians were in the minstrels' gallery, almost hidden from view by the heavy curtains on either side of it.

At six o'clock we feasted in the great hall and I had rarely seen such elaborate dishes. I thought how Clement would have loved to examine the contents of those massive pies and to test the quality of the crust. The leading families present had the pleasure of seeing their coats of arms and crests on the pies; the sucking pigs were brought in steaming hot on dishes which were carried around the tables by Kate's servants in the Remus livery; and when the sirloin was brought in we all stood up and made obeisance to the dish which had been knighted by King Henry.

Cakes had been baked and topped with ginger; in one of these cakes was a tiny figure in the shape of a king. These were distributed among the men; and the one to find the king in his cake was elected King of the Revels for the night or Lord of Misrule.

There was a great deal of amusement when Carey found the king's figure; it was clear that he was hoping that a very pretty girl, Mary Ennis, daughter of Lord Calperton, who was a guest with her father and her brother Edward, would win the queen's figure. He was well mannered enough to hide his dismay when Catherine won it.

Catherine laughed with delight and I could not help smiling, recalling how solemn she had been when wondering whether she ought to leave the Abbey and join in our frivolity.

She and Carey must needs now put their heads together and plan games and antics for our amusement; and this they did. There were charades and guessing games and we became very merry.

Carey and Catherine must lead us in the dance and they did so with some decorum though I overheard Catherine whisper to Carey fiercely: "And I'm almost as old as you in any case and everybody knows that girls grow up more quickly than boys."

I found myself dancing with Rupert.

"It is pleasant to be here," he said.

"I have not felt so content for a long time," I told him.

"This is how life should always be," he said. "Not just a little oasis of pleasure. But families gathering together like this."

"And yet, Rupert," I said, "even on such an occasion we must guard our tongues lest we betray something which could bring harm to us. It is only with our nearest and our trusted friends that we can be frank."

"Damask," he said, "how frank are you prepared to be?"

"In what way?"

"I wonder about you so much. I think of you constantly. Sometimes I brood on what it might have been if everything had turned out differently. Then I think of you at the Abbey there."

"Yes, Rupert."

"A strange life," he said. "How is it there, Damask? Are you happy?"

"I have the girls," I said.

"And they suffice?"

"They mean a great deal to me, but they will marry and have lives of their own. You should have married, Rupert. Then you would have had children."

"Who would marry and have lives of their own. But I should like children."

"You are young yet. Who knows, perhaps at this very gathering you will meet someone. You are in your thirties . . . some say it is the prime."

"Let us sit down," he said. "This conversation interests me so much that I prefer not to fit it to the dance."

So we sat and I watched my girls. Honey, breathtakingly lovely as all must think her, dancing with Edward Ennis, and Catherine with Carey, scowling at him now and then when he trod on her toe and yet her eyes aflame with excitement, for she loved to dance. And how well it suited her, far better than brooding on whether she should go into a convent, if, now that we were under a rigorous Catholic rule, one could be found for her.

"You know I shall not," said Rupert.

"What was that? I was thinking of Catherine."

"Marry and settle. And you know why."

I looked at him and seeing the expression in his eyes I was amazed that he had remained faithful all those years. I could not help my pleasure, which was wrong for it was no life for him to hope for a woman who was married to someone else.

"And Bruno?" he said.

"What of him?"

"He is all that you hoped he would be?"

"We generally ask too much of people, do we not?"

"And you asked too much?"

I hesitated and then I said: "Sometimes I wonder about our life at the Abbey. Sometimes it takes on the quality of a dream. It is so . . . unreal. We are living in an Abbey. . . . Many of those who live there were once monks. They had services in the church and those services are openly now the same as those which were conducted there long ago. As you know the Abbot's Lodging was made into a castle not unlike this. But there are the monks' dorter and refectory which still stand. I believe many of them behave just as they used to. We are an abbey which is not an abbey. Bruno is an abbot with a wife and family. Since King Edward died it has become more openly so. Sometimes I wonder what would happen if the Queen were to die. Simon Caseman was about to betray us at the time of the King's death. Poor man, it was he who met his death. It is a strange life."

"If you were happy you would think it worthwhile. You are not happy, Damask."

"What is happiness? Just a day or so here and there . . . a moment perhaps. . . . How often can anyone say, 'Now I am completely happy'?"

"That should not be so. A life of contentment should be within our reach."

"With the uncertainty which surrounds us! When we know not from one day to the next when some misguided word or act could lead us to the death!"

"All the more reason to take happiness when we can."

I sighed. "I saw my father taken. My mother has lost two husbands. By a quirk of fate I am not a widow now. Oh, it is a violent world we live in. Will it always be so?"

"It will change. Change is inevitable."

Suddenly I touched his arm. "Rupert, take care. Do not lean one way or the other for how do we know from one week to the next which is the safe way?"

"I am not a fanatical man, Damask. I keep a steady road . . . quiet, unexciting, I suppose."

I said: "I think we should dance."

And as we joined the dancers I knew that he was telling me that he loved me now as he had in the beginning and whatever happened he would not change.

As his hands touched mine in the dance, he said: "Always remember, whatever happens . . . I should be at hand."

It was a comforting thought.

Lord Calperton and his family were guests at the Castle for several days and I began to notice that young Edward was always at Honey's side. She blossomed; a radiance was added to her beauty.

I was afraid for her. The Ennis family was a noble one, and my Honey, of doubtful parentage, would not seem a very good match, I was sure. I did not want the child to be hurt and she could be more easily than Catherine, who had the security of being my own and Bruno's daughter.

All the same I was sorry when it was time for us to go back to the Abbey; and it was not long after our return when I received an invitation to visit Grebblesworth, the Ennises' place in Hertfordshire and to take the two girls with me.

Kate was also invited. She wrote to me jubilantly.

"Mistress Honey made quite an impression on Master Edward. I'm not surprised. That girl is a real beauty. She is fascinating. There is a kind of smoldering passion behind those glorious eyes of hers. But I must say I'm surprised. After all Edward is the Calperton heir. Well, we shall see.

"Of course we all know that Bruno is very rich and his situation is very fitting to our present way of life. I am truly eager to see the outcome of this."

Honey was enchanted. I realized that for the first time in her life she was at the very heart of everything. It was because of her that we had received this invitation. Catherine had been invited too, but simply because she belonged to the family.

I spent the next weeks with the seamstresses and we made gowns for Honey. She looked delightful in her riding habits with the little feathered caps we had had made for her.

I said to her as we tried on a lovely brocade gown, "Are you happy, Honey?"

She threw her arms about my neck and I had to protest that she was suffocating me.

She said: "Everything I have had and shall have comes from you."

I was deeply moved and I replied: "Whatever happens you and I will love each other."

The night before we left for Grebblesworth she was not in her room when I went to consult her about a ribbon for her hair.

I felt a twinge of alarm and went to Catherine's room to see if she had seen her. Catherine was sitting disconsolately in a chair studying a book of prayers in Latin. She looked very pleased to put it aside.

"Where is Honey?" I asked.

"I saw her go out half an hour ago."

"Did she say where?"

"No, but she goes often in that direction."

"What direction?"

"To the woods, I think."

"I don't like her being out alone. There are robbers about."

"They wouldn't dare harm anyone from the Abbey, Mother. They would be afraid of what my father would do." When she spoke his name a beautiful smile touched her lips. "It is wonderful to have a saint for a father."

I turned aside impatiently. I was asking myself often whether I was jealous of Catherine's devotion to her father.

I left Catherine and went back to Honey's room. I waited there anxiously until she came back.

"Honey," I cried. "Where *have* you been?"

"To see my grandmother."

"Mother Salter?"

"I call her Grandmother. She *is* my grandmother, you know."

I recalled the time when Honey had run away from me because she thought I cared more for Catherine than for her.

"I always go to her when something important happens. She wishes me to."

"And something important has happened?"

"Is it not important that we should be asked to Grebblesworth?"

"It could be, Honey."

"It is. I know it is."

"Honey, my dear child, does it make you happy . . . that they have asked you?"

"As happy as I never hoped to be," she answered.

Lord Calperton received us warmly. He was a widower of some years' standing and it was clear to me that this great mansion lacked a mistress. They were a good Catholic family and as Kate said "unworldly" but I for one liked them none the less for that.

I fancied Lord Calperton, like most men, was a little in love with Kate; perhaps that was one of the reasons why he had taken so kindly to the family.

It was not a large house party, which perhaps made it all the more enjoyable. We rode through the countryside; we danced a little; we played games and there were dinner parties when we met the local families. Carey sought out pretty Mary's company and that left Honey to Edward. Catherine and Thomas, the younger son of the household, played rather rough games together, and it was a very jolly party.

Kate was amused by the rapidly advancing friendship between Edward and Honey.

She whispered to me: "I verily believe that Calperton is so enchanted with us that he would ask a very small dowry for Honey."

"Do you really think they would consider her?"

Kate laughed at me. "How excited you are! Why, Damask, you are a matchmaking Mamma. I am surprised."

"I want Honey to be happy. She is very taken with Edward."

"And he with her."

"Oh," I cried, "I believe she would be so happy. She has always felt that she was not of the same importance as Catherine. Heaven knows I have done my best to convince her. But if this in truth became a marriage. . . . Oh, I can see her mistress of this house."

"If Calperton does not marry again of course."

"Kate, you are not thinking—"

"I have refused a Duke and two Earls. Do you think I should succumb to my Lord Calperton?"

"You might possibly love the man more than a great title."

"There speaks the old sentimental Damask. I do declare you amaze me. A scheming matchmaking mother one moment, gloating over the fine match her daughter will make, and then sentimentally talking of love. Let me tell you this, Damask. I have no intention of taking Calperton. As far as I am concerned Honey shall have the scene all to herself. But I know my Calperton. He wishes Edward to marry. He wants a grandson. Young Edward is completely enamored of Mistress Honey—and I am not surprised. My Lord will reason that he is more likely to get healthy sons with a young woman who so enthralls him. "I'll wager you that ere long there will be a discreet offer for Honey's hand."

I was so delighted, because I knew the state of Honey's feelings.

And when the offer came, I myself saw Lord Calperton. I told him that Honey was my adopted daughter; I myself would provide her dowry. She was well educated, a lady in every sense. She was the daughter of a woman who had served me but been a friend; and her father had worked for Thomas Cromwell.

He was satisfied.

Honey was married on that June day in the year 1557 when war was declared on France.

The marriage was celebrated at the chapel in Caseman Court. I had chosen this because after all it was my home and I made the excuse that it would do my mother good to supervise the celebrations. And it did; bustling about her garden, gathering herbs for this and that, practicing with her new salads and giving orders in the kitchen seemed to bring her alive again.

Bruno attended the wedding but he was aloof. As for Honey she had little to say to him; she had always avoided him.

We had the usual ceremonies with the bridecake and the mummers came in and performed. I was gratified to see my mother laughing merrily at their antics, and happy to pass Honey on to Edward Ennis, for it had given me the utmost pleasure to see her happily settled.

After the wedding we all seemed faintly depressed. My mother, deprived of all the tasks which the wedding had entailed, sank into melancholy once more; what surprised me most was how much Catherine missed Honey, far more than I had believed possible. She became moody—very different from the girl who had danced so gaily and teased Carey as Queen of Misrule.

Kate came to the rescue by suggesting that Catherine should come to Remus Castle for a spell and this was arranged. I was surprised by the alacrity with which she went.

It was soon after her departure that one of the servants brought me a message from Mother Salter. These messages were in a way like commands, and it did not occur to me to disobey them. I suppose deep down in me I was superstitious as most other people although my father's teaching should have placed me beyond such primitive thinking. Mother Salter was a witch but she was the great-grandmother of Bruno, child of a serving girl and a monk, who had risen to become head of a community, and of Honey who had married into the aristocracy; and when I considered this I realized that it was Mother Salter who had made the fortunes of both her grandchildren.

She was a power in her little cottage as Bruno was in his Abbey and the reason was that we all believed—in lesser or greater degree—in the extraordinary powers of these people. I no less than the most gullible of my serving girls.

So I lost no time in going to Mother Salter in the woods.

I was shocked when I saw her. She had always been lean, now she was emaciated.

I cried out: "Why, Mother Salter, you are ill."

She caught my hand, hers was cold and clawlike; I noticed the brown marks on her skin which we call the flowers of death.

"I am ready to go," she said. "My grandson's fate is in his own hands. I have provided for my granddaughter."

I could have smiled for was I not the one who had nurtured Honey and educated her so that she was a fitting bride for a noble gentleman? But I knew what she meant. She had insisted that I care for Honey; and if Keziah could be believed, it was Mother Salter who had planned that the child should be placed in the Christmas crib.

"You have done well," she said. "I wanted to bless you before I go."

"Thank you."

"There is no need to thank me. Had you not cared for the child I would have cursed you."

"I love her as my own. She has brought great joy to me."

"You gave much—you received much. That is the law," she said.

"And you are unfit to be alone. Who cares for you here?"

"I have always cared for myself."

"What of your cat?" I said. "I do not see it."

"I buried it this day."

"You will be lonely without it."

"My time has come."

I said: "I cannot allow you to stay here to die."

"*You*, Mistress, cannot."

"These woods are Abbey woods, and are you not my Honey's grandmother? Could I allow you to stay here alone?"

"What then, Mistress?"

"A plan has come to me. It will do much good, I think. I shall take you to my mother. She will care for you. She needs help for she is a sad woman. You will give her that. She is very interested in herbs and remedies. You could teach her much."

"A noble lady with old Mother Salter in her house!"

"Oh, come, old Mother Salter has not such a poor opinion of herself."

"So you give orders here."

"I care for the sick on my husband's Abbey lands."

She looked at me slyly. "You would not take me to my grandson."

"I would take you to my mother."

"Hee-hee." She had what I had always thought of as a witch's cackle. "He would not be pleased to see me. Honey used to come to me. She confided in me. She told me of her love for you and how she feared you loved your own child more. 'Twas natural. I blamed you not for that. You have done your work well and I don't forget it. But let those who heed me not take care."

My heart was filled with pity for this poor old woman, sick and near to death, still clinging to the powers which she had possessed or led people to believe she possessed.

I said I would prepare my mother to receive her and I went to her immediately. She agreed to take in Mother Salter once she had grown accustomed to the incongruous idea; she commanded her servants to prepare a room, put fresh rushes on the floor, and make up a pallet as a bed. Then she and I went together and we set Mother Salter on a mule and brought her to Caseman Court.

It was an unconventional thing to have done. Bruno was aghast.

"To take that old woman to your mother's house! You must be mad. Are you going to gather up all the poor and set them up in Caseman Court?"

"She is no ordinary woman."

"No, she has an evil reputation. She traffics with the devil. She could be burned at the stake for her activities."

"Many a good man and woman has met that fate. Surely you understand why I must give this woman especial care."

"Because of her relationship to the bastard you adopted."

Then because I could not bear him to refer slightingly to Honey I cried out: "Yes, because she is Honey's great-grandmother . . . and yours."

I saw the hatred in his face. He knew that I had never believed in the miracle and this was at the very root of the rift between us. Before I had implied my disbelief; now I said it outright.

"You have worked against me always," he said savagely.

"I would willingly work with you and for you. And why should facing the truth interfere with that?"

"Because it is false . . . *false* . . . and you alone whose duty it was to stand beside me have done everything you can to plant these false beliefs."

"I am guilty of heresy then," I said.

He turned and left me.

Strangely enough I had ceased to care that all love was lost between us.

I could not have done a better thing for my mother than take Mother Salter to her. When I next visited her I found the sick room fresh and clean. On a table beside the witch's pallet were the potions and unguents which my mother had prepared. She was excited and important and fussing over the old woman as though she were a child, which seemed to amuse Mother Salter.

Of course the old woman was dying; she knew it and she was amused to be spending her last days in a grand house.

My mother told me that she had imparted to her much knowledge of plants both benign and malignant. She would not allow my mother to write them down perhaps because she who could not write thought there was something evil in the signs that were made on paper. My mother had a good memory for the things in which she was interested and she became very knowledgeable during that time, which I was sure was ample payment for all that she had done for Mother Salter. But here was more than that. Whether the old woman had powers to bless or curse I cannot say, but from that time my mother really grew away from her grief and while Mother Salter was in her house I heard her sing snatches of songs.

Two or three days before she died I went to see her and was alone with her. I asked her to tell me the truth about Bruno's birth.

"You know," I said, "that he believes he has special powers. He does not accept the story that Keziah and the monk told."

"No, he does not believe it. He has special powers. That is clear, is it not? Look what he has done. He has built a world about himself. Could an ordinary man do that?"

"Then it was lies Keziah told?"

She gave that disturbing witch's chuckle. "In us all there are special powers. We must find them, must we not? I was born of a woodcutter. True I was the seventh child and my mother said I was the seventh of a seventh. I told myself that there is something different about me . . . and there was. I studied the plants. There was not a flower nor a leaf nor a bud I did not know. And I tried them out and went to an old woman who was a witch and she taught me much. So I became a wise woman. We could all become wise men or women."

"And Bruno?"

"He is my Keziah's son."

"And it is true that he was put into the crib by the monk?"

"It is true. And it was my plan. Keziah was with child. What would happen to the child? I said. He or she would be a servant, not able to read or write. I always set great store by writing. There's a power in it . . . and what is written can be read. To read and to write—for all my wisdom I could not do that. Nor could Keziah. But my great-grandchildren did. And that was what I wanted for them. The monk should not be blamed. Nor Keziah. She did what was natural to her and he dared not disobey me. So I made the plan; they carried it out. My great-grandson was laid in the Christmas crib—and none would have been the wiser if Weaver hadn't come. My great-grandson would have been the Abbot and a wise man and a miracle worker because these powers are in us all and we must first know that we possess them before we do."

"You have confirmed what I have always believed. Bruno hates me for knowing."

"His pride will destroy him. There is greatness in him but there is weakness too and if the weakness is greater than the strength then he is doomed."

"Should I pretend to believe him? Am I wrong in letting him know the truth?"

"Nay," she said. "Be true to thyself, girl."

"Should I try to make him accept the truth?"

"If he could do that he might be saved. For his pride is great. I know him well though I have not set eyes on him since he was naked new-born. But Honey talked of him. She told me all . . . of you both. Now I will tell you this. The monk before his part in this were known, was heavy with his sin. He said that the only way he could hope for salvation after his sin was to write a full confession. He could write well. He came here now and then. It broke the laws of the Abbey but they were not my laws and I had my grandson to think of. I must see this monk who was his father; I commanded him to come to me and he did, and he showed me the wounds he had inflicted on his body in his torment. He showed me the hair shirt he wore. He felt his sin deeply. And he wrote the story of his sin and hid it away that in time to come it should be known."

"Where is this confession?"

"It's hidden in his cell in the dorter. Find it. Keep it. And show it to Bruno. It will be proof, and then you will tell him that he must be true to himself. He is clever. He has great powers. He can be greater without this lie than he ever was with it. If you can teach him this you will help to destroy that pride which in time will destroy him."

"I will look for this confession," I said, "and if I find it I will show it to Bruno and I will tell him what you have said."

She nodded.

"I wish him well," she said. "He is my flesh and blood. Tell him I said so. Tell him he can be great but he cannot rise through weakness."

Our conversation was broken up by my mother who came bustling in and declared that I was tiring out her invalid.

A few days later Mother Salter was dead. My mother planted flowers on her grave and tended them regularly.

The Monk's Confession

The monks' dorter had become a place which I avoided. There was something more eerie about it than the rest of the uninhabited part of the Abbey; and although many of the Abbey buildings had by this time been demolished and so much rebuilding had been done, the dorter was a section which had been left intact.

Since Mother Salter's revelation I went there often. I wanted to find that confession which she said Ambrose had hidden there. If I could do this and present it to Bruno, he would then be face to face with the truth; and I could see, as Mother Salter had seen, that until he accepted it I could not respect him, nor could he respect himself.

Was this true? I asked myself. How difficult it is to test one's motive! Did I want to say, "Look, I am right"? Or did I really wish to help him?

Once he accepted the fact that his birth was similar to that of many others, would he start to grow away from myth? Would he build his life on the firm foundation of truth?

I did not know, for I did not understand Bruno nor my own feelings for him. I had been bemused by the story of his miraculous appearance on earth. I had been drawn into this union while in a state of exultation. It had not brought me happiness, except that it had given me Catherine.

Whatever the motive, I was urged on by some compulsion to search for the document which according to Mother Salter Ambrose had left behind.

As I walked up the stone spiral stairs with its thick rope banister I thought of all the monks who had filed down this stone stairway during the last two hundred years and it occurred to me that many of them must have left something of themselves behind.

At the top of the stairs was a long narrow landing and on either side of this were the cells. Each had a door in which was a grille through which it was possible to see into the cell.

Most of the cells were bare although some contained a pallet which had not presumably been considered worthwhile taking away by the vandals. Each cell was identical with its narrow slit without glass which was cut into the thick walls. It must have been bitterly cold in winter; the floor of each cell was flagged; and there were slabs of stone in the walls. No comfort whatsoever; but monks did not look for comfort, of course.

I had heard something from Clement and Eugene of what life in the Abbey had been like. I knew of the hours of penance which had to be performed in the cells and how at any time the Abbot would walk silently along the landing and peer through the grille to see what was going on inside.

"The watchful eye which came we knew not when," was Eugene's way of expressing it. I knew something of their habits, how there were long periods when silence was the order of the day; how they were not allowed to touch each other in any way; how they must perform their tasks and their devotion with equal fervor. A strange life, particularly for men such as Clement, Eugene and certainly Ambrose, who had broken free of it on more than one occasion.

I could imagine the anguish of that man, the soul-searching, the earnest prayers for guidance, the suffering and torment that must have gone on in his cell.

I don't think I should have been very surprised when I reached the top of that staircase to have come face to face with some long-dead monk who found it impossible to rest in his grave.

As I stood there on the landing I asked myself which of these identical cells had been that of Ambrose. It was impossible to know. Could I ask someone? Clement? Eugene? They would immediately report my interest to Bruno. I did not wish for that. No, I must find Ambrose's cell and if possible his confession by myself.

I went into the first cell. I caught my breath with horror as the door shut on me. I felt a panic such as I had rarely felt before. It is amazing how much can flash through one's mind in a short time. I imagined myself imprisoned in one of the cells. No one would think to look for me there. I should remain in my cold stone prison until there was no life left in me, and in time I should join the ghosts of the monks who haunted the dorter.

But there was no need for such panic. The door had no lock. I remembered Clement's explaining that. Doors could be opened at any time by the Abbot or any of his subordinates without warning, in the same way that they could peer through the grille.

I stepped back into the cell. I examined the walls. I could see no place where a confession could be secreted. I touched the walls, all the time looking over my shoulder, so convinced was I that I was not alone.

The cold dankness of the place chilled me. I looked into several of the cells—all alike. If only I could discover which one was Ambrose's that would help. A confession secreted in the wall! Why should Ambrose have confessed when his great desire was to cover up his sin?

I wanted to convince myself that there was no confession, and the reason was that I wanted to get out of this place and never come here again. I could not rid myself of the feeling that I was overlooked and that something evil was waiting to catch up with me.

There were forty cells on this landing. I looked into all of them; they were all alike, every one of them. How could I possibly tell which had belonged to Ambrose?

At either end of the landing was a spiral staircase. I reminded myself that while I was mounting one stairway, someone else could be mounting the other. Someone could lurk in one of the cells and leap out on me.

Who?

What was the matter with me? At one moment I was afraid of ghosts, at another I was looking for a human assailant.

I could not understand myself. All I knew was that whenever I entered the monks' dorter I was conscious of something warning me that if I were wise I should keep away.

*   *   *

Kate wrote that she was bringing Catherine back to the Abbey.

I replied that I would be delighted to see her as always, and I trusted that Catherine had behaved with the decorum which was now becoming necessary to her increasing years.

I looked forward to Catherine's return and the arrival of Kate with great pleasure. Both of them had a cheering effect on me.

I had not yet found the confession although I had been several times to the dorter. I would attempt to search and then some inescapable feeling of imminent danger would come to me. I should look through my grille expecting to find someone standing there and even when my gaze met nothing, the fear persisted.

I began to dread going there and yet had a great compulsion to do so.

I should have liked to confide in someone. Kate was not the one on this occasion. Rupert? I thought. No, I could not talk to Rupert. The fact that he had asked me to marry him and still thought of me tenderly debarred me from that for I could not speak openly to him of my feelings for Bruno. In fact I scarcely knew myself what they were.

I went again to the dorter. I mounted the stone stairs. I always hoped that this would be the time when I should find what I sought. I had examined six of the cells thoroughly, touching the stone slabs on the walls carefully to assure myself that nothing could be secreted there. My efforts had been without success.

Perhaps this afternoon, I thought.

How quiet it was everywhere on that afternoon. A pleasant June day; the sun was hot on the grass outside but the dorter was cold as ever.

My steps on the stairs had a hollow echo. I mounted them quickly and stood on the landing, and as I did so I thought I heard a sound from below. I stood still listening.

There was nothing.

I went into the seventh cell. Lightly I touched the buttress, then the walls which separated this one from that on the other side. I went to the long narrow slit and looked through the aperture in the very thick wall. Suddenly I felt the goose pimples rise on my skin because I knew that I was not alone. I swung around. A pair of eyes were watching me through the grille.

I heard myself gasp and putting out my hands grazed them against the granite wall.

The eyes disappeared.

I wanted to get out of this place but I had to know who was there in the dorter. But had I imagined those eyes peering at me? I thought of monks who had lain in their cells and suddenly looked up to see a pair of eyes watching them. That was the purpose of the grille—that someone outside could look in and catch the cell's occupant unaware.

I began to shiver. I went out into the corridor. I walked along it, looking into the cells. They were empty except for the pallets which had served as beds and which Cromwell's men had not thought worthy of taking away. I stood still and listened. Silence . . . and yet there was that uncanny awareness which clung to me and which told me I was not alone.

I pushed open the door of one of the cells. I stared aghast. Seated on one of the pallets was a man. I looked again to assure myself that it was Bruno. His eyes were cold, snakelike. He gave a sudden low laugh which had an unpleasant ring.

"Bruno," I cried, "what are you doing here?"

"I might ask what you are doing here."

"It was you who looked at me through the grille."

"Did that disturb you?"

"Naturally. It was so . . . uncanny. Why didn't you speak? Why didn't you let me know you were there? Why go away so dramatically?"

"Did you think it was a ghost who was looking through the grille at you? You had a guilty conscience, Damask. Why? Was it because you were doing something you would rather not be caught doing? What *were* you doing?"

I could not tell him. How far we were apart! We were enemies. And yet this man was my husband. How could I tell him that I was hoping to find something which he would go to great lengths to stop my finding?

"I . . . I was looking at the dorter."

"You find it interesting . . . suddenly?"

"Not suddenly. It was always interesting."

"You were here recently. You seem to make a habit of visiting the place. I wondered why."

"So you followed me."

"What I want to know is why you are so startled to be found here."

"Startled?" I countered. "Who would not be startled to see a pair of eyes watching them from the other side of a grille?"

"Sit down, Damask."

He moved along the pallet.

I was deeply aware of the silence of the place and a great urge swept over me to turn and run . . . to run away from my husband.

I said: "Not now."

"You are in a hurry? Surely not. You were making a leisurely search. Feeling the walls! What did you hope to discover? Were you looking for something?"

He had risen and was standing close to me. What was the meaning of the strange expression in his eyes? Did he know of the confession? Had Ambrose told him? Suppose he did know. Then he would guess that I was looking for it; and he would do all in his power to stop me. *All* in his power? He had great power. I knew that. I knew something else too. He would stop at nothing to prevent my finding that confession for in it would be a denial that he, Bruno, was the man he was determined to be—the prophet, the near-god, the superhuman man whom he wanted all those about him to believe he was.

Yet I assured myself that I *must* find that confession. I must make him accept the truth for I saw how right Mother Salter was when she said that his pride could destroy him, and perhaps us all.

I knew that he must not suspect that I was searching for the confession. He must not know that I was aware of its existence. If he did . . . what then? I dared not examine my thoughts too closely. I saw him clearly . . . too clearly for comfort . . . but he was my husband and I had loved him once. And a voice within me kept insisting: He must not know. You would be in peril if he did.

My wits came to my aid. I said quickly: "I was thinking to what purpose we could put this place. The building is so solid. It could make an excellent buttery."

"You have suddenly decided this?"

"I have been thinking of it for some time. I am constantly thinking of how we can put these places to good use."

"Doesn't the present buttery suffice?"

"It is scarcely adequate now that there are so many people here. I daresay that in the future you will be entertaining even more."

I was trying to sound matter-of-fact.

"Yes," he said, "that's true."

"Then what do you think of the idea?"

He was studying me intently and his eyes still held that cold snakelike quality. "It's worth considering," he said.

I felt a great relief flooding over me. I believed I had convinced him that I had been inspecting the monks' dorter for this domestic reason.

I went to the bakehouse. Clement was there with two of his scullions and when he saw that I wished to speak to him alone he sent them off to scour some pans in readiness for the day's cooking.

"Tomorrow," I said, "Lady Remus will be here. She is bringing Mistress Catherine home."

"Ah, I shall be glad to see the young mistress home. I'll make some of her favorite marchpane. There is no one that appreciates it but her now that Mistress Honey has left us."

"And for Lady Remus?"

"There shall be a game pie and I'll work the Remus coat of arms in paste for her. There'll be bacon and sucking pig. Those are favorites of hers."

"You will know how best to please her. Clement," I went on, "you must prepare almost as much food now as you did in the old days."

He nodded thoughtfully.

"Do you regret the old days, Clement?"

He narrowed his eyes, looking back. "This present day suits me well, Mistress."

"Do you ever go into the dorter, Clement?"

He shook his head. "Not since that day when the heretic"—he crossed himself—"Simon Caseman informed against us and almost took us to death."

"Before that did you go to your own cell and imagine the old days were back?"

He nodded, smiling.

"I was looking at the old cells not long ago. I thought we might make a buttery there. Those thick walls make it very cool. What do you think, Clement?"

"What does the master think?"

It was always so. They seemed afraid to express an opinion without Bruno's approval.

"I spoke to him of it. He thought it an excellent notion. Would you come and look at it some time and give me your opinion?"

There was nothing Clement liked so much as to be asked for an opinion. His face creased into smiles.

"When would that be, Mistress?"

"There is no time like the present. Could you meet me there in half an hour?"

He was delighted. I waited below for him. It felt different going up those stairs with him lumbering behind me.

"One of these must have been your cell, Clement."

"Oh, yes."

"Which one was yours?"

He led me along the landing.

"They are so much alike, can you be sure?" I asked.

"I'd always count," he said. "Number seven, that was mine."

"And who was next to you?"

"Brother Thomas that way. Brother Arnold there."

"I daresay you can remember the names of most of them."

"We were many years together."

"I have heard you talk of some of them. Eugene now . . . where was he?"

"He was there. And next to him was Valerian and then Thomas and Eugene."

"Where did you say Ambrose was?"

"Ambrose? I didn't say." He crossed himself again. "I said Eugene. But Ambrose was here opposite me. I used to hear him, praying in the night."

I hastily counted to myself. Seventh from the end was Ambrose's cell.

"Well," I said, "what do you think of my idea of the buttery?"

He thought it excellent. I had to listen to his views on storing salted meats for he thought these cells would be ideal for that purpose.

"The thick stone walls keep out the heat," he said. "I could keep salt pig in here for a very long time."

I listened; I agreed; and I longed to be rid of him; for now that I knew which was Ambrose's cell I was eager to get to work. I came back that afternoon. It took me an hour to examine the cell. Then I discovered that behind the crucifix which hung on the wall, one of the slabs was loose.

I removed it. Behind it was a cavity and in this I found Ambrose's confession.

I took it to my bedchamber. I shut myself in. It began:

"I, Brother Ambrose of St. Bruno's Abbey, have committed mortal sin and have imperiled my immortal soul."

It was the cry of a man in torment and I was deeply moved by the suffering he had obviously endured. He had written it all down: his dreams and longings, his erotic imaginings in that cell as he lay there on his hard pallet. He wrote of his great desire to purge his soul of lust and the hours he spent in prayer and penance. And then the coming of Keziah; the temptation which had been too great to resist; the hours of remorse that followed. The torment of the hair shirt and the lacerations of his flesh. He had indulged it; he would crucify it. But the sin was committed and then he knew that that sin was to bear fruit.

Doubly he had sinned. He had broken from the enclosed state; he had had speech with the witch of the woods, he had agreed to her monstrous plan to deceive the Abbot and everyone in St. Bruno's. And this he had done for yet another temptation had come to him—to watch over his son, to see him educated and raised to greatness. Again he had been unable to resist.

He would never expiate his sin; he was doomed to eternal damnation, so he had plunged headlong into sin and loved this son with the idolatry which should have been given only to God.

This confession he had made. It was for the generations to come. No one should read it while his beloved son lived for all must believe him to be divine.

He was guilty of lust and deceit; he would burn forever in hell but great pleasure had been his in the woman who tempted him and the son who was the result of their lustful union.

I folded it carefully and locked it in a sandalwood box which my father had given me years ago.

Soon I would tell Bruno that I had proof of what had happened at his birth not only from his great-grandmother, who had told me when she was dying, but by this confession of his father's.

But I must delay this until after Kate's return to Remus.

Revelations

When Kate arrived next day I thought she seemed more subdued than usual. Catherine was quiet too. I fancied that she was resentful toward Kate, which was strange; generally they were in harmony for they shared a gay and carefree outlook on life.

When I took Kate to her bedchamber she said she must talk to me soon. Where could we go for quiet?

I suggested the winter parlor.

"I will be with you in fifteen minutes," she told me.

I went straight to Catherine's room. She was standing at her window staring moodily out.

"Cat dear, what is wrong?" I asked.

She turned around and flung herself into my arms. I comforted her. "Whatever it is I daresay we can do something about it."

"It is Aunt Kate. She says we may not marry. She says that we must separate and forget and she has come to talk to you about it. How dare she! We shall not accept it. We shall. . . ."

"Catherine, what are you speaking of? Marry whom? *You* are only a child."

"I am nearly seventeen, Mother. Old enough to know that I want more than anything on earth to marry Carey."

"Carey! But you and he. . . ."

"Oh, yes, yes, we used to quarrel. But don't you *see?* That was all part of it. Quarreling with Carey was always more exciting than being friendly with anyone else. We both laugh about it now and we can never, never be happy away from each other. Oh, Mother, you must persuade Aunt Kate. She is being so silly. . . . Why should she disapprove of me? Are we not as noble as she is?

She is some sort of cousin of yours, is she not? And your parents looked after her or she might have been poor indeed and not had a chance to marry Lord Remus and have Carey. . . ."

"Please, Catherine, not so fast. You and Carey have told Aunt Kate of your decision and she refuses to sanction the marriage. Go on from there."

"She went quite odd when I told her. She said she would refuse to allow it, and she was coming to see you . . . without delay. And then right away she wrote to you and told you we were coming . . . and here we are."

"You are overwrought," I said. "I will go to Kate now and discover what this is all about."

"But you would not be so unkind? You would not say no?"

"I can see no reason why you and Carey should not be married except that you are so young, but time changes that of course and providing you do not wish to hurry into marriage. . . ."

"What sense is there in waiting?"

"A great deal of sense. But let me go and see what is worrying Kate."

"And tell her how foolish she is! I daresay she wants a duke's daughter for Carey. But he won't take her. He'll refuse."

I told her not to get excited and I went down to the winter parlor where Kate was already waiting—unexpectedly punctual.

"Kate, what is all this about?"

"Oh, Damask, this is terrible."

"I've gathered from Catherine that she and Carey want to marry and you are against the match."

"So must you be when you know the truth."

"What truth?"

"You were always so blind in some ways. They cannot marry because Carey is Bruno's son and therefore Catherine's brother."

"No!"

"But, yes. So is Colas. You didn't imagine Remus could get sons, did you?"

"But he was your husband."

Kate laughed, but not happily or pleasantly. "Oh, yes, he was my husband but not the father of my children. Is that so hard to understand? There were three of us, weren't there, playing there

on forbidden grass? And didn't you know how it always was between us? Bruno is not the saint he often likes to pose as being.
He loved me. He wanted me. And to you and me of course he was
the child in the crib. We deceived ourselves, did we not . . . most
excitingly? We were in the company of one of the gods who had
descended from the heights of Olympus. He was as pagan as that.
And yet he was divine; he was a saint. In any case he was different
from anyone else we knew. And he was important to us both. But
I was always the one, Damask. You knew that. He came to Caseman Court when the Abbey was disbanded. He loved me and
wanted us to share our lives but how could I share my life with
a penniless boy! And there was Remus with so much to offer. So
I took Remus but not before Bruno and I had been lovers. But
marry him, no! Marriage was for Remus. I think Bruno came near
to hating me then. He can hate, you know . . . fiercely. He hates
all those who lower his pride. Keziah, his mother; Ambrose, his
father; myself for preferring a life of luxury with Remus to a life
of poverty with him. So there was before my marriage a kind of
love between us—not wholehearted love. For us both it was over-
ruled by ambition—in me for luxurious living, for him by his pride
—his eternal overwhelming pride. I thought he could not then
give me what I wanted and by my rejection of him I wounded him
where he was most vulnerable. But the fact is that Bruno is the
father of my son and your daughter and there can be no marriage
between brother and sister."

"Oh, God!" I cried. "What have we done to those children?"

"The more important question, Damask," said Kate soberly, "is
what are we going to do?"

"You have told them that they cannot marry but given them
no reason?"

She nodded. "They hate me for it. They think that I am seeking an heiress of noble birth for Carey."

"It's the obvious conclusion. We must tell them the truth. It
is the only way."

"So thought I, but first I had to tell you and we must speak with
Bruno."

He stood there in the winter parlor, the light full on his face
with those wonderful features which even now looked as though
a halo should be shining on them.

I said: "Bruno, Kate has come with a terrible problem. Catherine and Carey want to marry."

I watched his face closely. He said: "Well?"

I could scarcely believe that he could be so unconcerned.

I cried out: "Kate has told me that Carey is your son. Have you forgotten that Catherine is your daughter?"

He looked almost reproachfully at Kate. "You told Damask that?"

"I thought it necessary as this has arisen."

He said coolly: "It should not be known. The marriage must be prevented for some other reason."

"For what reason?" I cried.

"Do parents have to give reasons to their children? We do not wish the marriage to take place. That will suffice."

I hated him in that moment. I had never seen him quite so clearly. He was not so much moved by the predicament of his son and daughter as at the prospect of how this would affect him.

I said: "It will not suffice. You cannot break people's hearts and not tell them the reason because it would be inconvenient to do so."

"You are hysterical, Damask."

"I am deeply concerned for my daughter, whom I regret is yours also. Oh, Bruno, come down to earth. Who are you, do you think, to take up this role of saintliness?"

It was Kate who said: "You are getting excited, Damask." It was as though we had changed roles. I had always been the calm reasonable one and it had been I who had in the past warned her to be cautious.

"Excited!" I cried. "This is my daughter's life. She is going to know the truth. She is going to know her father for what he is."

"You must not be jealous because Kate and I have been lovers."

"Jealous!" I said. "Not jealous. I think I always knew that I was the second choice . . . the one who had to come to you for yourself alone because Kate had refused to do so. It is all clear to me now. You had nothing to offer Kate except as a lover so, in her worldly fashion, she rejected you as a husband. Blithely she bore your son. Then, piqued, you went to London. There you either approached or were approached by foreign spies in this country who were interested in reviving what the King had destroyed."

"You are wrong."

"Indeed I am not. You . . . the god or whatever you think you are . . . are merely one of many little facets in the Spanish scheme. You went to the Continent on an embassy for the King, you tell us. You went to the Continent to take instructions from your masters. You were given money to acquire the Abbey and return it to what it was in the days before the dissolution. You were chosen because you were found in the Christmas crib in the Lady Chapel. Oh, it is all becoming very clear to me."

"You are shouting," said Bruno.

"And you are afraid that I shall explode your myth. Is it not time that myth was exploded? Is it not time that you were known for what you are? An ambitious man . . . who is not without his moments of lust and ambition and would sacrifice his son and daughter if need be to keep his pride intact."

Kate said: "What has come over you, Damask? This is not like you."

"It has been coming over me for a long time. I have seen so much of late. I have seen this man for what he is."

"But you love him. You always did. We are bound together. We three were as one."

"Not anymore, Kate. I am no longer close to either of you. You have deceived me, both of you. You will never do it again."

"You must not take this hard," said Kate. "It all happened so naturally."

"Is it so natural," I asked, "that a man should be unfaithful to his wife, that he should have sons, and his own daughter should want to marry one of them?"

"That is the situation to which we must give some thought," said Bruno looking coldly at me. "When Damask has finished pitying herself perhaps we could discuss it."

"Pitying myself! My pity is for those young people."

"It must not be known," said Bruno. "Catherine can be married suitably or Kate can find a wife for Carey who will make him forget Catherine."

"We are not all so fickle in our relationships as you are," I reminded him.

"They are young. They will recover. In a few months this will have been just an adventure to them," said Kate.

"How glibly you settle the lives of others! It is nothing to you to make a loveless marriage for the sake of expediency. Others do not feel the same. They must be told the truth."

"I forbid it," said Bruno.

"*You* forbid it. You may have no say in the matter. This is my daughter. They shall be told, for in their present mood they could run away together and marry no matter what we say."

"And if they did?"

"A brother and sister! What if there are children?"

Nobody spoke and I was horrified because I knew that Bruno was ready to let them marry and take the consequences rather than to tell them the truth.

I looked at him standing there.

And I could bear no more. I turned and ran from the room.

Catherine caught me on the stairs.

"Oh, Mother, what is happening?"

"Come to your room, my darling. I must talk to you."

I took her in my arms and held her against me.

"Oh, Catherine, my dearest child."

"What is wrong, Mother? What is Aunt Kate trying to do? She hates me."

"No, my dearest, she does not. But you cannot marry Carey."

"Why? Why? I tell you I will. We have said we will not allow any of you to ruin our lives."

"You cannot marry him because he is your brother."

She stared at me and I led her to the window seat and sat there with my arm about her. It seemed such a sordid story told simply.

"You see there were three of us, myself, Kate and your father. He loved Kate but he was poor then and she married Lord Remus but she had your father's child. So you see he is your brother. That is why we say you cannot marry."

"It is not true. It can't be. My father! He is. . . ."

She looked at me as though begging me to deny it.

"Men do these things," I said. "It is not an uncommon story."

"But *he* is not as ordinary men."

"You believed that, did you not?"

"I thought him divine in some way. The story of the crib. . . ."

"Yes, I suppose that is where it starts, with the story of the crib. My dearest child, you are young yet but your love for Carey and the tragedy of it has made of you a woman, so I shall treat you as such. You have listened to Clement and he has told you the wonderful story of how the Abbot went into the Lady Chapel one Christmas morning and found a child in the crib. That child was your father. It was known as the Miracle of St. Bruno's. You know that story."

"Clement told me. Others have talked of it. The people here all talk of it."

"And with the coming of the child the Abbey prospered. The Abbey was dissolved with others in the country but is rising again through the child in the crib. You believe that, do you not? And it is true. But you must know more of the truth and I believe it will help you to overcome your tragedy. All that you have been told is true. Your father was found in the crib but he was put there by the monk who was his father, and his birth was the result of that monk's liaison with a serving girl. I knew her well. She was my nurse."

"It can't be true, Mother."

"It *is* true. Keziah told the true version; so did Keziah's grandmother, and I have the monk's written confession."

"But he . . . my father does not know?"

"He knows it. In his heart he knows it. He has known it since Keziah divulged it. But he will not admit it and his refusal to do so has made him what he is."

"You hate him," she said, drawing away from me.

"Yes. I think I do. This hatred has been growing in my heart for a long time. I think since you were born and he turned from you because you were a girl and not the boy his pride demanded. No, it was before that. It was when Honey came to me and he resented her—a little child, helpless and lovable. But she was his sister and he could not bear to be reminded of the mother who bore them both. He hated Honey; he resented her. Yes, that was when I first began to turn against him."

"Oh, Mother, what am I going to do?"

"We will bear it together, my love," I cried, weeping with her.

* * *

There was hatred in the Abbey now. I was aware of it.

I looked from my window across the Abbey lands to the bastion of the castlelike structure which he had built to resemble Remus Castle. It must be as grand, nay grander, so that Kate should realize every time she looked at it that she could have had wealth and Bruno too.

Catherine had shut herself into her room. She would see no one but me. I was glad to be able to offer her some comfort.

She said of her father: "I wish never to see him again."

Kate stayed in her room writing to Carey.

Now that I had made my feelings clear to Bruno I was determined to show him Ambrose's confession, for I knew that we had gone so far that there was no drawing back. Bruno *must* face the truth. Even so I did not think it was possible to start a new life from there. I feel I had exposed my own feelings to such an extent that I understood them myself as I never had before.

I found Bruno in the Abbey church and wondered whether he had been praying.

"There is something I have to tell you," I said.

"You can tell me here," he replied coldly.

"It is hardly a fitting place."

"What can you have to say to me that cannot be said in church?"

"Perhaps it is fitting after all," I said. "It was here that they found you. Yes, it was here that Ambrose laid you in the Christmas crib."

"You have come here to taunt me with that lie."

"It is no lie and you know it."

"Oh, come, I am weary of your rantings on that score."

"I believe the evidence of Keziah and Ambrose."

"Extracted under torture?"

"Mother Salter told her story freely."

"An old witch from a hut in the woods!"

"A woman who would scorn to lie. When she was on her deathbed she told how she had bidden Ambrose to place you in the crib."

"So you believe everyone but me."

"No. I have Ambrose's confession which was written long before Rolf Weaver came to the Abbey."

"Ambrose's confession! What are you talking about?"

"I found it in his cell in the monks' dorter. Mother Salter told me where to look for it."

He turned on me then, his eyes blazing with anger.

"So that is why you were prowling about in the dorter. You lied to me. You said you wanted to make the place into a buttery."

"Yes, I did lie to you," I agreed. "I knew that if I had told you what I was looking for. . . ."

I paused and he said quietly: "Yes, go on. What if you had told me?"

"I knew that you would have tried to prevent me."

"Yet you deliberately went against my wishes."

"Yes. I wanted to know the truth."

"And you think you have it?"

"I have Ambrose's confession."

"His confession! What nonsense are you talking?"

"You know the truth. He confessed, did he not? Do you think he would have lied . . . and condemned himself?"

"Men will tell any lies if they think that by so doing they can save their wretched lives."

"This is no lie. It tells of his sin in begetting you and his further sin in putting you in the crib that there would appear to be something miraculous about your birth. He wanted his son to grow up to be the Abbot of St. Bruno's."

"I shall not believe this confession exists until I see it."

I was not going to fall into that temptation.

I turned away but he was beside me.

"If you have this confession, give it to me."

"You will see it in due course."

"What do you mean by that? When?"

"When you have given me your word that you will cast aside this make-believe, when you promise to face the truth, when you accept the fact that you are a real man."

"You are mad, Damask."

"I don't think so. It is you who are mad with pride. I ask you now, Bruno, to give up this mystery with which you console yourself. Accept the truth. You are clever. You are more than that. You have brought the Abbey to what it is. Why should you pretend to be possessed of supernatural powers when you have so many that are natural? Bruno, I want you to let it be known that this confession has been found. I want you to let everyone know that you are a man . . . not some mystic figure different from the rest of us. *Therein* lies madness."

"Where is this confession?"

"It is locked away in a safe place."

"Give it to me."

"That you may destroy it?"

"It is a forgery."

"Nay, it is no forgery. I want you to begin with those monks you have brought here. Tell them the truth. Tell them that Ambrose left his confession and that you are in fact his son and that of my nurse."

"Yes, indeed, your brain has been affected by madness."

"It is what I ask. Very soon it will be known that Ambrose's confession has been found. I would rather you told them before I did so."

"You have become a teacher to instruct us."

"Here is your chance, Bruno. Face the truth. You have a wife; you have a daughter. It might well be that they could learn to love you. You have men who serve you well. They will respect you for the truth. You have wealth. You could use it wisely, which I'll swear some would say you do now. But give up this alliance with a foreign power. Good God, don't you know how near you came to death in the last reign? And what now think you? Next year we could have a new sovereign. Have you ever thought what that would mean? This moment will not last forever. You have to choose."

He held his head high; it looked amazingly handsome; he looked in fact divine. He could have been carved out of marble, so pale was his face, so exquisite those proud features. I felt a sudden twinge of love for him. I almost wished that he would say: "Yes, I will cast out my pride. I will no longer hide from the truth as though it were the plague. I will tell the world who I am. I will make it known that Ambrose has written the story of the miracles of St. Bruno's Abbey."

I spoke gently to him. "Give all this up. I have Caseman Court and its rich lands. If you must give up the Abbey, do so. We will build a new life together founded on truth. . . . We have a daughter to be nursed through her tragedy. Perhaps we could forget all that has gone before and come to some happiness."

He looked at me scornfully. "The shock of learning that Carey is my son has turned your brain," he said. "If there is this confession of which you talk . . . and I doubt it, for I thought you were very strange when I discovered you prowling about the dorter . . . you should bring it to me at once. It is some hoax of course but such documents are dangerous. Go and get it that I may see it, and bring it to me here."

I shook my head. "You shall not have it. I beg of you, Bruno, consider what I have said."

I went out and left him.

What a strange brooding house it was. Kate had written to Carey and sent a messenger off with the letter. Catherine shut herself in her room and would eat nothing. In the old days I should have gone to Kate to pour out my sorrow to her. Now I kept aloof.

It was evening of that long day. I was sitting alone in my bedchamber when Bruno came in.

He said: "I must talk to you. We must come to an understanding."

"That would please me, but I must make you understand that I cannot go on sharing in this lie."

"I want you to give me Ambrose's confession."

"So that you can destroy it?"

"So that I can read it."

"A lie has been lived so long. There was no miracle at St. Bruno's. Since Keziah's confession I could never pretend that there was. Had you tried to be a man instead of a god everything would have been different."

"What would have been different?"

"Perhaps you would have told me that Kate had rejected you."

"What difference would it have made? You would have taken me!"

"Were you as certain of me as that?"

"I was certain."

"And when she rejected you for wealthy Remus your pride was deeply wounded. I understand, Bruno. You, the superhuman being, the god, the mystery, the miracle child had suddenly been reduced to an ordinary being, rejected lover, bastard of a servant and a monk. It was more than you could endure."

"Kate came to regret her decision." I saw the gleam of satisfaction in his eyes.

"Your pride was deeply wounded. You had to apply the soothing balm which was my consent to go with you wherever you wished . . . to live in a cottage if need be. That was what you wanted of me."

There was a knock on the door and Eugene came in with a tray on which was a flagon of wine and two glasses.

"So you wish us to taste your new brew, Eugene," said Bruno. He took the tray from Eugene and set it down.

"It's my best elder flower," Eugene told me.

"The one you were telling me of," said Bruno.

"And you particularly wish the Mistress to try it."

Eugene said this was the one. He went out smiling complacently and Bruno poured the wine into the glasses and brought one to me.

I was in no mood for drinking. I set down the glass and said: "It is no use, Bruno. I see this clearly. We cannot go on living this life. It is false. There is only one chance of our being able to make a life for ourselves and our daughter. We will let it be known that we have found the monk's confession. The miracle of St. Bruno's will be finished forever. It will be forgotten in time."

"And what do you wish me to do?"

"It is simple. We will tell everyone at the Abbey that we have found the confession. This will be the proof we need to show that Keziah's story was true. You must tell your Spanish masters that you can no longer go on with this falsehood."

"I tell you I have no Spanish masters."

"Then tell me this, too. How did you find the money to do all that you have done here?"

"This is where your story breaks down, does it not? So you have to provide me with Spanish masters. I tell you I have none. I have not received money from foreign countries to refound the Abbey."

"Then where did you find the money?"

"It came to me . . . as I told you, from heaven."

"You insist on this story!"

"I swear to you that the means of rebuilding the Abbey came from heaven. You are dabbling in matters too great for you, Damask. You do not understand. Come, drink up your wine. Eugene will want to hear what you think of his latest brew."

I picked up the glass and even as I did so I was aware of Bruno's gaze fixed on me. There was hatred in it. Oh, yes, he hated me. I knew then that it was because I had the means in my power to expose him.

What was it? Some warning perhaps. I was never to know. But I just felt that I must not drink that wine.

I set it down and said: "I am in no mood for drinking."

"Can you not take a sip or so to please Eugene?"

"I am in no mood to judge."

"Then I shall not drink alone."

"So he will not know your judgment either."

"I have already given it. It is of his best."

"Perhaps I will try it later," I said.

Bruno went out and left me.

My heart was beating fast. I picked up the wine and smelled it. I could detect nothing.

I took both glasses and opening the window threw out the wine.

Then I laughed at myself. He is proud, I thought; he is arrogant; he sees himself of greater importance than other men. But that does not mean he is a murderer.

I thought suddenly of Simon Caseman and I had a vision of his writhing in the flames. Bruno had sent him to his death . . . as Simon had endeavored to send him, as Simon had sent my own father.

Was not that murder? Simon had proved himself to be Bruno's enemy—as I had . . .

The next day I went to Caseman Court. My mother was delighted to see me.

"I was saying to the twins only today," she said, "that you would be coming to see me and bringing Kate too. I understand she is at the Abbey." She looked at me closely. "Why, Damask, is something wrong?"

I thought: She must know of course that Catherine and Carey cannot marry and she will have to know why. So I told her.

"A bad business," she said. "There was always something wanton about Kate. I often thought she was deceiving Remus. And the boys too . . . well he was as proud as a peacock at his time of life. It's a sorry matter. Poor Catherine; I will send something over for her. And you, daughter! Well, husbands are unfaithful . . . though a man in Bruno's position. . . . Well, well, your stepfather never believed in his faith. It was not the true faith, you see."

"Mother," I said, "be careful. Men and women are being burned at Smithfield for saying what you have just said."

"'Tis so, and that's a sorry matter too. Poor, poor Catherine. Such a child though. She'll recover. And Carey too. I would not have thought it of Bruno. He being so well thought of. Almost holy. Why Clement and Eugene used to genuflect when they spoke of him. It wasn't right. Your stepfather. . . ."

"It has been a great shock to me," I said. "But you have comforted me."

"Bless you, daughter. That's what mothers are for. And you will comfort Catherine."

"I shall try to do so with all my heart."

"Ah, I had a good husband."

"Two good husbands, Mother."

"Yes, I suppose that is a good tally."

"Indeed it is."

"I am going to give you some of my new cure. It is herb twopence and I know from Mother Salter that it will cure almost any illness you can name. When I was gathering it I saw Bruno. He was gathering herbs too. I talked to him and I was surprised what he knew of them. He said that when he was a boy he was taught the power of them. He had vervain for he said Thomas, one of his men, suffered from the ague and there is nothing like vervain for that. And he was getting woodruff for someone else's liver. Then I saw that among the herbs he had gathered was what seemed to be parsley but I knew it for hemlock and I said to him, 'Look, what have you there? Do you know that is hemlock?' He said he knew it well, but that Clement had gathered it for parsley and he was taking some back with him to show him the difference."

"Hemlock . . . that's a deadly poison, is it not?"

"As all should know. I'm surprised at Clement. Why, I remember one of our maids mistook it for parsley and that was the end of her."

I thought of the glasses of untasted wine and I wanted to tell her of my fears. Mothers, as she had said so often, were meant to comfort.

"There," she said, "what shall I give you? Something to make you sleep."

"No," I said, "give me an ashen branch, Mother, for you once said that would drive evil away from my pillow."

Dusk had fallen. The Abbey was silent.

I pictured Catherine in her room, face downward on her bed, staring into space at a desolate future which did not contain her lover. And of what did Kate think in her room? Was she reviewing the past? The wrong she had done Remus, the terrible consequences which meant that the sins of the parents must be borne by the children?

I laid on my pillow the ashen branch my mother had given me, but I could not sleep easily. I dozed a little and dreamed that Bruno crept into the room and stood over me and I saw that he had two heads and one was that of Simon Caseman.

I called out in my sleep and when I awoke the word "Murderers" was on my lips.

I started up. I was too disturbed to sleep. I kept thinking of Bruno gathering hemlock and bringing in the wine.

He hated me as much as that! He would have hated anyone who crossed him. His love for himself was so great that anyone who did not feed it was his enemy. He would not accept the fact that he was an ordinary mortal, and therein lay his madness.

If he had tried with the wine would he not try again? I thought of leaving him, taking Catherine with me to Caseman Court.

I rose from my bed and sat in the window seat brooding on my situation. Could I speak to Kate? No, for I no longer trusted Kate. All those years when I had confided in her she had been his mistress; for Colas must have been conceived on one of her visits to the Abbey. I imagined her sharing confidences with me and then going off to share Bruno's bed.

Whom could one trust?

It seemed only my mother.

I must have sat there brooding for more than an hour when I saw Bruno. He was making his way to the tunnels.

I watched him. I had seen him go that way before. I remembered a long-ago occasion when I thought Honey had wandered down to the tunnels. I had gone to look for her. Bruno had been there then and very angry to find me.

I had never been to the tunnels. It was one of the few parts of the Abbey I had not explored because Bruno had said it was unsafe there. There had been a fall of earth when he was a boy and he warned everyone against venturing down into that underground passage which led to them.

Yet he did not hesitate to go.

I thought afterward that it was foolish of me, but it was too late then. I was already out of bed, my feet in slippers, my cloak around me.

It was a warm night but I was shivering—with fear, I suppose, and apprehension, but something more than curiosity drove me. I had the feeling that it was of the utmost importance for me to follow Bruno that night. Mother Salter had told my mother that at moments in our lives when death is close we have an overwhelming desire to reach it. It is as though we are beckoned on by an angel whom we cannot resist and this angel is the Angel of Death.

So I felt on that night. Even by day the tunnels had repelled me; and now here I was at the entrance to them and I must descend that dark stairway although I knew that there was a man down there who, I believed, had had it in his mind to murder me.

There was a little light at the entrance to the tunnels—enough to show me the stairs down which I had fallen when I went to look for Honey.

I reached the top step and sliding my feet along the ground cautiously descended.

My eyes had grown a little accustomed to the darkness and I realized that ahead of me lay three openings. I hesitated and then I was aware of a faint light at the end of one of them. It moved. It could be someone carrying a lantern. It must be Bruno.

I touched the cold wall. It was slimy. My common sense said: Turn back. First count the tunnels and tomorrow come down, bring a lantern. Perhaps bring Catherine with you and explore. But that urge which I thought of as the Angel of Death was urging me on and I had to follow.

Carefully I picked my way, quietly sliding my feet over the stones in the passage. On and on went the light; it disappeared and appeared again. It was like a will-o'-the-wisp and a thought came to me. Perhaps it is not Bruno but some spirit of a long-dead monk who will punish me for prying into what might well be a holy place.

The light went out suddenly. The darkness seemed intense. But I still went on. I felt my way carefully with my hands, sliding my feet so as not to trip.

Then I came to the opening and there was the light again. I was in a chamber and the lantern was on the ground. A man was standing there. I knew it was Bruno.

"You dared . . .," he cried.

"Yes, I dared."

He came toward me and as he did so a figure loomed up behind him—a great white glittering figure.

I cried: "There is someone here."

"Yes," he answered. "There is someone here."

I stared at the figure. It had seemed to move because the light from the lantern had caught the glittering jewels with which it was covered. I saw the crown with the great stone which was dazzling in the dimness.

I had seen it before.

"I should have killed you before this," said Bruno savagely.

He came toward me menacingly and I shrank away, thinking: I am going to die here . . . now . . . and Bruno is going to kill me. Everything that has happened from the moment I went through the door in the Abbey wall has led me to this moment. And Bruno is going to kill me.

I had played into his hands. I had come of my own accord into the secret tunnels. He would kill me and leave me here and no one would know what had become of me. I should disappear here . . . beneath the Abbey.

"Bruno," I cried. "Wait. Don't act rashly. Think. . . ."

He did not answer. Time appeared to have slowed down. The silence seemed to go on and on.

"Bruno. . . ." I was not sure whether he had heard for although my lips formed the words I seemed to have lost the power to speak.

It was surprising that my thoughts could stray from this terrible danger; but I was saying to myself: It was here that he found his wealth. It was not from Spain. I am beginning to understand and that is why I am going to die.

There was no escape. I was trapped. Nothing could save me.

He was close to me now. His hands would be on my throat, pressing out life forever. I was lost.

But I was wrong.

The great figure looming behind him had moved. He, with his back to it, could not see this. It was my fancy. But, no. It swayed. It seemed to totter and then suddenly it fell.

It came crashing down toward us. Instinctively I leaped back, but Bruno had not seen it.

There was a deafening sound. I closed my eyes, waiting for death. I stood cowering against the cold stone wall. I waited . . . for what I was not sure. For death, I supposed.

Then I opened my eyes and saw that Bruno lay beneath that great image.

I forgot everything else but that he was my husband and I had loved him once.

"Bruno," I cried. "Bruno!"

I knelt beside him. I brought the lantern close. His body was crushed and his eyes were wide open, staring at me but there was no recognition in them.

I must get help, I told myself. I looked about me for the entrance to this place and I saw that I was in a kind of chamber. The sides of it were of rock, as was the ceiling. It had been built, I guessed, to store the Abbey's treasures. And this great figure lying on the floor ablaze with jewels I had seen before. It was the jeweled Madonna of the secret chapel.

It was comparatively easy to make my way out of the chamber but doing so I tripped over a lever of some sort and in that moment I heard a rumbling sound. I thought that it was due to a fall of earth, but this was not so. I turned. The chamber had disappeared. I knew that a door had slid down shutting it off and that I was on one side of that door, Bruno on the other. I set down the lantern and examined the door. I could see no handle on it, no catch, no means of opening it. Then just as I had had the compulsion to follow Bruno, so I had the intense desire to get away.

I was alone in those dark tunnels. I must try to bring help to Bruno for I could do nothing alone. Slowly I found my way back to the steps.

Who could best help? I thought at once of Valerian. I knew where he slept. It was in one of the old guesthouses where several of the monks had their quarters.

Still carrying the lantern I went to his room. It was as I expected —the crucifix on the wall, the hard pallet, a desk, a chair and no other furniture.

"Valerian!" I cried.

He started up from his bed and I said: "I have just come from the tunnels. I followed Bruno there tonight. There has been a terrible accident."

"Bruno is dead," he answered quietly.

"How can you know that?"

"I know it," he replied. He put on a fustian robe and went on: "We will go back to the tunnels."

I said: "I must explain to you. I followed him. I felt a compulsion to do so."

He nodded.

"I found him in a sort of chamber. There was a great glittering figure there. I had seen it before because he had shown it to me and to Kate when we were children. I think he was going to kill me. The figure fell . . . he was beneath it. I came away and a sort of door descended."

He did not speak but taking the lantern, led the way through the tunnels. I could see that he knew the way.

He paused at length and said: "This is where you entered the chamber."

"It would be here, but I see no sign of it."

"Here is what you call the door."

"We should bring him back to the house. He will need a doctor."

Valerian shook his head. "He will never need a doctor again."

"Open the door and go in."

"I cannot open the door."

"Please do."

"It is not in my power." Nevertheless he attempted to do so but his efforts were in vain.

He held the lantern so that he could see my face.

"You have been through a terrible ordeal," he said. "I must talk to you . . . now. But this is not the place. Come back with me to the scriptorium."

"There must be something we can do. Bruno needs attention."

"He is in the hands of God."

"You are sure that he is dead?"

"Yes, I am sure."

"How can you be?"

"I know these things. Come. We cannot enter the chamber. The way is not known to any of us. He was the only one who knew. But we must talk."

I followed him out of the tunnels to the scriptorium. There he bade me be seated and gave me a cordial to drink. It was hot and burned my throat but it revived me.

"The miracle must live," he said.

"There was no miracle. It was because I had proved this that he hated me and tried to kill me."

"Yet the miracle must live."

"How can it when it was not the truth?"

"It will be the truth in the minds of many, and it is what is in the mind which is important."

"He will be found there in the tunnels."

Valerian shook his head. "Only he knew how to open the door. The secret was told to him by the Abbot. Only the Abbots of St. Bruno's knew how to open that door and they passed the secret on to their successors. The code was written down and hidden— none knew where but the Abbots and those destined to take their place. Treasures of the Abbey have been stored there through the ages. Bruno would tell no one. The secret was his alone."

"It was there he found the wealth to rebuild the Abbey. It was from the jewels of the Madonna. He took them as he needed them. I can see it all so clearly now."

"They were such jewels that it was necessary to show the utmost caution in disposing of them. He had to let time elapse before he went abroad to sell the first and the smallest of them."

"That was why he came to us when he left the Abbey. He was biding his time, waiting until the hue and cry over the Abbey jewels had died down."

"That was so and the first and the smallest of them realized such a sum that he was able to buy the Abbey. He knew that he had a great treasure store and when he needed money he took a jewel and sold it abroad."

"So when Cromwell's men were coming to the Abbey they must have taken the Madonna down through the tunnels to that chamber. How could they have done this?"

"It must have been a great undertaking. All we knew was that it was in the sacred chapel one day and the next was gone. It was thought to be a miracle because a few days later Rolf Weaver's men came. I think I know what happened. The Abbot's giant servant could have carried her down. If her jewels were taken from her she would not be so heavy, of course. Among them, the Abbot, the servant and Bruno would have taken her there and replaced the jewels about her when she stood in the secret chamber. That is the only way it could possibly have been done."

"And only Bruno knew."

"The Abbot died. The servant was a mute. He is dead now. All three who knew the secret are dead. This is the end. I have seen its coming. I am aware of these things. Bruno is gone. We know where, but no one else must. This is the Madonna's answer. A new reign is almost upon us. We could not have survived as we are under a new sovereign. But the miracle must live . . . and this is the only way it can do so."

"You mean that no one must know what happened tonight?"

"I am commanding your silence. Go back to your room and say nothing of this night's events."

"But I must."

"Most certainly you must not. This is ordained. I know it.

Bruno is dead. He had to die to preserve the miracle and the miracle must live. He will have gone as strangely as he came and in the generations to come people will talk of the Miracle of St. Bruno's Abbey and good will come of it. Go now. You are distraught. You are weary. Go and rest. The cordial may make you sleep. In the morning it will seem more clear."

I went back to my room and waited for the morning.

Kate stayed with us all through that year. She did not wish to go back to Remus Castle now for Carey was there to reproach her.

For months after that night when Bruno had died in the Madonna's chamber his return was awaited. He had gone away before on those trips to the Continent to sell jewels, and at first it was assumed that he had gone away as he had on other occasions. But as the months passed and he did not return it began to be said that he had disappeared as mysteriously as he had come.

"It was a miracle," people said. "He appeared on Christmas Day in the Lady Chapel—a babe in a crib—and he disappeared in the thirty-sixth year of his life." It would never be forgotten.

Kate and I had returned to the old ways. She used to come to my room and talk of what was happening in the outside world just as she had always done: How the old Queen was dying of a broken heart because her husband Philip of Spain neglected her. How she declared that her heart had been broken in any case by the loss of Calais and when she died that name would be written across her heart.

"The name of Philip will be there too perhaps," said Kate, "if I may continue with such a flight of fancy."

She became gayer every day. "One cannot go on mourning forever," she said.

Honey was happy for she was to have a child; I insisted that she come to the Abbey that I might look after her. Catherine began to regain her spirits although she was never again the same lighthearted girl.

"Catherine will forget in time," said Kate. "So will Carey. You'll forget. I'll forget. Everyone forgets, so the sooner one starts to do so the better." She looked at me intently though and went on: "How strange that Bruno disappeared. Do you think he will come back one day?"

"No," I said. "Never."

"You know more than you betray."

"One should never betray all one knows."

"I often wonder," said Kate, "where he found the money to do what he did. I believe he was in the pay of Spain."

"One must have some beliefs," I told her.

"The only conclusion I can draw otherwise is that there was truly a miracle at St. Bruno's."

"It is not a bad conclusion to which to come."

That September the Emperor Charles, the father of Philip of Spain, died and in his will he exhorted his son to inflict even more severe punishment on heretics. The Smithfield fires would be intensified, said the people. They were in a sullen mood.

But in November the Queen died and a new sovereign was proclaimed at Hatfield where she had been living in a seclusion which could have been called a prison.

There was rejoicing throughout the land. The dark days are over, said the people. There will be no more smoke over Smithfield now that Elizabeth was Queen.

We took to our barge and went down the river to see the new Queen brought in triumph to London. Kate and Catherine, my mother, Rupert and I joined in the loyal shouts of "Long live the Queen."

She was young; she was vital; and she glowed with purpose. She told us that she would dedicate herself to her people and her country.

And we believed her.

I knew that as we were rowed back along the river leaving the grim gray fortress of the Tower of London behind us we were— every one of us—convinced that there would be changes in our lives and our spirits lifted and our hearts rejoiced.